Awakening

JOANN DURGIN

This book is a work of fiction. Names, characters, places and events either are products of the author's imagination or are used fictitiously. Any resemblance to actual events or persons living or dead is purely coincidental.

ISBN 978-0-9912252-0-0

All Scripture contained within is from the New American Standard Bible.

Text set in Garamond
Printed and Bound in the USA
COVER DESIGN BY Dino Piccinini

From the Author

My Dearest Readers,

Thank you for choosing to read **Awakening**. Bringing this book to you has been a true labor of love, and was first written more than a decade ago. It is loosely based on my love story with my own hero—my husband, Jim. A lot of the strength of character, unwavering faith and goodness in Sam Lewis is based on Jim (and yes, we even met in the great Lone Star State). Some of the feistiness and stubbornness in Lexa is based on yours truly, but I choose to believe I share her resourcefulness and resilience. In part, that's why you're holding this book in your hands now.

I thank Jim for his encouragement and support through the years to help make this dream a reality. To our children—Sarah, Chelsea and Matthew—may your mother's passion for writing inspire you, and leave a written legacy of faith for your own children in the years to come.

Thank you to my dear mother who looked the other way when, as a young girl, I crawled under the sheets with a flashlight, staying up into the wee hours to finish Nancy Drew's latest adventure. Reading those mysteries fostered my imagination, and my love of reading and writing, and I pay loving homage to the titian-haired sleuth in *Awakening*.

For my first readers, Joyce and Kathy, you are my rocks, and I couldn't do it without your faithful support. Thank you to all the friends and encouragers who read *Awakening* in its various forms on the way to publication, as well as the numerous prayer warriors. You know who you are, and I thank you most sincerely.

The Lord is truly my Partner. He has paved the way and opened the doors of His choosing in this fascinating journey. It never ceases to amaze me the miraculous way in which He works in all things to accomplish His perfect will. May you each receive a unique blessing as you read this book. As Hebrews 12:1-2 tell us, we should run with endurance the race that is set before us, fixing our eyes upon Jesus, the Author and Perfecter of our faith.

Until His Nets Are Full,
JoAnn Durgin

The Lord God has given Me the tongue of disciples,
That I may know how to sustain the weary one with a word.
He awakens Me morning by morning,
He awakens My ear to listen as a disciple.

Isaiah 50:4

Chapter 1

*L*EXA CLARKE WAS on a roll, and it wasn't even noon.

San Antonio—40 miles. The highway marker filled her with anticipation. Soon, she'd be a survivor of the four-hour bus trip from Houston. So far, so good. The guy with the beady eyes seated beside her reeked of knock-off drugstore cologne and offered her things, none of them legal. With nearly every seat occupied, she was stuck. Burying her head in her dad's old police union newsletter did the trick. Smart thinking, bringing that along.

The senior flirt across the aisle graced her with a gap-toothed smile and nudged her with his cane a couple of times. A young mother attempted conversation, but finally gave up when her two rambunctious boys demanded constant attention. When Beady Eyes snored—a loud, obnoxious wheeze— Lexa attempted to read her novel, but her thoughts always strayed to the upcoming eight weeks.

Maybe building houses in a summer predicted to be one of the hottest on record wasn't the smartest idea. Lexa swallowed her doubts and lifted her chin. When you want to make a difference in the world, you've got to make some sacrifices. The TeamWork driver would pick her up in less than an hour, and then the real adventure could begin . . .

The bus pulled into the Greyhound bus station along with Lexa's high hopes. Holding out one hand, the driver helped her to the curb and grinned with surprise when she handed him a generous tip. He hurried to retrieve her rolling suitcase. "Enjoy your stay in San Antonio, Miss."

Lexa broke into a grin, equal parts relief and excitement. "Thanks. I'm sure I will." It might be long hours of hard work with no pay, but it's how she chose to spend her summer. High hopes should count for something.

As she toted her designer suitcase through the terminal, Lexa's grip tightened when she glimpsed curious stares directed her way. A middle-aged couple waved and called to the frazzled mother with the two boys. Lexa's eyes misted with unexpected tears at the sight of their *Going to Grandma's* suitcases. Her version had been pink with daisies for all those weekend trips to Nana's house in Galveston. The man swooped the older boy into his arms and peppered his face with kisses while the woman bundled the toddler in a tight hug.

She squinted against the assault of late morning sun as she made her way outside. The sunglasses left on the dresser in her Houston townhome would come in handy about now.

Lexa jumped when a teenager's bulging backpack sideswiped her arm. With earphones strapped across his head, he was oblivious to the outside world as his thumbs worked furiously over some type of electronic gadget. A group of boisterous guys and girls piled into a compact car. Its tires squealed when it roared away from the curb, spewing a cloud of dust in its wake. Alone on the sidewalk, Lexa's throat clogged. She clamped a hand over her mouth, her other across her stomach, sputtering and choking. Nothing like coughing up a lung.

Recovered from her attack a few minutes later, Lexa spied a white Volvo station wagon putt-putting in her direction. A tall man in a cowboy hat sat behind the wheel. A trickle of perspiration made its slow, winding path down her back as the car simultaneously wound its way toward the curb. It stopped with a rumble inches from where she waited.

Lexa brushed a hand across her damp forehead and peered through the open passenger window. "Are you from TeamWork?"

He cut the engine. "Yep. Sam Lewis. At your service. You must be Alexis Clarke." Deeply-etched lines on either side of his mouth complemented a blinding smile and aviator sunglasses shielded his eyes from the blazing sun.

"Call me Lexa." Her neck craned upward as he climbed out of the car to his full height. She skimmed over the black T-shirt and faded jeans that tapered to well-worn boots. In spite of being covered in a layer of dust from the top of the black Stetson down to his toes, he somehow managed to look clean-cut. Truly, this man epitomized the urban, modern cowboy.

Sam towered over her as he reached for her bag. "Afraid you're going to have to let go unless your fingers are going in the back along with the suitcase." The drawl was deep and warm. "You can trust me. I promise I'll take good care of it."

Lexa relaxed her grip and tried not to stare. "Thanks." With his strong jaw line, defined cheekbones and those smile lines, Sam bore an uncanny resemblance to the rugged cowboy on the cover of the romance novel stashed in her purse. Her pulse picked up speed. Making a difference in the world should keep her busy enough for the next eight weeks. TeamWork expected her to work hard, and that's what she intended to do. Closing her mouth and not staring at the man like a lovestruck schoolgirl might be a good start.

"Hop on in." Opening her door, he removed his hat and parked it on the backseat with the reverence befitting a native Texan. Next came her suitcase, and Lexa was thankful he indeed treated it with equal care. When Sam raked a hand through his thick, dark waves, a few tinges of silver peeked out at the temples. In that total injustice that favored the male species, the silver only made him more attractive.

"Thanks." Good grief. Politeness aside, he'd think her only capable of mumbling one word or abbreviated sentences. Climbing into the car, she tossed her braid behind one shoulder and settled herself on the seat. Time to say something intelligent or witty.

"You look familiar. Have you ever modeled before?" She bit her lip. That sounded ridiculous, but making small-talk with a handsome cowboy wasn't a skill she listed on her professional résumé. She hoped he'd take it as the compliment she intended and move on. Judging by Sam's easy laughter, she needn't worry.

He closed the car door and leaned closer. "I've never been accused of that, no. How about you?"

That grin of his was pretty infectious.

Lexa inhaled a quick breath. Surely he noticed she wasn't exactly beautiful and barely tall enough to ride an adult roller coaster. Her mind sought a reply. "Well, then, I won't ask what you *have* been accused of since you're my ride to the TeamWork camp. You seem nice enough, and promised to take care of my suitcase." Not great, but hopefully it sounded halfway witty. She had to cool it, though, or he'd think she was flirting.

A wide grin slanted his lips, the smile lines deepened. As he slid behind the wheel, his long legs buckled at the knees, even though the seat was pushed all the way back. "Welcome to our TeamWork mission."

"Are you the leader of the camp?"

"I'm the director of this mission, yes." Sam waited until she buckled her seat belt before starting the car.

"How long have you been with TeamWork?" The rumble of the engine drowned out her words.

"Hang on." He gestured to the front of the car. "It'll calm down in a minute or two." They drove in silence a couple of miles until the engine quieted. "I'm hoping this car will get us through the next eight weeks, and then I'll put it out to pasture. It's old, but solid as a tank and loyal as anything." Sam patted the dashboard like a protective papa and readjusted the rearview mirror. "Now, let's try that again. What was your question?"

"I asked how long you've been with TeamWork." Lexa fanned her cotton blouse for a few seconds before she understood it was an exercise in futility and gave up.

"I've worked with TeamWork as a volunteer off and on since I was eighteen, and as a full-time summer director for seven years. Mostly in the United States, but I've also worked a couple of foreign missions. In my *other* life, I'm also an independent financial planner in Houston."

Small world. "Well, in *my* other life, I'm also a financial consultant with Alamo World Financial. In Houston."

"Did you feel the need to escape the financial planning world for a while?"

That question threw her a bit. Not sure how to answer, Lexa drummed her fingers on the open window. "I wouldn't exactly call it an escape. More like a break." If she told this man the truth, he'd think her misguided at best. Better to keep that little tidbit to herself.

"I completely understand the need to get away." Sam grinned. "After all, TeamWork is what I do for fun." He negotiated a turn. Other than a sparse scattering of trees, the narrow roads were flat, dusty and nondescript. Most didn't have posted signs. A couple of small, wooden shacks dotted the landscape. "What got you interested in financial planning?"

That one was easy. "I love working with numbers. It's that simple. I'm sure you can identify."

"I can. But I think the more important question is, do you like working with the *people* behind those numbers? The way I look at it, they put their trust in us, and we can't let them down."

"I like people, yes." Lexa shifted on the seat. "But numbers are easier." She'd never looked at it from that perspective before.

"Why do you think numbers are easier?"

Lexa sighed. "You're not going to let it go, are you?" She heard the edge of irritation in her voice, but it was way too hot for an inquisition.

"Sorry." Sam swiped a hand across his forehead. "My curiosity sometimes gets the best of me." The dark waves were tousled from the wind, his brow damp with beads of sweat.

Removing the sunglasses, he graced her with a direct glance. When intense, piercing blue eyes met hers, a tightness squeezed Lexa from the inside out. Her breath caught in her throat as she gulped dust blowing through the open window. It escalated into her second coughing attack of the day. Not so good. Lexa thumped a rapid staccato against her chest, as if that would help anything.

"Are you okay?" Concern laced Sam's voice. He replaced the sunglasses. "Do you have asthma?"

"I'm fine." Lexa forced a few slow, deep breaths. "Just inhaled . . . some . . . dust in my lungs." More like Sam in her lungs, but best to push that thought out of her head right now. This man was the leader of the camp, a man of God. The heat must be getting to her, seeping into her brain and muddling her mind.

"I've got water bottles in the back. Let me stop and grab one for you."

She waved her hand. "Don't bother. I'll be okay."

He still looked concerned and waited a few minutes before resuming any conversation. "So, feel like getting back to the whole number versus people discussion?"

Lexa sighed. "Let's stick with numbers. Remember, they're safer."

Sam looked her way, but he wasn't smiling. "Ah, now we're getting somewhere. You don't believe people are safe, Lexa?"

She shook her head, the grin fading. "Are you sure you're not the TeamWork shrink?" Even the TeamWork interviewer didn't ask such probing questions. Most people would ask what she liked to do, what she considered her strengths, or even her weaknesses. Sam wasn't like most people. He wanted to know her opinion of people and numbers. Sliding on the seat, Lexa anchored one foot on the floorboard and pushed herself higher on the leather seat.

"We've got some time until we get to the camp, and I'd like to find out a little about you. That way, I can better understand where you'd best fit in at the camp."

Lexa couldn't resist the bait. "Based on our discussion so far, do you have any suggestions?" Even with the windows open, it was stifling. Grabbing a tissue from her purse, Lexa blotted it across her forehead.

"I'm working on it." Slanting another glance her way, Sam grinned. "You'll get used to no air conditioning, believe it or not. Eventually you forget about it, and the constant heat becomes a state of being."

How comforting. Lexa pressed the tissue against her neck. "You'd think I'd be used to it, living in Texas my entire life. I suppose one takes modern conveniences for granted after awhile." She raised her face to the rush of warm wind caressing her cheeks, fully aware those blue eyes watched.

"Yes, I suppose one does." Amusement tinged Sam's chuckle.

Lexa tucked the tissue in the pocket of her capris. She'd have to watch the formal talk. Her grandmother coached her to speak properly, so it came naturally. It also came across as snobby.

A loud, sharp popping noise rang out somewhere nearby. Lexa jumped and a small squeal escaped. She slid down further in the seat. "What on earth was that?"

Oh dear God, please don't let that be a gunshot.

Chapter 2

$\mathcal{L}$EXA'S HEART THUNDERED in her chest. This was just great. She'd traveled to San Antonio only to come under attack on the way to the TeamWork camp. Surely, her life wouldn't end this way. First, she needed to *find* her life. Then, she'd take it from there.

It wasn't like she was the damsel in a stagecoach, Sam her heroic driver, and a rogue bandit with a sawed-off shotgun lurked on the side of the road. Although it wasn't the 1800s, it *was* Texas. Lexa darted a quick glance in every direction and blew out a sigh of relief.

"We've got a flat." Sam's jaw tightened, but his hands on the wheel remained steady as he steered the station wagon to the side of the road. Sure enough, the telltale thump . . . thump . . . thump shook the car everywhere and sent Lexa sliding across the leather seat toward the door. She grabbed onto the inside door handle as the car lurched to the right.

Shutting off the engine, Sam whipped off his sunglasses and tossed them onto the dashboard. A deep frown creased his brow as he looked at his watch. "I can use your help, if you don't mind." Without another glance in her direction, he flung open his door.

"I'm coming." Lexa almost tumbled headfirst out of the car. "Whoa!" Feeling silly, she steadied herself and took a few cautious steps along the uneven pavement as she cast a wary eye at the remains of the shredded right rear tire.

"We probably hit a nail or broken piece of glass. On this road, anything's possible." Sam pulled out a metal contraption Lexa assumed was a jack and knelt down in the dirt beside the car.

"Whatever it was, it did a thorough job on the tire. I need something fairly heavy. There's a stack of bricks in the back of the car. Please go find one and anchor it against the front tire for me."

Sam was in full boss mode now, his good humor blown along with that tire. But he said please, and his irritation was understandable, given the heat and humidity. Lexa resisted the urge to salute as she found a brick in quick order and carried it to the front right side.

"This tire?" It was a guess.

"Yeah. Thanks."

As Sam positioned the jack, Lexa lodged the brick. She was about to offer the use of her premiere auto club card, but he seemed more than capable. Not knowing what else to do, she leaned against the passenger door and watched.

"Please don't lean against the car." His exertion surfaced in his voice, but he didn't stop. Sam lifted the jack up and down with practiced ease, revealing mighty impressive upper arm muscles. Damp ringlets curled at the base of his neck. Even sweaty and covered in dirt, the man looked like he stepped from the pages of some western wear catalog.

"Oh. Sorry." Lexa wandered to the side of the road. One foot kicked pieces of asphalt, and they skidded a haphazard path across broken pavement. She shielded her eyes with one hand and squinted. Not a cloud in the sky, no breeze stirring, no birds anywhere. Texas backcountry at its best. At least it was daylight.

Sensing he watched, Lexa turned. Sure enough, Sam peered at her from behind the car. His eyes narrowed, and he grunted. "If you're looking for another ride, it's not gonna happen out here on this road. Afraid you'd be standing there a few days without seeing another soul. I've changed enough tires on this car that I can do it in my sleep. I'll get us on the road again soon enough."

He looked pretty sweaty. Maybe she should fan him or something. Hoping it wouldn't disturb his work, Lexa opened the back door and plucked the police union newsletter from the outside pocket of her suitcase. It was already coming in quite handy on this trip. She moved over to Sam and feverishly fanned the top of his bent head. *Whoosh!*

His hands paused their work, and Sam glanced up at her. "I appreciate your efforts to keep me cool, but it's pretty much a lost cause at this point. What I need most now is the tire iron. It's in the toolbox in the back." One brow raised and he swiped a hand across his forehead. "Interesting reading material. Are you an undercover cop in your spare time?" Sam's tone was teasing and implied he didn't believe it for a second.

"My dad was." Lexa folded and tucked the newsletter in her pocket. Poking around in the toolbox a few seconds later, she hoped she'd recognize the tire iron. If only her dad allowed her to help with his projects, maybe she'd know what it looked like. It wasn't like they routinely taught girls these things in school.

"Is there a problem?"

Lexa peeked around the corner of the car. "Um, which thing is the tire iron, exactly?"

"I'll get it." Removing the hub cap, Sam lowered it to the ground. Rising to his imposing height, he dusted his hands together and headed her way.

"Is it this thing?" When she pulled out the tool, it was heavier than she anticipated and her hands were clammy from all the humidity. Lexa watched in horror as it flew out of her grasp and slammed against Sam's denim-clad lower legs. It fell with a heavy thud in the dirt between his boots.   Wary of another coughing attack, Lexa waved her hand in front of her face. She trained her eyes on the ground, afraid to meet his eyes. She hoped he wouldn't bark like her dad when she tried to help.

"Yep. That's it." He didn't even flinch as a small cloud of dust swirled around them. Sam's voice sounded tight with frustration. Crouching down, he retrieved the tire iron.

"I'm so . . . sorry?" Lexa finally dared to look up at him, one hand covering her mouth, not sure whether to laugh or cry. Surely he understood it was an accident. She wished his smile would return. She liked it a whole lot better.

Sam's hands found his hips. "Miss Clarke . . ." The words were slow and measured. "I'm sure you understand we're going to be using tools for the next eight weeks." Shaking his head, he ran a hand through his damp hair. "Never mind. I'm sure I can find a way for you to help us out at the worksite." The encouraging signs of another grin tipped the corners of his mouth. "I suspect something with numbers or measuring things might be best."

Lexa tried her best to look him straight in the eye. It was rather difficult. When Sam lowered his head, she captured his gaze, holding it steady. The hint of a twinkle in those blue eyes surprised her. "I'm a fast learner. Give me something to do so I can help you."

Sam nodded, but he looked dubious. "Okay. I know just the thing."

~

Standing beside him, Lexa clutched the lug nuts in her tight fists, her expression a study in agitation. Stubborn as all get out, this one. No doubt irritated all he'd asked her to do was hand him lug nuts. But, it was all he needed if they were going to make it to the camp anytime soon.

Sam glanced at her impractical shoes and swallowed his grin. One foot tapped a steady rhythm, kicking up dirt. With her fancy clothes, Lexa looked more prepared to board a cruise ship than build houses. Even with those ridiculous shoes boosting her height, she still couldn't be any taller than five-foot-three, give or take an inch.

He stole another look as he worked. In odd contrast to the way she was dressed and those pink nails peeking at him beneath her shoe strap, Lexa was one of the most *natural* women he'd seen in a long time. His eyes followed the long, blonde braid down almost to her waist. That wasn't something you normally saw outside of a farm in the Midwest. Most career women couldn't be bothered. Fascinating.

A trail of faint freckles peppered her nose and sprinkled across her upper cheeks. Her features and that pleasing drawl held an inherent sweetness, an innocence all too rare. Guys would line up around the block for a woman like Lexa. But she gave off signals she wasn't interested. Even though he noticed, he wasn't *looking*. Big distinction. The two of them should get along just fine.

Once he was certain the new tire was secure, Sam repositioned the hub cap. "I hope you brought a pair of sturdy work boots. Especially out at the worksite, you don't want anything falling on those dainty toes."

If it was possible, Lexa's foot shifted into overdrive. "I hope that's not a crack because I hit you. I assure you, it was completely an accident." She sniffed and turned her head the other way. "For the record, I'm . . . I'm sorry."

Bless her heart, she sounded genuinely remorseful.

"Relax. It was simply an observation. And stop tapping your foot. You're stirring up trouble . . . I mean dust." Freudian slip. "Besides, I thought women liked being called dainty." Sam shot another glance at the tiniest feet he'd ever seen on a woman. "Those little wedgie shoes of yours aren't exactly practical for a work camp."

A pink flush slowly crept into her cheeks. It was gratifying to see a modern woman could still blush. "I brought steel-toed work boots, yes. And it's called a wedge heel, thank you very much. Not a wedgie. That's something else entirely." Her unexpected smile revealed a glimpse of the humor hidden behind that defensive façade. When she wasn't tight as a knot, Lexa Clarke was incredibly pretty.

Shrugging his shoulders, Sam gave her a half-grin. "Wrench, please." He held out his hand, waiting.

"Did you just call me a wench?" Lexa's voice rose, and the smile faded.

Sam laughed outright. Communicating with this volunteer might prove a challenge in itself. "Of course not. Careful, Miss Clarke. Your hackles are showing. I think that particular term went out with the Middle Ages and is only used at Renaissance Fairs. I simply asked for the *wrench*. Since the tire iron proved a bit unwieldy, I thought maybe I'd use the wrench this time. You *do* know what . . ."

"Of course, I do." Lexa darted to the back and returned in five seconds flat. Without another word, she handed him the wrench. Her look of self-satisfaction said it all. He wouldn't bother telling her he meant the bigger wrench. He could make do. For a brief second, Sam wondered what her hair looked like loose and flowing. He averted his gaze. Now she really *was* stirring up trouble, but trouble of an entirely different nature. The kind he was trying hard to ignore and avoid.

Giving each lug nut a solid, full turn to make sure they were equally tight, he lowered the car to the ground and removed the jack. "That should do it." He checked the tire one last time, satisfied it was secure. "We'd better get moving. We're already behind schedule." He gathered the old tire and tools and piled them into the back of the car.

Not waiting, Lexa flung the door wide and climbed back in the car. It was a surprise when she leaned across the seat and pushed his door open. "I'm sorry if picking me up at the bus station put you behind schedule. I could have just flown in on an airplane like a normal person and grabbed a taxi to the camp."

Easing behind the wheel again, Sam replaced his sunglasses and decided to ignore the normal person comment. From the fancy suitcase and clothes to her overall demeanor, Lexa seemed pretty pampered. Maybe the humidity made her irritable. It had that effect on a lot of women. He hoped she'd get used to it sooner than later or he'd be better off to steer clear. A narrow line between her brows surfaced and she crossed her arms.

Starting the engine, Sam pondered her comment. He cleared his throat, searching for something to say that might not offend her. "First of all, I would have opened the door for you."

Judging by her deepening frown, that wasn't the best comment. He pulled out on the road again and avoided looking at his watch.

"Not that I don't appreciate your gentlemanly, old-fashioned chivalry, but I thought it'd get us on the road quicker if I'm self-sufficient and don't stand on ceremony."

"And also for the record, picking you up at the bus station didn't put us behind. It's more the matter of a nail in the road causing a flat tire. And no way would a taxi driver be able to find his way to the camp. All roads definitely do not lead to the TeamWork camp. Let's just say it's the road less-traveled." Lexa kept her eyes trained out the window as if there was actually something to see, but Sam could tell she listened. "If I've learned anything in my life, it's that God always knows what He's doing."

"Are you saying God made the tire go flat?" Her tone sounded more curious than defensive as she turned to look at him again.

"No. I'm saying He allowed it to happen. He has His reasons. It's up to us to try and figure out what He's trying to tell us." Wow, that sounded high-handed. Lexa met his gaze before lowering her lids. The luminous, blue-green color of those eyes reminded him of the Mediterranean. He'd flown over it enough times to appreciate the beauty of the sunlight reflected in its waves.

A vision of eyes similar in clarity and brilliance still haunted him, but Sam pushed the thought to the back of his mind. He had a job to do, houses to build. But mental fortitude couldn't prove a match for the sudden pumping of his heart. This woman might prove to be trouble in more ways than one. *Texas-sized* trouble.

Lexa Clarke intrigued him whether he liked it or not. As he drove them closer to the TeamWork camp, Sam resolved to keep his thoughts occupied with something other than the fascination sitting beside him on the front seat.

Chapter 3

THEY DROVE IN silence for a few minutes. Sam was probably figuring out where to place her in the TeamWork camp that wouldn't endanger any of his more experienced volunteers.

"I hope you realize you'll be working around a lot of people at the TeamWork camp."

Lexa blew out a heavy sigh. Could the man talk about nothing else? "When I signed up with TeamWork, I thought I'd be going to Europe. But all the overseas positions were filled by the time I applied."

"So, you signed up for the adventure of it all, thinking you'd be traveling to some foreign destination." It was more a statement of fact than a question.

"Sorry if that offends you, but yes. TeamWork is supposed to be a *foreign* missions organization from what I understand." Seized by a sense of how egocentric that sounded, Lexa twisted her hands in her lap. She was looking for so much more than adventure.

"It doesn't offend me. Not at all. Especially since you decided to come here, even though it's not your first choice."

Lexa struggled to sit up straighter in the leather seat and glanced over at her companion. "There's more to it than that, of course. It's not like I expected to traipse through the Alps, singing and skipping around like a carefree Von Trapp in *The Sound of Music*, you know. Favorite movie aside, I did some research. I like how TeamWork's helping people around the world in lots of different ways, putting their faith into meaningful action. I'm hoping I can contribute something to the cause."

"Well, that's an admirable goal. I mean, sure, it's not Europe or Africa, or outside the United States. Or even outside of Texas." A grin tugged at the corners of Sam's mouth.

"Okay, here's the thing. The lady in the TeamWork office told me this was where they most needed me. So," she said with a shrug, "here I am."

He nodded. "I appreciate your willingness to help. Trust me, we need all we can get. It's where God has planted us for the next eight weeks, and these people need our assistance."

"Because God knows what He's doing."

"Right. He has His purpose."

"And are skipping and singing like a carefree Von Trapp allowed?" Her grin escaped. In return, Lexa was rewarded with one of the most genuine smiles she'd ever seen.

"Singing is definitely allowed. Just don't expect me to skip. Never gonna happen in my lifetime, unless . . ." The expression on Sam's face appeared wistful, as though he harbored a delicious secret.

"Unless what?" Lexa prompted.

"Unless the Lord blesses me to one day hold the hand of my daughter. That's the only thing that could ever justify skipping." He grunted and straightened on the seat as if to deflect from his tender sentiment by infusing it with a healthy dose of masculinity.

Tears stung her eyes at Sam's unexpected words as Lexa stared blindly out the window. What would this man say if she told him she wasn't sure God even loved her? That He took her mother way too soon and left her with a father who couldn't tell his only child he loved her and wanted no part of God?

Not that she blamed God. Her father wasn't a bad man. He always provided for her, but Michael Clarke didn't have a clue how to raise a motherless girl. He didn't know how to comfort her when she cried herself to sleep every night for nearly a year after her mom died. He preferred to wallow in the misery of his own loneliness. And he certainly never skipped with her.

If anything, Lexa hoped TeamWork could help her find her way back into the graces of the Almighty. Maybe if she did something good for others, He'd find favor and bless her life in some way. It might make up for all the years spent apart from Him, away from the church. Then again, maybe that's not how it worked. Her shoulders slumped under the burden of inadequacy.

"So, I'm sure the TeamWork recruiter told you our specific mission here in San Antonio is to rebuild eight homes destroyed by flooding a few months ago."

Lexa nodded. "Right. Eight homes in eight weeks seems awfully ambitious."

"You'll be surprised how quickly we can rebuild. They're not large homes. We were here at the same camp three years ago, doing the exact same thing." Sadness laced Sam's words. "This particular area is prone to flooding after a drought followed by sudden heavy rains. For some reason, the residents always come back and rebuild in the same place."

She could understand. Until signing up for the TeamWork mission, she'd been hesitant to step outside her own comfort zone. "I guess it's their home and they simply don't want to leave. Old habits die hard, and people sometimes find it difficult to change."

"Where's *your* home, Lexa?"

That question was surprising. Sam didn't seem the type of person to forget much of anything. "Houston." She darted a glance in his direction.

"I'm not talking about *that* home."

She raised a brow. "I'm not sure I understand what you mean."

"Where's home in your heart?"

"Home in my heart?" Lexa repeated, feeling silly.

"I sense hesitation in there somewhere. Or maybe uncertainty."

"Give me a minute." She chewed the inside of her lip. "Not all of us can be as quick on our feet as you."

"I'm not that quick. Just tall." Those smile lines had a life all their own.

"Look, no matter why I signed up, or what I'm afraid of, or why I'm here . . . or where home in my heart is, I need a change of pace. I need to establish priorities in my life, and do something worthwhile. I want to help people less fortunate, and I want to be needed." The edge of irritation slipped back into her voice. "Does that answer all your questions?"

Lexa imagined this man was just getting started. Crossing her arms, she realized she acted and sounded like a petulant child. And why wouldn't her bottom stay anchored to the seat? Pretty soon she'd be staring up at Sam from the floorboard of this old bomb. It had to be the leather seats. They were downright slippery.

"Oh no, red alert. Hostile body language." Sam's tone was wry.

"You really do this for fun?" Lexa shot back.

Raising his arm, Sam gestured at their surroundings. "Why not? Wide open spaces, a great opportunity for ministry, and plenty of interesting *co-workers*."

The last part of that sentence was clearly intended for her benefit. She stared out the window. It seemed like they'd been in the car for hours on end. Whether or not they'd ever arrive at the TeamWork camp was becoming a distinct question in her mind. "Are we almost there?" Lexa didn't expect the hearty laugh elicited by that question.

"Be patient. We'll be there in a few more minutes." Sam sounded the tiniest bit placating.

Drumming her fingertips in a slow march on the edge of the open window, Lexa glimpsed the occasional ramshackle house, a cow, a few abandoned cars and dilapidated signs advertising places long gone. Her stomach churned a bit, fear squeezing her from the inside out the closer they drove to the camp. Would the other volunteers welcome her? Accept her? Was she crazy to sign on for something when she had no idea what to expect? No one said making a difference in the world was easy.

A combination of hot pavement, freshly-mown grass and a foul stench from something in the animal kingdom assaulted Lexa's nostrils and contributed to her queasiness. Leaning her head back against the seat, she wrinkled her nose and closed her eyes. Inhaling a few deep breaths to try and calm her nerves was a mistake and did *not* help.

Without warning, Sam swerved the car and slammed on the brakes, jerking both of them forward. The engine cut off and silence engulfed them. Somewhere in the distance, a cow mooed, and a horse fly buzzed through the car and landed on Lexa's shoulder.

"What . . . ?" She opened her eyes and batted in annoyance at the pesky fly. Looking up in surprise, she shoved escaping strands of hair away from her eyes. A goat stood in the middle of the dirt road. The ornery animal stared them down, as if daring them to come any closer. Massaging the back of her neck, she stole a glance at Sam.

Lowering the sunglasses, he gave her a startled look. "Sorry about that. Are you okay?"

A rumble of laughter began somewhere deep inside, bubbling up and bursting forth in an embarrassing fit of giggles. She didn't care. And then she laughed even harder, releasing the pent-up frustration. A few tears escaped. Beside her, Sam laughed almost as hard as she did.

Wiping tears from her wet cheeks, Lexa lifted her eyes heavenward. Squeezing her eyes tight, she breathed the first silent prayer she'd said in a very long time, asking God to help her get to the TeamWork camp intact. Opening her eyes a few seconds later, she caught Sam watching her with a definite sparkle in those blue eyes.

"I think our adventure has already started." His smile sobered. "Really, Lexa. Please tell me if anything hurts." His concern for her welfare was touching. Of course, he didn't need a lawsuit against TeamWork. Might as well put his mind at ease.

"I'm fine. Just embarrassed you've had to ask me that same question twice in the last forty minutes or however long it's been since we met. I didn't expect a goat crossing out here in the middle of Nowhereville."

Glancing out the window, Lexa cried out in alarm when she spied the goat right beside her open window. It was too late. That crazy old goat worked its jaws and wound up like a major leaguer as it hurled a sticky wad of spit mixed with dry grass through the open window, dead-on in its aim for her cheek.

"Oh! Ew!" Lexa recoiled in shock as it oozed a downward path toward her jaw. Her hand flew to her face. She snatched it away in disgust and stared at her goopy fingers. "Couldn't you have yelled incoming or something to warn me?" Reaching for her purse on the floor by her feet, she fumbled for a tissue.

"I'm as surprised as you, trust me. I thought only llamas liked to spit. Here. Allow me." Sam leaned across the seat and retrieved the package of tissues at the top of her purse. "Normally, I would never invade a woman's sacred property, but you obviously need a little help."

Lexa's pulse picked up speed when she remembered the romance novel stuffed in her purse. She prayed Sam hadn't seen it. She wasn't up to any explanations. It was clear he was trying not to laugh as he pulled out a tissue and held it up to her face. Stunned speechless, Lexa turned her cheek toward him. Anchoring her chin with firm fingers, Sam dabbed away the offending slobber with a surprisingly gentle touch. Funny thing, he didn't appear awkward about it in the least.

"I've been called upon to perform many duties as TeamWork director, but this is a first." Sam grinned and eased his hold on her chin. "If nothing else, I think you're definitely going to challenge me this summer."

"I don't know what to say. That was a first for me, too." Relaxing a bit, Lexa cracked a grin. "Thanks for de-sliming me." She wiped off her fingers and carefully deposited the tissue in the plastic bag he handed to her. Glancing out the window, she spied her bovid assailant ambling through a nearby field.

"You're welcome. I'm the oldest of six in my family. Growing up, we had dogs, cats, birds, turtles, frogs, rabbits and the occasional guinea pig, so I'm used to cleaning animal . . . stuff." Sam chuckled. "The way I see it, that goat was mighty sweet on you, Miss Clarke. I'd take it as the highest form of compliment."

Lexa laughed, and relaxed even more. "You're out of your Freudian mind, Mr. Lewis."

"Oh, I'm sure old Sigmund would have some interesting observations about it. There's bound to be a metaphor in there somewhere. Just a tip. As a self-protective measure—and since you seem to attract all creatures, great and small—you might want to roll up the window until we get to the camp in a few more minutes. It's almost time to hit the bovine crossing." His brows lifted.

With a smirk, Lexa rolled up the window. For good measure and all.

As they headed down that never-ending dirt road again, Sam was quiet for another few minutes before slowing the car and glancing her way. "It's now or never. Last chance to back out before we get to the TeamWork camp." His expression was hard to read, and she couldn't tell if he was teasing or not. He already thought she was incompetent with tools, and an animal magnet. And liked numbers more than people. And wore inappropriate shoes.

A nervous giggle escaped and she settled back against the seat. "Dream on if you think you're going to get rid of me that easy. If we ever actually *reach* the TeamWork camp. I'll have you know I was voted Most Resourceful Volunteer at a Habitat for Humanity project last summer. So, it's not like I haven't helped with this type of thing before." That sounded boastful and totally self-absorbed. She really needed to learn to be quiet sometimes.

Sam smiled. "I don't doubt it for a second. If I may ask, what task were you assigned at the Habitat worksite?"

Lexa bit her lip. She looked out the window and avoided those probing eyes.

"Lexa?"

She shook her head. "Let's just say I stretched the food budget and fed seventy-five people with provisions for fifty." She shrugged. "Simple mathematics and reasoning."

"So, you multiplied the loaves and fish?"

"Guess chicken and potatoes, and you're getting somewhere."

"Well, if our food supplies run low, I'll know to come to you. You've proven yourself pretty hardy. You've already passed the dust-in-the-lungs attack, the flat tire and the goat spitting thing. Those are impressive feats all on their own."

Lexa dropped her gaze from those probing eyes. "May I ask why you're looking at me like that? Surely I don't look like the proverbial deer caught in the headlights."

"No. But you do look sort of like a . . . oh, I don't know . . . maybe a *goat* in the headlights or something."

"Very funny. Just drive, Mr. Lewis."

He chuckled. "Your wish is my command."

Maybe that old goat actually did her a favor. After the eventful trip from the San Antonio bus station to the campsite, she felt inspired and ready to face any challenge TeamWork threw her way. She'd survived a spit assault by a major league goat, so anything was possible. It was downright empowering.

"One other thing. I hope you don't plan on wearing any perfume other than bug spray while you're at the TeamWork camp. It might attract . . . certain creatures, too."

What in the world did he mean by that? Was he flirting? Lexa decided to ignore it. "Sam?"

"Yep?" Another grin tugged at the corners of his mouth.

"Bring it on." Okay, maybe that was flirty. He didn't seem to mind. Lexa slid further down into the seat, but not before she spied what must be the TeamWork camp in the distance. It was about time.

Sam echoed her thoughts. "Ready or not, TeamWork, here we come." Sam pressed harder on the accelerator, sending another cloud of dust swirling around the station wagon.

She was ready. So far, so good. Bring it on, indeed.

Chapter 4

$\mathcal{T}$HE SIGHT OF several ugly, gray concrete buildings sprawled across the flat landscape greeted them. Relief flooded through Lexa. She'd started to think the road to the TeamWork camp was some never-ending loop, and she'd be stuck in the old Volvo station wagon with this inquisitive but distractingly handsome giant the rest of her life.

Small groups of men and women walked across the campsite. They looked to be a good mix of ages, although mostly young, and a variety of ethnicities. As Sam drove them further into the campsite, some waved and smiled.

Parking beside a small concrete building, Sam stepped out of the car and stretched his arms in a high arc above his head. "Gotta work out the kinks." He shot her a grin. "Stay put. Chivalry's at work. Be there in a second." She stayed put. A few seconds later, the door of the Volvo creaked a little as he opened Lexa's door. "Sounds like it needs oiling again to get out *its* kinks."

"Hi, Sam!" A tall, slender girl with long blonde hair walked toward them. Lexa bit her lower lip, feeling dwarfed and dowdy by comparison. This gorgeous creature could put on a potato sack and make it look like designer wear. Most likely there was a beauty queen crown in her closet. But her smile was as friendly and genuine as they come.

"Hey, Beck. This is Lexa Clarke." Lexa darted a glance at Sam. At least he didn't display that idiotic, besotted expression most men adopt around a beautiful woman.

"Hi, Lexa." Her voice had a distinctive, southern drawl, genteel and cultured. "It's nice to meet you. I'm Rebekah Grant, one of your roommates while you're here for the summer." She gathered her close in a quick hug. "Welcome to TeamWork."

"It's nice to meet you, too." Somewhat embarrassed, Lexa surveyed their surroundings. "Exactly how many roommates do we have?"

"Six others besides us. Don't worry, you'll get used to it. None of us snore or have any disgusting habits. We have Sam for all that," Rebekah teased with a wink in Sam's direction. With an amused grunt, he hoisted Lexa's suitcase over one shoulder and started walking across the campsite toward a row of the gray, one-level buildings a short distance away. Lexa hastened to catch up to him, a near impossible task since his strides were so long.

Pausing, Sam turned back toward her. "This is actually an old prisoner work camp."

Lexa gulped. Was the prisoner tale some rite of initiation? Perhaps they gave the new volunteers that line to gauge how gullible they are. "Well, as long as I don't run into the old chain gang, I'm good. But if that happens, all bets are off."

Sam and Rebekah both laughed. "It really *is* an old prison work camp," she whispered as they resumed walking, "but that was a long time ago."

Something in Sam's expression revealed an ease of familiarity around Rebekah. Lexa wondered if there was more to it, but she seemed pretty young. She couldn't be much older than twenty or twenty-one. Judging by the faint lines crinkling the corners of Sam's eyes, and the tinges of silver at his temples, he must be in his late twenties or early thirties.

"What kinds of ministry . . . things do you do around here, Rebekah?"

"I do a little bit of everything, like most of us here at the camp. We all pitch in where we're needed most. It helps break the monotony, and you get to know everyone better. Most of the time, I work with the children in the schoolroom, keeping the preschoolers occupied and out of trouble so their fathers and mothers can help rebuild the houses destroyed by the flood." Pushing a few strands of long hair behind one ear, Rebekah looked over at her. "What area of ministry are *you* most interested in?"

Lexa hesitated as she thought of an appropriate response. She really should work on an answer to that question. It was bound to come up again.

"I'm sure once Lexa has the opportunity to check everything out, she'll be able to plug in and help us out tremendously."

The unexpected show of support was surprising, and Lexa darted a grateful smile in Sam's direction. "How many new TeamWork volunteers do you have this summer, Sam?"

"Seven. I've worked with most of the other volunteers on at least one other mission."

Either TeamWork or this man inspired loyalty. Maybe both. Lexa turned her attention back to Rebekah. "Are you a schoolteacher?"

"You guessed right. I'm planning on being an elementary teacher. I'm from a small town outside Baton Rouge, and I'll be a senior this year at LSU." Rebekah the Teacher would be a first love for all the smitten boys, and the girls would adore her. Her apparent calm, patient manner should be a plus when dealing with children.

Opening the screen door of one of the nondescript, long, narrow buildings, Sam held it open and waited. Lexa made a mental note that it was Building Seven. Considering the fact the concrete structure housed eight women, it was a bit cramped, but serviceable. In a quick glimpse, she surveyed a few single beds, a couple of bunk beds and what she hoped was a small bathroom with running water.

"There's a bathroom with shower in each dorm, and a washer and dryer in the building two doors down to the right. It's always the first question women ask," Sam advised with a grin. The TeamWork leader was uncanny in reading her mind sometimes.

"We're going to paint the walls this weekend, if you want to help. We also saved you one of the single beds." Motioning to one of the beds that looked not much better than a glorified cot, Rebekah stood aside as Sam lowered Lexa's suitcase. Considering how much she'd crammed into it, Lexa was grateful he didn't make a crack about bringing everything she owned. He handled it like it was featherweight.

It was considerate of the other women to think of her needs and not stick her on the top of a bunk bed, not that she would have minded. Rebekah took a couple of minutes to explain the basic daily routine and showed her the small bathroom and lockers where they could store personal items. Out of the corner of her eye, Lexa noticed Sam lounging against the door frame, lightly twirling his Stetson and whistling under his breath.

"Are you two going to stand around talking all day or are we going to lunch?" he asked a couple of minutes later when they finished. "They've probably started without us."

Lexa was surprised Sam waited in the first place. Surely the TeamWork director had more pressing things to do.

Rebekah rolled her eyes and shot an apologetic glance Lexa's way. "Doubtful they'd start without our fearless leader. Relax, Mr. Taskmaster. We're coming. Besides, we're not that late. How long have you been standing there eavesdropping?"

Sam laughed and followed them out the door of the small building, replacing his hat as soon as he stepped outside. He was right about one thing. The rest of the volunteers were already eating when they arrived at the dining tent. Lunch was a quick, bustling event with ham sandwiches, salad, chips and iced tea or lemonade accompanied by an abundance of rowdy laughter and good-natured teasing.

Rebekah explained that specific individuals were in charge of the cooking, but everyone was expected to take turns pitching to help set the long tables, serve the meals and help with cleanup. Food supplies were brought in by truck a couple of times per week from a grocer in San Antonio.

Most of the workers seemed well-acquainted and enjoyed an easy camaraderie she hoped to share soon enough. It could be that a number of them knew each other from home churches or previous TeamWork camps. Preferring to stay quiet beside Rebekah, Lexa listened to the conversations around her as she ate, not really tasting anything. Her mind was muddled from all the names and faces of the people she'd be working alongside for the next eight weeks.

As the volunteers talked about the various assignments in the camp, it hit her that this mission would be tough in some respects—a physical challenge, sort of like boot camp. The TeamWork representative who interviewed her in Houston told her in no uncertain terms that it would be long hours and hard work. So, it wasn't like she wasn't forewarned.

San Antonio was also a fun city with lots to see. The TeamWork orientation leader explained she'd have two free weekends during the eight-week assignment. Maybe then she'd have time to explore the Alamo, the Riverwalk with its winding walkways and open-air cafes, and the festive street markets with their colorful wares. The old missions outside the city also intrigued her. For the most part, the TeamWork experience was going to be the side of San Antonio most tourists never see.

Hearing someone call Sam's name, Lexa glanced his way. Very animated, engrossed in conversation, he gestured with his hands. He possessed a natural, effortless charisma. But Sam had a bit of a grouchy side, too. Hitting him on the leg with that heavy tire iron hadn't helped. To be fair, that would irritate most people. He'd have a nasty bruise to show for it in a day or two. Sam alternated between teasing her, being nice to her, fussing at her, and asking thought-provoking questions that challenged her. He was an enigma in some ways, but overall, Sam came across as genuine, and seemed to care for all his volunteers.

Maybe it was part of Sam's job to make everyone at the camp feel welcome. She wondered why he'd been the one to pick her up at the bus terminal. Was it only because she was a first-time volunteer? If Sam picked up every one of his volunteers, he'd spend every blessed minute of the first few days running around in that old car. The thought made her grin.

Leaving the dining tent, Lexa's heart fluttered as her eyes met Sam's. She focused on moving her feet forward when he fell into place beside her. When she darted a quick glance his way, she saw compassion in those blue eyes. *He knew.* Knew how scared she was. Frightened the others wouldn't like her, wouldn't accept her once they found out she didn't go to church or know much about the things of God. Their God. But was He also *her* God?

"Don't worry, Lexa. It'll be okay." When she paused, Sam placed a light hand on her forearm. Unbidden tears welled and threatened to escape. He couldn't know those were the exact words her mother said before she passed away from cancer when Lexa was a scared eight-year-old, fighting the fear of abandonment. Six words meant to comfort and give her hope for the uncertain future. Words that meant so much for her heart.

"I'm not worried." Lexa fought to keep her voice even and blinked hard. "Why would you think that?" Not sure she wanted to hear what came next, she started walking again. Dropping his hand from her arm, Sam kept pace beside her again. He was a persistent man. That didn't exactly come as a surprise.

"Try not to take everything so personally." Before she could respond, he continued on. "I'm sure it's hard, being thrust in the middle of something so unfamiliar."

Lexa fought the urge to cross her arms. Sam was only trying to be nice and spoke the truth. "It was completely my choice to come. I'll adapt." She tilted her head to one side. "You seem to have a lot of questions about me, Mr. Lewis. Isn't there a file with my volunteer application or something? Surely that should fill in some of the blanks."

Sam nodded. "Yes, there's a file. Confession time. I haven't had a chance to actually look at your file yet, but I will. I'm much more interested in what's *not* in your file. Your driver's license and social security card only prove your identity, but they don't show me who you are." He sighed. "I only arrived a couple of days ago myself, and it's been hectic getting everything set up. Most of the other volunteers arrived yesterday, and I've been a little busy."

"You don't owe me any explanations."

"I still wanted you to know." Sam pulled his sunglasses from his pocket and positioned them on his face. "I'm taking a crew over to the building site in a half hour if you want to join us and get started on one of the houses. It'd be a good opportunity to meet some of the other volunteers. But if you want to stay in the dorm—unpack and get oriented to the camp—that's fine, too, especially since you just arrived."

When she didn't answer right away, Sam plundered on. "How handy are you at swinging a hammer?"

"As handy as you are at charming the girls, I'm sure." Lexa turned away as her cheeks grew warm. She resisted the urge to put her hands on either side of her face. Nothing like snippy, sarcastic comments to keep men at bay. It had always proved a surefire method before. She had the feeling this particular man was different and looked at her as a challenge.

He didn't miss a beat. "Nah. These girls around here are only interested in me for my brawn, not my brain."

Lexa tamped down the laugh threatening to erupt. "That doesn't appeal to you?"

It was Sam's turn to laugh. "No, Miss Clarke. I'm looking for a *real* woman." With his deep drawl, it sounded exactly like the kind of thing a Texas cowboy would say. Bring on the horse, the barking canine companion and the cattle drive. Time for the roundup.

Lexa couldn't resist the bait. "And what qualifications must a *real* woman have to gain your attention?"

Sam's expression sobered. "The only qualification, as you put it, is that she has to have a strong commitment to the Lord."

Whatever she expected to hear, it wasn't that. "That's it? Seriously?"

"Yep. That's about it."

"What about looks?" That might sound shallow, but surely looks ranked high on the list for a man like Sam.

"What about them?" he countered, pinning her down with that blue-eyed gaze. "I've been around long enough to know that beauty is surface gloss, only an added bonus. It's what's in here that counts." He put his hand above his heart. "Beauty is all in how a woman responds to life's challenges, and grows from her experiences."

"Well, that's a perfectly lovely sentiment, and no offense, but it sounds like something straight out of Dating 101 for Christian men." Perhaps she should have thought that one out before spouting it out. "I didn't mean to sound so derogatory. Of course, you have a right to your opinion." Only dating strong Christian women and not caring about looks? No way on earth could she accept that as the truth about this man.

"No offense taken. If you want to know the truth, I personally like a little spice in a woman."

Lexa threw her head back with laughter. "Spice? Like what? A little salt, perhaps?" She started to walk away, but not before she glimpsed his wide grin.

"No." He caught up to her in one large step. "More like paprika. Someone to keep my eyes wide open and on my toes." Sam stopped walking. "Are you flirting with me, Miss Clarke?"

"Never!" she protested, grinning back at him over her shoulder as she moved forward. "I don't know why you'd think such a thing, Mr. Lewis." In the course of only a few hours, she'd said something similar to him at least twice. This was getting ridiculous.

No matter his protests to the contrary, a man like Sam wouldn't fall for just any solid Christian woman either—plain Jane or not. If that was the case, he would have married a long time ago. Any one of the girls in Sam's TeamWork camp should qualify. He didn't wear a wedding ring, and he didn't strike her as the type to ever divorce a woman. No, he'd stick it out in a loveless marriage. He'd be faithful and loyal to the end. Besides, no woman in her right mind would ever divorce a man like Sam.

Lexa didn't want to consider the possibility he was a widower with a dead wife and a slew of kids back home in Houston. She wouldn't wish something like that on the poor guy, pining away for some saintly but deceased woman who'd stolen his heart and left him with a bunch of kids to raise all by his lonesome. Sounded like the plot of a romance novel or some sappy television movie.

Sometimes she thought she could write her own romance novels with all the crazy thoughts dancing in her mind. What in the world was she thinking? Lexa shook her head and tried to hide her soft laughter.

"Definitely spicy."

Lexa heard it clear as a bell before Sam caught up to her again. Her heart beat wildly in her chest. This was not a good sign. Not at all. Talk about a hopeless romantic.

"So, are you game to come along with my group this afternoon?"

Again, she couldn't resist a grin. "Why not? I think that's why I'm here, after all. Besides, it doesn't look like I'll have a better offer the rest of the afternoon. Unless that old chain gang decides to show up, of course."

He laughed. "I'm meeting everyone in front of the dining tent in half an hour. Remember, the afternoon sun can get really hot." His gaze brushed over her fair arms. "Be sure and put on some sunscreen, but water is provided."

Lexa nodded. "I'll be there, ready to work." She felt Sam's smile all the way down to her toes.

"Good."

He tipped his hat as she turned toward Building Seven. Her head high, Lexa sensed a certain pair of light blue eyes on her the entire way. She focused on picking up her feet and not stumbling. Heaven help her when she put on those heavy work boots back at the dorm. That would be the real test of walking.

It was unnerving knowing the TeamWork leader watched. Lexa dared not look back over her shoulder this time. If she did, she feared she might just turn to dust or at least be rendered unsteady on her feet and incredibly weak in the knees.

Chapter 5

*T*WO HOURS LATER, Lexa sat back and wiped her wet brow with the back of her hand. It was so humid, she felt sticky all over. She'd changed into denim shorts and an Astros T-shirt for the worksite, but the backs of her knees were practically fused together. Even though it was equally hot in Houston, she wasn't used to manual labor under the blazing sun. It was sweaty and hard. But another part of her loved it. It was a rewarding release of energy and cathartic in several ways.

"Here, have a drink of water."

Lexa accepted the cold cup of ice water from Rebekah with a grateful smile. Tipping that cup over and letting it fall on her head sounded like a pretty good proposition, too, but thirst won out. She remembered Sam's comment about getting used to the heat. Right now, that didn't seem possible.

"Thanks." She drained half the glass before stopping. "I definitely needed that."

"Yeah," Rebekah agreed, swinging her long, tanned legs around to sit beside Lexa on a stack of cement blocks. "You have to keep hydrating yourself in this heat, and you'd better get a hat or you'll get a serious sunburn. We blondes have to stick together. Did you bring a hat?"

Lexa shook her head. "No, as a matter of fact. Call it an unfortunate lack of foresight." She frowned. It was pretty careless not to think of something so practical. Not to mention sunglasses. Served her right for not following the suggested packing list.

"You can't be expected to think of everything. I'll check around and see if anyone has an extra. If they don't, maybe we can get Sam to run us into town in the morning. Well, I'd better go see if anyone else needs a drink of water. See you later." Rebekah tossed a wave over her shoulder as Lexa called out her thanks.

"Lovely girl, isn't she?"

Squinting in the blinding afternoon sunlight, Lexa shielded her eyes with one hand while nodding in agreement. "Yes, she is." She rose from her position to gain a better view of the blond man standing beside her. "Nice, too."

"I suppose she's nice enough if you're not related to her." He extended his hand. "Josh Grant." His smile deepened the color of his Oz-like emerald green eyes. A lot of women would follow that proverbial yellow brick road all the way home if it led to this man.

"Rebekah's brother." One eyebrow raised. He did bear an uncanny resemblance to her statuesque, blonde roommate. "Twin brother, to be exact. Of course, I'm the better looking of the two of us."

"And certainly the most humble. Nice to meet you. I'm Lexa Clarke."

"I know. Beck pointed you out at lunch, but things were kind of hectic so I didn't get over to meet you. My mistake." His grin was playful. "Is this your first TeamWork mission?" Those green eyes looked at her with unabashed interest.

"Is it that obvious?"

"No, but I'm sure I'd remember if I'd met you at a TeamWork camp before."

Smooth operator, this one. Lexa handed him a hammer. "Here. Channel all that charm and make yourself useful. I need some help." Josh laughed and winked. She explained the job of hammering thick strips of wood together. Together they made much quicker work of the assignment than she could have done by herself.

An unsettled feeling came over her at one point. Glancing up from her work, Lexa spotted Sam standing about a hundred yards away. He'd changed into khaki shorts and brown, sturdy work boots. Caught staring, Sam raised his hand. Even so, the look on his face struck her as odd. Call it intuition, but Lexa wondered if it had something to do with the man working beside her. Returning Sam's wave, she lowered her head and tried to focus on Josh's latest story.

Like his sister, Rebekah's twin kept up a steady stream of conversation. He asked her questions about her work and life in Houston. Ambitious and forward-thinking, Josh already graduated college a year ahead of Rebekah and planned to begin law school the week after their TeamWork mission ended.

Not wanting to lose her concentration, Lexa nodded as they worked to indicate she listened. As much as anything else, she wanted to prove her worth as a hard worker. To herself as much as to one extremely tall cowboy.

~

"I've got to grab a quick shower before dinner." Lexa walked alongside Rebekah as they returned to the dorm late in the afternoon. At least the sun wasn't quite so high on the horizon, and a slight breeze broke the monotony of the heat.

"We take about three showers a day around here." Another girl jumped off her bed and moved forward. "Hi, Lexa. I'm Amy Jacobsen. We met in the canteen earlier, but I don't expect you to remember my name." Amy pushed a strand of shoulder-length, dark hair behind one ear and gave her a friendly smile.

"It's nice to meet you." Lexa returned the other girl's smile. "There's so many names to learn, and forget about last names." After all, she was better with numbers, not people.

Amy nodded. "It seems impossible, but you'll surprise yourself at how quickly you'll learn. Don't give up. Here you go." Grabbing a piece of paper tacked by the front door, she thrust it in Lexa's hand. "This is a list of everyone here in the camp. It'll help you. Do you need soap for the shower or anything?"

"I think I have everything I need, thanks." Lexa glanced down at the long list of names, knowing they wouldn't mean anything until she could associate them with faces. She unzipped her suitcase and retrieved a bath towel. That shower was going to feel so good, and the hot water would soothe her tired, aching muscles. Nonetheless, it was true—hard, honest labor was incredibly satisfying.

"I understand you met my notorious twin brother." Finished with their showers a short time later, Rebekah scooped her long hair into a pony tail as Lexa braided her damp hair in front of the small square mirror mounted on the wall.

"Josh is very nice."

"Watch him, Lexa. He makes people laugh and they end up smashing their fingers with hammers and stuff like that. In other words, he's a work hazard, dangerous to be around when you're working." Rebekah hastily threw everything into a bag and shoved it underneath her bed.

"Thanks. I'll take it under advisement."

"Don't say I didn't warn you." With a parting wave, Rebekah headed out of the building with Amy.

"Do I have time for a quick nap before dinner?" Lexa asked the other girl sitting alone on another single bed in the otherwise empty women's dorm.

She nodded her short-cropped, dark head. "Ye–ye–yes bu–but only a–a sh–sh–short one." Her voice was quiet and accompanied by a shy, but very sweet, smile.

Dropping down onto her bed, Lexa sighed. "Maybe I'll read then," she commented, more to herself than the other girl. If she didn't nap long enough, she'd get grumpy. She wanted to be as agreeable as possible for this summer assignment. As it was, the high humidity wasn't doing any favors for her disposition.

It wasn't long before the dinner gong sounded. Her roommate closed her Bible and put it on her pillow. Her bed was incredibly neat, the sheets and lightweight blanket tucked in at the corners with near-military precision.

"I'm Lexa. What's your name?" They walked out of the building together in the direction of the dining tent.

"Sh–Sh–heila," came the soft reply.

Lexa looked over at her and smiled. "Are you from Texas, too?"

Sheila's dark eyes widened and she shook her head, but it was hard to determine her response. She met Lexa's eyes for a split second before turning away, avoiding her gaze. But not before Lexa caught the look of fear in her deep brown eyes. It was only there for a fleeting second, but there was no mistaking it. *What's this girl afraid of?* Even the way Sheila walked, with her shoulders hunched and her head down, she looked afraid of her own shadow.

Entering the large dining tent, Lexa heard her name being called. Josh waved an arm in her direction. It was like being invited to sit at the popular kids' table in school. Intending to invite Sheila to join her as she threaded her way among the long tables, Lexa watched her head off in another direction.

"Ah, Miss Clarke. I'm so glad you've decided to join us this evening. I trust you feel refreshed?" Josh grinned, Rebekah rolled her eyes, and the others within range laughed. "Here, sit by me." He moved over on the bench and patted the seat beside him.

"Thanks." Lexa glanced around the table at the other smiling faces. As she waited for the blessing, Lexa's focus settled on the person she'd unconsciously been seeking. *Sam.* Sitting a few tables away, he faced her, engaged in conversation with a man she recognized as another new volunteer. A shock of wavy dark hair fell across Sam's forehead beneath the ever-present cowboy hat.

Watching him, Lexa wished she could tuck his hair out of the way of those piercing blue eyes. *Stop it, Lexa.* She'd never had the desire to run her fingers through a man's hair before. Why now? Why here? It made no sense.

She drew in a quick breath when his eyes met hers. He nodded and gave her a small salute, sending her pulse into overdrive. This, too, was getting ridiculous. Besides his obvious good looks, what was it about this man that intrigued her? Shaking her head and trying to regain her concentration, Lexa listened to the various conversations around the table.

"Where's Sam?" Josh looked around the tent. "He'd better pray soon, or I'm going to have to do it. We can't sit around starving all night, waiting for him to finish his conversation." He motioned to Sam. "Hey Sam, pray for this meal already, will you?" Spontaneous laughter and a smattering of applause broke out as everyone turned in Sam's direction.

Rising to the occasion, their leader rose to his feet. The smile lines were very much in evidence as he removed his hat, clasped it in front of him, and bowed his head. "Let's pray."

Glancing around as everyone around her bowed, Lexa admired the respect Sam commanded from his crew of volunteers. It was as though he was their leader in an army. It *was* an army of sorts, kind of like God's army. A snippet of a song from childhood Sunday school class floated into her mind. Maybe some things you don't forget. They just get pushed back a bit in the mind. It was something about being in the Lord's army . . . shoot the artillery . . . fight in the cavalry . . . Closing her eyes, Lexa bowed her head and concentrated on Sam's words.

"We thank you for bringing these wonderful people here to help us out in our work this summer. We thank you for bringing our newest volunteers to us today. We pray for your watchcare over us, and we thank you for this food that's been prepared. Most of all, Father, we pray for the salvation of those we're here to help. Help us to impress upon them the need for the Savior in their lives so that they might see your mighty power and the glory of your name."

A rousing chorus of amens echoed throughout the group in the tent as Sam sat back down and the meal began.

Looking around the group of about sixty workers, Lexa spied Amy pouring drinks. Three other girls and two guys served the barbecued beef sandwiches. It was only a matter of time before she'd be expected to pitch in and do her part. Good. Being on a list would help her feel included, a part of the group. She'd look forward to it.

"Those sandwiches smell great," Rebekah commented as one of the servers brought the plate of steaming food to their table. Lexa didn't realize how hungry she was until she took her first bite of the sandwich. Soon, she ate with relish, marveling at her own voracious appetite.

"It's something about the heat and hard work." Rebekah nodded at Lexa's empty plate. "People either lose their appetite or find themselves incredibly hungry. It seems to have the latter effect on you."

"I'm going to have to watch it or I'll gain weight this summer." Lexa chose an apple from the bowl of fruit on the table.

"That's doubtful." Amy rejoined their group after finishing her serving duties, at least for the moment. "With all the work we do around here, you're going to need the food for sustenance. Believe me, you'll work it off, so my advice is to eat up."

Lexa shot her a grateful glance. Without a doubt, this bubbly girl had been a cheerleader. Her enthusiasm was infectious. At the worksite earlier in the afternoon, Amy kept the group in stitches with her anecdotes, from what little snippets Lexa's overheard in-between Josh's stories.

"Coming to the bonfire tonight, Lexa?" Josh took a long, slow sip of his iced tea. Those green eyes were too good to be true. He needed to stop looking at her like that. And the winking thing even more so. Besides, he was too young for her. Still, he entertained her with humorous stories, and she liked being around Josh and his sister. Both were so nice and made her feel welcome in the TeamWork camp. Everyone had, as a matter of fact.

"I don't know," Lexa began, shooting Rebekah a question with her eyes. For the first time, Lexa noticed Josh's twin's eyes were every bit as deep green with little flecks of amber dancing around in those orbs. "I didn't know we were having a bonfire." What in the world would they do there? For starters, Lexa imagined they'd sing and pray.

"We have one every night," Josh told her. "You'll love it. It's a chance to kick back, relax, sing, share a testimony, get to know each other better, and grow closer to the Lord."

It sounded pretty good until the last part about growing closer to the Lord. What had she gotten herself into here? What in the world was a testimony? Suddenly, the truth washed over her—she was a phony. An imposter. She didn't know anything about being a Christian, and here she was with this wonderful group of people who accepted her without question and believed she belonged to their group.

Lexa stood on the outside looking in. Sam Lewis already had her number, and it wouldn't take long for the rest of his volunteers to surmise the same. Lexa silently absorbed the lively banter around her, aware that Rebekah eyed her with a curious expression.

As she left the dining tent a short time later, Lexa stared at the ground and kicked up dust with her boots as she shuffled along. She made a conscious effort to pick them up and not stumble. Even though they were important for the work she was there to do, she felt ridiculous wearing them. It was called forsaking vanity for practicality.

"Coming to the bonfire tonight, Miss Clarke?"

She tried to control the wild fluttering inside. *Just keep walking, Lexa.*

Chapter 6

$\mathcal{L}$EXA STUMBLED FOR a split second before catching herself. All she needed was to fall on her face, in the dirt at the TeamWork director's boot-covered feet. That would pretty much complete her humiliation. For whatever reason, Sam liked seeking her out. While flattering, it was unnerving. That blue-eyed gaze traveled down to her feet, and the already familiar grin surfaced.

"I'm not sure. I'm kind of tired." It was only a half-truth, but Lexa didn't know what might be expected. If she had to say anything—or was expected to share her feelings with the others—she preferred the option of being able to slip away unnoticed. So, it was better not to go. End of story. She'd pretend to be exhausted at the end of a long first day and then go to bed early. She didn't know what her excuse would be after tonight, but she was creative and would come up with something.

Lexa looked around at the barren landscape of the camp. "There's not much to look at, is there?" She avoided looking at Sam, but it was tempting. That question sounded leading, and she shouldn't have asked it.

"Oh, I wouldn't say that, exactly." She heard the smile in his voice. "And whenever you have an answer to the home in your heart question, I'm waiting to hear it."

Here we go again. "You're like an elephant and never forget anything, do you?"

"I try not to." Sam laughed. "There's always something that helps me remember. Take you, for instance."

Her brows shot up. "Me? What do you mean?"

"Braid. Numbers. People. Something about you that's different, what you're about, and what you're afraid of."

"That's pretty simplistic. And I didn't say I'm afraid of people. I only said numbers are easier and safer . . . than people," Lexa stammered. "Numbers are finite, although they can certainly change. But I can always depend on them."

"Ah-ha. Bingo!" His tone sounded triumphant.

Her curiosity got the best of her. "Okay, Mr. Freud. What does that say about me?"

"Numbers don't disappoint the way people can." Compassion resonated in that deep, masculine voice.

Lexa shrugged. "Disappointment's a big part of life. I'm a big girl. I can handle it."

"You don't always have to be so defensive, Lexa. You're among friends here." His eyes met hers, holding them steady.

Her breathing grew shallow. He had her pegged. Biting her lower lip, Lexa resolved not to reveal her vulnerability to this man. Sam was unusually perceptive, not to mention intuitive. Had he tipped Rebekah and Josh off about her, asked them to befriend her? Were they only acting like her friends as a favor to him? She didn't want to think things like that, but her mind was clouded, confused. Struggling for an answer, she gave him a helpless shrug.

"From what I've seen so far, you're getting to know the volunteers and fitting in. Feel free to join us at the bonfire tonight. I think you'd have a good time." Sam turned to go.

"Sam?" Lexa hated the slight tremor in her voice. It betrayed her every time.

"Yes?" Those baby blues looked kind, drawing her in.

"Thanks." It sounded inadequate, but she wanted him to know she appreciated his efforts to make her feel comfortable in the camp.

"For what?" He sounded genuinely puzzled.

"Thanks for taking an interest and making me feel welcome." A question came to her mind. What did she have to lose? "Sam?"

"Yes?" A grin of amusement upturned his lips.

"Tell me something. Do you personally pick up all the camp volunteers at the bus station when they arrive for duty?" Goodness, she made it sound like boot camp. She might as well embroider *Private Clarke* on her blouse, salute the leader and march back to her barracks.

He pulled the Stetson low on his head and ran anchoring fingers around its rim. "Nah. Only the spicy girls. It's inherent in my position as director." The smile lines deepened, and the faint lines around his eyes crinkled as Sam gave her a respectful tip of the hat and pivoted on his boot.

Such a cowboy, this man. Half the women in the TeamWork camp must secretly be in love with the director. Lexa swallowed hard, grateful Sam missed the open-mouthed stare he left behind.

~

Removing his glasses, Sam shook his head and ran a quick hand through his hair. It was muggier than usual. Even his hand was damp when he picked up a pencil. Frowning, he reached for the roll of paper towels he kept near the desk and wiped his hands. Through blind eyes, he stared at the file folder in the middle of his desk. With one finger, he lifted the edge of the folder and opened it. Alexis Clarke's folder.

Rubbing one hand over tired eyes and sitting back in his chair, Sam thought about the woman who captured his immediate attention. She appeared insecure and timid one minute and then turned all spicy and defensive the next. He was curious and more than a little surprised by his own instinctive reaction to her. Maybe he should take some time to examine why that was. But not right now.

A knock on the office door startled him. "Come on in," he called, closing Lexa's folder. "Hi, Beck. What's up?" Motioning for her to have a seat in one of the chairs opposite his desk, he watched as she closed the screen door and sat down.

"I'm curious about Lexa."

"Join the club."

"She's obviously not the usual TeamWork volunteer."

"You can say that again. I was just starting to look at her file now. I haven't really had a chance to look at her application."

"Oh, I'll leave you alone then." Rebekah started out of the chair.

"No, it's all right. Stay." He motioned for her to take her seat again. "The bonfire's over an hour from now, so I've got plenty of time. Besides, you know I always have time for you." Sitting back in his chair, he crossed his arms behind his head. "Tell me what's on your mind."

"Lexa seems somewhat uncomfortable, and I get the feeling she's not . . ."

"Not a Christian?"

Rebekah's green eyes grew wide and Sam heard her quick intake of breath. "I'd never say that, Sam. You know that's not what I meant."

"I know what you mean. This work camp is totally outside Lexa's realm of normal. But no matter why she's here, the Lord's put her here for a reason." Seeing Rebekah's eyes cross, he laughed. "I know, sometimes I sound ridiculously pious. But it's true, all the same."

"Maybe you should have pursued full-time church ministry. If you ask me, you're well-suited to it."

His smile sobered. "This is my ministry for now. You know how much I love my TeamWork camps. And Lexa told me she researched TeamWork and wants to help us make a difference. But, in spite of me griping at her when I was changing a flat tire, and being spit on by a goat," Sam said, pausing as Rebekah laughed, "she didn't tell me to turn the car around and take her back to the bus station. The woman's got spunk and determination." Among other things.

"Are you serious? A goat really spit on her?" Rebekah laughed and shook her head in disbelief. "That must have been pretty gross."

Sam laughed. "It was, but she handled it with uncommon grace."

Rebekah tilted her head, surveying him. "You like her."

Sam sat up straighter in the chair and clasped his hands together on the desk. "I like all my volunteers." He avoided her eyes. She knew him too well.

"This is different. Even though you're trying not to look at me, I saw it. You've got that same look in your eye when you talk about Lexa that you did when you talked about Shelby."

Sam grunted. "That's neither here nor there. Besides, I just met the woman." He hoped she'd drop it.

Rebekah was quiet for a long moment. "It's been three years. You need to let Shelby go."

"I let her go a long time ago."

"Look at me, Sam."

Sam moved his eyes upward to meet Rebekah's, but it took awhile. Patience was one of Beck's best virtues. He knew she'd wait, and she didn't disappoint.

"Shelby was one of my best friends. We both loved her. But she's gone." She paused. "You're thirty-one. It's time to start living again. You need a companion."

"I don't know . . ." Sam shook his head. There was so much about Shelby that Rebekah never knew, never suspected, but he wasn't going to be the one to tell her. Maybe she was right. One of these days, maybe he'd slow down and focus on trying to find another woman. But, at this point, that was a mighty big *maybe*. Just because Lexa Clarke intrigued him didn't mean she was the right one.

"I seem to be doing fine all on my own. I don't need a woman complicating my life."

She wasn't buying his protests for a second. Rebekah's gaze softened as he met her eyes again. "You know Josh and I look at you like an older brother, Sam. You're also smart enough to know the right woman won't complicate anything." She leaned across the desk, making sure she had his eye contact. "The right woman will only enhance your life and ministry. You're too good a man not to find love and share your life with someone. Besides," she added with a coy grin, "it's about time you finally started raising little TeamWork volunteers of your own."

Sam shook his head. "No offense, Beck, but I have a mother. She does a fine job of reminding me of that constantly, all on her own." Not to mention his three sisters had jumped on the old let's-get-Sam-married bandwagon. It was getting rather annoying.

"All I'm saying is, I hope you'll at least open your eyes to the possibility of allowing yourself to love another woman." Rebekah hesitated. "I like Lexa. She might be different from most of the women here, but she's smart, and has a sharp wit. And she's here for the right reasons. In other words," she said, standing once more, "she's got an awful lot of potential. It just needs to be tapped. Do you want me to take her under my wing, show her the ropes around the camp?"

Sam looked up with a grateful smile. "That would be great. From what I've seen, you've done a terrific job of that so far." He shook his head. "I have the feeling I might have to keep an eye on Lexa out at the worksite. She's pretty independent, so I'll have to try and not be obvious about the fact that I'm watching her."

Rebekah saluted with a small grin. "*Pretty* being the key word there, my friend. From what I've seen, you're already doing a good job of keeping your eye on her."

Sam ignored her knowing glance, not wanting to give her the satisfaction. Admitting an attraction for one of his newest volunteers, even to one of his dearest friends and confidantes, wasn't exactly the wisest move. As the work camp director, his behavior needed to be above reproach at all times. He had a job to do, and TeamWork depended on him to get it done.

"I'll leave you to your reading. Enjoy."

"Thanks, Beck."

Her smile always brightened his day.

"You're welcome. Anything to help. That's what TeamWork's all about, right?"

How right she was. Sam's thoughts drifted to earlier in the day. He'd been as obvious as an adolescent boy with a crush on the new girl in school when Beck showed Lexa around the women's dorm. He might as well offer to carry her books and ask her to the Friday night dance.

He was happy when Lexa joined his group at the worksite. If nothing else, he was grateful for the chance to keep a close eye on her. Something in the stubborn demeanor, the defiance in those lovely eyes, alerted him. He needed to make sure she didn't get into too much trouble. Unsupervised, that seemed like a distinct possibility.

In the dim light of his small, cramped office, Sam opened her file folder. Retrieving his glasses, he glossed over the parts about Lexa's family background, but read enough to know she was an only child. Her mother died from cancer when she was a young girl, and her father within the last few years. The interviewer indicated Lexa was more or less an orphan except for a few scattered cousins.

Sam couldn't begin to imagine what his life would be like without the love and support his large family offered. Their hearts and arms were always wide open, ready to embrace any one of them. As the eldest child and namesake of the Lewis clan, he accepted the responsibility to model Christ-like behavior to his siblings and now to his TeamWork volunteers. He didn't look upon it as a burden, but as a high privilege and honor. Still, it was a lot to live up to, and he hoped never to disappoint any of them.

Stopping to read Lexa's answers on the application about her personal testimony, Sam rubbed a hand over his brow. Straining forward to decipher the TeamWork interviewer's handwritten notes in the margin, he read that she asked the Lord into her heart when she was a child of eight. The same age she'd been when her mother died. She listed no home church in Houston on the application.

Removing his glasses, he folded and tucked them into the pocket of his shirt. Sam knew what he must do. What the Holy Spirit prompted him to do. It started with the devotional tomorrow morning. Even if Lexa chose not to come to the bonfire tonight, he hoped to see her there in the morning. It was at the top of his personal prayer list, the one he shared with no one but the Almighty.

Chapter 7

"COMING WITH US, Lexa?" Amy pulled a lightweight sweatshirt around her shoulders and tied the sleeves together across her chest with a casual, practiced move. It was the same way the preppy kids in college wore their sweaters, bouncing along to the tennis courts or club activities. Lexa had seen it all before with her clients. It was the unconscious gestures that gave Amy away—tying the sweatshirt, the tilt of her pinky when holding a cup, certain inflections in her voice. She was generous and unassuming, but this girl had a trust fund.

Lexa shook her head. "Not tonight. Maybe tomorrow night."

Amy shrugged and smiled. "I understand, believe me. You'll get used to the pace here. It won't take long." She called to Rebekah to wait and followed her out the door.

Alone at last. Having so many people around constantly with all the commotion and chatter was draining. Even though part of her enjoyed it and liked the companionship, she also craved the solitude. That's why she didn't share her townhome in Houston with anyone else. Not even a cat.

Sitting on her bed and staring at the empty walls, Lexa weighed her options. She could read the romance novel in her suitcase or go to bed. But she wasn't quite ready to retire for the night and felt restless.

Since she hadn't been to any kind of camp since she was a young girl, Lexa didn't like the imposition of guidelines or curfews dictating what she could—and couldn't—do. She wasn't a rebel in any sense of the word, but she was independent and feisty enough to balk against being made to obey rules. She was an adult, capable of managing her own life and making her own decisions. After all, isn't that what she'd been doing the last seven years, four years in college and then living on her own?

Pulling the book from her suitcase under the bed, Lexa sat down on the mattress and began to undo the laces of her work boots. They were quite dirty after working at the worksite. Yanking the boots off her tired feet, Lexa grimaced when she glimpsed her filthy socks. Peeling them off and draping them across the boots, she pushed them beneath her bed, out of sight. Combined with the heat and hard work, she'd be paying a visit to the laundry room sooner than later.

Lexa plopped down on the bed with a tired sigh. She almost laughed aloud when she turned the book over and spied the virile-looking cowboy who bore an uncanny resemblance to the TeamWork leader. Perhaps she shouldn't read this particular book since there was a living, breathing example of a man like this right here in the camp. But considering it was the only vice in her life, she felt somewhat justified.

After a few minutes, she heard the door to the dorm creak open. Putting a finger in the book to keep her place, Lexa frowned and looked up to see which one of her roommates was coming back inside.

"Hi." Shoulders slumping, Sheila headed straight for her bed. Picking up her Bible, she bowed her head and started to read. Sensing Lexa's stare, she looked up a moment later with a timid smile. It relaxed the drawn lines on her face. Beneath all the worry, Sheila was quite pretty, but it was difficult to judge her age.

"You seem to really like reading your Bible." Lexa turned on her side and propped herself on one elbow. She hoped she didn't make it sound like a bad thing, but more as a simple observation of truth.

Sheila nodded, her smile growing brighter. "Ye–ye–yes." Unlike most of the other women, this roommate was a woman of few words. It might be a result of the stuttering, but Lexa suspected there was more to it. At least she didn't look scared of her own shadow for the moment. Reading and studying her Bible seemed to give her a sense of calm and peace.

"Well, I won't keep you."

Sheila nodded and resumed her reading. A sting of shame nipped at her conscience, and Lexa moved one hand over her novel and nudged it beneath the pillow. The bare-chested cowboy on the front might be great-looking, but she didn't want the other girls to see it. If they did, they might run straight to Sam and plan a TeamWork intervention. Even so, they'd be loving and gentle about it. The thought made her smile.

Feeling somewhat claustrophobic, she decided to take a walk. A slight breeze wafted through the open window, beckoning her outdoors. It had cooled things down enough to make the act of breathing easier. Shoving her feet into tennis shoes, Lexa left the dorm and strolled across the work camp, following the sounds of laughter coming from the bonfire a short distance away. The logs on the fire snapped and a man started to sing, his voice rich and strong.

Lexa headed closer, straining to hear the lyrics of the song. It was about belonging to the Lord as one of His children. She listened, entranced by the clarity and conviction of the man's voice. It sounded familiar. Standing a few yards away, behind the circle of volunteers sitting on benches in a semi-circle, she paused.

She should have known. *Sam.* It wasn't so much the quality of his voice that drew her closer, although he carried the tune well. It was more the pure emotion he poured into the song. He meant every word he was singing, in his heart, his very soul. His eyes reflected the brightness of the moonlight and the leaping, orange-red flames.

Lexa clasped her arms tightly about her, transfixed, shivering even though she stood closer to the fire than before. It must be incredible to feel something with such a depth of emotion. Turning away as his song ended, she thought about sitting on the ground behind the circle or retreating, hoping no one would see her.

Sneaking away on tiptoe in the stillness of the night, she heard Sam begin another song. The others joined in. *Amazing grace, how sweet the sound, that saved a wretch like me. I once was lost, but now am found, was blind but now I see . . .* The lyrics of the old, familiar hymn flooded her mind, and Lexa sang them quietly under her breath. Some things you don't forget, after all. She hadn't sung those words in years, and yet they came back to her easily.

With one last glance over her shoulder, she made her way back toward the dorm. Her steps slowed and she listened as she walked, still humming under her breath when she no longer remembered the words. She felt comforted and warm all over. She couldn't explain it, but she did.

~

"Lexa! Time to get up, sweetie." Someone gave her arm a gentle shake.

"Huh?" Lexa opened her eyes, dazed with sleep. "Where am I? What time is it?" She clamped a hand over her mouth as she yawned.

Amy laughed. "It's almost five-thirty. Looks like we've got ourselves a hard sleeper, girls." Holding out one hand, she helped pull her to a sitting position.

Lexa rubbed her eyes and ran a hand through her tousled hair. She wasn't exactly a morning person. Under these conditions, it might be a difficult eight weeks.

"I guess I did sleep pretty hard." She darted a groggy glance around the room, seeing the other girls busy with their morning preparations. Most of them were dressed and appeared ready for the day's events. How did they manage to be so alert at this unearthly hour of the morning?

"You didn't get a chance to meet the rest of your roommates yesterday," Rebekah began before Lexa interrupted.

"Why don't we wait until I'm a little more awake." She yawned quite loudly.

"Nonsense. This is Natalie Combs, Kim Lawless, Monica Porter and Winnie Doyle." Still in a fog, Lexa nodded in the direction of the four girls, but knew she probably wouldn't remember any of their names by the time she got into the shower.

"Nice to meet you." Lexa's eyes opened wider. "What day is it?" Sitting up and stretching her arms wide, she kicked aside the lightweight sheet with one leg.

The pretty blonde with a ponytail and big blue eyes laughed. Lexa thought it was Winnie. "It's Sunday, and breakfast is served in thirty minutes. Time to rise and shine!" Perky Winnie definitely was the Mother Hen of the group. At the moment, it was equal parts comforting and irritating.

Groaning, Lexa rolled out of the bed and planted two unsteady feet on the hard concrete. Even at this early hour of the morning, the floor was already warm from the rising temperatures.

"Whew! Is it going to be a hundred degrees in the shade today?" Lexa fanned her face with one hand.

"Only a hundred and five," Amy joked, reaching out a hand to pull Lexa off the bed. "Come on, you can do it!" Amy pulled her to a standing position.

"All right, I can do it." Being part of this crew wasn't such a bad thing.

Rebekah caught Lexa's eye and winked. "Sam leads a Sunday morning Bible study after breakfast, if you'd like to come."

"Thanks. I'll think about it." Was it Sunday school all the time at the TeamWork camp? Occupied with unzipping her suitcase, she avoided looking at Rebekah. She wasn't up to answering any questions.

Showering and dressing in record time, Lexa braided her damp hair with practiced movements. A quick glance in the mirror reflected a tinge of pink in her cheeks, a new sparkle in her eyes. Not pausing to think about why that was, Lexa headed off for the dining tent a step behind the others.

Breakfast was another quick event with cereal and milk, and coffee and juice, before everyone dashed off to the meeting circle. It must be the popular spot to congregate for both the evening devotionals and the Sunday morning Bible study. "Come with us, Lexa." Winnie pulled her along behind the group of volunteers headed toward the circle.

Lexa pasted a smile on her face, masking her annoyance. "Don't do me any favors," she mumbled under her breath.

"What?" Winnie didn't ease the hold on her arm, but she graced her with a sweet smile.

"I said . . . it's such a nice morning." Lexa forced a brightness into her voice from somewhere deep inside. Nothing like being coerced into going to the Bible study against her will. Still, she felt no inclination to fight and could think of worse things than staring at a handsome man for however long the study lasted. Maybe she'd learn something.

Rebekah hooked her arm through Lexa's, keeping pace with them. "Enjoy today. Sunday is the one day where we can actually get a little rest in the afternoon if we want."

Opening a chorus book after everyone was settled around the circle, Sam retrieved a pair of wire-rimmed glasses and led a chorus of *Praise the Name of Jesus*. The voices of those sitting around Lexa rose in song, some strong, some soft. Glancing around the circle for Sheila, she spied her huddled on the outer edge. She didn't know the words either.

Moving across the circle, Lexa dropped down beside her. Sheila graced her with her usual shy smile. She wanted to befriend this quiet, withdrawn woman. Something about her reminded Lexa of herself, the introverted part that found it difficult, if not impossible, to open up and let anyone else share her life.

As Sam asked them to open to a verse of scripture, Lexa noticed most of the others carried Bibles. *Strike two.* She chided herself for not unearthing and bringing her old Bible to the TeamWork camp. Who goes to a Christian camp without a Bible? What an oversight. She wasn't even sure where it was—maybe stuck at the top of a closet or in the bottom of a drawer. Or she might have donated it somewhere along the way to Goodwill or the Salvation Army.

Lexa doubted she could recall any of the verses of scripture she'd learned all those years ago, or recognize the hymns or songs. An overwhelming feeling of inadequacy pervaded her senses. Shaking her head, she hung her head and closed her eyes, torn between feelings of self-recrimination and doubt. What was she doing here? What had she gotten herself into? She hoped this group would give her more than three chances. She'd need them. At least they didn't seem judgmental, even for someone as hopeless as her.

"Jonah wondered what in the world he was doing there, in the belly of that huge fish," Sam said at that exact same moment, echoing her own thoughts. Lexa's head snapped up, and her eyes settled on the self-assured man standing in the center of the circle. "Here he was, sitting in the belly of a fish, pondering his options."

Clamping a hand over her mouth, Lexa nearly cried aloud. *Just like me!* Holding his open Bible, Sam talked about how that was the exact place where God wanted Jonah, to teach him and the other men onboard the ship a lesson about the power of the Almighty. She tuned out Sam's voice for a long moment. *Is that what you're trying to teach me, God? How powerful you are?*

Focusing on Sam a few seconds later, Lexa found blue eyes on her. Maybe he just happened to look in her direction. Then again, it could be the reflection from his glasses. But, no. Lexa suspected Sam stared at her for a reason. Did he think she needed to hear this lesson? The very idea made her bristle. The audacity of the man! He didn't know anything about her, so how dare he make assumptions? She shivered and crossed her arms over her chest in spite of the fact the temperature reached almost ninety degrees.

Chapter 8

WHEN THE TIME of prayer began, Sam sat down. His gaze traveled around the circle until it rested on Lexa. His words stirred something inside her. Angered her, judging by the fire sparking in those eyes when they looked up and met his. Beautiful eyes that held a sadness and masked a deep, inner pain to trigger her defensiveness. Sam shifted his position. Now he was an armchair psychologist.

Lexa was a challenge. The other female volunteers in his camp were strong Christians since the womb. They knew the books of the Bible by heart—could practically recite scripture verses backwards and forwards—and stayed active in their home churches. Any of the TeamWork women around the circle might qualify as a wife and lifelong partner, but is that what he really wanted? He'd been seeking the perfect Christian woman for years. But he was honest enough to admit no such woman really existed except in his own mind. He thought he'd found her in Shelby, but she'd disappointed him greatly. And then she died.

Lexa Clarke wasn't strong in her faith. As far as having a strong commitment to the Lord—from what he could tell, she left something to be desired in that category. Not that it was a bad thing. But did she understand what she'd done so long ago when she asked Jesus into her heart? Did she want to gain a deeper understanding of what it means to have Christ as the Lord of her life? Desire to find the power and unbelievable freedom to be found in surrendering her will to the authority of the Almighty? That was often the hardest thing for people to do.

He'd noticed Lexa standing on the perimeter of the bonfire circle the night before. The look on her face was intriguing. Almost wistful. He wondered what she thought as she listened to their singing. He wanted to call out to her, but he couldn't very well do that without drawing undue attention to her.

More than anything else, Sam prayed Lexa would start to feel comfortable and join them. At least she'd ventured out of the dorm and come outside, drawn to their bonfire circle. That was a good sign. Lowering his head to pray, Sam heard none of the other prayer requests, lost in his own.

"Lexa! Wait up!" Sam called as the prayer time ended. He thrived on interaction with his volunteers, the challenge of following up with intensive study and research. Answering one of the newer volunteer's questions, he kept one eye on Lexa as the group scattered.

His conversation ended a couple of minutes later, Sam spied her in the same place, a few yards away. Her back was turned, and one foot dug in the dirt. She appeared vulnerable, prepared to bolt at the slightest provocation. He'd need to tread carefully. "Thanks for waiting."

"No problem." With a shrug of those slender shoulders, Lexa slid her hands down into the pockets of her khaki shorts as they walked together.

The top of her blonde head hit somewhere in the middle of his chest. She was tiny all over. Petite. That was the word for it. But even though she was diminutive in stature, she was well-proportioned with long legs and feminine curves in all the best places. She looked dainty, delicate— like she could barely lift a hammer—but he'd seen how strong she was at the worksite. Not to mention she could wield a flying tire iron with the best of them. In spite of her seeming fragility, Lexa possessed an underlying strength, emotional as well as physical.

"I wanted to ask how things are going for you so far." He tried to keep his tone casual. Glancing her way, he caught her looking at him. Stealing glances was becoming a habit with both of them. Sam's normally slow, steady heartbeat betrayed him. "Are you finding everything you need?" That sounded pretty insipid, and he hoped she wouldn't find him a complete imbecile.

When Lexa smiled, it was encouragement enough to keep going. "Considering there's not much to find, I'm managing fairly well, thank you."

"Please don't tell me you find our little work camp boring, Lexa." When he quirked an eyebrow, she laughed. It was such a great laugh, lilting and surprisingly deep. Pleased he'd made this interesting creature happy, Sam hated to think his next question might chase away that laughter, that entrancing smile.

"It's growing on me."

"I'm glad you came to the Bible study this morning. Did you enjoy it?"

Lexa's eyes narrowed and her smile faded somewhat, as he suspected it would. "Yes, I guess you could say that."

"I thought you might be able to identify with Jonah and his predicament."

Stopping in her tracks and turning to face him, Lexa's eyes blazed. The wrath was coming. Although he'd risk her anger by bringing up the subject, he had to know. Had to know where this woman stood in her spiritual walk. No matter how hard he'd tried to get Lexa out of his mind since meeting her only the day before—the image of those eyes, that mouth—popped into his mind. Maybe he was wrong and physical looks meant more to him than he realized. Surely he wasn't that vain.

"Exactly what predicament are you referring to?" Lexa stared, wide-eyed, her pretty mouth an unyielding straight line.

Sam covered with a lighthearted glance, attempting to keep the mood as light as possible. "All I mean is, this whole missions thing, is new to you, isn't it?" That much was obvious. He was bungling this already.

"Okay," Lexa said. She crossed her arms and planted her feet apart in a stance of preparing to go into battle. "What exactly did the TeamWork interviewer tell you about me? Go ahead, I want to know." When she caught Sam's look of surprise, she blurted out, "It's obvious she either told you something—or wrote something on my application—that's given you cause for concern."

"I wouldn't call it concern." Sam guided her aside, away from the curious stares of the others.

Shaking off his arm, Lexa glared at him, her cheeks flaming. "I told you yesterday when you picked me up from the bus station that I'm here to help. If that doesn't fit the criteria for helping out with this mission, then I might as well go pack my bag now and head back to Houston. Just because I don't know every chorus or bring a Bible with me . . ." Her voice trailed.

From her mortified expression, Sam could tell she'd just admitted something she didn't want him to know. Her gaze dropped to the ground, and she released a shuddering sigh that ran all the way through him.

Lexa turned her head, but not before he glimpsed her tears. "I don't need your pity." Her words were barely more than a whisper. "Just let me stay and help with the building project or whatever else it is you want me to do, but don't pressure me into anything else, okay?"

"Okay. Deal." Feeling like an idiot, but not knowing how else to react, Sam thrust out his hand as if to seal the agreement. Accepting his hand with obvious reluctance, Lexa's eyes moved back to his. Her frown conveyed her confusion.

Her soft, warm hand fit perfectly. The sensation of her much smaller hand in his triggered instincts and affected him deeply, in places and ways he didn't expect. Protective instincts, but it was much more than that. Holding on a few seconds longer than necessary, Sam's heart raced. He slowly released her hand, overcome with the emotion of not wanting to let go. Ever.

"I'm sorry, Lexa. And," he added with a sidelong glance as they began walking again, "for the record, it's not pity. It's interest with a healthy dose of compassion and sensitivity thrown in, I like to believe."

"Is that right?" The irony in her tone only reinforced the ridiculousness of his words. She must think him a pompous windbag, overblown with his own ego.

"Believe it or not, I admire you."

Lexa stopped, quiet for an extended moment. "How can you admire me when you don't even know me?"

"I know firsthand how hard it is to leave a job, your home and security for eight weeks. That takes a major commitment. Other than working with Habitat, I get the impression it's the first time you've ever done something like this. Am I right?"

Lexa's cheeks grew pink again, but at least she didn't look away. Sure enough, those arms crossed in front of her. For an independent woman who didn't hesitate to speak her mind, she sometimes seemed tongue-tied. "You're pretty good at reading people."

"I try. Maybe it's annoying at times, but it helps me be a better leader." Sam grunted. "Listen, I was actually wondering if you'd like to go out with me sometime. But," he added, arching a brow, "since you don't want to be pressured into anything else, I guess a date is out of the question." After deciding he wasn't going to ask Lexa out, the words slid off his tongue, unbidden, of their own accord. Maybe it was the Holy Spirit prompting him. Then again, maybe it wasn't.

"I . . . I," Lexa spouted, unsuccessful in hiding her shock. "I certainly didn't expect *that* question."

Sam scratched his head. "Neither did I, to be honest. But it's out there, so we might as well deal with it." He hadn't asked anyone out in more than three years. Under normal circumstances, he preferred getting to know a woman better before asking her on a date. Since Lexa also lived in Houston, common sense would dictate waiting until after the TeamWork camp was over. But normalcy and common sense had long since flown out the window.

She tilted her head to one side, but didn't appear angry. "Was I just insulted?"

"No. That didn't come out the way I intended. I believe I just asked you for a date. I hope you have an answer." Leaning his head down, Sam attempted to regain her eye contact. The woman looked a million miles away. He was beginning to recognize that look, and it was only the second day of the camp. It might be an exhilarating eight weeks ahead. Or it could be quite awkward if things didn't go well.

Lexa started to cross her arms, and Sam felt a measure of satisfaction when she dropped them to her sides. Her mouth twisted in what looked like a serious attempt not to grin. "I'm sure you're a man used to getting what he wants."

"Neither do I ask for something I don't want." Where that line came from, he had no idea. But he meant it. If only those eyes of hers weren't so incredible. Big, luminous pools of blue-green drawing him in and wrapping around his emotions, his mind. He could drown in those eyes. No woman had ever affected him this way, not even Shelby. Knowing what was best, Sam avoided looking at Lexa's mouth. No answer seemed forthcoming, so he turned to go.

"I didn't say no."

Sam took his sweet time in turning back around to face her. "I'm not sure how to interpret that answer. Reading a woman's mind is not my strong suit." When Lexa met his eyes, he was half afraid she was going to turn him down flat.

"I suppose my answer is . . . yes." It almost sounded like a question. He wasn't sure which of the two of them was more surprised by the turn of events—the question *or* the answer.

He nodded, and a grin escaped. "Good." It was way better than good, but he had to keep his image intact. Jumping up and down like a kid didn't seem appropriate. *Yes* never sounded so promising. Lexa's answer thrilled him more than he wanted to admit. Sam nodded and ran a hand through his hair. It was a nervous habit. Not that it was a bad thing, but he needed to watch it.

The look she gave him told him he might have jumped the gun. It was pretty obvious she thought he was a fast worker. In this case, he had to agree. But the die was cast. Sam was determined to play out this little scenario, enjoy the ride and see what happened.

"Forgive me, but I have to ask. Do you make it a habit to ask out your new volunteers?" Lexa giggled, a sound as surprising as it was charming.

He laughed. "Not usually, no. Even then," he added, fighting the nerves twisting inside, "only the . . ."

Amusement slowly widened Lexa's grin. "The spicy ones?" She crossed her arms and shook her head, and it swung her braid like a clock's pendulum.

Great. Now she'd think he was a player when nothing could be further from the truth. He had to keep talking before Lexa came to her senses and changed her mind. "We could get away together for a little while either tomorrow night or the next. I can ask one of the other guys to cover the bonfire and give everyone a break from me for one night." He grinned. "If you'd like, we can go down to the Riverwalk and grab some dessert."

Sam prayed Lexa couldn't tell how his loud his heart thundered, how shallow his breathing had become. This was something he really wanted, but he wasn't exactly sure why. Just the way she looked at him made him want to know more about her. He sensed a hesitancy, as if she somehow felt unworthy. But unworthy of God's love, or something else, he couldn't guess. That's what he wanted to find out. On the other hand, he could be totally misreading her.

"I love the Riverwalk, but I'm not sure how many desserts you can simply reach out and grab." Lexa dug the toe of one boot into the barren ground again, shoving her hands in the pockets of her shorts before finally looking back up at him. It was the same thing she'd done earlier. Maybe she was more nervous than she let on.

Sam laughed. "I can see you're a literalist. I'll need to watch my syntax around you."

Lexa shook her head. "Syntax is the study of the structure of a sentence. I simply meant to watch what you say, Mr. Lewis. There's a difference."

Watching her walk back into the women's dorm, Sam shook his head and smiled. "I'll do that, Miss Clarke."

Would he ever.

~

Lexa didn't look back. The fluttering in her stomach tickled her from the inside out. It was undeniable although she hadn't felt it in a very long time. The first time it happened, she was seventeen and the guy in her senior class she'd crushed on for years caught her eye and smiled. But, of course, that's all it was. One little moment frozen in time—complete with scratched goggles and glass beakers in a chemistry lab.

The second time, it was with a man named Nick she worked with in Houston. After she devoted almost a year of her life to him, he'd tarried with her emotions and moved off to greener pastures in Colorado without so much as a decent good-bye. Lexa wasn't sure she'd ever recover from the hurt. Nick claimed to be a good Christian man, but based on what she'd heard from friends, he'd found someone to satisfy his more basic, primitive urges. At least anger made it easier to forgive the hurt.

No man was going to claim her heart easily. Most men weren't available in terms of emotion, or else they'd tarry with her affections like Nick and then leave. Weren't all men the same? Her thoughts strayed to a very tall man with wavy dark hair, killer smile lines and almost unbelievably blue eyes. Combined with the glasses, the tinge of silver at his temples lent an air of authority and confidence. He was a good leader, a man after God's own heart. And he'd asked her out on a date.

In twenty-five years, no one ever told her they admired her. Her mother didn't live long enough to tell her. Her father never told her. Neither had her teachers, bosses or co-workers. Sure, they thought she did a good job, but never once did they use the word *admire*. But here was the director of the TeamWork camp—a man she'd barely met—telling her he admired her. The compliment was as wonderful as it was hard to believe.

Opening the door of the dorm, Lexa tried to dismiss such musings. No man was perfect. Not even Sam Lewis. Something had to be wrong with him. Only the guys in romance novels were dependable. Yeah, right. Lexa knew it was a lie, but it was all she had to cling to at the moment. Until proven otherwise, she needed to keep believing it.

Chapter 9

A BIBLE SAT on top of her pillow a few hours later. Lexa smiled when she opened the front cover and spied Rebekah's name inside, scrawled by a child's hand. With its dog-eared, yellowed pages, it had been treasured. *Loved.* Just the night before, Rebekah handed her a straw hat. How wonderful to find such a good friend to watch over her so soon in the TeamWork camp.

"You—you're cer—cer—certainly in . . . a . . . a . . . goo—good m—moo—mood."

Lexa whirled in a circle, surprised. A slow smile slipped out. "Yes, I guess I am." She plopped down beside Sheila on the bed and dangled her feet over the edge. "So, what do we do on a quiet Sunday afternoon around here? I mean, do we rest or do we work?" She'd go crazy staring at the four walls of the dorm or making small talk with the other girls for an entire afternoon.

"M—mo—most of us re—rest, b—but S—S—Sam does—doesn't st—st—stop th—th—the oth—others th—that wa—wa—want to d—do ex—extra wor—work a—around th—the ca—camp—campsite. B—but he for—forbids any—anyone t—to go to th—the work . . . worksite."

Lexa tilted her head to the side. "He *forbids* it? Seriously?" Interesting.

A look of warning surfaced in Sheila's dark eyes. "He st—strong—strongly ad—advi—advises a . . . again—against it."

Lexa grinned. "We'll just see about that."

~

Two hours later, alone at the worksite, Lexa wondered what in the world possessed her to do something so foolhardy as to venture out by herself in the blazing heat. What was she trying to prove? Perhaps the important question was whether she was trying to prove something to herself or to a certain man named Sam Lewis. The answer was both, but more so to Sam. She wanted to prove to the TeamWork director that she was a hard worker and could swing a hammer with the best of his dedicated volunteers.

With increased determination, Lexa pounded another nail into the board she'd been working on the day before. It was mindless and rote, but therapeutic in a surprising way. She'd made some decent headway. Lexa squinted as she looked up at the wood frame of the house. It was the third out of six they were to rebuild. Two waited to be painted since they'd been constructed by others before the arrival of the TeamWork crew. Her eyes scanned the three other homes in the early stages of construction. Sam must be proud of what TeamWork would accomplish here. The residents needed the help—financially and physically—to rebuild their homes.

Even though she'd never been good at judging heights or distance, Lexa figured the height from the top of the frame to the ground was about twenty-five feet, give or take. Not a great distance, but she didn't want to know if it was any higher. She could do this. All she had to do was swing herself up there and hammer in some nails. Piece of cake. She'd always been pretty well-coordinated and a good climber. Sam would discover a little leprechaun had been busy working on the house . . . on Sunday, no less.

~

Sam knocked on the door of the women's dorm. He felt somewhat like a suitor standing on the doorstep holding a flower in his hands. He cleared his throat. "Beck? You in there?"

"Hey, stranger. Come on in. What brings you to our humble abode this afternoon?" Rebekah held the screen door open and beckoned him inside.

"I'm looking for Lexa." Sam scanned the room. Although he tried to cover his disappointment at not finding her, he should have known he couldn't fool Beck.

She crossed her arms and gave him one of her knowing looks. "So, I was right. You have a little crush on your new TeamWork volunteer. The petite blonde one with the braid." She shot him a wry grin.

"Trust me, no one's more surprised than me." He ran a hand through his hair. "Am I that transparent?"

Rebekah nodded. "Afraid so, my friend. And put your hand down. Your nerves are showing. Just be careful. You and I both know Lexa's skittish." Her brows drew together. "She's afraid of something, but I don't know what. Did you learn anything from reading her application?"

"A few things, yes, but you know I'm not at liberty to discuss any details."

Rebekah laughed. "Of course not, being TeamWork director and all."

He crossed the room. "Isn't this Lexa's bed?"

"Right." She eyed the small, black leather book in Sam's hands. "What's this? Your little black book?" Her green eyes teased.

"Something I'm not using anymore. I want Lexa to have it."

Rebekah nodded. "And am I supposed to let on that I know who brought this gift if she asks me?"

Sam shook his head, heading toward the door again. "I think she'll be able to figure it out."

With a grin, he tugged his Stetson over his head and whistled the entire way back to his office.

~

Hammering away, Lexa paused when she realized she hummed the chorus she'd learned at the morning service. It came naturally, and had a catchy tune. Hearing an odd noise, something unidentifiable yet couldn't be human, Lexa peered down at the ground. She screeched when she spied what had to be the biggest, ugliest armadillo in the world. It settled directly beneath her elevated perch. Having lived in Texas her entire life, she'd seen countless armadillos before, but in the road and . . . well, dead.

"Hello there, big fella! Go on your way now. There's bound to be something better for you down the road. Over there! Shoo!" Lexa motioned with her arm, waving as if the animal could see her much less understand what she was telling it to do.

The absurdity of her situation hit. She started laughing and couldn't stop. It was like that ornery old goat staring at her from the middle of the road. She hadn't laughed so hard or so long in years, and the release felt good. *Really* good.

Oh, this was rich. Here she was, sitting twenty-five feet up in the air, laughing her head off, with an armadillo waiting for her on the ground. No way on earth was she climbing down until that ugly creature left the area. Do they bite? If she climbed back down from her perch, would it attack her?

"Okay, it's either you or me, big guy!" Lexa considered the possibility of throwing her hammer to scare it. After all, she'd proven herself pretty decent at throwing tools around—on purpose or not. Not wishing to hurt the armadillo, Lexa decided to work a little longer. Swinging the hammer high, she brought it down again and pounded her left thumb. Hard.

"Yowza!" With the force of her yelp, she bit her lip. Hard. Oh, bother.

Wincing, Lexa stuck her thumb in her mouth and sulked. The worst part of it all was that she deserved it. This would teach her to do something foolish just to prove a point. She leaned over, hoping the creature might be scared off by her outburst. Nope, she wasn't so blessed.

"You're not about to leave first, are you?" Frowning in disgust, she crossed her arms and pouted, prepared to wait out her standoff with the armadillo. What a fine situation.

~

Sam scooted over as Rebekah dropped onto the bench beside him. Almost finished with dinner, he planned on a quiet evening studying the plans for the house they'd finish in the next few days. They kept such a grueling pace during the week, it was nice to observe a quiet day, taking the Lord's Sabbath to heart. It might be an old-fashioned concept for some, but it worked for him.

"Sam, I'm a little worried about Lexa."

He finished the last bite of peach cobbler. The peach was truly God's greatest fruit. Smacking his lips and wiping his mouth with the napkin, Sam turned his full attention to Rebekah. "I'm sure she's fine. Is there any reason to think she's not?"

"She's missing." Rebekah's arms crossed on top of the table, and she frowned.

Sam blinked hard. His heartbeat increased tenfold. "What do you mean, she's missing?"

An exasperated sigh escaped. "She wasn't in the dorm all afternoon, and you didn't see her here for dinner, did you?" Rebekah waved her hand around the tent.

"Is her suitcase gone?" Had Lexa already packed it in and given up on their camp? Maybe he'd scared her off with the whole let's-grab-dessert thing. But she hadn't seemed adverse to the idea. Where could she have gone? Other than the dorm, dining tent and laundry facilities, it was all wide open spaces. She couldn't hide, even if she wanted. "Maybe she's doing laundry or went into town." Sam tried to keep his breathing even.

"Relax, Sam. I didn't mean to get you all worried." Rebekah put a hand on his arm and squeezed. "After all, why would she leave now when she's caught the attention of our fearless leader?" She caught his look and shrugged. "I checked the laundry room, and she's not there. If she went into town, she didn't tell any of our roommates about it. Besides, how would she get there since you're the only one with a car?"

"You know the reason for that."

She nodded. "Sorry. Of course, I do. Do you think we should send out a search party?"

"No need for that yet. We don't want to jump the gun. I'm beginning to think anything's possible with Lexa. She probably wandered off somewhere and forgot about the time. I'm sure she'll be back soon. We still have some time before nightfall." He nodded at a couple of the men across the dining tent and forced a smile he didn't feel.

"Wandered off . . . where? Surely you're not going to wait until nightfall to look for her?" Rebekah's voice was incredulous.

"No, I suppose not." Sam's heart raced. While not wanting to overreact, he wanted to know where Lexa was. Wanted to know *now*. An unsettled feeling washed over him. The woman came to his camp looking for adventure. She was feisty and impetuous. Who knows where she might have gone, what she might have done, what kind of trouble she might have managed to find. Or what kind of trouble might have found *her*. He scowled.

Leaving the table, Sam dumped his empty plate in the trash can. He turned in a slow circle to face Rebekah. His hands found his hips, his forehead creased with concentration. "Are the other girls in the dorm now, do you know?"

"Yes, I think most of them are." Rebekah hurried to catch up with his long strides as Sam headed in the direction of Building Seven.

"Fine. We'll start by asking them if they've seen her, what they know." The innate leader had taken control once more.

When he started to open the door of the dorm, Rebekah stretched an arm around him and held it firmly in place. "Excuse me, but since when do you barge in here without so much as a knock?"

"Oh, I didn't think. Sorry." Throwing a look back at Rebekah a split second later, he hollered, "Ladies, I hope you're decent because I'm coming in now!" Flinging the door wide, Sam stomped inside.

Chapter 10

*F*IVE PAIRS OF eyes stared at him, wide-eyed, as Sam stormed into the center of the room. Thank the Lord they were decent in spite of his impulsive act of barging in on them. The braided wonder was already making him crazy, in more ways than one. Normally, he never would have rudely barged into the women's dorm unannounced. As Sam focused on Lexa's still-empty bunk, he waited a moment until his eyes adjusted to the dim light.

"Have any of you seen Lexa this afternoon?"

Winnie, Amy, Natalie, Kim and Monica all shook their heads and stared at him without saying a word. "No one's seen, heard from, or even talked with Lexa this entire afternoon?" Again with the head shaking. "Well, she's got to be somewhere!" His voice was gruff with impatience. Sam shoved the screen door open without ceremony and stamped back outside. He almost mowed down Sheila in the process. "Sheila!"

The timid girl shrank away from him, her shoulders more hunched than usual. "Ye–yes–yes?" Shaken, her eyes cast downward at the ground.

Pausing, Sam tamped down his rising frustration. "Have you seen Lexa this afternoon? She didn't show up for dinner, and Rebekah and I are a little concerned."

Sheila shifted her feet and appeared anxious, but remained silent.

"Sheila, please tell us if you know anything, have any idea where she might be." Sam wanted to take her by the arms and force her to look at him, but it would probably scare the poor woman to death. He'd noticed how Lexa befriended her at the morning Bible study. If Lexa had spoken to any of them, it would have been either Rebekah or this one.

Why was his heart racing like it was going to fly out of his chest? Even though Sam knew his reaction was extreme, he couldn't help himself. He didn't like feeling out of control.

"I–I–I s–s–saw h–her."

Sam strained forward to hear. "You did? Where? What did she say?"

"I–I," the girl stuttered, swallowing hard and closing her eyes to concentrate, "I th–th–think I– I kno–know wh–wh–where sh–she is."

"Where, Sheila? Where's Lexa?"

"Th–th–the wor–worksite," she sputtered. Dark eyes finally met his.

"Thanks. I appreciate your help." He hoped his tone sounded less gruff. "You did the right thing telling me. I just pray she's all right."

"Me–me, t–t–too."

He was touched by the concern in her timid voice. Smiling to reassure her, Sam turned to go.

"Are you taking the car?" Rebekah followed him back out the door.

"It's probably best, in case she needs medical attention." He ran a hand over his brow. "Beck, what in the world is Lexa doing out there on her own? Doesn't she know how dangerous it can be in this heat if she doesn't have enough water . . ." His voice trailed, his brows drawn tight. "What's she trying to do, trying to prove?"

Rebekah shook her head. "Beats me. Lexa Clarke seems to operate under her own set of rules. Your guess is as good as mine. Do you want me to come along?"

Sam shook his head. "I think I can handle this one on my own. Just say a prayer for me to hold my tongue once I find her. Lord help her then."

"Down, boy. Something tells me Lexa already learned her lesson if she's been out at the worksite by herself all day. That sun's pretty brutal. Like you said, I hope she had a water bottle."

Rebekah's frown worried him even more. They shared a look. She thought of Shelby, just as he did. He couldn't afford to lose another volunteer on his watch. It was *not* going to happen.

"Bring her back safe and sound, Sam."

"Thanks, Beck. I'll do my best," Sam promised with a mock salute. Spurred by an overwhelming sense of urgency, he sprinted to the station wagon parked beside his office. Sliding behind the wheel, he dug into the pocket of his shorts for the keys. Remembering they hung on a ring on the pegboard in his office, Sam grunted as he flung open the car door. Back at the car in less than a minute, he revved up the engine and sped off in a swirl of dust for the half-mile drive.

As he drove the short distance, he prayed for the Lord to keep Lexa safe. At least until he got there. Then she'd probably need protection—from the wrath of Sam.

~

Staring at her swollen thumb, Lexa shifted her feet. They'd fallen asleep again. Every time she started to climb down from her position, the armadillo made its indescribable sound and moved in her direction. How silly to be so intimidated by one of God's creatures, no matter how incomprehensible it seemed that the Almighty could create something so odd.

"This is absolutely ridiculous!" Her words carried off into what little wind stirred. "I'm actually scared of an armadillo." She raised her knees with extreme care and rested her chin on them. Oh, where's a good cowboy when you need one? She was going to grow old before this thing either left or her prince in shining armor came to rescue her.

Lexa called to the armadillo. "Are you my prince in shining armor?" After all, he *did* have an armor of sorts. "Sorry, but you're not exactly what I had in mind." She sighed. Of course, it was supposed to be her *knight* in shining armor, but she might as well set her sights a bit higher. Why settle for a knight when a prince would do quite nicely?

Without a doubt, she was certifiable. Not to mention dehydrated. The heat from the sun made her loopy. The sting of her arms was uncomfortable after sitting even closer to the sun for hours on end. Thank goodness she possessed enough foresight and brain cells to tug the hat over her head and guzzle a gallon of water before climbing to her perch. Still, at the rate she was going, they'd find her all shriveled up, still sitting on this beam in the morning when the TeamWork volunteers returned to the worksite. Or else in a crumpled heap on the ground below. Lexa shuddered at the thought.

~

After speeding into the worksite in a swirling cloud of dust, Sam stepped out of the car and watched as a spooked armadillo waddled off into the brush as fast as it could go. Hearing something from above, he glanced up at the top of the house. The last thing in the world he expected to find was Lexa Clarke sitting on the highest beam of one of the houses, talking to herself and laughing. From what he could tell, she'd attracted an armadillo to her collection of admirers and was afraid to climb down for some reason. He couldn't help the laugh that escaped.

Lexa leaned over to look at the ground below. In her shock at seeing him, she lost her balance and pitched forward, arms and legs flailing. A scream escaped, and a terrified look crossed her face. My, oh my, that sweet voice held amazing lung power as she cried out his name and fell toward the hard ground. Danger was always a good motivator. Thank goodness he was close enough to hopefully reach her in time, and the Lord blessed him with long limbs. At the moment, they were made for one purpose only.

Rushing into action, Sam ran with outstretched arms and positioned himself directly below her. As Lexa fell into the cradle of his arms, they both tumbled to the ground in a sprawling tangle of limbs. At least his much larger body cushioned her fall, but she was right on top of him.

"Ouch," Sam muttered a moment later, gasping as he tried to catch his breath. All that came out were sputtering coughs.

"Ouch." Lexa tossed her braid behind one shoulder and echoed his cough with a hearty rendition all her own. Sam avoided touching her as she painstakingly extracted herself. She sat up on her knees and massaged the back of her neck. He was glad she'd moved. It was . . . unsettling. Her cheeks were flaming red, but it wasn't from sunburn. Served her right. At least she had the decency to look remorseful.

"Are you okay?" When Sam didn't immediately answer, Lexa crouched over him and touched the middle of his chest with a cautious finger. "Are you okay?"

she repeated, more urgent this time. "Speak to me. Oh, good heavens, you're not dying are you?" Her voice sounded panicked.

"Stop poking me. I'll live," Sam answered, his voice testy. He couldn't ignore the way her touch electrified him. Sent every nerve ending into instant overdrive. That small hand rested right above his heart, bunching up his shirt. Swatting her fingers away before she moved them and caused even more trouble, he struggled to sit up on his elbows. "Alexis Clarke, what do you think you're doing out here by yourself?"

"You mean on a Sunday, don't you?" And there it was. That saucy, I-dare-you-to-tell-me-what-to-do expression. Crossing her arms, she glared at him with that increasingly familiar defiance.

"I repeat, what are you doing out here by yourself? It was a very foolish thing to do. I hope you realize that now." Maybe he should quiet his tone, but she needed to learn a lesson.

"Yes, Mother." Lexa dusted off her hands and rose to a standing position. "Here." She offered her hand. "The least I can do is give you a hand up. After all, I suppose you saved me."

"Don't do me any favors." When she roared, he shook his head. The woman confounded the bounds of normal propriety. "You're a very strange woman. I don't quite know what to make of you. Are you always this much trouble back home in Houston?"

Waving away her hand, Sam pulled himself to his feet and dusted his hands. His pulse throbbed, his heart pounded in his chest. He was dizzy, but not from having the wind knocked out of him. He didn't care to stop and examine the reasons why.

"Don't you dare laugh at me, Sam Clarke." That defiant chin tilted upward.

"Lewis." He towered over her, but every defense crumbled as Sam lost himself in those challenging eyes, those tempting lips. She looked like she wanted to slap him or . . . More than anything on earth, he needed to play this one out.

"Lewis, what?" Lexa stepped backward—a slow, baby step. Her eyes grew wide, and she shook her head and averted her eyes. He liked that she was rattled enough to say the wrong name. Liked her off balance.

"My name. You just called me Sam Clarke. My name's Lewis. *Yours* is Clarke." His voice sounded odd—husky and thick. Sam understood it meant trouble, but nothing was stopping him now.

"Do you realize what you just said?"

Part of him wanted to run in the opposite direction, but Sam kept both feet firmly planted on the ground. Oh no, he wasn't going anywhere soon. Neither was she since she made no move to flee. He lowered his head, his lips hovering above hers, only an inch away as he searched for a clue to what she wanted. Sam glimpsed his own hunger mirrored in those gorgeous eyes.

"Together, you and me, we're Lewis and Clarke," Lexa mumbled. "You know, the explorer team?" Her question held a sense of wonder. Her eyes swept across his face and fell on his lips.

Unless he was misreading her—and that was a distinct possibility—Lexa wanted it as much as he did. "I've heard of them." He was only interested in exploring one thing. Hauling her into the circle of his arms, Sam ran out of patience. It was a move worthy of The Duke in one of his western movies. He'd never wanted to kiss a woman more in his life. He might regret what he was about to do, but nothing was stopping him now.

"I'm going to kiss you, Miss Clarke. If it's possible, please be quiet and try to enjoy it." That statement even *sounded* like The Duke. Sam's fingers tightened around her tiny waist, pulling her even closer, his lids lowering. They felt heavy, as if under the spell of a potent drug. He was powerless.

"Make me," Lexa challenged, her voice husky now, too.

Bringing his lips down on hers, Sam covered her mouth with his own and kissed this feisty woman with passionate abandon. Something about her brought out long-dormant instincts. For one thing, she poured her energies into a heart-stopping kiss. He could feel the tension slowly easing from her body as Lexa relaxed in his arms and sighed a little against his lips. Sam wasn't sure how he stayed on his feet, but he needed to keep them upright. Never in his life had he felt so alive. Or so out of control.

He needed to stop. He needed to back away from her now and not look back. But she responded to him in the way he hoped yet dreaded she would. Her lips were so lush and soft, and Sam wanted so much more. Things he shouldn't think about as a Christian man, a leader and mentor for the younger men. If needed, he'd pray for forgiveness . . . later. All he could concentrate on was the woman in his arms. As he kissed Lexa like a starving man at a feast, he lost track of time, dizzy with her nearness and the undeniable force of their attraction.

In that moment, Sam knew he was lost.

Forcing himself to finally back away, he released her. How long had it gone on? His stare met hers as he tried to regain his shaken composure. "I'm sorry," he muttered, half under his breath. In his heart, he wasn't sorry, but he didn't want Lexa to think he intended to take advantage of the situation. Didn't intend to devour her lips, but he'd certainly claimed them.

They'd only known each other for two days. He'd already asked her out, and now he'd practically mauled her with his lips. What on earth was wrong with him? He'd never acted this stupid or impulsive around a woman in his entire life. He didn't regret it for one moment, but he had a reputation to uphold in the TeamWork camp.

Serious prayer was definitely in order. He'd be on his knees tonight. Lexa Clarke would keep him on his toes, but the signs were already there she'd keep him on his knees on a regular basis.

"I said I'm sorry, Lexa." His gaze focused on the ground although he knew she watched. Seemed that kissing quieted this intriguing woman. He'd have to tuck that tidbit away in case it came into play later on. A full minute passed without either of them speaking.

"Sorry for what, exactly?" Lexa blinked hard, those lush eyelashes fluttering against reddened cheeks. Her fingers moved to her mouth and she left them on her lips.

If her muddled emotions were anything like his, Lexa must be more than confused. But it was also pretty great in a lot of respects. His mouth still stung from their prolonged kiss. He'd feel it for a long time, forget it never. Sam scratched his head, knowing his dazed expression must mirror hers.

"I'm sorry for telling you to be quiet. I've never said that to a woman before." There was more to it than that, but he wasn't talking. Not about that. Not now.

"I'm afraid I provoked it. And, for the record, you *did* say please."

"Yeah, well, we'd better be getting back to the campsite." Walking past Lexa, Sam retrieved her hat and waited for her to catch up. Together, they silently hobbled back toward the station wagon. "Are you okay?" He tugged open the passenger door and waited. "If you're hurt, please tell me."

He wondered if he should fill out an incident report. As TeamWork leader, he should, but he didn't want her to get in trouble for breaking the rules. It might send her running all the way back to Houston. Sam didn't want to risk that happening. She was equal parts annoying, fascinating, challenging . . . and fun. Oh yes, he wanted to keep her around all right.

"Other than having a bad sunburn and hurt pride, I think I'll live." Lexa climbed into the car. Leaning her head back against the seat, she released a deep sigh.

"Just do me one favor." Sam slid onto the seat beside her.

"Depends." Lexa crossed her arms again. "Okay," she relented. "I'll try my best. What's the favor?"

"The next time you decide to do something foolish, ask someone else to come along. And here," he said, reaching into the backseat and thrusting a water bottle in her hands, "drink some of this. Your mouth must be a little dry by now."

His humor recovered, Sam laughed when Lexa gaped at him. "Didn't your mother ever tell you it's not polite to stare?" he teased, pulling out of the clearing in yet another cloud of dust.

Chapter 11

*A*FTER HER SHOWER, Lexa sat cross-legged on her bed, towel drying her hair. Even though she'd been a fool and falling on top of Sam at the worksite had been the ultimate humiliation, she smiled. She'd never been kissed like that in her entire life. Never *kissed* a man like that. Her breath slowly filtered back into her body. As difficult as it was for her to believe, Lexa suspected Sam hadn't kissed a woman in a long time. He must be making up for lost time. In a *big* way.

Noting a lump under the bedcovers, Lexa pulled aside the lightweight blanket and spied yet another Bible. Did everyone at the Bible study notice she didn't have one? This one was well-worn in the extreme. Fingering its binding with reverence, she recognized its owner before she turned it over and saw Sam's name embossed on the front cover.

Judging from the Bible she'd seen him hold at the bonfire and again this morning, Lexa figured he must have gone through a dozen of the Good Books in his lifetime. It was something he treasured. Because his faith and God's Word meant so much to Sam, she appreciated his thoughtfulness in giving it to her. It was a precious gift.

Opening to the dedication page, Lexa ran her finger over his handwritten name. *Samuel J. Lewis, Jr.* She wondered if the small, precise lettering was his. Wincing because of her sore thumb, Lexa stopped when she reached the book of Jonah. She read how the Lord commanded Jonah to go and preach in the city of Nineveh as a result of the wickedness there. Instead, Jonah took off in the opposite direction and headed for Tarshish. He boarded a ship and the Lord sent a storm upon the ship—a storm so great the sailors cried out to their own gods to save them. Confronting Jonah, the sailors demanded to know what he'd done to so anger God.

Closing the Bible, Lexa's brow creased. Was God mad at *her?* Mad because she'd pushed Him out of her life for so long? She certainly didn't hate Him, but she had so many unanswered questions. Why had He taken her mother away, leaving her with a father who couldn't show his love for his only child? Maybe it wasn't her place to question God's purpose.

Perhaps Sam was right, and she was more like Jonah than she wanted to admit. When she'd asked Jesus into her heart, she wanted to belong to Him, wanted Him in her life. But then what did she do? She pushed him away for years, running in the opposite direction. Just like Jonah.

Winnie sat down quietly on the bed beside Lexa, holding a bottle of aloe. "You look like you could use some of this." Her soft voice was as soothing as the gel Lexa needed on her neck, arms and every other part of her exposed to the sun at the worksite. "Don't worry, I won't ask what happened, sweetie. I just hate it that you're going to really hurt tomorrow. Do you want me to help you rub in the gel?"

"I'd appreciate it. Thanks, Winnie." Lexa looked at her with grateful eyes. The coolness of the gel eased the stinging of the sunburn, but Lexa knew it was fleeting. She winced as Winnie spread the gel over her arms. In the morning, she'd be left with a glaring reminder of her foolishness and resemble a crustacean. She had no one to blame but herself.

"You're welcome. I'm going to leave the bottle here on the floor beside your bed. Use as much as you need. We've got lots around here." Winnie climbed under the sheets of her bed. Pulling them up around her, she gave her a sweet smile.

"Good night." Watching her, Lexa thought what a wonderful mother Winnie would make someday. She was so nurturing and kind to all the TeamWork volunteers. Earlier in the evening, she'd brought her a sandwich from the canteen supply, knowing she'd missed dinner.

Would there be a storm in her life one day like the one God sent to Jonah's ship? One that brought her to her knees and forced her to make a decision whether to follow God's will or reject it? She'd made a decision all those years ago, but choosing to follow His leading was another story now. In her heart, Lexa wanted to believe God cared about her. She *needed* Him to care about her.

Turning off the light anchored on the wall above her bed, Lexa vowed to read more in the Bible the next night. And the next. Before she fell asleep, Lexa wanted to try and pray. She might not say the right thing, and she might feel pretty stupid. Still, she wanted to try, and hoped the Almighty could hear her prayer. And so, she prayed.

~

Lexa awoke on her own the next morning without anyone tugging her out of bed. She caught Rebekah and Amy exchanging amused glances. Sheila kept her nose stuck in her Bible as usual, peering over the top at her every now and then.

"I hear you had yourself a little adventure yesterday." Josh kept his voice low as he seated himself beside her at the breakfast table. He laughed under his breath when she stared at him.

"Don't worry. No one else needs to know." He leaned close. "Beck went to Sam when you went missing."

A frown tugged the corners of her mouth. "Everyone probably has their suspicions. I honestly don't know what possessed me. I was bored, and foolishly thought I could get a little work done. I suppose I was also rebelling against Sam's rule of no work at the worksite on Sundays."

Josh laughed. "Well, he wasn't the first one to think of that particular rule. It's also a commandment."

"Give me a break, Josh," she snapped, sounding more harsh than she intended. "We're not kids here."

Josh looked at her askance. "And you don't like being told you can't do something."

Lexa blew out a sigh. "I certainly deserved that. Look, normally I play by the rules. I guess I decided to do my own thing for a change. And look where it got me."

"So, you learned your lesson. Because you had something to prove."

Lexa opened her mouth in protest, but faltered. The man might be young, but he was smart and intuitive.

Josh watched her with an odd look in those green eyes. His gaze traveled to her arms. "It looks like you got a painful sunburn, too. That must hurt." He touched her arm, but withdrew his hand when he caught her warning glance. Even the brief touch left white finger marks on her arm. He murmured appropriate sympathies as she cringed.

After one of the men prayed for their breakfast, Josh turned to her with his most charming smile. "Care to walk to the worksite with me this morning, gorgeous?"

"I can't," Lexa told him with genuine regret. "I'm pledged to help out in the schoolroom today. Stop being so kind. I know I'm anything but attractive this morning."

Josh looked straight into her eyes. "You're a lovely woman, Lexa. Don't let anyone ever tell you differently."

She tried to hide her surprise. Was Josh looking for more than friendship?

He watched as she took a bite of toast. "Maybe later this week you'll lend a hand with the building, and we can work together again. I think we make a pretty good team."

"As long as you promise to keep the pesky armadillos at bay." Lexa laughed, but it rang hollow. This work camp was getting more interesting by the moment.

~

The one-room school was hot, cramped, and bustling with nearly thirty school age children ranging in age from about seven to thirteen. The children over thirteen were expected to help their parents and the volunteers with the building project. Lexa sat in a corner and watched as Rebekah led everyone in singing a few fun songs. Then she stood with the others as they recited the Pledge of Allegiance before they broke into smaller groups and separated into different corners of the room. Rebekah assigned Lexa to assist Natalie and Amy with the youngest group.

"Are we allowed to teach Bible stories?" Lexa whispered to Amy.

"Here." Amy handed her a stack of papers, a box of crayons and some colorful stickers. Satisfied a few moments later that all of the children were busy coloring, Amy walked over to stand beside her. "We've got a mix of kids here. Some are them belong to the people whose homes are being rebuilt. Others are the children of migrant workers. To be honest, they're lucky to get what little education we can offer them. But to answer your question, the parents are all made aware from the start that we're going to teach Bible lessons and songs as well as the usual subjects." She grinned. "Especially with Sam in charge."

"I thought we were here to help rebuild homes destroyed by the floodwaters."

Amy nodded. "It started out that way, but then Sam recognized the need for more than what was in the original plan. Especially since there's so many kids, he expanded the operation to include this school. It's a good way to keep them occupied so the parents can help in the rebuilding effort. The kids adapt well to the loose but structured learning environment here." She leaned her head toward Rebekah. "Beck's a big help since she's training to be a teacher, and Natalie's a kindergarten teacher."

Pausing to answer a question, Amy turned back to Lexa. "Most of the younger group speak English. We primarily speak English here in the schoolroom to help build their vocabulary and communication skills."

Lexa helped Natalie pass out papers a few minutes later. "Are those some of the mothers?" Lexa nodded her head toward a small group of women on folding chairs at the back of the room. They were respectful and quiet and watched their activities with interest. She smiled at one, but the woman lowered her head in a shy manner and looked away.

Natalie nodded and clapped to get the attention of a group of giggling children. "Right. The ones who are pregnant or can't help at the worksite for whatever reason often come and visit." She leaned closer. "Some of them benefit from the lessons, too." After introducing Lexa to the group, Natalie began their lesson.

One little girl couldn't take her eyes off Lexa the entire morning, and stared at her long braid. Amy told her the child's name was Margarita. She was seven, but small for her age with big brown eyes that threatened to swallow the rest of her pretty, delicate features. Dangly earrings swung from her ears every time she moved before getting lost in a mass of dark, wavy hair. Margarita's multi-colored dress was old but clean, and she shuffled around in tennis shoes three times the size of her small feet.

"Do you like my hair?"

Margarita nodded and surprised Lexa by nudging aside her arm and scooting onto her lap. Laying her head against her chest, she closed her eyes.

Amy smiled. "She's the youngest one in the group and gets tired about mid-morning. Just hold her. She gives good love."

Lexa stroked her hair, so soft and silky. It seemed to give the girl a measure of comfort. She sighed and stuck a couple of fingers in her mouth. She listened as Lexa hummed a quiet song and nestled even closer. A warmth flooded through her, and Lexa's arms tightened around the precious child. Margarita was so trusting, so innocent. God must have known they both needed a moment like this.

A short time later, Rebekah called everyone together and dismissed them for lunch following a short prayer. "We'll meet here again at three o'clock and then go until five-thirty in order to get in the required number of hours per day," she told Lexa. "Margarita's really taken to you. She's a very loving little girl. It's a shame about her, though."

"What do you mean?"

Rebekah looked around the room to make sure the children and mothers were all gone. "She has several older brothers and sisters. Two of them come here to the school, but they don't pay her much attention." A sadness surfaced in her green eyes. "Apparently, sweet little Margarita was an afterthought. The parents dote on the older children, but sadly neglect their youngest."

Lexa sighed. "Attention is what she seems to crave right now. At least she was dressed neat enough."

"Yes, today she looked pretty good. Other days, not so much."

Lexa turned away so Rebekah wouldn't glimpse her tears. She busied herself collecting stray crayons from the floor and straightening chairs around the long tables. Amy and Natalie worked together in another section of the schoolroom.

As the group walked back to the campsite for lunch, Lexa's thoughts centered on the small girl. Such large, lonely eyes. She vowed to pay as much attention to Margarita as she could for the duration of the TeamWork camp. She understood the pain of loneliness, especially for a child, and wanted to somehow protect the little girl. Even for only a moment in time, she wanted to shield Margarita from the hurts caused by the world.

It was the same way she felt drawn to her quiet roommate, Sheila. Both seemed lonely and a little lost. Just like Lexa herself a short time ago. But now it was different. Something had changed.

Or could it be that *she* was changing?

~

After lunch, Sam summoned the seven newest members of the TeamWork crew into his office. Walking with the others, Lexa's heart rate picked up speed at the thought of seeing Sam again.

"Come in!" Sam threw the door wide and smiled. His eyes settled on Lexa as she ducked beneath his arm on the way inside. She turned her head and tried to focus on what another girl was saying. The newest volunteers were each assigned to different dorms among the more seasoned crew. It was an effective way to help them get to know everyone better and ease into the camp routine.

For the better part of the next hour, Sam distributed various handouts listing the names of the others at the camp and the available assignments. He explained the camp procedures in more detail and answered their questions. Lexa leaned against a tall file cabinet in one corner, studying the paperwork and darting quick glances at Sam.

"You've already been here a couple of days and no doubt have a better idea where you'd most like to serve. Don't feel pigeon-holed. If you wake up one morning and want to test your culinary skills and make peach cobbler, or help serve meals, I'm sure they can use you in the canteen. However, if you feel the urge to build something, we can use your help at the worksite. Of course, the children can always benefit from more willing volunteers in the schoolroom."

"We have enough volunteers and positions to fill, so don't worry about signing up on a list for any particular day. However, I reserve the right to move you around if we have a pressing need somewhere else. One of the perks of being the director," he teased, and they all laughed.

"These things always have a way of working themselves out." Sam paused, looking around the room. "I commend you all. I've noticed some of you trying out the various positions in the camp, and you're doing a great job."

Sam told them more about his expectations for the newest group of volunteers. "It's not going to be easy." His words echoed those of the interviewer in the TeamWork headquarters in Houston a few months before. "But it's also very rewarding work." Sam's gaze encompassed those squeezed into his cramped office, missing no one. His eyes found hers.

Averting her gaze, Lexa stared blindly at the paper in her hands. Sam had a unique way of making each volunteer feel valued. He shared an easygoing camaraderie with the men that commanded their respect. But he also possessed the uncanny ability to see straight into a person's soul. It was as wonderful as it was unnerving.

When he spoke next, the words were quiet. "I thank you from the bottom of my heart for your willingness to help this summer. We've got a terrific group of people. I trust when we leave at the end of the work camp, we'll consider ourselves a family. Not just the family of Christ, but people who love and care for one another. Not because we feel we have to, but because we want to." Sam nodded. "*That*, my friends, is what TeamWork is all about."

Those assembled broke into spontaneous applause. The men slapped each other on the back as they filed out of the office, laughing and talking. The director stood at the door, shaking hands and answering a few lingering questions.

Hoping Sam might want a word alone with her, Lexa hung around until the others all departed. By this time, he was once again seated behind his desk, the glasses in place, busy reading some report or other. According to Rebekah,

Sam's intense concentration was legendary. That must be the case now, and she hoped he wasn't purposely ignoring her. Not wanting to disturb him, feeling awkward, Lexa turned to go. A creaking floorboard alerted Sam to her presence as she crossed the office. Darting a glance in his direction, she saw him look up.

A slow grin spread across that way-too-handsome-for-his-own-good face. "Well, hello there, Lexa Clarke." Those smile lines captivated.

"Hi." She couldn't help returning the infectious grin. From anyone else, it might irritate her that he kept calling her by both her first and last name. "I was wondering if your offer of dessert and the Riverwalk was still open." Where she found the boldness to ask that question, Lexa didn't know. But she had, so now she had to face the consequences.

Leaning back in his chair, Sam plopped his boot-covered feet on top of the desk and crossed his arms behind his head. The smile never left his face. "It sure is. We can go tonight during the bonfire time, if you'd like. Does that suit you?" His tone was flirtatious, teasing. Stinker.

"Fine. I think I can fit it into my busy social calendar." Lexa sidled to the door, feeling as self-conscious as a tiny ballerina at her first dance recital. Sam watched as she moved across the room. Caught in a paradox, she both loved and hated it. Turning back to face him, she refused to give into the grin threatening the corners of her mouth. "Please stop staring. Didn't your mother ever tell you it's not polite to stare?"

The glint of amusement shone in those incredible eyes. "I thought you rather liked it, Lexa."

She liked the way he said her name. She liked his voice with its deep, native Texas drawl. She liked *him*. Sam possessed an inner strength and conviction she'd never known in any other man.

Lexa paused, one hand on the doorknob. "Sam, tell me something. Did yesterday really happen?"

He chuckled. Removing his glasses, he rose to his feet. "If you're referring to the armadillo incident, it most certainly did. I saw him, too. Like I said, you seem to have an uncanny knack for attracting all kinds of creatures."

Lexa wondered if Sam included himself in that assessment. Judging by the look on his face, it was a fair assumption. Moving around the desk, Sam inched toward her, his steps slow, purposeful. Lexa's heart quickened with every step of those dust-covered boots. "That's not what I'm talking about it, and you know it."

Sam loomed above Lexa, his eyes never leaving hers. "If you're talking about the fact that you fell from the top beam of one of the houses and I came to your rescue—yes, it also happened, Miss Clarke. I actually have the beginnings of a few bruises to prove it. Wanna see?" he teased, starting to lift his shirt.

"Nope." Lexa shook her head. *Put that shirt back down.*

Grasping her chin with a firm hand, Sam studied her face as though memorizing every detail. Thank goodness he didn't feel the need to point out her obvious sunburn, a glaring reminder of her foolishness. His gaze swept from her eyes, down to her nose, and lingered on her mouth. Lexa's breath caught in her throat, lost in his smile.

"Okay, then." Sam leaned near, his face only an inch from hers. "If you're talking about the fact that I kissed you, you're absolutely, positively out of your mind. Raving lunatic. Never happened." He released her, his grin entirely too smug.

"You!" Lexa cried, stomping out the door after first slamming it in Sam's face. "And stop staring!" she yelled in mock disgust, laughing all the while as she scurried back across the campsite to the women's dorm.

The TeamWork director's laughter followed her all the way.

I could get used to this.

Chapter 12

$\mathscr{L}$EXA SHIFTED FROM one foot to the other. She waited for Sam in the dorm, as giddy as a shy teenager on a first date. It proved frustrating to choose something to wear considering her TeamWork wardrobe consisted primarily of shorts and coordinating tops or T-shirts. She finally chose a khaki skort since it was the closest thing she had to a real skirt, and topped it with her dressiest pale pink knit top.

Even though her roommates acted curious, none asked any questions as they headed out the door to the bonfire. Throwing a wave over one shoulder, Rebekah called to her to have a nice evening. The grin on her face was interesting. Josh's comment tipped Lexa off that he and Rebecca knew she'd been at the worksite. Which meant they probably knew Sam came after her, too. But their TeamWork director didn't seem like a kiss-and-tell kind of guy.

A light rap on the door startled her. She saw the outline of Sam standing on the opposite side of the screen door. "Excuse me, but do you know where I might find a lovely lady by the name of Alexis Clarke?"

"She's right here." Lexa pulled her purse over one shoulder and stepped outside. Sam was clean-shaven and wore khaki pants with a red polo which brought out the intensity of his eyes. The thick, dark hair was combed back neatly with no black Stetson. Her eyes traveled to his feet and she tried not to laugh. At least he'd polished the work boots as best he could. Goodness, did this man ever clean up well. Lexa accepted his proffered arm with a shy smile. As they began walking, she caught a whiff of cologne. That surprised her somewhat.

"I like your hair that way."

Lexa tucked the compliment in her heart, pleased he'd noticed. It took nearly a half hour to add a few curls to the ends of her stubborn, straight hair. She'd thrown the curling iron in her suitcase as a last minute afterthought. Kind of like her dad's old police union newsletter. It didn't really make any sense at the time, but now it did.

Maybe Sam meant he liked her hair down since he'd only seen the braid. She needed to stop second-guessing everything. It was time to enjoy a relaxing evening with a nice man. An incredibly handsome man. Lexa willed her pulse to slow down, but it was a lost cause. When she glanced his way, she caught his smile.

A few volunteers passed by, tossing curious stares their way. No doubt they'd be a hot topic of discussion and speculation. People liked to talk, even in a TeamWork camp. She reached for the car door.

"Allow me." Sam hastened to open it for her.

She'd been doing it for herself so long, Lexa reminded herself to allow Sam to play the gentleman. It was nice to be pampered and treated like a lady. "If you're trying to impress me, it's working. You TeamWork directors are quite mannerly." She climbed into the car and lowered her gaze.

Sam pulled his long frame into the car beside her. "I have to do my best to correct your impression of me. I'm not usually so . . . impetuous."

"It's good you can take a night off every now and then. I hope we don't have any car mishaps this time."

"Or run-ins with animals. Kind of gives new meaning to animal magnetism." Sam laughed when she smirked. "Sorry. I can be pretty corny sometimes."

"At least I know what a tire iron is now." Lexa frowned at her slightly swollen thumb. "I just have to be careful with tools—especially hammers."

"Does it still hurt?" He sounded concerned. Then again, maybe he wanted to kiss it and make it all better.

"A little." She could literally feel the color creeping into her cheeks again. They always betrayed her.

"If it's any consolation, you're doing a great job out at the worksite."

Lexa smiled, pleased by the unexpected compliment. It was too hot and stifling in the car to ride without the windows down. Three minutes down the road, her hair was straight again. Even at the relatively slow speed of the station wagon, and at this hour of the evening, it was still extremely hot and windy.

In stark contrast to the first time they'd been in the car together, Sam didn't initiate conversation. But it didn't feel awkward. The countryside wasn't so bland and uninteresting as it had been a couple of days ago when he picked her up at the bus station. She looked at everything with a fresh, new perspective.

She was falling hard for Sam Lewis. Lexa tried to push the thought from her mind. Her imagination sure was fanciful since coming to the TeamWork camp. All those romance novels must finally be infiltrating her brain. Still, she was on a date with the man. And, in her heart, there was nowhere she'd rather be.

~

"Not much to look at, is there?" Something about Lexa brought out Sam's teasing nature. Other than his little sister, Caty, and sometimes Beck, he rarely teased a woman. It seemed too intimate and familiar. Shelby didn't like teasing. Then again, her temperament was as opposite from Lexa's as night and day. But Lexa—well, Lexa was different. He liked teasing her.

"Oh, I wouldn't say that." The way Lexa scrunched her nose and her cheeks turned pink was adorable and could get addictive. The woman was witty. She didn't miss a beat and could probably meet him at every turn in conversation. Keeping up with her was a challenge he welcomed. Lost in thought, Sam drove them onto the main road leading into town. From the corner of his eye, he saw Lexa shift her position to turn toward him. She anchored one hand on the open window.

"Sam, should we maybe talk about that kiss?"

It was hard to hear with the rumbling of the engine, but he heard her question. Maybe he didn't have a decent answer. He opened his mouth and then closed it. What was there to talk about? Why did women always have to talk about these things? The kiss was better than good. It was so great, it actually blew his mind. Lexa must feel the same way. She was sitting beside him in the car, wasn't she?

He cleared his throat and hoped for the best. "I think that's one of the reasons we're sitting here in the car together right now. Before you can ask the question, yes, it really happened. I won't deny it this time. If you're asking me if I want to try it again sometime . . ."

"That's not what I meant."

Sam knew he'd have to avoid looking at Lexa if he didn't want to get distracted while driving. His senses—*all* of them—were reacting to her. He needed to be in full control of his faculties. "Just tell me what you're thinking, Lexa."

"Aren't there TeamWork rules against such things?"

"Not specifically, no. Granted, there are plenty of rules, but none that prevent kissing." A vision of Shelby popped into his mind, but he pushed it to the back of his mind, wanting to bury it so deep it wouldn't resurface. Not while he was with Lexa. Shelby was long gone, but Lexa was here, flesh and blood, sitting beside him. Looking all pretty and sweet, but still feisty as ever. He liked that about her. He liked her independence. Her intelligence was obvious. He liked flirting with her. Especially liked that shy little smile that surfaced every now and then.

"Aren't you kind of like my boss while I'm at the camp? Not to mention we haven't known each other very long."

All of a couple of days, as a matter of fact. It seemed like much longer. "Is that a problem?"

"What?" Lexa shook her head, confused. "The boss part or the not knowing you long part?"

"Listen, we don't need to overanalyze this. We're just going to share some dessert and conversation, get to know one another better."

"Don't you worry. I'm not overanalyzing anything." She sounded huffy now. "I want you to know I didn't come to the TeamWork camp to find a man, Mr. Lewis."

Sam bit his lip not to laugh. "Well, that's a relief." He paused for effect. "If it makes you feel any better, I didn't sign on for this mission specifically to find a woman either, Miss Clarke."

Surprising him, Lexa laughed. "Good. As long as we understand each other." He wasn't sure what to think about that statement. She slid down in the seat again. Maybe she needed to tighten her seat belt.

"Believe it or not, I'm thinking of your reputation. I don't want to get you into any trouble, that's all."

"I'm a big boy. I can handle trouble." That was an understatement, especially when it came to the woman sitting across the seat from him. "Besides, TeamWork is a volunteer organization. Like everything else, kissing is voluntary." Sam avoided looking at her, swallowing his grin. But he caught her smile.

~

Drinking in the sounds and charming ambiance of the festive Riverwalk, Sam walked beside Lexa as they descended the stone steps to the walkway bordering the canal. Slow-moving tourist boats floated through still waters beside them.

It was a bit crowded, but the pace was conducive to quiet, shared conversation. Sam shoved his hands deep into his pockets to stop from capturing her small hand with his. It was too soon for something like that. That struck him as odd since they'd already shared that unbelievable kiss. It hadn't been ordinary by any stretch of the imagination. Holding hands with Lexa now seemed almost as intimate. The woman beside him was reawakening needs, emotional as much as anything else. If he reached for her hand now, he might not relinquish it—ever.

A wistful smile crossed Lexa's face. She waved back with enthusiasm and smiled at a little boy in one of the boats.

"Judging from your expression, I'd say you've been here before."

"Yes, but it's been years. I was only eight when we visited. Right before my mom died."

"You haven't been back since then?"

Lexa shook her head. "No. But I remember the open-air markets and all the terrific southwestern art and pottery. I also remember this annoying little boy who kept following us around and wouldn't leave me alone."

He chuckled. "So, you had male admirers even then."

Lexa smiled. "No, I don't think it was that. He just wanted to get my parents to go into his grandfather's tourist shop. If I recall correctly, they did, and spent a small fortune."

"So, the boy's plan worked. Pretty crafty, I'd say. Should have hung on to that guy, Lexa. He's probably the president of an ad agency or Fortune 500 company."

Lexa shot him a sidelong glance. "No, I'd rather hang out with a missions group for no pay, get all dusty, dirty and sunburned, smash my thumb with a hammer and get accosted by an armadillo. Not to mention ridiculed by the heartless leader of the group." She darted another quick glance at him before lowering her gaze. "Even if most of those things were my own doing."

"I wouldn't agree that I'm heartless." Sam met her eyes. "I think there's a heart deep inside me. As a matter of fact, I know there is since it's beating pretty fast right about now."

"Glad to know the old ticker's working."

Lexa's humor and sarcasm must be her defense mechanism, protecting her from getting too close—or allowing anyone to get close to her.

"Why don't you tell me why *you're* a financial planner, Sam."

Putting a hand on her elbow, he steered her to one side of the walkway as a throng of senior citizens passed by them. Standing directly behind Lexa, he caught a whiff of her sweet-smelling hair. It reminded him of his mother's roses. He nodded and smiled at a few tourists as he guided Lexa back onto the walkway. His eyes strayed down to her feet, and he grinned when he spied pink nails peeking up at him. Again, he was being way too obvious.

"Like you, I enjoy numbers and moving them around so they make sense for someone's future. It's thrilling to help people discover how sound financial planning can enrich their lives instead of confining them. I like to show clients how to embrace what's ahead by careful planning and foresight. Expand their horizons by highlighting the possibilities."

Lexa stared at him like he had three heads. "Did you memorize that from some kind of financial planners' guidebook?"

"Yep. *Financial Planning for Dummies*." Sam's grin widened. "You know what I mean. In some ways, it's very similar to the work I do for TeamWork. Instead of planning finances, I'm working on securing eternity and helping people see that what's ahead is something to look forward to. It isn't frightening. At least it doesn't have to be. Don't you agree?" He shot a curious glance in her direction. Lexa didn't answer. Judging by her furrowed brow, she found it thought-provoking.

"Tell me more about yourself, Lexa." They sat across from one another at a small table in one of the charming cafés bordering the Riverwalk. A gentle breeze lifted her hair, and a long, blonde strand blew across her cheek. Even though the braid was practical for the worksite, Sam liked her hair down. It looked shiny, feminine, soft. Touchable.

Lexa didn't try to mask her beauty, but she had no idea how gorgeous she was. That faint sprinkle of freckles across her nose and the rosy bloom in her cheeks made her look younger than her age. Unlike before, she wore some kind of lipstick. Probably to keep him at bay. When Lexa hesitated, Sam wondered why this woman found it difficult to talk about herself. He wanted to know everything about her—her past, her dreams, and especially about her relationship with the Lord.

"What do you want to know?" Her voice was soft, and those lovely eyes avoided his.

"What are you afraid of?"

She looked up at him for a long moment. "You don't beat around the bush, do you? I'm afraid of armadillos, I guess. I just never really knew that until yesterday."

Sam chuckled before his eyes narrowed and his smile sobered. "I'll tell you my greatest fear."

Lexa raised her head with a gleam of renewed interest shining in her eyes. "I find it difficult to believe you could be afraid of anything."

Leaning closer, he lowered his voice. "I'm afraid I'll somehow miss God's true calling in my life."

She looked surprised. "Isn't that why you're here in San Antonio, directing the TeamWork camp?"

"Yes, but I feel there's something more to do. I just don't know what it is yet. I'm thirty-one, but I don't believe financial planning is what I'm meant to do the rest of my life."

Lexa nodded. "I'm sure you'll figure it out soon enough. But I know how you feel. I'm twenty-five, and one of the reasons I came here is to try and figure out who I am and what I want from life. I know there's more to it than working all the time and going out to eat with my friends once a week." She inclined her head toward one of the boats gliding through the nearby canal. "I'd say in some ways we're pretty much in the same boat, you and me."

Sam leaned one hand on his chin and noted how Lexa lowered her eyes. Was she afraid he'd somehow see too much? That he wouldn't like something he discovered about her? The waitress approached their table. Lexa ordered strawberry cheesecake and coffee, and appeared amused when he asked if they served anything with peaches.

"Sounds like one of your passions in life is peaches." Lexa graced him with that shy little smile. It got his heart pumping, that smile. So pretty.

"How can you tell?" Sam chuckled. "Is there anything better? I love them and always have. Any way they come. For the record, what's your favorite fruit?" His eyes trailed to her lips, and he tried not to stare. It was difficult to look at her and not remember those lips, the way she sighed, the *feel* of her in his arms. He shifted in his chair. He was quickly becoming the romantic fool.

Lexa thought about it for a moment. "I believe I'd have to pick . . . the apple."

"Good choice. Just not as good as the peach." Sam's smile sobered again. "Come on, Lexa. Name one thing you're afraid of." Sitting back, he waited. He'd wait all night, if needed.

She seemed unaware he watched her every movement. Her profile was lovely. Yes, Lexa was beautiful in her own, unique way, but didn't know it. That in itself attracted him. Something stirred inside. A woman like this could make him change his mind on any number of things. In some ways, it thrilled him. In other ways, it scared him to death. Oh, yes, he was lost all right.

Chapter 13

*E*VERYTHING ABOUT SAM Lewis screamed of deep honesty and integrity. The man wasn't lying when he said he wanted to get to know his volunteers. But Lexa doubted he asked the other new volunteers the same questions he asked her. The TeamWork director viewed her in a different way or she wouldn't be sitting across this table from him now. On a date. *Answer the man.*

"I'm afraid," Lexa began, swallowing hard, "of not making a difference in the world."

Sam's eyes softened. "Are you thinking TeamWork will help you make a difference?"

Lexa nodded. "I'm hoping it will."

"Are you talking about making a global difference, or a difference in the lives of a few people?"

Lexa held his gaze. "I'd like to think my life means something to someone else. Whether it's one person, or a few people, or more than that—it doesn't really matter."

"Why is it so important to you to make a difference in the world?" Sam's voice was quiet, his expression thoughtful.

"Because it's not all about me. I want to impact someone else's life. I hope that doesn't sound selfish on some level." Lexa shrugged. "I suppose it will help me feel closer to God, more worthy of His love, if I'm doing something to help someone else other than myself." There. She'd said it. Let him deal with that statement however he wanted.

Sam surprised her by smiling. He moved his arm so the waitress could put their dessert and coffee on the table. When she asked if they wanted cream, both nodded. "Do you mind if I ask a blessing?"

People pray before dessert? Lexa bowed her head and listened to Sam's rich voice, struck again by his depth of reverence, this man's deep faith. It practically radiated from him. She was surprised he wasn't the pastor of a church.

Finished with his prayer, Sam eyed the peach pie. He looked like a child anxious to open his biggest birthday gift. He was an intriguing man, and it was more than obvious he wanted to get to know her better. The thought warmed Lexa from the inside out.

"Sam, why did you ask me what I'm afraid of instead of, say, something I love?"

He took his first bite of the pie. "You can learn so much more about someone when you discover the root of their fears. Don't worry," he added, "I'll find out what you love soon enough."

"You're a deep thinker, Mr. Lewis. Your turn," she prompted, stirring the creamer into her coffee before adding a packet of sweetener. "Tell me something else you're afraid of." Looking at him over the rim of her cup, Lexa watched as he added the same to his coffee. His hands were strong and masculine, with long, tapered fingers and well-groomed nails in spite of the fact that he worked hard alongside his crew at the worksite.

Sam grinned. "Don't think for a second I'm going to leave that last comment alone."

"I know." Lexa raised her face, embracing the light breeze ruffling through the trees along the Riverwalk. She closed her eyes for a few seconds.

Sam thought about his answer for a couple of minutes, his brow furrowed as they enjoyed their coffee together. He took another hearty bite of the pie. "Warm, just the way I love it. Please, taste yours," Sam encouraged, watching as she used her fork to cut a tiny piece before tasting it. "I have to say, you are about the daintiest eater I've ever seen in my life. But your smile is the most genuine I've ever seen in my life, too." He grinned. "It's positively . . . effervescent."

Lexa felt the warmth of color invading her cheeks. Must he say things like that? Did he do it to get a rise out of her? The worst—or best—part was that she liked it.

"Okay, you asked me a question. Time for an answer," he told her a minute later. After sipping his coffee, Sam leaned across the table. "I hate knowing a lot of really good people are going to spend an eternity in hell, especially if I have the power to help change the outcome."

No matter how Lexa thought he might answer, it wasn't that. Maybe he *should* be a pastor since that sounded like something she imagined one would say. She stared at him, unsure how to respond. A rising feeling of dread rumbled inside. "You're not *judging* anyone, are you, Sam?" Was he judging *her* when she said she wanted to feel closer to God and worthy of His love? Wasn't it the job of Christians not to judge, but to love and accept others as they are?

Sam frowned and lowered his fork. "I don't want to think that's what I'm doing. It's just that, based on what I know, what I've seen and heard, a lot of my friends don't know the Lord personally." A look of great sadness crossed his face and he lowered his head.

"Have you tried asking them? Maybe they're Christians but have fallen away for some reason . . ." Lexa's voice trailed. "Perhaps they accepted the Lord when they were just a kid, but then didn't have the opportunity to go to church for some reason." She shifted in her chair and put her fork on the edge of her plate, her desire for the cheesecake gone.

"What I'm trying to say," she said slowly, "is that there are any number of reasons why people don't know the Lord, or don't grow in the Lord. Reasons that sometimes are beyond their power, their reach, their ability to do anything about it."

Sam fixed her with the intensity of his gaze. Reaching across the table, his hand covered hers. "Is that what happened to you?" When she didn't respond, he pressed, "I really want to know. Please tell me." His voice sounded earnest, his hand squeezed hers. Her answer was very important to him.

Withdrawing her hand, Lexa lowered her gaze and stared at her hands twisting together on her lap. "Yes." Tears stung her eyes. "My mom used to take me to church, but I was only eight when she died. Dad didn't want me in church for reasons known only to him." She shrugged. "That's just the way it was. I didn't have a choice."

"But when you were on your own, old enough to go to church of your own volition?"

A surge of anger mixed with sadness, and even guilt, flooded her mind. Lexa stared at Sam with wide eyes, shaking her head. She forced a few deep, calming breaths. "Sam Lewis, have you been living in some kind of sheltered Christian cocoon your entire life?" Noticing that others at nearby tables turned their heads in their direction, she lowered her voice. "You've probably lived this perfect Christian life and don't even know the struggles others face. It's not always easy," she stammered, her cheeks growing warmer by the minute.

Swallowing hard, Lexa forced herself to continue. She'd started to let it out, so she might as well finish now. "You want to know the truth about me?" Lexa's eyes blazed. "I'm sorry if I don't fit into this little spiritual mold or whatever it is you're looking for. The truth is, I've never had anyone take an interest in me spiritually to show me *how* to have a personal relationship with Christ—not that I'm blaming anything on anyone else. I've lived a good moral life, and I acknowledge the fact that God is in control, but, simply put, I don't really know how to *live* like a Christian. All I know," she sputtered, "is what I know. Which isn't very much." Her voice sounded small and defeated. Tugging her purse over one shoulder, she started to walk away from the table. She held her head high, but tears threatened to spill over onto her cheeks.

"Wait. Don't go." Sam stood up and reached out to stop her. *"Please."*

Pausing and looking down at his hand, Lexa struggled between wanting him to remove it and wanting him to pull her close and never let go. How she longed for someone to shelter her forever, keeping her safe, warm and protected. *Loved.*

"You haven't even had much of your cheesecake yet." The slightest tinge of humor surfaced, but Sam's brow furrowed.

Lexa looked up at the deepening night sky and forced several deep, calming breaths. She finally took her seat opposite him again. Eyeing her strawberry cheesecake, she wondered if she'd have the stomach for it.

"I suppose I deserved that." Sam held up one hand. "Truce. Listen," he continued before she could respond, "I really want to see the Lord through your eyes. I can't do that unless I know where you stand spiritually. I need to know if you're living for yourself or living for Him. It's not wrong, and please know I'm not judging you."

"Why?" Lexa sat back down in her chair, her dessert untouched, waiting for his answer.

Sam looked into her eyes again in that way he had of disarming her. "I like you, Lexa. Very much. I want to know you better. As more than a TeamWork volunteer. But in order to do that, I need to know where you stand spiritually."

Lexa could barely contain her agitation. "So you've already said. I suppose it's only fitting that the apple is my favorite fruit," she seethed.

"Why do you say that?" Sam shook his head. His expression was one of confusion and dismay.

"The whole Adam and Eve thing." She waved her hand. "I'm like tempting, forbidden fruit to you. I'm not the type of woman you want or need in your life. If you take a bite from the apple I'm offering you, you'll be entering a world of earthly sin, your eyes will be opened and you'll be banished from God's perfect garden. Or something like that." Lexa crossed her arms and turned her head, impatiently wiping away a tear that coursed down her cheek. "I don't know how to talk to you. I'm afraid I'll say the wrong thing."

"That's not fair, Lexa." Sam closed his mouth, and looked at a loss.

Her breath strangled in her throat, and she struggled for control. Feeling a chill, Lexa shuddered and rubbed her hands up and down her arms, knowing it wouldn't touch the hurt welling up inside. "Far be it from me to hold you back from following God's great plan in your life. Besides," she continued, her voice rising, "I just told you where I'm at spiritually. And if you're so concerned about where I'm at, then maybe you'd be better off examining just exactly where *you're* at!"

Flinging her napkin down on the table, Lexa paused. Rising to her feet, she gathered her thoughts and her dignity and tried to calm down. It proved difficult, and anger won the inner battle raging within. She lowered her voice and leaned close. "The next time you ask a girl out with some hidden agenda, I suggest you think twice about putting her through the third degree. Good luck finding the perfect Christian woman you're looking for, Sam Lewis, but I don't think you'll ever find her!"

He appeared genuinely shocked. "I know you're hurt, and I'm really sorry, but did you ever stop to think you might be jumping to conclusions?"

His eyes widened as she stepped around the table and leaned close to him, practically nose-to-nose. Sam leaned back further in his chair as she stared him down. Gulping, Lexa blinked hard to stem her tears.

"Instead of pulling this sanctimonious, holier-than-thou act, maybe you should think about what Jesus would do in your shoes. I understand that's what Christians do." She gave him one final glare. "I don't think Jesus would act the way you just did." Turning, she fled into the night.

Chapter 14

*W*ITH TEARS STREAMING down her face, Lexa flew back up the stone steps on the way to the street. She didn't have a plan other than to get away from Sam and try to find a quiet place to collect herself. Then she'd worry about getting a cab or a hotel room or whatever. At the moment, she debated heading straight back to Houston.

Seating herself on a stone wall in a quiet spot further down the Riverwalk, Lexa raised her face to the sky, closed her eyes and put one hand over her mouth, stifling her quiet sobs. Shivers ran through her and she rocked herself in a self-comforting motion. Maybe she should say a prayer. She didn't know what else to do, and it felt somehow appropriate for the situation. The prayers she said at night seemed to make her feel better, so why not? It couldn't make things worse than they already were.

Lord, I don't know what I'm doing. I'm miserable. I came here tonight thinking I'd have a romantic evening with a handsome man—a man who belongs to you—but now everything's a big old Texas mess. I want to know you, Father, but I need your help. I want to serve you, and I really don't want to leave. Please show me how I can become a better person through you, how I can help others, and how you want me to serve. In Jesus' name.

Looking around at her surroundings, Lexa pondered her options. In spite of this disastrous date with Sam, she wanted to go back to the work camp. She cherished the time spent with Margarita. Liked the camaraderie with the other ladies. Enjoyed the Bible studies at the bonfires and helping at the worksite and in the canteen. Working for no pay was never so satisfying. She was beginning to feel like she *belonged* with these people.

Lexa sat up straighter and dried her eyes. She'd never been one to allow a man to stand in the way of her goals. She'd just been sidetracked a little in her quest to make a difference in the world. But now, it was time to get back on track.

~

As soon as the words were out of his mouth, the uneasy stirring in the pit of Sam's stomach alerted him he might very well have dug the proverbial hole even deeper for himself. Seeing Lexa's tears punched him right in the gut. He hated that he'd made her feel this way. Something deep inside twisted, squeezing tight. How could he make her understand? Her eyes sparked with such a fiery anger. They were unbelievable in their beauty, but made him miserable with guilt.

Still, talk about a rush to judgment. Either by his words or his actions, he'd made her feel somehow unworthy. Or made her feel even more unworthy than she already did. And what did she mean by that apple and temptation comment? Did Lexa think all he wanted was to tumble into bed with her? Maybe his undoubtedly strong physical attraction for Lexa *was* confusing the issue.

Sam frowned and rubbed his hand across his brow. He was messing this up royally. He found it difficult to communicate with this woman. It was definitely uncharted territory. Now she was offended and he didn't know what to say, what to do, to make things right.

Standing a short distance away, hidden from view, he watched Lexa sitting on the wall. It looked like she was praying, and it touched his heart. He'd blown it with her, and he'd be lucky if she gave him another chance sometime in this lifetime. He'd only dated Christian women before, and Lexa was so unlike most of them in a number of ways. But in the ways that counted most, she was their equal and more. Lexa was good, honest, with a purity of heart and spirit. She had a genuine desire to serve the Lord. Weren't those the things that mattered the most?

The hardest part to swallow was that she was right. He'd been evaluating— yes, perhaps even judging others—for too long. That in itself was a sin. Sam prayed his own silent prayer, but dared not close his eyes for fear he'd reopen them only to find Lexa gone again. He couldn't take that chance, so he kept his eyes trained on her as he prayed under his breath for the Lord to keep her there with him and his TeamWork crew in San Antonio. After only a few days in the camp, Lexa was growing and learning. Sam asked the Lord for the wisdom to know the right words to say to this intriguing woman, the right things to do so he didn't push her further away.

At that precise moment in time, he had his own private mission— protecting Lexa from the seedier element that sometimes hung out around the Riverwalk. He had to keep her safe and take her back to the camp. He only prayed he hadn't scared her off so she'd run all the way back to Houston and never look back. Dear God, he didn't want that.

After a few more minutes passed, Lexa raised her head. Wiping her eyes with a tissue, she sniffled and blew her nose in a most unladylike fashion. From his hidden stance, watching her, Sam almost laughed aloud. He'd best not reveal his hidden presence or she'd never forgive him.

Standing and smoothing her clothes, Lexa pushed her long hair behind her shoulders and raised her head before looking around. He glimpsed that defiance etched into her expression. That dare-you-to-get-to-me look which was becoming all too familiar, but which Sam understood masked her insecurity and vulnerability. She'd definitely be mad to know he suspected such a thing. When she moved her head in his direction, he ducked behind a stone wall, his heart pounding hard, afraid she'd see him.

Lexa started walking, and he followed a short distance behind. Memories of playing hide and seek and his younger brothers, Will and Carson, came to mind. He needed to keep her in view while he thought of a plan of action. At least she was walking in the general direction of the car. He should have time to dart back over to where he'd parked the station wagon on a side street. Surely she wouldn't be foolhardy enough to hitchhike. Lexa might believe she could get a cab, but he knew better. Not in this more remote area at this hour of the evening, even on a weeknight. All the cabs in the Riverwalk area would already be busy with customers.

Darting her head in either direction, Lexa clutched her shoulder bag and quickened her steps. It was as though she sensed someone's eyes upon her and didn't want to take any chances. Above all, Sam didn't want to scare her to death. When the Volvo came into view, he detoured in its direction, keeping Lexa in his sight. Turning the key, he muttered under his breath when the engine rumbled but didn't turn over.

"Come on. Don't fail me now." He waited a few excruciating seconds before trying again. The engine sputtered before choking and dying. "Great. Just great." By now, Lexa's figure was fading from his range of vision. His fingers tapped an impatient dance on the steering wheel. Deciding to give it one more try before he took off after her on foot, Sam chewed his lip, willing the engine to turn over. Thank goodness it obeyed and roared to life.

Pulling out so fast the tires squealed, Sam drove in the direction Lexa walked when he last saw her. His eyes scanned the roadside. A rising panic tore through his chest and his breath grew short. Slowing the car to a near crawl, Sam looked in every direction. *There!* She'd decided to go down yet another side street.

Turning off the lights, Sam soon rode alongside her. If Lexa was scared, it didn't show. Better not to let her worry that it was someone else. He cleared his throat loud enough for her to hear. "Care for a lift back to camp?"

"No, thank you." Lexa didn't pause and walked with her head held high, shoulders back, and a purposeful stride. My, but she was the most stubborn woman he'd ever encountered. While Sam liked her spunkiness, the defiant act could get plenty annoying sometimes.

"Um, I hesitate to mention this, but there's not exactly a stream of cabs in this neighborhood right about now." He struggled to keep his voice calm and steady.

"I'll manage to find one. There's bound to be one around here somewhere." Even though her voice never wavered, Sam thought he detected a slight element of fear in her voice. It was his fault. Waves of guilt washed over him.

"Come on, Lexa. Get in. I promise not to say another word the entire way back if you'll just get in the car." He felt like begging, but only as a last resort. He had *some* pride left.

Her steps slowed only for a moment before resuming their brisk pace. She picked up speed and practically marched. She didn't bother gracing him with even the slightest glance. "No thank you, Mr. Lewis."

"Okay then." Sam tried to mask his aggravation with this beautiful, obstinate creature. "Guess I'll have to keep pace with you. If we're lucky, we'll make it back to camp about, say, three o'clock this morning." He paused, and his head darted back and forth between the road ahead and Lexa by the side. "Sure will be awfully hard trying to work tomorrow in the blazing heat if you're tired. Nope. Not a good combination at all."

"What do you think you're doing following me?" Lexa demanded. Stopping, hands on hips, she glared at Sam. "Slumming?"

"Okay, that's it!" Irritated with her taunt, he shoved the gear into park. Leaving the keys in the ignition, he jumped out.

Seeing that he was heading straight for her, Lexa turned and started to run away again. "Oh, no you don't!" Her cries of protest were drowned out when he lifted her and put her over his shoulder, being none-too-gentle about it.

"What do you think you're doing?" she cried, her voice indignant. "Put me down!"

Tight fists pummeled Sam's back as he carried her over to the car. Depositing her in the seat without ceremony, he slammed the passenger door and hurried around to the driver's side, tamping down the irresistible urge to grin.

"Two can play this game!" Lexa spouted through clenched teeth. She hopped out of the car again before Sam could put it back in gear. "See you back at the camp, Bucko!" Slamming the door equally hard, she stalked away from him, headed back this time in the direction of the Riverwalk.

Watching her in the rearview mirror, Sam noticed her steps slowed a few hundred yards down the street. When she turned, he shifted the car in reverse. It skidded backward in her direction and stopped beside where she stood in the middle of the quiet street. The car rumbled, sputtered and threatened to die right then and there.

Her hands traveled to those tiny hips in a firm stance of battle, David to his Goliath. "In spite of your best intentions, *you* can't single-handedly save the world, Sam Lewis. Some battles aren't yours to be won."

He inhaled a quick breath and raked his fingers through his hair. Frustration with Lexa Clarke was going to turn him mental. "And if you'd stop being so defensive all the time, maybe you'd actually learn something." He pinned her down with his eyes this time. "Some battles *are* worth the fight, Lexa. Even if they're an uphill climb. Just get in the car. *Please.*" He struggled but kept his voice low and controlled.

"I'll be fine on my own, thank you very much." No tremors, no fear now. Just that stubborn defiance.

"Okay, fine," Sam said, his voice tight with frustration.

He could tell he shocked her when her eyes widened. The corners of her mouth tugged downward.

"Suit yourself. See you later, sweetheart!" He sped off into the night.

~

She didn't think he'd really leave. Now what had she done? Standing in the middle of the street and gaping wasn't going to help her situation. Her foot tapped a steady rhythm. Seeing the tail lights of the station wagon still visible in the distance, Lexa felt like screaming Sam's name and begging him to come back for her. Would he really leave her out here by herself, defenseless in the night, in an unfamiliar city?

A group of teenagers hanging out in a nearby driveway called out to her. Oh, this night just kept getting better. She ignored them and headed back in the direction of the Riverwalk. Even though they called out indecent proposals, she forced her steps to be confident. She was only a few blocks away from more civilization. But they were following her.

The boys laughed as she picked up her pace and kept walking. Their voices grew louder. She heard their footsteps and knew they were right behind her. Fear seized her. Inhaling a deep breath, she somehow moved her feet forward. Where was Sam? The man saved her from an armadillo, but where was he when she *really* needed him? Granted, he'd also saved her from serious bodily harm when she fell from that rooftop. But *now* would be an opportune time for the tall cowboy's chivalrous ways.

"Hey, pretty lady. What's a great lookin' woman like you doin' in a place like this? Need a date, sweetheart? Lookin' for a man?" A kid who couldn't be more than sixteen or seventeen shot around to one side of Lexa, close enough to smell alcohol on his breath. She shrank back, not daring to look him in the face. The group of boys hemmed her in.

She was trapped, and her heart thundered. It was a mistake to look a potential attacker in the eye. Her eyes unseeing, she fought to keep her breathing even. *Don't let them see your fear. God, please help me!*

"Leave me alone," Lexa managed to get out between tight, clenched jaws. "My ride will be here in just a minute." She hoped it sounded convincing, but it fell flat. The knuckles clutching her purse were white. Maybe if she threw it down on the pavement, they'd grab it and leave her alone. Replacing lost documents would be a pain, but it was preferable to being raped . . . or worse.

Maybe they only wanted to scare her, but she couldn't take any chances. Twinges of regret squeezed her. She should have enrolled in that self-defense class with her co-workers a few months ago. Too late now. It would still be five against one on this dark, deserted San Antonio street. As if she had a chance. That thought started her heart pounding even harder.

"Sure thing, honey. We'll leave you alone once we're done with you. You look real sweet. We just want you to play nice with us for a while." Rivers of fear ran through Lexa at that statement. She stared straight ahead and focused on a distant tree.

Another boy ran one finger along the length of her bare arm, leaving a path of shivers in his wake. Lexa flinched and jerked her arm away from his touch. They were only boys, but they were also men in the physical sense with an appetite for women. Her mind was numb, her legs unsteady.

In that moment, she vowed to give Sam Lewis a good piece of her mind . . . and more . . . *if* she survived this ordeal. She pushed aside the thought that he'd gone so far as to manhandle her in order to put her back in his old bomb of a car. So, the blame was hers alone. Again. But first things first.

"I think she's feisty, boys." The first boy inched closer.

Please don't let me faint. Where's Sam? Everything within her wanted to curse and scream his name. Curse him for leaving her on this deserted street, and scream for him to come and save her. Yes, Lexa Clarke wanted to be saved. By Sam Lewis. If God Himself wasn't going to help her out of this mess, then maybe He'd send His messenger.

Chapter 15

*R*EMORSE MIXED WITH ebbing anger flooded his soul as Sam drove around the block at a low speed and tried to regain control. Never had a woman so attracted and infuriated him at the same time. Why couldn't Lexa get in the car without protest? Once in the car, why couldn't she stay put? Why did she always have to be so combative? Chewing on his lower lip, Sam decided to let her stew a couple more minutes before going back to get her. Only a heel would leave her unprotected. She just needed to learn a lesson.

It was pretty clear she was sticking to the street and should only be a little further down than she was a few minutes ago. Switching off the headlights again and turning the corner, Sam's heart stopped at the sight. Lexa was standing in the middle of the street, surrounded by a gang of teenage boys.

Oh, no. His foot slammed into the floorboard as the station wagon sputtered a little and roared down the street. "This should be good." He halted the car with a rumble near the group and hauled himself out of the car and rose to his full height—slowly, for the effect of it all. Six-foot-five didn't faze them. Okay, time to employ the swagger. Hands on his hips, Sam stalked in their direction. The boys didn't scatter and stood their ground. So, they wanted to play tough.

Lexa's eyes widened as she looked up at him, but not before Sam glimpsed her obvious relief. She might not say it, but the woman was grateful. All he wanted to do was pull her close and tell her all was okay with the world. Punks. He'd show them.

Sam glared down on the group. Being so tall came in handy sometimes, and no more so than when saving a damsel in distress. Not that he didn't think Lexa couldn't take care of these kids all on her own by virtue of sheer stubbornness. But that didn't change the fact that she could use his help now. She needed him even though she'd probably never admit it.

"Is there a problem, boys?"

"We're just talkin' to her. Buzz off, jerk."

Sam's jaw tightened and his fists clenched. He never liked fighting, but he'd do it, if needed. As much as anything else, Lexa was one of his TeamWork volunteers and needed help. He'd do it for any one of them—although most wouldn't find themselves in a similar situation.

"I'm going to ask you nicely to leave. You're not going to get another chance." Strolling toward the instigator, Sam poked a long finger into the middle of his chest. "You don't want to mess with me. You can trust me on that one."

The spokesman punk snorted. "Yeah, right. Dirty Harry's here to save the world." He motioned with one hand for the others to follow. "Relax. We're leaving. If I were you, though," he called back over his shoulder, "I'd watch out for my woman a little better. She shouldn't be walkin' out here all by herself, if you know what I mean. Things can happen to a woman like that in this part of town." His leering stare raked Lexa up and down in an invasive manner.

Even under the cover of darkness, Sam saw the slow flush of color creeping into her cheeks. No doubt it ran all the way down to her toes. Lexa swayed, and her knees started to buckle.

"Whoa!" He rushed to her side and swept her into his arms. She couldn't weigh much more than a hundred pounds.

"Shall we try this again?" This was ridiculous, standing in the middle of the deserted street, holding the most defiant woman he'd ever met. And the prettiest. One hand splayed against his chest like out at the worksite. Her eyes searched his for the briefest of seconds before she snatched her hand away as though touching a burning flame.

The urge to kiss her seized Sam all over again. At the moment, she looked small, vulnerable. *Don't do it.* Talk about a flame. That little voice inside him warned he might get his face slapped if he dared press his lips to hers. He restrained himself. It wasn't the time. From the cradle of his arms, Lexa's expression was dazed, indecipherable. Feeling her tremble, he tightened his hold.

"For once, I honestly don't know what to say."

That was difficult to believe. The woman could probably engage a mime in animated conversation. "Yeah, well, thank you might be a good place to start." With her still in his arms, Sam marched over to the car. It surprised him that she didn't squirm to escape his hold, didn't move. Those warm, small hands of hers inched around his neck, burning a path the entire way. Lord help him now.

"Can you stand up on your own long enough to get in?" His voice was gruff, but he couldn't help himself. He avoided looking at those full lips in case they pouted and wore down his defenses even more. It wouldn't be a hard thing to do at this point. Irritant or not, the woman entranced him.

Lexa nodded. "I think so."

"Good." Depositing her on the ground, Sam opened the car door. When she stood there for a moment, still not moving, he grunted. "Look, you'd better get in if you're going to because I don't know how much longer this old car is going to last. No more games, no more anger." His voice was thick with exhaustion. They'd both had enough.

Hopping in, she sniffled, slamming the car door before he could reach it.

"I'm getting a sense of déjà vu, Miss Clarke. I do believe trouble follows you." Sam was beginning to think he'd need to take out an individual liability policy on her alone while she was on this TeamWork assignment. Climbing back into the car, he closed his door, being careful not to slam it. He hoped she'd get the point. Grabbing a lightweight jacket off the backseat, he handed it to her. "Here. Put this on. You're shaking, and I suspect it's not from the temperature."

Lexa accepted the jacket without looking over at him and tugged it around her slender shoulders. "I didn't need you and your big old white horse to come rescue me, you know." Her voice was quiet, and she didn't sound so combative now. Her hands twisted together where they rested on her lap.

The muscles in his jaws flexed as he stared with blind eyes out the front window. "Yes, you did, and you know it. And don't call me Bucko. It's Sam. Just Sam." He made sure her seatbelt was on before starting the car and pulling out. He was scared to think what might have happened if he'd arrived on the scene another minute or two later. A shudder ran through him at the thought.

They drove in silence for a few miles. The car was too noisy for conversation, anyway, and sounded like a roaring lion in stark contrast to the stillness of the night.

"Thanks for not leaving me out there all alone."

When he looked over at Lexa in surprise, Sam couldn't believe it. Her shoulders were shaking. Was she crying? Pulling the car over to the side of the road, he watched, stunned into silence. Lexa's sobs were quiet, unlike anything he'd ever seen or heard. At least she wasn't wailing like some kind of wounded animal.

Sam didn't like the feeling of helplessness invading his senses. He didn't know what she wanted from him, wasn't sure how to comfort her. If he'd learned anything, Lexa wasn't like most women. Short of beating on his chest with both fists and shouting a Neanderthal mating cry, Sam wanted to shelter her from the hurts of the outside world. With all the mixed signals he got from her, he didn't know what to think anymore.

"I don't cry often," Lexa sobbed, dabbing at her eyes with a tissue. Those tissues sure were coming in handy on this TeamWork mission.

"Maybe you should try it more." That suggestion must not have been the right thing to say, judging by her glare. He blew out a sigh. Coping with crying women was an acquired art. He wanted—he needed—to somehow ease her fear.

"Please don't cry, Lexa. It makes me hurt to see you cry." That must have been better since she looked up at him so fast it made his heart jumpstart in his chest.

"That's quite possibly the sweetest thing you've ever said to me." Sniffling, she dabbed daintily at her nose.

Sam rotated his sore shoulder and leaned back against the seat. "It's okay to admit you were scared. I'm not afraid of some young punks, but it scares me to think what could have happened. And don't go thinking I'm so sweet. That wouldn't be so great for my reputation, for one thing. You've only known me a few days."

When he glimpsed new tears welling in her eyes, Sam leaned closer, letting Lexa give him the cues she needed. She didn't disappoint. Scooting closer, she leaned toward him. Without hesitation, Sam bundled her into his arms, cradling her head against his chest. Holding her this close was better than nice. Underneath all the defiance, Lexa Clarke needed comfort. Security. It was his prayer she'd find it in a growing relationship with the Lord. And maybe with him. Only the Lord held the answer, but she sure fit nicely in the curve of his arms. Interesting.

Her shoulders rocked with more quiet sobs. Bless her heart, those kids scared her more than he'd known. With one hand, he smoothed her long hair and patted her shoulder a few times. Although a bit awkward, the gesture appeared to give her a measure of comfort.

At least Lexa didn't swat his hand away, and didn't seem to find his actions inappropriate. Sam tried to keep his touch gentle but innocuous. He wondered how he'd comfort his youngest sister, Caty, if something similar happened to her. The acute awareness this wasn't his sister bordered on painful. This was Lexa, a woman to whom he was drawn with each passing moment, his every breath.

For once, Sam understood what it meant to get a woman under his skin. With all the conflicted feelings churning inside, he could pen a country song. Perhaps he should—sell it for royalties and pour the money into TeamWork. Maybe get another used Volvo out of the deal.

How long they sat there, he couldn't be sure. Waiting until her sobs quieted, Sam pulled back, his gaze melding into hers. The sides of his thumbs brushed gentle arcs over damp cheeks. Lexa's gaze swept back and forth over his face. He liked seeing her like this, soft and feminine. Vulnerable. *Sweet.*

"You don't always have to be so tough, Lexa."

She nodded. "I've been doing it too long."

"Since you were eight?" It was a guess, but her look told him everything. As much as he wanted to keep this woman at a safe distance, it seemed she was always doing something to get his attention or force him to take some kind of action. For the second time in as many minutes, Sam wondered what God's plan was in all of this. He also knew it would be revealed sooner or later. He was grateful Lexa was safe. But, for now, he had to get moving or else he'd kiss her again.

"It's getting late. We'd better head back to the camp." Extracting his arm from around her shoulders, Sam turned over the engine. At least it started. If it hadn't, he might have released a shout borne of sheer frustration.

Driving along the quiet road a few minutes later, Sam stole a glance her way. Her shoulders were swallowed by his jacket, and she pulled it tighter about her, snuggling into it. Slumping down further in the seat, Lexa's arms crossed over her midsection.

"You've got to stop doing that."

"Doing what?" Lexa stared out the window. "I thought you promised not to talk."

"You've got to stop crossing your arms like that. It's hostile body language. I thought we were making some headway with that. Until tonight."

Lexa sniffed. "Maybe you should think about what prompts me to do such a thing in the first place, Mr. Lewis."

From her tone, Sam could tell she was teasing this time. Then again, maybe she was half-serious. He hoped for the telltale upturn of her lovely mouth, but it wasn't there.

"Oh, trust me, Miss Clarke, you've given me plenty to think about tonight."

"Good." Lexa sank even further down in the seat, but not until first uncrossing her arms.

Chapter 16

WITH A START, Lexa awoke a week after her date with Sam in San Antonio. Willing herself to go back to sleep, she tossed and turned for the better part of an hour. Her lips curved in a smile as she remembered her outrage when Sam's big, warm hands gripped the backs of her legs as he put her in the car. While humiliating, it was not unlike a scene she might read in one of her silly romance novels. Still, let him think what he wanted. She wasn't giving in that easy.

While not purposely avoiding Sam, she needed to sort out her feelings. She didn't measure up to his ideal of the perfect Christian woman. She was embarrassed she needed Sam to rescue her. Ashamed he'd seen her so vulnerable when she cried. But loved it when Sam swept her up in his arms like some kind of brave romantic hero. Adored it when he pulled her in his arms and comforted her.

Then Lexa remembered how he told her how her tears made him hurt. That statement alone revealed uncommon sensitivity and compassion. His gruff manner masked inner emotions the same as defensiveness masked hers. Oh yes, they were a lot alike.

Sitting up on the bed, Lexa's eyes strayed to Sam's Bible on the end of her bed. She cherished her time alone each day to read new passages. The highlighted portions—and the notes in the margins—were insightful when she could make out his tiny, precise handwriting. She'd also taken the Bible to the bonfire the first few times, but found it too difficult to see. That's why Sam always read the passages of scripture aloud and encouraged his TeamWork volunteers to read them later.

For his part, Sam seemed content not to seek her out. He didn't try and explain himself further, or try to talk with her more about it. That hurt. But that same sparkle was still there whenever he turned her way. Whenever he met her eyes, Lexa's heart pounded and her breath caught in her throat. There was also a hesitancy in his manner.

It wasn't like she encouraged any of the banter, the lighthearted teasing or even the barbs they'd traded during her first week in the camp. *Call it what is was, Lexa. Unabashed flirting.* She'd never admit it out loud, but she missed it.

"Are you going anywhere on your weekend off?" Winnie asked as they handed out ice cream sandwiches at the worksite a few days later.

Lexa frowned. "I haven't even thought about it. I suppose I could go home to Houston." But what was waiting for her there? Maybe she could find a church to attend. It hadn't been a priority for her before, but now she wanted to focus on that aspect of her life. A church with a thriving singles program would be ideal. A place where she could meet more people her own age who shared her interests and lifestyle while learning more about the Lord and deepening her spiritual walk.

"You're welcome to come with Amy and me. We're going to stick around here, maybe go to some of the missions. You know, sightseeing and shopping. It should be fun."

Lexa smiled. "Sounds great. Can I let you know tomorrow?"

"Sure. No rush. We're flexible."

The more she thought about it, the more the idea of staying put around camp and then sightseeing during the day in San Antonio sounded like fun. Until Winnie told her that Sam might be tagging along for part of it. "He's driving us into town Friday night. He's got some business to do for TeamWork on Saturday, but he said he'd like to join us when he can."

"Oh," Lexa muttered, disgruntled. Did Sam know she might come along, too?

Winnie eyed her curiously. "Is that a problem?"

"No," Lexa protested, perhaps a bit too insistent. "Of course not. Why shouldn't Sam come along?"

"Considering he's our only free transportation around, it's the best offer we have."

"Right. I just hope that old station wagon lasts the rest of the summer," Lexa commented under her breath, handing an ice cream sandwich to Josh.

"How are you?" He flashed his brilliant, trademark smile, oozing that all-too-easy charm.

"Just fine, thanks." Lexa returned his smile. Josh sat by her in the dining tent as often as possible. Now that she thought of it, he managed to sit beside her at the bonfire a lot. Maybe he flirted with all the women. It was flattering, but she couldn't take it seriously. Still, if she made the slightest move in his direction, Lexa suspected Josh Grant would be more than willing.

~

Sam's eyes strayed over to Lexa as he finished his lunch. He couldn't stop looking at her. Since their night together in San Antonio, she was more compelling than ever. He'd kept his distance, but witnessed her volunteering for more assignments, growing more comfortable with her surroundings and their work at the camp. It thrilled him to see it.

She had relaxed more and enjoyed herself in many activities at the camp, getting to know the others. As he led the devotions, Lexa was one of his most avid listeners. She asked thought-provoking questions which clued him in that she was reading and studying her Bible.

The one thing Sam *didn't* like was Josh Grant sitting by her almost every night. His eyes focused in on Lexa as she talked with Josh now. At the bonfire, it was customary for Josh to sit on one side of her with Sheila on the other. Sam liked the fact that the shy, quiet woman was bringing out the caring instincts in Lexa, just as little Margarita brought out Lexa's innate motherly instincts. He didn't know what else to call it. He remembered the small boy waving to her from the boat at the Riverwalk. Children gravitated to her. So did grown men. He scowled when Josh touched Lexa's arm.

Rebekah tipped him off to the fact that Margarita's parents paid little heed to their youngest and that the child was drawn to Lexa. In fact, she thrived under her attention and personal instruction. One afternoon, stopping into his office before heading out to the worksite, Sam spied Lexa sitting with Margarita on the ground outside the schoolroom, leaning against the wall. They sat side-by-side and Lexa stroked the girl's hair as they read together. He watched as Lexa encouraged Margarita to read a passage from the book, waiting patiently as the girl stumbled over the words.

Sam looked forward to the weekend since Amy told him Lexa planned to go with them into San Antonio. Perhaps then he could tell Lexa he was sorry for the way he'd acted, the way he'd treated her. He shook his head and winced at the memory.

Maybe Lexa was right when she teased him about being their heartless leader. But Sam knew he had a heart. It pounded every time Lexa smiled, every time she looked his way, every time he thought of her soft lips raised to his, waiting for his kiss.

He'd acted like a complete and utter fool at the Riverwalk that night, and wanted the opportunity to make it up to her. If only she'd let him. And Sam knew that was a mighty big *if*. They'd shared a special moment when he'd come to her aid with those young thugs. Then again, she wouldn't have been in that position if he hadn't made her run away from him. More than ever, Sam was determined to make it up to Lexa.

He sighed as he finished his meal and rose to leave. Yes, he'd be on his knees again tonight with some very specific requests to lift up to the Heavenly Father.

Chapter 17

*T*HE SCHOOL SESSION dismissed early on Friday afternoon, and Lexa walked to the worksite alongside Amy and Natalie. Of course, it had to be the hottest part of the day. She pulled the brim of her hat down further over her perspiring forehead and kicked up dust with every step.

"Aren't we about due for a storm?" She peered up at the sky through narrowed eyes.

Natalie laughed. "Sounds like you're really hoping for one."

"I am. A good, soaking downpour sounds great about now."

Amy laughed. "Be careful what you wish for, Lexa. You might just get it."

"Fine by me." They laughed together, but Lexa understood rain might have the opposite effect of what she wanted. It might escalate the humidity, although that didn't seem possible. A drip of sweat ran down the length of her back as if for emphasis. Even God had a sense of humor.

Covering the short distance to the worksite within minutes, the girls marveled at the progress the TeamWork crew had made in such a short time. The house she'd worked on that fateful Sunday afternoon was now finished and ready to be painted. Maybe that was something she could help them do. When they'd painted the dorm walls a pale yellow, Lexa enjoyed it. She had an affinity for painting.

Sam walked toward them with a smile as they crossed the threshold of one of the houses. Lexa avoided looking directly at him but was never more aware of his masculinity. His red tank was soaked through to the skin so that it clung to him. Those muscular arms glistened, his thick hair plastered to his head in dark waves. But it was those devastating, light blue eyes so prominent against the tan skin—and the ever-present smile reaching his eyes—that tugged away at her heart.

What is this man doing to me?

She was falling in love with Sam Lewis. She couldn't meet his eyes. If she did, he'd see how much she cared. Her mouth was dry, and Lexa prayed she wouldn't hyperventilate. Any minute he'd be telling her not to stare and offering her water.

Sam assigned Amy and Natalie to a group in another room of the house. Walking into the kitchen with them, he called back over his shoulder for Lexa to stay put. "I have something special picked out for you."

Waiting for him to return from helping her friends, Lexa shifted from one foot to the other, hardly an easy feat in the heavy boots. Just what did Sam have up his sleeve? The thought that he wasn't wearing any sleeves struck her as amusing, and she smiled.

"At least I see your smile is still intact." Coming back into the room to stand beside her, Sam wiped a towel across his forehead.

"It never really left. More like the sun hiding behind the moon." Lexa avoided his probing gaze. As perceptive as he was, she didn't want him reading her mind now.

"I'd also like to see your eyes sometime, too, if that's possible." Sam leaned his head down in an exaggerated manner. "That is, if they're not hiding behind the moon, too." He ran the towel over his head, back and forth a few times to absorb some of the moisture.

Lexa looked up and met his gaze. All that thick hair stuck out at crazy, odd angles yet he never looked more appealing.

"Oh good," he said, feigning relief. "I was afraid someone had stolen away those beautiful eyes."

"Enough with the compliments," Lexa groused, but grinned nonetheless.

"Lexa, you're a beautiful woman, inside and out." He leaned close. "Just the way God made you." Maybe the man was laying it on thick, but he sounded sincere.

She shrugged. "I've always had a hard time accepting compliments. Thank you. So, what's this big job you have for me?"

Sam motioned for her to walk with him as he led the way to another home nearer to completion. "At first, I thought I'd put you on armadillo watch, but then decided your talents would be better utilized elsewhere." He ducked to miss her playful swat.

"Glad to see your sense of humor is still intact."

"Always. Here." He handed her a paint roller. "Since I witnessed the product of your handiwork in the dorm, I decided you could help me paint. Seems safe enough, anyway."

"Funny thing, I was just thinking the exact same thing." Accepting the paint roller, Lexa moved over to where the other supplies were clustered. When he didn't leave, she smirked. "I suppose you're going to stand and supervise."

Sam threw his head back and laughed. "Every single stroke." Those blue eyes positively sparkled.

"Well, in that case, here." Lexa flung a roller into his unsuspecting hands.

He caught it and shook his head, laughing again. "Watch it, Miss Clarke. You're throwing things at me again. It's not heavy this time, but it could get a little messy."

"You might as well make yourself useful. Leaders are more effective when their subjects see they're willing to work alongside them, you know." She gave him an exaggerated wink, and they both laughed as others came over to lend them a hand. Lexa enjoyed meeting some of the women whose houses they were rebuilding, and Sam talked with the men. Every now and then, he caught her eye across the room and winked.

~

"Man, do I need a good, hot shower." A couple of hours later, Sam took a step back to appraise their workmanship. Grabbing a nearby towel, he wiped more sweat from his face and neck. He'd probably lost five pounds. When he offered the same towel to Lexa, she crossed her eyes. Sam handed her a clean paper towel, and she accepted it, dabbing at her forehead daintily.

He surveyed their work with a satisfied nod. "Not bad at all. Alamo World Financial should be worried. I'll make a housepainter out of you yet." Lexa started to make a comeback, opening her mouth before closing it. Her smile faded so quickly, Sam wondered what he'd said, what she was thinking.

Reaching for her hat, she tugged it down on her head. "If that's all for today, I think I'll go back to the dorm now. I need a shower, too, especially since we're heading into town for the evening."

"I'm driving everyone in, as a matter of fact."

"I'm aware of that."

Sam couldn't tell if she was pleased by the prospect or not. Lexa turned back around, slowly pivoting on one foot. He needed to apologize so they could move past this impasse. The mood was set. It was time.

"Lexa," Sam began, walking over to stand in front of her, "I owe you an apology. I know I acted like a jerk that night on the Riverwalk. I've been beating myself up about it ever since." He paused as she stepped nearer, and his heart rate increased the closer she came. "You have to understand my relationship with the Lord has always been the most important one in my life. I don't take a relationship with a woman lightly. If I'm even thinking of starting something, I want to be sure she shares my faith." Maybe he shouldn't have used the word relationship, judging by the tentative look in her eyes.

"I'm not the type of Christian woman you've been looking for. That's what's bothering you, isn't it, Sam?"

The words were quiet, not accusatory or full of hurt as he might have suspected. His eyes widened.

"You can admit it. You thought you'd find . . ."

He held up one hand to stop her. "Not that I've been actively seeking anyone, but you're right. I thought I'd eventually find a woman who's been a Christian as long as me, a woman who's as strong in her commitment to the Lord as I like to think I am. But you know what I found out?" He needed to keep going before Lexa had a chance to turn away from him in frustration or anger. Given the opportunity, Sam suspected that was exactly what she'd do.

"What?" Her tone held no challenge. It was sweet, really.

"How arrogant that kind of thinking is, for one thing, and how dangerous. It doesn't matter how strong your faith is. If it's there, and it's a growing commitment, that's all I care about. You see, sometimes Christians can get sort of . . . stagnant. We have to work at keeping our faith alive and fresh. When I told you I want to see the Lord through your eyes, I wanted to know how it feels to be young in your faith. I wanted to see Him through the eyes of someone who has a sincere desire to learn, to become a better person through Christ, to help others for His sake."

"And you see all that in me?" This time, she sounded uncertain.

"I do." Sam prayed she also understood he wasn't a man of idle words. "The strength of your commitment has nothing to do with how long you've known the Lord. And, at the risk of angering you, I didn't say anything about you not being the kind of Christian woman I need. You assumed that."

Lexa nodded. "You're right. I guess that's an insecurity on my part. And that whole Adam and Eve thing . . ." her voice trailed. "I didn't mean I was sinful or anything," she sputtered, looking totally embarrassed. "You must think I'm crazy." When she put one hand on her hip and the other over her face, hiding her eyes, she never looked more adorable, especially with that splotch of blue paint on her cheek.

"No worries. Trust me, I don't think you're going to lead me down the road to ruin." She was mighty tempting all right, but he didn't want her to think she was a temptress. Big difference.

The color of her eyes deepened, her lips parted slightly. "Are you saying you want a relationship . . . with *me*, Sam?" Disbelief laced her question.

Those eyes beckoned, and Sam could barely breathe. He nodded and reached somewhere deep inside for his voice. "I'd say it's definitely something worthy of consideration." He was rewarded by another shy little smile. Good thing, since he sounded pretty inane. Amazing how such a petite woman held such power over him.

He lightly touched her nose before taking her hand in his, turning it over, studying it like a work of fine art. It was, in many respects. Oh, but he was losing ground fast with this woman. Lexa looked up at him with renewed surprise, and he glanced around the room. Several of the other workers were still there. It was obvious they were trying not to listen to their conversation, but it wasn't as if the room was large enough to afford privacy.

"As my mother would say, you have piano fingers. Long and lovely." It was unusual for her fingers to be so long and thin. "Do you play?"

Slowly withdrawing her hand from his hold, Lexa smiled. "I've been known to tickle the ivories every now and then. I'd better go now. I'll see you in a little while."

"Before you go, Lexa, I have to know something."

She paused, turning back. Her brow raised, but she remained silent.

"Am I forgiven?" Sam's heart raced, but the look on her face was encouraging.

"I'll think about it. A little more groveling might be nice."

He laughed as she flipped that impossibly long braid over one shoulder and strolled out the door into the bright sunshine. Moving to stand by the window, he watched Lexa greet the other girls for the walk back to the camp. The happiness on her face flooded his heart. Sam lifted a silent prayer of thanks as the sound of the girls' laughter floated back to him.

"She's a good woman, Sam."

He turned away from the window, unable to hide his smile. Kevin Moore stood right behind him. A quiet man, Kevin didn't offer opinions freely. But he was a godly man, solid and grounded. And one of the best judges of character he'd ever met.

"Yes, she is." Good for *him*.

Leaving the worksite with Kevin and some of the other men a short time later, Sam knew the sun's rays reflected the lightness of his own heart. No doubt, the smile plastered on his face was pretty goofy. But, as surprising as anything else, Sam didn't care.

~

"I think Josh is disappointed you're not interested in him," Rebekah confided a few minutes later as Lexa prepared for her shower. "He's quite smitten, you know."

Lexa smiled as she retrieved her makeup case and bath towel. "I guessed as much. He's just so young, Rebekah. Besides, I'm sure there's plenty of girls who are interested in your brother, and would welcome his attentions."

Rebekah laughed. "There are, but don't tell Josh. It'd swell his head, and heaven knows, we don't need that. There wouldn't be enough room left in the camp." They laughed easily together. "I can tell Sam likes you. Do you like him?"

Time to sidestep that question. "Have you known Sam long?"

Rebekah laughed and shot her a knowing grin. "About five years. We met at a Christian camp outside Houston. My youth group was one of several from Louisiana, and Sam was one of the leaders. He told everyone about this wonderful summer program he worked with called TeamWork. I was too young for one of the summer missions since you have to be at least eighteen. Still, I remembered what Sam said about the work being done through TeamWork, and knew I wanted to be a part of it. So, as soon as I graduated from high school, I came on my first summer work team."

"Have you worked with TeamWork every summer? With Sam?"

"Every summer but one." A cloud passed over Rebekah's face. "He wasn't leading the group two summers ago. We were in Costa Rica that year."

"Why wasn't Sam there?" The look on the other girl's face started her heart beating fast. Rebekah looked away for a quick moment, and lowered her head. Maybe her innocent question wasn't quite so simple, after all. Although she didn't know why, Lexa suspected the answer might just change her life.

Chapter 18

*R*EBEKAH STARED AT the ground for a few seconds before lifting her head and meeting Lexa's eyes. "Maybe Sam should answer that question for you."

Lexa sighed in exasperation. "Why? Is it some big secret or something?"

"No." Rebekah shook her head and twirled long strands of hair around one finger. "It's not a secret, but it's just . . . well, it's just something I think *he* should tell you, that's all." That said, Rebekah turned to leave the dorm.

"Hold up a minute!" Lexa hurried over to the door. Putting one hand on Rebekah's arm, she turned her around. "Please tell me, Rebekah." Sensing hesitancy, Lexa tried again. "I'm not asking for selfish reasons. I'm asking because I care about Sam, in answer to your question. You're scaring me. I have the feeling that something happened. Am I right?"

Clearing her throat, Rebekah nodded. "Yes. My first TeamWork mission was here in San Antonio three years ago, in this very camp, rebuilding homes just like we are now. I brought along one of my best friends from church, Shelby Hanson. She was five years older than me, and she set her sights on Sam. He didn't pay much attention to her at first, thinking she was much too young, a little girl with a crush. But, by the end of the summer, he'd fallen for her, too. It wasn't hard. She was gorgeous and sweet as anything. Near the end of the camp, Sam asked Shelby to marry him." A look of great sadness crossed Rebekah's face.

Feeling her chest tighten, Lexa swallowed hard, wanting to know but also *not* wanting to know. "Why do I have the feeling that something terrible happened . . . to Shelby?" Her voice dropped to barely more than a whisper. Rebekah turned away, but Lexa could see tears drop onto her cheeks. She let them fall without bothering to wipe them away.

"I'm so sorry I upset you, Rebekah." Running over to Sheila's bed, Lexa retrieved a few tissues and thrust them into her hand. Helping Rebekah over to her own bed, Lexa sat the shaken girl down and sat beside her, putting a comforting arm around her shoulders. "You don't have to tell me. It's obviously too painful for you, and I'm really sorry I pushed."

"No, it's okay," Rebekah protested. "I just," she said between sniffles, "I just haven't thought about it for a while, and it all came rushing back, you know?" She looked over at Lexa with a feeble smile. She blew her nose and dabbed at her eyes.

"It was late one August night, about a week before the TeamWork project was over, and Shelby was invited to go for a ride with one of the other guys who happened to have a car for the summer. They were picking up supplies for Sam in town. The rest of us were sitting around the bonfire, like usual. And then . . . then," she continued, sobbing and taking a deep breath, "there was this horrible crash."

Another cry escaped and Rebekah covered her mouth, fighting for control. "We could hear it from the camp because it was so quiet outside. The crash was so unearthly, so loud. After that, there was this deathly silence." Rebekah's eyes were far away as she recalled that terrible, fateful night that changed the lives of the TeamWork volunteers.

"What happened?" Lexa sat stunned, dazed. She'd come upon the scene of an accident once in her life. She knew how it felt to dare to look, but not want to see the reality. But she didn't know the victims, and couldn't imagine the horror if she had. Lexa's hold on Rebekah tightened.

"There was a group of local teenagers. They'd been in town drinking. They were barreling down one of the dirt roads outside the camp, and didn't see Jake's little silver sports car until it was too late. Broad-sided them. It was heartbreaking."

Rebekah sniffled. "It was like Sam knew as soon as we heard the sounds of the crash. And then quiet. Nothing. It was as if Sam knew in his heart that Shelby was gone. We all did. Jake survived, but Shelby was killed instantly." She dabbed at her eyes with the tissue and sobbed a little, leaning against her. Lexa murmured soothing words and smoothed Rebekah's hair away from her face. Her eyes were red-rimmed and full of emotion, and her lower lip trembled.

"Sam took the next year off from TeamWork and buried himself in his work in Houston. Then the Lord got hold of him again, and he was back in place with TeamWork. That's another reason why Sam made the rule that he was the only one driving to and from town when we're here in this particular camp. I know to someone new, it might seem a little dictatorial, but he doesn't want to take a chance on anything happening to anyone else ever again." Rebekah darted a glance at Lexa. "Especially someone he cares for very much."

"Oh, Rebekah," Lexa moaned. "I'm so sorry." She shook her head. Her heart ached, especially for Sam and Rebekah. "You'd never know it to look at Sam today that he's been through so much." She understood about the car, and maybe it gave him a small measure of comfort. A TeamWork volunteer—one to whom he'd been engaged—had been killed on his watch, even if it was under circumstances beyond his control. What a horrible thing for Sam to have endured. For all of them.

"When you've been with Sam in the car, I'm sure you've noticed how he always makes sure you fasten your seat belt before he starts driving."

Lexa nodded and looked over at Rebekah. "Yes. I've always admired how safety-conscious he is. It's a good trait, especially in a leader."

Rebekah lowered her head and wiped away another tear. "Shelby wasn't wearing her seat belt that night and was thrown out of the car. She probably would have survived otherwise. At least Jake had his on. But," she said with a shuddering sigh, "don't let Sam fool you." She gestured for Lexa to hand her another tissue. "The man's pretty serious. His humor is one way he manages to keep going."

She attempted a feeble smile. "Sam likes you, Lexa. I know he does. I can see it in the way he looks at you, the way he talks about you. He always looks around for you when you're not there, and then acts all nonchalant about it." Rebekah smiled and dabbed again at her still-watery eyes. "I didn't think I'd see that look in his eyes again for a long time, to tell you the truth. But it's there now. It's different from the way he looked at Shelby, too. He lights up all over and his voice goes all soft. You bring out the best in him. And," she continued, releasing a shuddering sigh, "in your own way—even unconsciously—you're helping Sam to heal."

"He talks about me? I mean," Lexa stammered, not wishing to sound like a high school girl with a crush. Inside, her heart was soaring. She had no reason to celebrate. Still, if it was true that she was helping Sam heal from the aftermath of losing Shelby, it could be a positive thing.

"Well, of course he does, silly. He has to talk with someone, doesn't he? Shelby was one of my best friends, and since Sam met her because of me, we bonded, especially after she died. It's not anything romantic between us, if that's what you're thinking. It's more of a mental connection or whatever. We shared something no one should ever have to share. We're both stronger because we survived it together. In many ways, Sam is like an older brother to me and Josh." Rebekah sighed. "I'm sure you've noticed how he's a mentor, and friend, to *all* the TeamWork crew. Until he has kids of his own, I guess we're all kind of like Sam's kids."

Lexa nodded. "I can tell Sam pours his heart and soul into TeamWork. It's more than just a job to him."

Wiping her eyes, Rebekah took a deep breath. "Right. It's a ministry he's absorbed into his *soul*. But," she added, giving Lexa a rather coy smile, "I think part of the healing process is that Sam's finally starting to realize he wants to share his life with someone."

"I'm sure Sam's had more than his share of girlfriends." Maybe she was fishing, but as much as anyone, Rebekah might have the answer.

"No, not really." That was surprising. "I mean, sure he's dated. Look at the man." She laughed a little, wiping her pink nose. "He's probably left a trail of broken hearts around Texas. But, as far as I know, no one caught him, so to speak, before Shelby."

Lexa couldn't resist. "What do you think it was about Shelby that caught Sam's attention, besides the fact that she was sweet . . . and gorgeous?" That was hard to say. Was she actually jealous of someone no longer among the living? Surely not . . . that would be positively morbid. Poor Shelby.

Rebekah thought about the question. "It could be that he hadn't slowed down enough. Maybe he hadn't taken the time to really get to know a woman. He was concentrated on getting his undergraduate degree, making a success of his financial planning business, and working with TeamWork." She looked at Lexa again. "Before and after Shelby, Sam simply hasn't taken the time to devote to a relationship."

Lexa nodded. That explanation made sense from what she knew of Sam Lewis.

A tiny grin surfaced as Rebekah elbowed Lexa. "Maybe it's something about this particular camp. I think there might be romance in the air or something." She nudged her arm. "Maybe it just took the right woman. In God's perfect timing."

Lexa ignored her last comment. She couldn't think that way. "I'm glad you and Sam could comfort one another, Rebekah, and again, I'm so sorry about Shelby. Thanks for telling me about her. I know how hard it was for you." Pulling the younger girl into her arms, Lexa enfolded her in a long hug of comfort and friendship.

"I'm glad you're here, Lexa. You're good for us, all of us," Rebekah murmured.

The words warmed Lexa's heart. With her arms wrapped around Rebekah, she wondered if it would hurt Sam if she asked about Shelby. Then again, she had no reason. It wasn't jealousy she felt, really. It was more a pervasive sadness that he'd suffered and lost someone he dearly loved.

Jumbled thoughts crowded Lexa's mind as she showered, allowing the hot, steamy water to soothe and comfort her. Sam had been engaged. Lexa couldn't help wondering what Shelby Hanson looked like. She must have been the kind of strong Christian woman Sam wanted. She must have been special to attract the attention of a man like Sam.

Lexa didn't stop to think what that said about *her*, too.

~

Sam rinsed his shaver under the warm water and laid it on the side of the sink. He eyed the aftershave. Grabbing it before he changed his mind, he sprinkled out a little and pressed it against his cheeks. Headed into the bedroom, he grabbed a white polo and his one good pair of jeans from the closet.

As he continued getting dressed, pulling on the jeans and tucking in his shirt, his thoughts strayed to Lexa. Images of her invaded his mind at any given moment throughout the day.

He hoped she understood a few things. Like he'd told her at the worksite, he didn't want to date for the sake of companionship. Casual dating had no place in his life. After searching his heart, he knew Rebekah was right. It was time to move past Shelby and get on with the business of living, learning, loving. With Lexa in the TeamWork camp, he'd started to believe a lifetime love might be possible. In some ways, it was as frightening as it was exhilarating.

Lexa hadn't set out to snare him on purpose, with any kind of intent to hook him. Others had tried, but he'd ignored them. Lexa managed to do it all on her own, by virtue of a sweet, innocent sassiness that reached out to his heart unlike any other woman. They were barely into the work camp. It was amazing, really.

As Sam finished dressing, he went back to the closet and pulled out the navy blue sportcoat, the nicest piece of clothing he'd brought to the camp. Lexa might like to see him in it. He wanted her to see him dressed up a bit. Not that it was a date. But, somehow it sure felt like one. He needed to make up for the Riverwalk disaster. Hopefully tonight he could get a few minutes alone with her.

Glancing in the mirror, he smiled. "Lexa Clarke, you ain't seen nothin' yet." Tossing his keys in the air before pocketing them, Sam smiled. He headed out of the office in the direction of the station wagon, full of high hopes.

Chapter 19

"YOU LOO–LOO–look re–re–real–really pr–pretty tonight, L–L–Lexa."

Lexa turned around with a grateful smile, fixing one of her earrings. "Thanks, Sheila." It was a nice compliment.

"I–I h–ho–hope y–you ha–have a g–goo–good ti–ti–time."

"I hope so, too." Earlier in the week, Lexa invited her to join their group going into town to Maxie's, a popular coffee house in downtown San Antonio. It didn't surprise her when Sheila declined in favor of staying at the camp. Rebekah also opted not to come. Guilt tugged at Lexa. Rebekah might be too exhausted after telling her about Shelby. She tried to get her to change her mind, but couldn't.

An hour later, Lexa sat squished with four others in the backseat of the Volvo as the car bumped along the dirt road. She was already overheated, but it was good to get out of the camp and have free time in town. For the most part, Lexa listened to the lively, laugh-filled banter.

Glancing up to the front a couple of times, Lexa saw Sam watching her in the rearview mirror. When he winked, she almost winked back—then chickened out and felt the telltale warmth in her cheeks. She had the feeling Sam did it to get that very reaction. Turning her head, not bothering to hide her grin, Lexa looked out the window. Daring to look back a couple of minutes later, she saw Sam raise a brow and give her a wide grin. She laughed under her breath. Others around her engaged in lively conversations while Sam talked in low tones with the guy in the passenger seat.

Dropping the group off on a side street, Sam asked them to meet him in the same location four hours later. Most of the guys took off as a group, and Lexa watched as Sam departed with a wave, headed back to the camp to pick up the second group of volunteers. She wondered if tonight Sam might regret making the rule stipulating he was the only driver in and out of the camp. She reminded herself that tonight wasn't a date. All the sparks flying around between them in the car might indicate otherwise.

It was fun to poke in and out of the tourist shops and open air markets with Amy and Winnie. Fanning themselves with cheap paper fans, they tried their best to keep cool as they walked. They gloried in and lingered longer in the air-conditioned shops. Lexa wished again for rain, especially if it would help cool the temperatures even just a little.

"Look at this turquoise necklace, Lexa," Amy called from the other side of one of the shops. "Isn't it pretty? I think my younger sister might like it for her birthday." She held it up. "It's a little more than I want to spend, but Celeste loves jewelry. What do you think?"

Lexa nodded, although she'd never been fond of turquoise except as a color. "If it comes from you, Amy, then I'm sure your sister will love it."

Amy gave her a bright smile. "Thanks. I appreciate that."

Waiting while Amy purchased the necklace, Lexa wandered outside. She found it intriguing that a girl with the trust fund was so cost-conscious. It was a good trait and would serve her well. Hearing a woman's loud voice, she turned her head. Her eyes widened as she realized the woman was berating a child. And it wasn't just any child.

Margarita.

Starting in their direction, something held Lexa back. She stopped and stared, taking in the unsettling scene unfolding in the marketplace. A man was shouting at the woman and she, in turn, was yelling at the little girl. Lexa could only assume the woman was Margarita's mother. The child's eyes spilled over with tears and she shook her head, her hair flying wildly. But she didn't say a word.

The two adults spoke Spanish so fast, Lexa couldn't keep up. How could they even understand each other? They screamed in anger, trying to be the loudest and most belligerent. Yanking something from Margarita's hands, the man thrust it in the woman's face. It was some kind of painted pottery, a small jar perhaps.

Amy came to stand beside Lexa. "Isn't that your Margarita?"

Lexa nodded without speaking.

"What's going on?"

"I'm not sure, but I don't like it." Lexa stepped forward.

"Wait a minute. Maybe we shouldn't interfere." Amy put a hesitant hand on her arm.

Lexa stopped, not daring to blink. By now, a small crowd gathered to watch. It didn't bother the man or woman as they continued their shouting match, leaving the scared little girl cowering between the two.

Margarita spied Lexa and ran in her direction, her arms opened wide. It was a second or two before the adults saw her and then they, too, were right behind the girl, unwittingly catapulting Lexa in the middle of their quarrel. Margarita clung to Lexa's bare legs, hanging on for dear life, burying her head against her stomach. Lexa stroked Margarita's hair in the gesture familiar and comforting to the frightened child.

Lexa looked up with eyes blazing. She had no intention of joining in their screaming match, but Margarita must be defended. Maybe she was God's messenger this time, like Sam had been with her when she was accosted by those teenage thugs.

Without a word, the woman reached out. Snatching Margarita by the wrist, she wrenched her away. All the pent-up emotion poured out of the little girl, and she kicked and screamed as the woman dragged her away. Lexa felt a bit of her heart breaking as Margarita turned sad, pleading eyes on her.

When the woman raised a hand to strike Margarita, Lexa could no longer remain silent. Time for action. "That does it!" Lexa shouted, running for the girl with Amy close behind. "Listen, I don't know who you are, but you have no right to treat this child in such a deplorable manner!" Lexa stood in front of the couple. Her heart was beating with uncontrollable abandon, and her legs felt like jelly, but she had to help Margarita. She was only a defenseless child. At least the woman lowered her hand before making contact with Margarita.

Lexa addressed the woman. "Do you speak English?" It wouldn't help matters if they needed an interpreter to communicate. Her limited knowledge of Spanish wouldn't help in this volatile situation.

"*Sí,*" the woman answered after momentary hesitation. "Yes." She stared at Lexa as though astonished by the boldness of an outsider who dared to intrude.

Lexa swallowed hard. The small crowd started to disburse now that the shouting was over. "Are you Margarita's mother?" She'd never seen this woman at the schoolhouse since Margarita arrived and left with her older brother and sister most days.

"What's it to you?" The woman pushed an insolent finger into Lexa's arm.

"I'm Lexa Clarke, one of her teachers." Standing her ground, Lexa met the woman's dark-eyed, unwavering stare. "Mrs. . . . ." Her voice trailed.

"Martinez." The voice was low.

From the corner of her eye, Lexa could tell Amy had backed away. It didn't seem like a good time for introductions, in any case.

"Mrs. Martinez, I don't know what the problem is here, but you can't solve it by hitting Margarita. She's a very sweet little girl. I'm sure whatever's happened is something that can be solved without violence."

The woman scoffed. "You got any kids, lady?"

Lexa shook her head. "No."

"Well, then," she said, turning away in obvious dismissal, one hand anchored on her hip, "you got no business telling me how to raise mine!" Pausing, she turned around as fast as her large frame would allow, eyebrows raised. "Hey, you! Wait a minute!" she snarled. "You the teacher that keeps putting all those crazy thoughts in Margarita's dumb little head?"

Lexa felt like striking the woman down on the spot, right then and there. She'd never hit another woman with her bare hands—never hit a woman at all—but she was sorely tempted now. Clenching her teeth, her fists curled at her sides, she forced herself to count to three under her breath before trusting herself to speak.

"I pray to God you don't ever use that term about your daughter again." Her voice was bold and firm with a conviction stronger than she'd ever felt before. Maybe this is what it meant to have the Holy Spirit take over. "Margarita is a beautiful, very bright child, Mrs. Martinez. She deserves to be treated with respect." Why did God give children to people like this in the first place if they don't treat them with the love and respect they deserve? Whether ignorance or neglect, there was no excuse.

"Let me tell you what this beautiful, bright child just did." The tone was hostile, the words clipped as she glared at Lexa. "Did you see the pot that man was holding? The one he grabbed from Margarita's hands?"

Lexa nodded, noticing the man was nowhere to be seen. Margarita stopped whimpering, and stood to the side of the woman, staring up at her with those big eyes that tugged at her heart. Lexa swallowed hard and gave her a little smile of encouragement.

"Well, Miss Lexa whatever-your-name-is, your little teacher's pet just stole it from that man's store!"

"I'm sure she didn't mean to steal it," Lexa began before being cut off mid-sentence.

"Oh yeah, she did. She stole it because she wanted to give it to you!" The woman stood back, and it was obvious she relished the stunned look on Lexa's face. "You encouraging Margarita to steal, lady?"

Lexa shook her head vehemently. "I'd never do that, Mrs. Martinez." If anything, it was this woman teaching her to steal. "Look," she said, pushing a stray strand of hair from her eyes, darting a quick glance around, looking for Amy, "I'm not a thief and neither is Margarita. If she took it, I'm sure it was a mistake. If it wasn't a mistake, she wanted attention. *Your* attention. Why don't you try giving her a little of yourself every now and then?"

Lexa shut her mouth, realizing what she was saying, what she was doing—engaged in verbal warfare in the middle of the open-air market with a woman she'd never even met before. Was she crazy? But Lexa stood her ground. It was right to fight for Margarita, no matter the consequences. The little girl was defenseless against her own mother. If God—or anyone else—had a problem with it, she'd deal with it later and face the consequences.

"Leave me alone, and leave Margarita alone or you'll be sorry!" Grabbing Margarita by the arm, the woman dragged her away.

Part of her wanted to run after Margarita, but what could she do? Helplessness was a horrible thing. Lexa turned her back, and her eyes filled with tears. She stood rooted to the concrete, collecting her thoughts and attempting to calm herself. Biting her trembling lower lip, she stared straight ahead and forced deep breaths.

"Hey, you okay?" Amy walked over from where she'd been watching outside a nearby shop.

Frustration threatened to spill over. She could have used an ally in Amy. Then again, she also understood. A few weeks ago—even as recently as a couple of days ago—she might have reacted in the same manner and retreated to the background if something like this happened. Face-to-face confrontations were never easy. But in this case, it wasn't a choice. Lexa prayed Margarita would be okay once that woman got her behind closed doors. She shuddered and her heart hurt. *Lord, keep Margarita safe.*

"What's happening to me, Amy?" Lexa shook her head, not expecting an answer.

Amy looked baffled. "I don't understand."

"This mission. Ever since I came to the TeamWork camp, things have changed. *I've* changed. I'm saying things, and doing things," she stammered, "that I've never done before."

"Well, if you ask me, they're only changes for the better. I mean, you're opening up to us more now, making friends with the other workers, and really becoming a part of the group. That can only be a *good* thing, right?" Amy leaned her head briefly against Lexa's shoulder, squeezing her arm as together they headed to the prearranged rendezvous spot to meet Winnie.

Amy spoke the truth. "You're right. I *do* feel a part of the group. I don't think I would have had the guts to talk back to someone like that even a few weeks ago. Not that I was a meek little mouse when I went for the TeamWork interview in Houston, but I'm surprised I was even approved for this project in the first place."

"Maybe that's why you're here."

"What do you mean?"

"I mean, maybe the interviewer saw unique potential in you, Lexa. Maybe he or she saw someone who needed TeamWork as much, if not more, than the project needed her. All I know is, I'm glad you're here, and I know the other ladies are, too." Amy smiled. "What you did for Margarita was really cool. You're my heroine."

"Maybe you wouldn't feel that way if you knew what I'm thinking about Margarita's mother right now."

"We need to pray for her. That's the best thing we can do right now."

"Oh, I'll pray all right. But I'm praying for Margarita to grow up quickly to get away from a bad mother like that." Lexa frowned.

"I know. It's a bad situation for a kid." Amy released a long sigh and shook her head sadly. "Unfortunately, there's not much more we can do about it."

Lexa wasn't satisfied with that response. It wasn't good enough. Margarita deserved better. *There's got to be something we can do, and I'm going to try and find it.*

Chapter 20

$\mathscr{A}$SHORT TIME later, the trio walked into Maxie's. It was on a quiet street not far from the scene of her disastrous first date with Sam on the Riverwalk two weeks earlier. As they were seated at a table in the crowded, popular club, Lexa tried to be nonchalant as she glanced around the room, hoping to catch a glimpse of their TeamWork leader.

"Don't worry. He'll be here." Winnie patted Lexa's hand in her motherly, comforting way. Either Winnie was very astute or she was being way too obvious. Lexa slanted her a sheepish grin. Listening to the alternative rock band, they traded skeptical glances. She felt old and was tempted to stick her fingers in her ears to block out the loud noise. Amy and Natalie seemed to enjoy it, and their heads bobbed in rhythm.

A server stopped by their table and took their order for soft drinks, tortilla chips and salsa. When she returned a short time later with their food, the trio happily munched away. They didn't even attempt conversation.

"Save some of those for me, will you?" The familiar deep voice startled Lexa, the warm breath tickled her ear. Turning her head with a welcoming smile, she unintentionally grazed Sam's lips as he dropped into the empty seat beside her. Talk about timing. A few of the other TeamWork men seated themselves at the table behind them, smiling at the women. Josh was conspicuous in his absence, and Lexa felt relieved. She'd rather not fend off his flirtations tonight. Tonight was about Sam. She hoped they'd get some time alone.

"That's the loveliest greeting I've had in a long time." Sam's bright smile reached his eyes. "I could definitely get used to it." He licked his lips. "Tasty, too. A little salty." He grinned as Lexa shook her head and laughed.

She was grateful for the dimness of the coffee house. She tried to cover her sudden attack of nerves with a casual air and handed him a chip as the band completed their set. At least now they could share conversation without having to shout. Lexa prayed she could carry on a coherent conversation with Sam sitting so close. It was disconcerting, but altogether wonderful.

"When did you get here?"

"Just now. I made a beeline for you. Missed me, did you?"

"Don't flatter yourself. Salsa?"

"No, thanks. How quickly they forget. Remember, I prefer my spice in my women." Biting into the chip, Sam leaned his chin on one hand, staring at her, unashamed in his flirting. "Like that greeting a minute ago. It was great."

"Flirt."

"Takes one to know one. Another chip, please."

Turning back around, she heard Sam's low chuckle. She also caught the shared grin between Amy and Winnie as they bantered with some of the TeamWork guys. Lexa concentrated on the new band taking the small stage. As they began their set, Lexa recognized some of the songs as covers of current Christian pop hits. Natalie and Amy played a Christian station on the small radio in the dorm, often to the point of overkill. Recently, she'd hummed those songs under her breath out at the worksite and shared them with Margarita and some of the other children in the schoolroom. Most of the songs were based on verses of scripture, and it was a delight when she found them in her Bible reading.

As they listened, Lexa felt the vibrations on the wooden floor, both the sounds from the band as well as from Sam's foot tapping in rhythm. She caught the sound of his voice as he sang along. It sounded in-tune and rich, just as it did at the bonfire. Lexa stole a glance when he turned to speak with the guys. He looked great in his jeans and white polo and a lightweight, navy jacket perfectly tailored for those strong, broad shoulders. This man was more ruggedly handsome than any male model she'd ever seen.

Lexa inhaled a couple of deep, calming breaths. Seemed she'd been doing that a lot in recent hours, first learning about Shelby and then the incident in the marketplace. Her smile sobered, and she frowned. She couldn't allow the incident in the marketplace to spoil the rest of the evening.

"Do you like Christian music?" Sam helped himself to another chip during a break between songs and offered one to her.

"I haven't really had the opportunity to hear a lot of it," Lexa admitted, accepting the chip. "I like it better if I can understand the lyrics."

"Good point. It loses power and meaning if you can't understand what they're singing." He nodded his head in the direction of the door with an inviting grin. "What do you say we get out of here?"

"What, and miss all this marvelous entertainment?"

Sam chuckled. "I think they'll do just fine with four fewer hands to clap for them at the end of the set."

"But what about the others? Can we just leave them here at Maxie's for a while?"

"Why not? They're big girls and boys. They don't need me to chaperone. Trust me. They'll understand."

Clasping his big, warm hand around hers, Sam pulled her up with him. He didn't even give her a choice. Not that she cared. Lexa shot a quick look at Amy and Winnie. She almost laughed out loud when she glimpsed their beaming faces. If she didn't know better, she'd think they were the world's biggest matchmakers. With a small wave and a smile, Lexa followed Sam as he threaded his way among the small tables as they left the coffee house together.

"Now, that's infinitely better." Sam exhaled a deep breath when they reached the outdoors.

The sounds of the night enveloped them, and Lexa glanced upward at the lovely twilight sky. There was nothing in the world like the wide expanse of a Texas sky on a hot summer evening.

"Well, I suppose it is if you like high heat and humidity." The air stifled and threatened to overwhelm her as they stood to the side the entrance. Sam still held her hand. It felt good, it felt *right*. She left her hand in his, and smiled when he squeezed a little.

"I mean this is more like it. And I'm not talking about the temperature, or the percentage of humidity." His eyes met hers.

"What's more like it?"

Sam sighed. "Must you always answer everything with another question?" Keeping his hand wrapped around hers, Sam strolled with her to the nearby walkway.

Her heart thrilled at his gentle smile as he watched her. "I can't help it. I'm a naturally curious person."

"And just what are you naturally curious about right now?"

Lexa gave him a sly grin. "People, for one. What makes them do the things they do, say the things they say, that sort of thing." Sam wanted her to admit to something more personal, but she wasn't ready.

"Ah, a student of psychology . . . or is it sociology?" He stopped walking and turned to face her.

"Both, probably. How about you? What are you curious about?"

"Lots of things."

In one fluid motion, Sam surprised her by reaching his hands around her waist. He lifted and then carefully lowered her onto the stone wall behind them. He paused a moment to collect his thoughts and planted his hands on either side of her. She didn't feel trapped. She felt protected.

"I want to know why God gave birds wings to fly but gave man two feet and made us learn to walk. I want to know why women are so emotional and men so logical." Catching her bemused grin, Sam was quiet a long moment. Then the line formed between his brows.

Lexa wanted to reach out and smooth away his frown, but left her hands in her lap instead.

"I want to know how man can soar through the atmosphere to the moon and back, but not come up with a cure for the common cold." Sam bowed his head, and when he lifted it again, his eyes were bright with emotion. "I want to know how we can legally kill unborn children, and then execute someone for killing a grown man." Leaning back against the wall, he crossed his arms over his chest and blew out a sigh. "I guess I want to know *why*."

"You don't wonder about much, do you?" Her smile teased, but her voice was quiet. "You're a deep thinker, Mr. Lewis."

Covering Lexa's hand with his own, Sam stared into her eyes as though trying to read her mind, her heart, her very soul. Lexa's smile faded as she memorized his face—those incredible, expressive eyes, the passionate full lips. Lexa wanted to experience the thrill of his kiss again, his lingering touch.

"I sense you're bothered by something tonight, Lexa. Everything okay?" He jumped up to sit on the wall beside her.

She struggled with how to answer him. She didn't know men could be this sensitive. Sam had an uncanny way of reading her emotions. Should she tell him what happened with Margarita and her mother? "It's nothing." Lexa averted her gaze, not wanting anything to spoil this night. It seemed something always happened to put a damper on their time together, and she didn't want it happening again. Not tonight. It wasn't the time or the place.

"Well, if you decide you want to talk about it, please know I'm here for you."

Lexa smiled, touched by his sensitivity. "Thanks. I know."

"Want to take a little walk?" Sam suggested after they sat in silence a couple of minutes, enjoying the night and each other's company. When she nodded, he slid back down from the stone wall, reaching to pull her back down from the wall. Lowering her gently, his warm hands around her waist, their eyes locked and held.

The way Sam stood there, not removing his hands, Lexa felt sure he'd take the opportunity to kiss her again. She was more than ready, and she sensed he knew it. Instead, he reached for her hand, and turned to resume their walk. As they strolled along the tree-lined walkway together, Sam told her about his plans for various TeamWork missions in the coming years.

"You really put your heart and soul into TeamWork, Sam. It must be wonderful to be so passionate about something." She hoped her tone conveyed her admiration for his dedication.

He nodded. "It's my life's true work, more than the financial planning. I've seen so many needy people—emotionally, physically and spiritually needy people—come to Christ through our work, I can't even fathom not doing these projects."

Watching Sam talk about his work, his eyes alive with excitement, Lexa loved the resonance of his voice, adored the smile lines around his eyes and mouth, and simply loved being in the company of this honest, compassionate man.

"It's refreshing to be with someone who feels things so deeply."

He held her gaze. "There's something else you have to know about me, Lexa."

"What's that?" Lexa forced a calm into her voice. She only prayed it would be good. This night was too special otherwise. She took a quick breath and waited.

Chapter 21

I'M FINANCIALLY SOUND, but I'm frugal. I have to be, especially working with TeamWork every summer. I get a small stipend, but I'll never get rich doing it." Sam laughed. "You've seen the car I drive, after all." Relief was etched into her expression. He wondered what she'd expected him to say.

"Earthly riches don't bring happiness, love or forgiveness, Sam. They don't give strength of character or conviction."

He nodded, pleased by her sentiment. "I've done most of the talking. That wasn't my intention. Tell me more about your family, your work, your hopes, your dreams." He wanted her to feel comfortable enough with him to share such personal things.

"How much time do we have?" Lexa reached out and squeezed his hand. From the look on her face, Sam could tell she surprised herself by the instinctive reaction. Starting to remove her hand from his warm grasp, she smiled as he resisted and held on tight.

"You reached for my hand because you wanted to, Lexa. Leave it there. Please. It was a great instinct."

"Well," she began, taking a deep breath, "I was an only child. I was pretty spoiled. Rotten, I'm afraid. Bad to the core. Seriously, I think my mother would have given me the moon if I'd asked for it." Lexa paused, and when she looked back up at him, tears shone in her eyes. "I wasn't as close to my dad, but he loved me in his own gruff, quiet way."

"What about your grandparents? Were they around much?"

She shook her head. "Only my grandmother on my mom's side. The others died either before I was born or within a year or two. Nana was very special. Dad took me to her house most Saturday afternoons. She lived in Galveston. We did all sorts of fun things together—string pearls, paint by the numbers, read books together, watch movies, pick apples from the tree and make a pie . . ."

"Maybe that's where your fondness for the apple began."

Lexa smiled. "Maybe so. Nana had this little summer porch in-between the messy garage and the rest of her interesting house. But she didn't care about the clutter. She cared more about investing herself in my life and spending time with me. I was her only grandchild. She taught me so much, and I cherished every minute with her. We'd sit out there on that summer porch for hours, talking and drinking iced tea. I loved riding with her in the car. Especially at Christmas, she told the best stories about Santa's Toyland at the North Pole."

Sam encouraged Lexa to share more memories of her family as they started back in the direction of the coffee house. He nodded, listened, and asked questions every now and then. Lexa's eyes misted as she talked more about her mother and grandmother. Pausing outside the entrance to Maxie's, Sam leaned back against the steel railing, listening. He loved the sound of her voice with her native drawl. He could listen to it forever. He'd heard her sing at the bonfire some nights, and her voice was clear and sweet, but surprisingly low, like her enchanting laugh. Their voices would probably blend well in a duet.

"Nana loved to tell me all about what she expected to find when she went to the happy hunting grounds." Lexa's laughter was quiet. "That was her term for heaven."

"She must have loved you very much."

"Yes, and I loved her with all my heart. She showed me in so many ways."

"And your dad continued to take you to your grandmother's house for weekend visits, even after . . ."

Lexa lowered her eyes. "Yes, even more so after Mom died. He didn't know what to do with a little girl. It was easier to take me there and have Nana take care of me than try and figure out how to act like a real dad."

Sam brushed her cheek with a whisper of a kiss. "I'm sorry, Lexa." It made his heart hurt for the little girl she'd been with a father who couldn't share his love. And he ached for her losing her mother so young. "Where's Nana now?"

She smiled. "Wreaking havoc in the happy hunting grounds, most likely. I'm . . . I'm a lot like her." When she reached to wipe away a stray tear, Sam gently moved her hand and kissed her. Breaking away, Lexa cried softly and then leaned against his shoulder.

"Sometimes I thought Nana loved me more than my father did, but now I realize it was an unfair comparison. My dad just didn't know how to show love." She let out a long, shuddering breath, and lowered her eyes. "I think Mom was tempted to leave Dad a few times."

"Why?" It was major for Lexa to share something so personal with him. It revealed more than she'd ever know. She trusted him with her secrets. It was hard for her, letting him get this close. But she'd done it.

Lexa hesitated. "He wasn't abusive or unfaithful that I know of, but he neglected her." She shook her head. "Dad was a workaholic, dedicated to his job, and he put it before his family."

Her slender shoulders lifted in a shrug. "It had to be lonely for my mom even though she never said much. She was the type to suffer in silence." She paused, and Sam moved aside as a few patrons emerged from Maxie's. The sounds from inside the coffee house—music, and voices mixed with kitchen noises—invaded the quiet of the evening.

"Your dad was a cop, right?" Taking her by the hand, Sam led her away from the door. He didn't want their time together to end, but their time in town was all too quickly drawing to a close.

"Right." Lexa released a prolonged sigh. "He prided himself on protecting and saving virtual strangers, yet he couldn't see his own marriage dissolving in front of his eyes. He was blinded to it. I realize that sounds harsh, but it's true. It's like his identity was wrapped up in being a cop."

He'd heard that was sometimes the case with public servants, but Sam didn't voice that thought aloud. It would only serve to reinforce Lexa's sadness. "Why do you think your mother stayed with him?" Maybe that was too personal, but she didn't seem to mind.

Lexa looked at him through bright eyes. "Because she wasn't a quitter. She was a fighter, and a strong Christian woman. She had no solid, valid reason for leaving him, so she stayed." Her voice faded. "For better or worse, she simply . . . stayed."

"And do *you* think she should have left?"

Lexa glanced down at their joined hands. "I honestly don't know. I've never really thought about it from that perspective." The sadness surfaced in her voice and her eyes when she looked up at him again.

"Was your dad a Christian?"

"I don't think so. If he was, he certainly didn't model Christ-like behavior around me." He briefly wondered why Lexa brought the police union newsletter to the camp. Perhaps it was her unconscious way of staying connected to her dad.

"I'm afraid most of us fall short a lot of the time. It's a tall order." He squeezed her hand.

"You're the strongest Christian man I've ever met. Sometimes, I sit in awe during the devotional time, wondering how you know so much, how you can get up there in front of everyone else and preach."

"I've studied a lot, and for a while, I thought of going to seminary. Then I found TeamWork." Sam shook his head. "I honestly don't know how I could have gotten through some of the toughest times in my life without the love of Christ in my heart."

~

One of those tough times in Sam's life was when Shelby Hanson was killed in the tragic accident outside the TeamWork camp. It had to affect him in a profound way, being here in the same surroundings, with the memories of her and what they'd shared. Should she let him know Rebekah told her about Shelby, and that he'd been engaged? Not wanting to spoil the mood, Lexa decided against it. If Sam wanted to tell her, he would. But hopefully not tonight.

The air was still and calm as Sam walked Lexa back to her dorm a couple of hours later. The others had all returned to the camp and disbanded. He asked her to wait up for him, if she wasn't too tired, so they could continue talking after he finished some paperwork. They'd enjoyed such a wonderful evening together, neither one wanted it to end.

After their time of shared conversation and getting to know one another, Sam was so much more than the handsome face, the smiling eyes, the teasing words. He was Sam Lewis—her friend, passionate mission worker, and a man after God's own heart. And so, Lexa waited.

She sat on her bed reading, all the other girls asleep, when he knocked quietly on the screen door. Startled even though she expected him, she slipped out the door. "I must admit, I feel rather sneaky doing this."

A slow grin upturned his lips. "Should I say good night here, then, and let you go back into the dorm?" Sam started to walk away. "Good night, beautiful girl."

"Come with me, cowboy." With a small smile, Lexa tugged him by the hand, leading the way to the lonesome tree on the west side of the camp. Behind her, she heard his soft laugh. Looking up at the moon, Lexa saw it was obscured by fuzzy-looking clouds.

"Maybe it's finally going to rain tonight," she mused, running her hands up and down her arms even though she wasn't cold. Not in the least. "My dad always said fuzzy clouds over the moon mean rain is imminent."

"Really?" Sam removed his hat and held it between his hands. Leaning against the tree, one knee propped, he watched her with a lazy grin. "What else did your father tell you?"

She'd heard about that kind of lazy grin. Coming from him, it started her heart pounding hard. Lexa leaned her head to one side. "Oh, he told me to be careful of a smooth man with a line for every pretty girl who comes down the pike." She took a few small steps toward him, her eyes never leaving his face.

"And what else?" Sam prompted, still grinning. That deep voice was quiet as he hung his Stetson on a low-hanging branch. He pushed away from the tree and came closer.

The look on his face, combined with all the rest of the man, was doing untold things inside her. "Oh, let me think." She grinned. "Things like don't kiss a man until you're sure you really, *really* like him."

Taking another step closer, Sam reached out with one hand, lacing her fingers through his as if he'd never let go again. Ever. "And tell me, Miss Clarke, do you always follow your father's advice?"

"Sometimes I do . . . and sometimes I don't, Mr. Lewis."

Walking his fingers slowly up her bare arm, his eyes never strayed from hers. Sam pulled Lexa to him. Gentle fingers pushed her hair behind one ear. He touched the side of her face with the back of his hand, gazing at her with a look of wonder.

Leaning his head toward hers, Sam stopped, his lips hovering in the same tantalizing way as before in his office. "And what would your father tell you to do now?" His whispered question was a sweet caress, gentle and husky.

"Shut up, please," Lexa demanded, reaching up with one hand to pull his head down. "And I'm not about to apologize for saying that either." Her fingers found the curls on the nape of his neck and smoothed them. Even with only the light from the stars overhead, Lexa saw those blue eyes deepen. His skin was warm, and Lexa trembled from his nearness. It was intoxicating. *He* was intoxicating, captivating every sense and fiber of her being.

Her eyelashes fluttered against warm cheeks as she raised her lips to his— anticipating, wanting, *needing* Sam's kiss.

He smiled as those lips drew even nearer, only a heartbeat away. "Definitely spicy," Sam murmured, lowering his head as his hungry lips met hers.

Chapter 22

"Lexa, you told me it was nothing." The door of the dorm slammed shut as Sam stormed in the middle of the women's dorm. Removing his Stetson and tossing it on a nearby table, Sam's hands found his hips. His eyes darted around the dorm.

"We're alone. Why don't you tell me what you're talking about." Sitting on her bed, Lexa put aside her notebook and looked up at him, dumbfounded. He was obviously in TeamWork director mode now.

"Can you please enlighten me about the scene at the open air market last Friday night? The one with Margarita?"

"I know which one." Lexa scowled. "I hardly thought it was worth dredging up."

"Well, maybe it was." Sam pulled a chair across the room and sat down beside her bed. "I need to know what happened. It's important." At least his voice sounded less harsh.

Lexa blew out a heavy sigh. "All right. Margarita's mother and a shop owner were engaged in a terrible shouting match, and she was caught in the middle. It was horrible, Sam. When she raised a hand to strike Margarita, I couldn't just stand there and watch. I had to do something, had to take some kind of action to protect a defenseless little girl."

"What did you do?"

"All I did was give that woman a piece of my mind. She's neglected Margarita far too long. Someone needs to stand up for her rights." Lexa turned blazing eyes upon him. "You can't tell me it was wrong to defend her."

"I'm not telling you that, Lexa. But *you* need to know that Mrs. Martinez has filed a formal complaint against you and TeamWork."

"She *what*?" Lexa gasped.

"She feels you're a bad influence on Margarita," Sam told her, sounding too matter-of-fact for Lexa's liking. "I understand there was also a piece of stolen pottery involved in this little incident in the market."

Lexa stared. "Apparently, she *did* take it, but probably only to get attention, and that's what I told her mother. There really wasn't any harm done, and I hope Mrs. Martinez talked with Margarita about it. Having met her, though, she probably found an alternative way to *talk* to her daughter." Lexa crossed her arms with a frown, "You should have seen her, Sam. She was awful."

"Well," Sam said slowly, "even if she *was* awful, we need to be careful. Mrs. Martinez is still Margarita's mother. As representatives of TeamWork, we're also representatives of the Lord. Everything we do is being watched by others, whether you realize it or not. We can't afford to let our witness be tainted."

"Well, excuse me for doing what I thought was noble, fair and right!" Lexa said through clenched teeth. "I don't think the Lord is going to fault me for what I did. As a matter of fact, I think the Almighty might be downright proud of me!" Rising from the bed, she quickly crossed the room and put one hand on the door. If he dared invade her space like this, then she would have to be the one to leave.

Sam was right behind her. A firm, strong hand reached around her and closed the screen door, preventing her escape. "Don't go running away from me again, Lexa. I'm not saying you didn't do the right thing. I know you did what you thought was right, and I admire and applaud your wish to protect Margarita. What I'm saying is, there might be a price to pay, so to speak."

"What do you mean?" Lexa whirled around to face Sam. "Are you telling me I might be fined . . . or that I might have to leave the camp?" Up until now, she hadn't considered the possibility of being forced to pack up and leave. Was there such a thing as a TeamWork dropout or flunkie? She hated the sudden nervousness in her voice that betrayed her.

"You're jumping to conclusions again. All that will happen is a written report. Hopefully, that will be the end of it. If it's any consolation, these things don't usually amount to much."

Lexa looked up at him, her eyes wide. "I certainly hope it doesn't happen often."

His blue eyes met hers, softening. "No, it doesn't."

"And what's involved with this report? Who writes the report?"

"I do, as director of the work camp and since you're a volunteer under my direction. The report is based on my conversation with you, and a statement of the facts as you've told them to me. If you'd like to file your own version of what happened, you have every right."

Lexa snorted and crossed her arms again. "Do I also have the right to remain silent? Are you going to tell me that anything I say may incriminate me and be used in a court of law, or whatever it is the police always say when they read the citizen's rights speech?"

"You should know the answer to that one since your dad was the cop."

Her eyes widened with the sting of hurt. Sam was right, though. As usual.

"You're just about the feistiest woman I've ever met. And the prettiest, especially when you're mad." Sam leaned forward to plant a quick kiss on the end of her nose. "There's one more small thing I hesitate to mention."

"Oh, no. I should have known. Do I really want to know what it is?" She tamped down her irritation and stifled a low moan.

"It's not that bad," Sam assured her. "It's only the small matter that your second weekend privilege might be revoked because of the marketplace incident, and uh, you're sort of on probation for the next two weeks."

Those last few words were rushed and mumbled, but she heard them just fine.

"The price I might have to pay," she muttered, under her breath. "Hey, wait a minute." Lexa's eyes narrowed with suspicion. "Who made these rules and regulations, anyway?"

Sam avoided her gaze and grunted, retrieving his hat. "I think you know the answer to that one. I have a board who works with me, you know. It's not like I decide these things all by myself, and they're set in stone."

"You mean you're not really Moses and they're not really the Ten Commandments?"

"No." Sam laughed.

"Still, I was right," she grumbled. "I've been drafted, and this is boot camp." Sam's attention turned to her bed where something peeked out from underneath her pillow.

Oh, no. Lexa reached out to stop him, but it was too late. Following close behind, her cheeks grew warm with shame. She watched helplessly as Sam pulled out the corner of the romance novel. Lexa's hands dropped to her sides, and she hung her head. She hadn't been so humiliated since the whole incident when he'd rescued her from the thugs in San Antonio. And before that, there'd been the armadillo incident. She supposed she should be grateful to Sam since he must not have written her up for the offending incident of going out to the worksite by herself on only her second day in the TeamWork camp. What a fool she'd been. A few times over. But somehow, the man still seemed to like her.

Sam's words brought her back to the present. "What do we have here?" He chuckled under his breath, and his eyes held thinly-veiled amusement. Considering the shirtless Sam look-alike on the cover, Lexa knew her cheeks must be positively flaming. Surely this moment qualified as the most humiliating incident.

"I'm not really reading it." The protest sounded weak. It was a useless defense although true. After all, it was the same book she'd started since coming to the camp. Under normal circumstances, she would have been on a fourth or fifth romance novel by now. "Besides, my bed, my pillow, and certainly this book," Lexa muttered, seizing it from his hands, "is my personal property, thank you very much. At least while I'm here in the TeamWork camp," she stammered.

"But it is *your* book, right?"

"Just shoot me now." Lexa buried her face in her hands.

Sam surprised her by laughing. "I won't say a word except to say the guy on the front looks vaguely familiar. He has a rather ugly mug, wouldn't you say?"

Lexa stared at him, not bothering to hide her surprise. "For the record, I bought that book a long time ago. If it makes you feel any better, I've spent a lot more time reading your Bible than this silly book." Although he said nothing, Sam's expression was far too smug. She blew out a quick breath. "Go ahead. Tell me. I'm sure you have an opinion you're just dying to share." She motioned with her hands. "Let me have it."

Carrying the chair back across the room, Sam returned to where she once again sat on the edge of the bed. "Okay, but only since you asked."

Lexa tilted her chin. "I'm listening."

"I don't really know much about those kinds of books except that they're full of situations that should be reserved for a marriage relationship, if even that."

He looked embarrassed, as though wondering why he'd voiced his opinion in the first place. Pulling Lexa quickly to her feet, Sam wrapped his hands securely around her waist. His slightly rough jaw brushed against her cheek as he leaned close. She loved his nearness, the smell of the outdoors resonating from him, the feel of those strong arms holding her, completely encircling her.

"I also know something else, Miss Clarke." With his whispered words, Sam's lips, soft and warm, brushed over her temple. "Real life is a whole lot more fun."

With a final wave and a parting smile, Sam was gone. Watching him replace the Stetson on his way out the door, Lexa slumped back down to the bed, covering her head with the pillow to stifle her escaping moan.

Chapter 23

*L*EXA DEPARTED THE bonfire early a few nights later, suffering a headache. Slipping into the darkness alone, she headed to the dorm. As soon as she entered the building, she sensed something amiss. Although she couldn't put her finger on it, Lexa knew by instinct something wasn't right. It didn't *feel* right.

The only light came from moonlight streaming in through the window. Lexa fumbled her way over to the bed, her eyes adjusting to the dimness. Reaching for the small lamp on the wall above her bed, she paused, thinking she heard a muffled sound from Sheila's corner of the room. Turning her head, Lexa strained to see.

"Sheila? Are you there?"

"Ye–ye–yes." Her voice sounded different.

"Are you okay? You sound strange." Lexa's eyes opened wider as she heard more muffled sounds. A burly, dark-haired man dressed in black from head-to-toe darted across the room and out the screen door before Lexa had a chance to be afraid. He pushed the door with such force that it made a horrible cracking sound, ripping clean off its hinges.

"Sheila! Are you all right? Who *was* that?" Lexa demanded, waiting a few seconds until her eyes adjusted to the darkness. Crossing the room, she dropped onto the bed beside Sheila.

Discovering the other woman's hands tied behind her back in a sloppy, loose knot, she took in a quick breath. "What's going on here? I can tell that guy wasn't a Boy Scout," Lexa muttered, loosening the rope to free her hands.

Clutching her sore wrists, Sheila darted her a grateful look, tears shining in her dark eyes. "Th–that w–wa–was m–my hu–hu–husband."

"Your *husband?*" Lexa had no idea Sheila was married. She'd never noticed a wedding ring, and Sheila never mentioned him. Witnessing the man firsthand, she could understand why he wasn't a frequent topic of conversation.

"What's going on?" Lexa repeated, catching her roommate's eye. Lowering her voice, she smoothed the other woman's messy hair away from her face. "You can trust me, Sheila. I want to help you."

"I do–do–don't . . . w–wa–want t–to . . . t–t–talk a–ab–about it."

"You're shaking like a leaf." Lexa grabbed the soft, light blue blanket from the end of Sheila's bed and tossed it around her shoulders. Putting her arms around her, Lexa rocked back and forth with her for a few minutes until the other girl's shivering stopped. "You don't have to talk about it now, if you don't want to, but please know I'm here for you if you decide you need to confide in someone." Lexa prayed Sheila would trust her enough to tell her the truth.

"D–do–don't . . . t–t–tell any–anybo–anybody, L–L–Lexa. O–O–Okay ?"

Pleading eyes implored hers, and Lexa nodded with reluctance. Her instincts told her—as leader of the TeamWork camp—Sam should be notified. But she also didn't want to get in the middle of another scandal that could get her kicked out of the mission. Including the armadillo offense, this could be counted as the third incident, even though the last two were circumstances beyond her control.

Why did these things keep happening to her? The Lord would have to answer that one. Just as she needed to help Margarita in the marketplace, she needed to protect Sheila now.

As she climbed into her own bed a short time later, after first making sure Sheila was all right, Lexa pondered the change in her own thinking. For the first time in her life, she truly belonged somewhere. Surely God Himself led her to the TeamWork camp. She was part of a group working toward a common goal, helping others and making lasting friends along the way. It felt good. But it was about more than making herself feel good. It was about serving the Heavenly Father. By doing that, she showed others how much He loves *them*, too. And *that* felt right.

Then there was a very tall, handsome man named Sam Lewis. Lexa smiled as she pictured him in her mind. The hole in her heart was mending, a void in her life slowly being filled. After what Rebekah told her about Shelby, Lexa hoped she could help Sam fill the void in *his* heart. They needed each other. At least for now.

~

Margarita missed the first few days of school following the incident in the San Antonio marketplace, but started coming back later in the week. Lexa noticed with relief that the girl looked all right and her spirits were what she'd consider normal. While never giddy with happiness, Margarita participated in class and worked hard.

Every now and then, the little girl's eyes fell on Lexa. Those eyes were way too young to look so haunted. Full of sadness. Lexa spent as much one-on-one time with her as she could. Sometimes in the late afternoon, Margarita would grow weary, and she'd crawl onto Lexa's lap. Stroking her long hair, Lexa sang quiet songs and stole a kiss on her forehead every now and again. Snuggling closer, Margarita put one finger in her mouth and closed her eyes.

Pray for her, Lexa. It was that same small voice that whispered, more and more in her mind, in her heart.

Lexa wrestled with confiding in either Rebekah or Sam about Sheila. The scene with her husband—if that's who he really was—didn't sit well. The whole thing seemed shady, with him all dressed in black and tying Sheila's hands behind her back. In the dark. No, this wasn't good at all.

After debating it all the next day, Lexa decided she had to tell someone, for Sheila's own good. Working with Josh at the worksite, she sensed he could tell something was bothering her, but respected her silence. The Lord would honor her decision if she told Sam, not as breaking a promise to someone, but in order to protect that person from possible physical harm. As the leader of the camp, Sam should know.

"Sam, I need to talk with you about something." Lexa opened the screen door to his office that evening with barely a knock, and stepped over the threshold without waiting for his invitation.

"Come in, come in," Sam welcomed, gesturing with one hand. "You're just the kind of welcome interruption I love. Sit down, please." He pulled out a chair for her. Dropping down beside her, his smile was expectant.

It was good to see him so relaxed, and Lexa prayed what she had to say wouldn't upset him. "You're certainly in a good mood."

"I just found out TeamWork has added a major new source of funding. Which means," he said, his smile widening, "we can keep going for at least the next three years."

Lexa frowned. "Was there ever any doubt?"

Sam's broad shoulders lifted in a shrug. "Let's just say we were in a moderate amount of danger. Even though the volunteers all pay their own way, there's still an enormous amount of expense with building materials, food supplies, that kind of thing."

"Not to mention the upkeep of the transportation."

Sam laughed and his eyes sparkled. "You're good for me, Lexa."

"I'm thankful for this new source of funding. It makes me happy to see *you* so happy." His smile grew brighter as quickly as Lexa's faded. She mulled over how best to broach the subject of Sheila. She'd gone over and over it in her mind. Best to plunge right in. She inhaled a quick breath.

"What's up?" He leaned close, one brow quirked. "Something's bothering you. Speak to me."

"I walked into something disturbing when I went back to the dorm last night. I left the bonfire a little early," she admitted.

"Was I that boring?" Sam teased, crossing his hands behind his head.

He did that a lot, along with raking his hand through that gorgeous mane of hair and chewing on his lower lip when he was worried. That last one was particularly endearing. Shifting in the uncomfortable chair, Lexa focused on what she needed to tell him.

"I had a headache and was really tired, so I left. This is serious, Sam. Obviously, I walked into a situation I wasn't supposed to see."

"Sorry." His smile sobered. "I noticed you leaving. I missed you. I was hoping we could do some more . . . talking after the bonfire. Tell me what happened." Sam leaned his elbows on his knees, and his fingers tapped his chin as he waited.

Lexa drew in a deep breath. "When I walked back into the dorm, it was dark. I thought I heard an odd noise, and then, all of a sudden, this big guy—dressed all in black, mind you—darts across the room. Well, lumbers is more like it. Anyway," Lexa continued, shaking her head, "he goes tearing out of the dorm like a tornado, ripping the door right off its hinges. Then, I found out he tied Sheila's hands behind her back. Not very well, I might add. This man was certainly no Boy Scout."

Pausing, Lexa looked up at Sam to gauge his reaction. Those piercing eyes watched as he gave her his full attention. So far, he didn't look surprised. Concerned, yes, but surprise didn't register in his expression. "Doesn't that sound strange to you? Sam?" Lexa insisted, impatient when he didn't respond as quickly as she expected. "It was obvious this guy wasn't up to any good. And, even more than that, Sheila admitted he's her husband." She didn't intend to reveal that specific bit of detail, but he needed the facts.

"Yes," he said, "it sounds strange, but not altogether hard to believe. That probably *was* Sheila's husband, especially if she told you it was." The words were slow, measured. "You're right in that he's up to no good. And I wondered what happened to the door, but I figured it was the wind since it was pretty strong the other day." He sighed. "It's probably a good thing you showed up when you did. I'm thankful Sheila wasn't hurt. Or you."

"What is he, an ex-convict or something? He looked the part, I'll say that much."

"Bingo."

Lexa stared at him. "Are you serious? The guy really *is* an ex-con?"

Sam nodded. "His name's Howard Morris, and he's got a record a mile long. Mostly things like felony robberies, although he attacked a woman a couple of years ago. They think the attack was motivated by robbery, and not anything more sinister. He got off on some legal technicality."

Lexa tilted her head, trying to catch Sam's full attention. He avoided eye contact with her. It was uncharacteristic. She didn't like it. "What is it you're not telling me? And why is it that Sheila's allowed to stay here in the camp, knowing it's a strong possibility this man might show up unannounced?"

Sam's eyes moved back up in a slow path to meet hers. "You're getting to know me pretty well already, Lexa. I'm not sure I should tell you, to be honest."

"Well, I told you about Sheila even though she begged me not to. That way, I figure we're even." Lexa tamped down the irritation creeping into her tone. "Not that I'm keeping score." Lexa shot him a helpless expression.

"I'm glad you did. And thank you for not crossing your arms in that annoying way you usually do when you're all spunky and mad. And it's about time you started telling me things."

"Meaning?" Lexa fought the overwhelming desire to cross her arms, but let them fall to her lap instead.

Sam chuckled. "Meaning I want to be part of your life, if you'll let me. It's what being in a relationship means, after all." His eyes held hers, unwavering. "You're becoming very important to me. I want you to feel comfortable coming to me with things that are on your mind, bothering you. I have the feeling that's something you found very hard to do. Am I right?"

Lexa hesitated for a long moment before nodding. "Okay, I'll give you that much. You're right. I've always been rather hesitant to open up to others in the past."

"No way!" Grasping one of her hands, Sam squeezed it and studied her fingers as if they were the most fascinating things in the world. The man seemed to have a great fondness for holding her hand. She certainly wasn't complaining.

"You know, Sam, you asked me what I was afraid of." Lexa watched as he traced the pathway of a line etched into her palm. "I've been afraid of too much in my life. Being here at the TeamWork camp just this short amount of time, and meeting you, has shown me that much. I think one of the things I've always been most afraid of is being hurt."

"And if you open up to someone, you'll be hurt? Is that part of why you're afraid?"

Lexa nodded, not trusting herself to answer as he raised her palm and planted a quick, soft kiss. It was sensual in its sweetness. He couldn't know its powerful effect on her. With everything he did, everything he said, Sam showed her he was falling in love with her. It was in the way he looked at her, sometimes when he didn't realize she was aware. Maybe Sam didn't understand it himself. Was it too soon? Granted, she didn't have a lot of experience with matters of the heart. But one thing Lexa did know—the feelings she held for him were honest and real.

Sam opened his mouth to speak again, but hesitated. Lexa presumed he planned on telling her about Shelby, but he must have changed his mind. Finally, he spoke. "I need to tell you something. Something about my past." The words were quiet, spoken with conviction. It was like he had to get them out quickly before deciding against it.

"I'm listening."

"Not yet. How about we meet tonight after the devotions, if you're not too tired."

"How can I be tired, knowing I'll be meeting you?"

Sam's hold on her hand lingered before releasing it. "I'll see you tonight then, if not before. And thanks for telling me about Howard."

"Howard," Lexa repeated, shaking her head. "Howard's not a name for an ex-convict. Howard's a name for a bookworm, a college professor. Or a computer nerd." Preparing to leave the office, Lexa rose from the chair.

"Trust me. This Howard's an entirely different breed. Be careful, Lexa." He walked with her toward the door.

"Are you going to tell me more about Howard tonight? You were very deft in not answering all my questions."

That tiny frown line surfaced between his brows again. "As far as Howard is concerned, please always be on the alert. The board has discussed the situation with Mr. Morris several times. We decided to monitor it, believing the benefits for Sheila being here at the camp outweigh any possible danger." He paused. "Trust me, keeping my TeamWork crew safe is my top priority. We don't believe Howard will really hurt Sheila. Put it this way—he has an ulterior motive. Sheila has something he wants." Sam stepped closer. "Please promise you'll let me know if you ever see him lurking about the camp again."

Lexa nodded. "I promise. But may I make a suggestion?"

"Sure. Lay it on me." Sam leaned against the doorframe, arms crossed.

"Maybe you could assign one of the guys to keep an eye on Sheila every day. Schedule some kind of rotation. Just to make sure she stays safe, especially now that we've seen Howard lurking around. The fact that he made it into the women's dorm is very unnerving. Husband or not, I think Howard should be seen as a potentially serious threat. If it's okay with you, I'll mention it to Rebekah and my other roommates. I'll tell them only as much as you think they should know, but they'll help keep an eye on Sheila."

Sam nodded. "I agree. Go ahead and tell them whatever you feel is best. I know you'll handle it better than I could."

Lexa lifted her chin, meeting his eyes. "I feel strongly this is something we *must* do."

The slightest hint of a grin upturned his lips. "Anyone ever tell you that you're a very wise woman?"

Lexa laughed. "Not really. I didn't expect to hear it from you, either, to be honest."

"Well, you are. Take it as a compliment, and don't deny it. I'm beginning to see you're one of the wisest women I've ever known."

"Better stop right there," Lexa teased with a grin, holding up one hand. It might be his hormones guiding him, but it was flattering. "In the mind of Sam, you certainly didn't think that when you first met me."

"Be quiet and accept it, Lexa. First impressions are hasty and usually incorrect."

"Thank you, Sam."

"That's much better, but we'll have to keep working on it." He nodded. "I'll speak to some of the other guys and put a TeamWork watch into place. I haven't wanted to say too much about Sheila's situation to the group as a whole, not wanting to alarm the volunteers unnecessarily, but you're right. Now that Howard's managed to infiltrate the camp and actually get to Sheila, wife or not, we need to be extra vigilant in protecting her."

Sam shuffled his feet and looked down at the floor. "In answer to your most recent question, no, I'm not going to talk about Howard Morris tonight.

There's something you should know. Something personal I need to tell you. It's time." His eyes looked far away.

"Right. From your past." It sounded so ominous. "Well, mister, as long as you weren't once a woman or something like that." *As if.* Her lips lifted in an attempt at a grin, but it fell far short. Teasing seemed so inherent in their relationship, and something was missing when it wasn't in place.

He surprised her by pulling her into the circle of his arms. Anchoring one firm hand behind her neck, he lowered his mouth to hers. The kiss was tender, full of emotion, but over all too quick.

As Lexa slowly opened her eyes, Sam was on his way back behind the desk. "I'll see you tonight." He was dismissing her.

She blinked hard, dazed by the power of his kiss. Something was on Sam's mind, and he was preoccupied. Most likely, it was a lot more than Sheila's situation. Lexa's heart pumped a little faster. Whatever it was, she'd know later that night.

She found her voice. "If you're lucky."

With a short grunt, Sam flung a balled-up piece of paper in her direction. But he didn't look up, didn't smile. Lexa darted out the door before it could hit her. This time, Sam didn't laugh as she walked away.

Neither did she.

Chapter 24

$\mathcal{L}$EXA, WITS ABOUT you, girl!" Natalie gave her a gentle nudge as they worked side-by-side cleaning up after dinner early that evening. "Where are you, anyway? You look like you're a million miles away. Everything okay?" Concern laced her question.

Lexa continued picking up discarded cups and plates, tossing them into the bag Natalie held. "I've just got a lot on my mind. Thanks for the wakeup call."

Natalie respected her space as they worked together in companionable silence. From Connecticut, she had long dark hair, luminous deep blue eyes and was quieter than most of her other roommates. She told Lexa in the schoolroom one morning that she'd met Amy, a native of Pennsylvania, at a New England TeamWork event. The two had bonded and worked a couple of TeamWork missions together the last few years. Both were also close with Winnie, a native of Texas, and the three always bunked together at the work camps.

While Lexa appreciated Natalie's thoughtfulness and sensitivity, she couldn't voice her uncertainties and fears. Maybe it wasn't the best thing for her emotional or mental state to keep everything bottled up inside. Still, she'd been doing it for so long, it was second nature.

Tell the Lord, Lexa. Trust Him as your best friend.

What did Sam have to tell her? Why he couldn't tell her in the privacy of his office, she had no idea. Anything was possible. As she helped Natalie gather the trash and the soda cans for recycling, Lexa prayed Sam didn't have some startling new revelation to unload. Another thing she'd never particularly liked was surprises. Good or bad. In her experience, they usually weren't good.

"Consider Jonah again," Sam told them that evening. "Remember how he fled in the opposite direction from where God wanted him to go? Is that what you're doing tonight? Are you fleeing from God and what He wants for your life? My guess is that simply because you're sitting around this bonfire tonight, you're exactly where God wants you. You're here, supporting yourself financially, or with the help from others. You're giving yourself, your time, your abilities, your all to TeamWork. And why? Why would you give of yourself so unselfishly for the good of others?" Sam paused, holding his open Bible in his hands, his eyes moving from face to face. The embers in the fire crackled, breaking the stillness.

"Because you're followers of Jesus Christ. Because you want to show others the kind of love Christ showed us by dying a horrible death upon a wooden cross on Calvary. How wonderful we can call Him Savior and Lord. Have *you* shared Him with someone today?" Another pregnant pause. Watching him, drinking in his words, Lexa admired how Sam captured the full attention of everyone gathered around the bonfire circle.

"Have you told someone about the impact Christ has made in your life? Sometimes we get sheltered, especially in this camp environment. We're like our own little holy huddle, if you want to call it that. But as Matthew Chapter Twenty-Eight—verses nineteen and twenty—tell us, it's our responsibility, our duty, our great commission to go out into the world and tell the nations about Jesus Christ. Out into the world means outside your own personal comfort zone. But all it takes is one person at a time. One person telling another, then another, then another . . ."

Sam pointed to several of the volunteers seated on benches around the circle. "It's that complicated, and yet that simple. One at a time," he reminded them as he finished.

Sheila's head rested on Lexa's shoulder. Taking Sheila's hand in hers, she held on tight as they prepared for the closing prayer. On the other side of her, Josh's large hand captured hers and squeezed as they bowed their heads.

Lexa glanced at her watch an hour later, dismayed by how late it was. She and Sam had talked with a group of volunteers for over an hour following the bonfire devotions. When she suggested they talk in the morning, he made it clear he wanted a little private time with her.

"Your message tonight was a very good one." Sam looked especially tired. Josh mentioned how hard Sam had been working on the houses. He'd also met with most of the homeowners to discuss more particulars of the construction. Lexa reached for his hand, pleased when he squeezed and held on tight as they walked toward their special tree.

"Thanks. I thought it was time for a personal challenge. It's the midway point, and often the time when some of the volunteers start to slump. I need to try and keep their spirits and morale positive."

"Well, I trust you'll tell me if I start to slump." Lexa smiled up at him and noted the circles beneath his eyes.

"May it never happen." He'd dropped her hand to rub his eyes, and Sam reached for her again now. It was amazing how easily they both reached out for the other. "From what I can tell, you're learning and growing by leaps and bounds. Some of the questions you've asked at the bonfires and the Sunday morning studies floor me. Your insights are unique, Lexa, and you're helping the other volunteers see new ways to interpret scripture. I think you're also teaching them about their own faith."

Sam moved his arm around her shoulders, drawing her closer. "I know you're teaching *me* a lot."

"Surely you're not talking about being . . . stagnant." Lexa found it difficult to believe she could teach anyone about the Christian faith since she was newly discovering it for herself.

He stifled a yawn. "I'm sorry." He gave her a sheepish grin. "Some of us have been Christians for so long, we think we know most of what there is to learn. I think that's part of what God teaches us. We need to always be teachable, willing to see what new lessons He has for us. It should be a lifelong process." He chuckled. "You, Miss Clarke, certainly keep me on my toes. You keep me sharp. I certainly need that. We all do."

"In my case, it's certainly not iron sharpening iron." Lexa shook her head. "There's so much to learn, Sam. It's overwhelming, to be honest."

He stopped walking. He tilted her chin, his thumb lightly caressing it. "Don't ever sell yourself short, Lexa. You have so much to share. So much to give. You've opened your mind to all the possibilities of the Lord." His eyes softened. "It's a great thing to witness firsthand."

Swallowing hard, Lexa headed toward the tree, tugging him along behind her. She loved Sam's humility in including himself when talking about his volunteers. "One of these days, I'll get you to skip, cowboy."

"Not anytime soon, beautiful girl." He grinned and dropped to the ground, patting the spot next to him. When she sat down, Sam nestled her close. "You *are* beautiful," he murmured, his eyes bright in the moonlight.

"Why, thank you." Lexa gave him a shy smile.

"And you're getting better," he teased.

"I beg your pardon?"

"You accepted the compliment graciously, without too much embarrassment."

"Oh, my cheeks are red. You just can't tell because it's dark."

"*Very* beautiful, in fact." It was a sweet compliment from an even lovelier man. Such contentment she'd never experienced except maybe with her mother and grandmother all those years ago. Her dad never sheltered and protected her the way Sam already did.

"I'm sure you're wondering what I wanted to talk to you about."

"The thought crossed my mind."

Sam looked away for a moment, gathering his thoughts. Lexa waited, knowing that whatever he had to tell her was important and close to his heart. It was obvious she was becoming important to him or he wouldn't tell her. Several minutes passed without either speaking.

"Sam, you're scaring me just a little bit."

"Sorry." He drew in a deep breath. "I was engaged a few years ago."

Lexa waited as he paused again. She wasn't about to admit Rebekah told her about Shelby.

"Her name was Shelby Hanson, and she was a close friend of Rebekah's. But she was killed three summers ago." He motioned with one hand. "Here, on the dirt road outside the camp." His brows were drawn, and he hung his head as he drew in the dirt with one finger. "The reason I'm telling you this is because you've come to mean a great deal to me. I wasn't looking for anyone else, and to be honest, I didn't think I'd find anyone for a long time. If ever."

He hesitated, and she looked up, meeting his gaze. When Sam laid a gentle hand on the side of her face, Lexa turned into its gentle curve. "I'm so very sorry, Sam." She leaned her head on his shoulder, and moved her hand to rest above his heart. The sound, the feel, of his strong, steady heartbeat filled her in a moment of breathtaking intimacy. She waited for him to speak, to open his heart to her a little more. Sam's arms encircled her in the way she adored, and he rested his head against hers.

"Because of Shelby, I knew I could love a woman unselfishly. It was a learning, growing experience. But I did a lot of things wrong. She was older than Rebekah, but still very young. We were both too young in a lot of respects." His voice sounded far away.

"I didn't imagine for one minute you haven't had your share of girlfriends."

She could feel his smile as he tucked aside her braid and kissed her temple. His lips were warm and tender.

"That's another story for another time. I know enough to see a diamond in the rough, so to speak, right in front of my eyes."

Lexa turned back around to face him again. "Is that supposed to be a compliment?"

Sam laughed. "All I mean is, you have your rough edges, just as I have mine. But polish you up, and man, do you shine. Do you ever."

"That's truly one of the more . . . unusual . . . and *precious* compliments I've ever heard."

"Then you must not have dated much yourself. Personally, I think the one about how beautiful you are should rank right up there with the best."

Lexa covered his hand with hers and smiled into his eyes. "Thank you for telling me about Shelby. I know she meant a great deal to you."

"She did." Sam stared at the ground. "It took me a long time to get over it, to get over what happened." He released a deep sigh. "But I need to tell you more about it. It's time."

"There's more?" Her pulse raced and she struggled to sit up straighter.

"We argued the night she died. Shelby was mad at me, and it was a horrible fight. Generally, she was pretty even-keeled, but she had a temper. I found out late in the work camp how . . . volatile and emotional she could be. She stormed away from me in the middle of our fight, and asked another volunteer to take her somewhere. Shelby wanted to escape the camp, wanted to get as far away from *me* as possible." Sam's voice faded to a whisper and Lexa strained to hear his words.

"Why did you argue?" Maybe it was an unfair question, but Lexa suddenly had a burning need to know. Plus, she wanted to steer the conversation away from a morbid recounting of the events of that night. It wouldn't serve any good purpose for either one of them now.

"Shelby was having an affair." Sam's voice was so low, she almost couldn't hear.

"A *what*?" Lexa choked on the question.

"You heard me."

"You mean . . ." Lexa couldn't even finish the sentence. Not that the idea of someone having an affair was something she'd never heard of before. To the contrary. But the thought that Shelby could betray this incredible man was too much to grasp, especially since she was blessed enough to be engaged to him. It was impossible to comprehend. Either Rebekah was unaware of this part of the story, or it was an intentional omission. If that was the case, Lexa knew Rebekah must have her reasons. That wasn't important now.

"Yes, I mean a physical affair. I honestly don't know how emotionally involved she was with the other man, but they were good friends. But, please don't think for one minute that Shelby and I had an intimate, physical relationship."

"No, of course not." Lexa sat motionless, numb with an overwhelming sadness.

"As it was, we'd only been engaged a few days when she was killed." Sam shook his head and raked a hand through his hair. "It all happened so fast. Sometimes it still seems unbelievable. Learning about the affair tore me up and made me question my faith, but only for about a week or two. It didn't take long to understand what happened was simply the old sin nature rearing its ugly head. Shelby was awfully young, after all."

Lexa nodded, but she felt her heart breaking for the pain Sam endured because of a woman's betrayal, no matter how young or beautiful Shelby was. It didn't excuse a horrible betrayal like that, and she ached with compassion for Sam.

He sat with his hands resting on his propped knees and stared down at the ground before finally looking back up at her. "The hardest part to accept is that the other man with whom Shelby had the affair is right here at this camp as we speak. I see him every day, and it's a reminder of Shelby and all that was lost." He traced another circle in the dirt. "In a lot of ways, it's made it more difficult to get past the memories."

The surprises were coming from all directions now. "Sam, I don't know what to say." The silence between them grew even longer. "Does this man know you're aware of his affair with Shelby?"

"I don't know, to tell you the truth. If he is, it's not because it came from me."

Lexa stared at him. "He's one of your TeamWork volunteers, and you never even *talked* with him about it?" Incredulity laced her tone.

Sam lowered his head into his hands, and they sat in silence for a few minutes before he spoke again. "I don't know what to say. Shelby's gone. To a great extent, I feel responsible for her death. First, she stormed off because of our fight. And then she died." Sam's shoulders slumped even further.

"The whole situation has eaten me up inside for the better part of three years. He loved her, too, and he's a hard worker who gave into physical temptation. It happens. He's been a good friend to me in all other respects, and I simply can't bring myself to hate him. I know you might think that sounds crazy, and I know that's not how the world operates, but it's *my* way."

Sam reached for her again. Settling her into the curve of his arms, he needed her support and comfort, not questions or disbelief. "Trust me, I've gone over it in my head a lot, and the guilt has eased somewhat. The Holy Spirit's still working on me, and I'm learning I can't feel responsible for Shelby's death. He allowed it to happen for whatever reason, and I have to get on with the business of living." He kissed the top of her head. "After all, there's a lot to live for in the here and now."

They sat together again for several long minutes. "I'm sorry to hit you with all this at once." Sam's hold on her tightened. "I feel so close to you, and I thought you should know."

Lexa sat dazed, shaken. In spite of what he'd said, she had a hard time accepting his reasoning. Was any man *that* forgiving? "It must be so unbelievably hard for you, having this other man constantly around. How can you do it?"

Sam shook his head and stared up at the night sky. "If Christ died to forgive my sins, how can I not forgive this man? Of course, it hasn't been easy. I'm human. I was furious, livid, mad with rage when I first found out."

Lexa wondered how he found about the affair. "So, you confronted Shelby about her affair? The night she was killed when the truck hit them?"

Sam nodded and then looked over at her quickly, his face pale even in the darkness.

"You *knew*?"

The words were quiet, brimming with anguish. Lexa couldn't speak. Her breathing slowed and caught in her throat.

When she nodded without speaking, her head down, afraid to look him in the eye, Sam demanded, his voice insistent. "Who told you? Did *he* tell you? Did *he*?"

Lexa stared at him, not understanding his change of mood and sudden anger. "No, but someone who loves you did." *Because Rebekah knows how much I care for you. She knows I love you!* But she couldn't say the words aloud.

Sam rose to his feet, his fists clenched. The muscles in his cheeks flexed wildly, the set to his jaw firm and unyielding.

"They didn't want to tell me," she protested, struggling to her feet, reaching for his hands. Sam turned away from her touch. He looked stunned, his face contorted with disbelief. *Betrayal.* A deep feeling of dread washed over Lexa, threatening to drain the very breath from her lungs. "I practically ordered them to tell me because of my own selfishness, my own morbid curiosity. They wanted me to talk with you about Shelby, but I was the one who insisted on knowing. Please don't be mad, Sam."

Sam stared at Lexa long and hard, as though he didn't know her at all.

"You're not having an affair with him, too, are you, Lexa?"

With that one question, Sam wiped out their closeness, their friendship, and especially Lexa's trust. That was it. He managed to destroy everything she thought they'd established together. Something wonderful, passionate and lasting. She was wrong.

Sam Lewis was no different. He *was* just like every other man.

Standing, Lexa trembled with rage. Fists clenched, she glared at him, willing herself to say something, anything. She couldn't even begin to verbalize what she was feeling. Maybe it was better not to say anything until she calmed down. Until they both calmed down. And that might take a very long time. If ever.

Turning, Lexa fled into the night, her heart breaking with each stride of her long legs as she realized this time, Sam Lewis wasn't coming after her. Not now, and quite possibly never again.

That dreaded word. *Never.*

Father, help me! With tears streaming down her cheeks, Lexa stormed over in the direction of the worksite, not caring if that old armadillo waited for her there. He'd be better company than anyone else right now. Not knowing where else to go, she needed time to think, time to be alone.

She broke into a run and didn't look back.

Oh, Lord, why did you bring me here? Why did you bring me here?

Chapter 25

$\mathcal{H}$E'D MADE A terrible, maybe even unforgiveable mistake. Once again, he'd hurt her. The look on Lexa's face would be forever imprinted in his mind. She looked more hurt than angry, but unbearably so. Sam berated himself, asking himself over and over how he could have asked her that horrible, accusatory question that sent her running off into the night. Away from him. Away from his heart.

He couldn't explain it, even to himself. An overwhelming jealousy clouded his judgment. His words were rash, unfounded. It must have been Beck who told Lexa about Shelby. It was only natural it might have come up at some point since Beck was friendly with Lexa. What was the harm, really?

Poor Rebekah. She had no idea Shelby had betrayed him, had betrayed *her* in a way, too. How could he tell dear, sweet Beck that his fiancée—and her best friend—betrayed them both with Beck's own twin brother? No, he couldn't do that to her. As much as he loved Rebekah Grant, it would need to be Josh who told her.

Then came the matter of trust. Lexa told him he was the strongest Christian man she knew. And look how he'd blown his testimony. He'd shattered her faith and trust by his thoughtless, stupid accusation. Sam didn't like the word stupid, but he could think of no better term for this particular situation. His words had been unfounded, pointless, without provocation. They slipped out from somewhere not of the Lord. In the long run, telling someone like Lexa *the devil made me do it* wouldn't wash with her.

Not knowing what else to do, Sam followed the path he knew best—he prayed and meditated on scriptures. He talked to himself, doubled his efforts at the worksite, ate only when he remembered and was gruff and short with anyone who dared to ask him a question. Sleep was elusive most nights, but when exhaustion finally overcame him, it was a blessing.

So, what could he say or do to make things right? Teasing banter and romantic overtures couldn't make up for what his thoughtless tongue had destroyed. As he recalled the verse of scripture about the tongue being a double-edged sword, it made Sam want to weep. A desperate man, he fell to his knees in the end and prayed. And continued to pray that somehow the Lord would show him the way to forgiveness—from himself and from Lexa. Sam prayed she'd understand his words that night were rash and reckless, motivated by nothing more than a hurting heart.

Sam loved Lexa. Loved her with a depth of emotion and passion he'd never felt for Shelby. Lexa was strong, intelligent, witty. He loved her sense of humor. She was insightful and determined. She had strength of character. She'd captured his mind as well as his heart. Sam wanted to protect her and take care of her forever. Wanted her beside him as he stumbled his way through life. She made him a better man and kept him straight.

But now, every time she caught him looking at her, Lexa turned away with such a look of hurt that it tore him up inside. Her father hurt her by never opening up to her in an emotional way, and now he'd hurt her by acting like he didn't trust her. It was almost too much. It made Sam hate himself a little. But the deep, abiding emotion of love is stronger than hate.

Please help me, Father. Help me find the way back to Lexa before it's too late for us.

~

Lexa felt numb, as if she was simply going through the motions. Sam tried to talk with her several times, but she made sure never to be in a position where she was alone. She came late to lunch and dinner and left early, and either skipped the bonfire devotionals or left before the prayer ended. She wasn't proud of her behavior, but avoiding Sam was the only way she could stay in the TeamWork camp and continue working. Otherwise, she would have left the very night he accused her of having an affair with the same person as Shelby.

She might have packed her bags and called for a taxi that night. But even in the midst of his anger, Sam sent Kevin Moore out to the worksite in the station wagon to find her and bring her back to the camp. Always the leader, always the protector, Sam made sure she was safe.

Then there was the other man who so bewitched Shelby that she'd carried on an affair. As hard as it was to believe, it had to be someone within the TeamWork organization. Someone at the work camp. But which man? While she didn't want to make any assumptions, Lexa kept a wary eye on everyone. Trying to figure out which man didn't serve any good purpose, so she decided to let it go and give it over to the Lord's capable watchcare.

Lexa devoted her time to helping at the schoolroom and the canteen, and immersed herself in studying her Bible. If nothing else, Sam's words gave her the gift of self-discovery. She prayed and spent time with the Lord like never before. Whenever she had a short break, Lexa walked with her Bible, the one Sam had given her. She'd sit beneath the tree, reading and meditating on God's Word. It gave her a comfort nothing else or no one else could—not even Sam. Gave her hope for a future without him. But her heart ached almost unbearably.

From the corner of her eye, Lexa sometimes glimpsed slight movements a short distance away. Someone might be watching as she sat beneath the tree. She suspected it might be Sam, but couldn't be sure. If it *was* him, he never approached her. He'd tried several times to talk with her, but she wouldn't let him close, and surrounded herself with the other ladies.

Lexa's heart was breaking, piece by little piece, every day when Sam rose to lead the group in prayer. No matter her personal feelings, Lexa acknowledged he was in his element as the TeamWork director. It suited him and his spiritual gifts. How could she not admire a man who followed his dream, followed God's plan for his life? Sam told her he prayed he'd recognize God's calling for his life. Was it his work for TeamWork, or was it something else? Lexa prayed the Lord would make his life's purpose clear.

Sometimes Lexa wondered why God put Sam in her path to tease her with love and romance. But God doesn't tease. Meeting Sam proved she was capable of loving someone. Perhaps it was more important for her to learn she was capable of *being* loved. It filled her with a self-confidence that hadn't been there a few short weeks ago. How her life had changed since joining the TeamWork mission and meeting Sam Lewis. She wasn't as timid in approaching new situations, challenges and people. Even though things with Sam had gone terribly wrong, being a part of the TeamWork crew was special, a blessing like none other.

She made slow but sure progress in befriending Sheila. One afternoon, as they worked side-by-side at the worksite refilling water bottles for the workers, Sheila confided Howard was the first man who paid her any attention. She claimed not to know anything about his unsavory background, and her family forced her to marry him when she became pregnant with his child. So, not only did Sheila have a husband, she also had a child.

She hadn't yet discovered where or with whom the child lived while Sheila served at the mission—or whether it was a boy or girl—but she figured it was only a matter of time. Sheila would tell her if and when she wanted.

Most days, Lexa devoted her time assisting the children with their schoolwork. It was an avoidance tactic since Sam was usually at the worksite. At least Margarita thrived under Lexa's special attention. She looked brighter and responded more to the other children. Her English improved every day, and she communicated better with Lexa and the other teachers.

Sometimes when she caught Margarita in a moment unaware, she glimpsed the sadness in the little girl's face. How could anyone neglect this precious child? Since Lexa didn't hear anything further about the complaint against her and TeamWork filed by Mrs. Martinez, she assumed everything was all right. She couldn't work up the nerve to ask Sam about it, but neither did he broach the subject. Lexa decided to leave well enough alone.

~

After two weeks passed, Sam decided he'd suffered enough punishment. He'd beaten himself up mercilessly and figured Lexa should have cooled off enough to give him another chance. The ache in his heart was heavy and threatened to overwhelm his concentration on TeamWork matters. And *nothing* interfered with TeamWork. Enough was enough.

Surely Lexa wouldn't dismiss him from her life forever because of callous remarks in a moment of heated discussion. There was too much at stake between them, too much passion, too much everything. He wanted this woman with every fiber in his being. He'd make it up to her if it was the last thing he did.

It was time to take the first step toward reconciliation. Lexa didn't have that much time left with the mission before she went back home to Houston. No way on earth was he going to let her leave the TeamWork camp without making it right between them. He resolved to talk with her, make her see how sorry he was for the remarks that had driven such a deep wedge between them. Sam believed she'd ultimately forgive him. He couldn't face the alternative.

Of more importance, he needed to show Lexa he trusted her. He *loved* her. Telling her was one thing, but proving it was another beast. Especially after letting her believe he didn't trust her, he couldn't start spouting words of love or she'd laugh in his face—or possibly spit on him like that ornery old goat the first day they'd met. Sam needed to be able to back up his words with action. He prayed for the Lord to show him the path back to Lexa's heart.

Getting time alone with Lexa might be harder than he thought. He could ask her to meet him in his office. She could refuse. He could have Rebekah bring her. Lexa might catch on and resent her. He could sit down beside her at the dinner table and force a confrontation, and then ask her to meet him later. But he didn't want to embarrass her in front of her new friends.

Then there was Josh Grant. Once Josh knew things had cooled between him and Lexa, he didn't hesitate to make his move. He continued to sit next to her in the dining tent and made sure he was right beside her at the bonfire. It made Sam's blood boil one night when Josh sat so close it looked like he wanted to pull Lexa onto his lap. Thank goodness, she had the presence of mind to resist Josh's charms.

The man was his own worst enemy, but couldn't see it. That's usually the way it worked. Since confiding in Lexa about Shelby, it weighed heavily on his mind that he needed to have a serious, heart-to-heart with Josh. He'd always pushed it aside because he'd been too close to the situation with Shelby. He'd been in prayer about it, and the Holy Spirit was prompting him to address the situation and do what he could to help Josh.

Rapping out a fast rhythm with his pencil on the desktop, Sam's frown deepened. Yes, he had to talk with Lexa, and he had to act now if he was going to have any chance at all with her. Time was not his friend. Once she left his TeamWork camp, his chance might be gone. Houston was a big city, but it would be lonely and tortuous without her in his life.

Lexa was also his friend. He'd enjoyed their talks under the tree. He missed them. He missed *her*. He'd shared things with her he'd never told anyone else—not even his little sister Caty, his closest confidante in the world. He'd opened his heart to Lexa, and she'd opened her heart to him.

"All the thinking in the world isn't going to win her back, old man." As the screen door of his office slammed behind him, Sam stormed outside. He was rewarded by a creak of protest as it came partially off its hinges. Looking back for a split-second, he spied it hanging cock-eyed, barely attached at the bottom. Shaking his head, he continued on his way with a mental note to reattach the door later.

Several workers walking about the campsite stared as he passed by. He didn't care. He couldn't stop to make small-talk. Lightning streaked across the sky, and thunder boomed as he strode across the campsite. He had a one-track mind as he rapped on the door of the women's dorm.

Chapter 26

"COME IN. AT least you knocked this time. Well, aren't you a sight." Rebekah shot Sam a wry grin after he barged inside.

Stopping in his tracks, he grimaced, running a hand over his unruly hair. "I haven't exactly been thinking about my appearance lately."

"That much is obvious. From the looks of you, you aren't getting enough sleep, either."

"Gee, thanks. Sorry I offended you. Tell me how you really feel, Beck. Give me a break."

"Sam, what's gotten into you lately? The same thing that's bothering Lexa, I assume?"

"Seems like you answered your own question." Hands on his hips, Sam stood in the center of the room, shaking his head and rubbing a hand over his rough jaw. Beck was right. He needed a good, close shave.

"Care to tell me what happened?"

It surprised him that Lexa hadn't confided in Beck. But Lexa wasn't like other women. For one thing, she apparently liked to suffer in silence. Just like her mother. It was hard for her to open up to others. The painful truth pierced his heart all over again that she'd opened up to him and he'd hurt her by betraying the trust she'd placed in him.

Sam looked at Rebekah long and hard, trying to decide whether or not to confide in her. "Let's just say I blew it by saying something infinitely stupid." She didn't answer, and waited for more information. "Basically, I foolishly misled Lexa to think I didn't trust her."

"Well, that *is* a tough one." Rebekah whistled under her breath.

"So, tell me what to do, Beck," Sam pleaded, his eyes searching hers. Desperation flooded his thoughts, his posture, his expression–a reflection of his inner torment. He was a man in love with a woman who didn't return his love. Deep down, Sam knew Lexa cared. Did he dare believe she could love him? The only man she'd ever truly loved—her father—couldn't show his love. Spurred on by that thought, Sam was willing to do whatever it took to win her back.

"Have you tried telling her the truth, asking for her forgiveness?"

Rebekah's words stirred him back to reality. "Sort of. I mean I tried a few times, but she's avoiding me like the plague. I can't seem to get within ten feet of her. For one thing," he plundered on, regardless of the consequences, "that brother of yours seems to be monopolizing her company. A guy can't get a word in edgewise."

"Well, then, talk to Josh. Tell him to lay off."

"Since when has Josh backed off from a woman he really wants?" Sam snarled, looking down at the floor, his mind racing.

"What's that supposed to mean?" Rebekah crossed her arms as she glared at him.

"Nothing," Sam muttered, shaking his head.

"Sounds like pure jealousy to me." Rebekah sniffed, turning away.

Forcing himself to hold his tongue so he wouldn't say anything further about Josh, Sam turned to go. "Sorry. I just have to work this out in my own mind." And then he had to convince Lexa.

"Lexa's really grown a lot since she's been here. In a lot of ways." The words were spoken so softly that Sam had to turn back to hear them. "I like her a lot. She's come out of that shell she had around her when she first came to the camp."

Sam nodded, the beginnings of a small smile playing about his lips. "Yes, she has."

"In the beginning, she was sort of like that old armadillo she bonded with out at the worksite." Rebekah smiled a little. "But, like I said, Lexa's crawled out from beneath her own shell. And I think," she said, pausing to make sure she had Sam's attention, "a certain TeamWork director has something to do with that."

Sam grinned. "You think so?"

Rebekah nodded. "I *know* so. You love her, don't you?"

Sam nodded, his eyes full. "You know me too well."

"I can tell it's different than with Shelby, too. I think you've met your match with Lexa."

Sam pulled Rebekah to him in a tight hug. "I love you, too, you know."

Rebekah kissed his cheek. "I know, my friend, but we're talking about an entirely different kind of love here. Go get her, Sam. And don't let her go. Ever. Know I'll be praying."

"Thanks, Beck. I need it." With a parting grin and salute, Sam waved and left the dorm. Standing just outside the door, he glanced up at the dark, menacing sky. Even the stillness in the air was ominous. Another streak of lightning followed by a clap of thunder confirmed his suspicions.

Dark clouds loomed overhead and a few large raindrops started to fall as he hurried in the direction of his office. There was no doubt they needed rain. Unfortunately, the rain usually made conditions more humid and muggy instead of cooling the temperatures down.

Somewhere in the distance, a cracking, splintering sound pierced the eerie silence. A tree going down, hit by lightning, no doubt. Quickening his steps, Sam entered his quarters and closed the screen door, securing it as best he could considering the broken hinges, hoping it wouldn't bang or fly off altogether if there was much wind with this particular storm.

Outside, he glimpsed a few of the workers running around the camp, scurrying for shelter. Standing in the doorway of his office, Sam watched Lexa run back to her dorm with Natalie and Winnie. His heart quickened at the mere sight of her. The rain was heavier now, her long hair plastered to her head. Her clothes were soaked through to her skin and clung to Lexa, revealing more than she could possibly ever know, but confirming what he already knew.

Sam released the light groan trapped in his throat and forced himself to tear his eyes away. Half-praying that Josh Grant didn't see Lexa before she reached the women's dorm, he trudged across the wooden floorboards to his desk. He crossed his elbows behind his head and leaned back in the creaky chair, closing his weary eyes. One of these days, that old chair was going to collapse under all his weight.

~

It was still raining quite hard when the dinner bell sounded a short time later. Standing in the doorway of the dorm and peering outside, Lexa shook her head. "I suppose the bonfire devotionals are canceled with rain like this," she observed to no one in particular.

"Yes." Natalie joined her. "Not to mention the building at the worksite if everything's all muddy, although some of the guys can be die-hards."

A great commotion outside startled them. Several men ran toward Sam's office, hollering at the top of their lungs.

"What's going on?" Winnie stood behind Lexa and Natalie, peering over their shoulders.

"I'm not sure." Lexa pushed open the screen door and strained to hear.

"Fire at the worksite! Fire at the worksite!" Josh ran into the center of the camp in the direction of Sam's office. Sam flung open the door and came running out to meet Josh and the other men. This time, the screen door flew completely off its hinges, landing on the ground a few feet away, forgotten and abandoned.

Running outside, with Rebekah and her other roommates close behind, Lexa approached the men huddled together outside Sam's office. "How can we help?" A number of the other women joined them, and they stood behind the men, watching Sam for direction.

"Call 9-1-1," Sam instructed. "Tell them we don't have access to the hydrants near the worksite and need help. Tell them to hurry." One of the other girls ran back into the dorm to call.

"How can there be a fire with all this rain coming down?" one of the guys yelled above the rest of the voices.

"Because everything was so dry in the first place. It might not be raining as hard at the worksite as it is here. The rain, not to mention the weather, is very fickle here in this area." Turning to some of the other men, Sam called out commands. In circumstances like this, it was good he was so tall, his voice resonant and commanding.

Lexa listened, wondering how else she could help. As soon as the men began to scatter to their various posts, she quickly caught up to Sam as he headed for the station wagon. "What can we do?" She reached out her hand to touch his arm, but then dropped it to her side.

Sam fixed her with a grim look through the pelting rain as she hurried to keep pace. But those blue eyes were kind. "Pray. Pray hard, Lexa."

She nodded as he jumped inside the car and slammed the door. Drenched with rain, Lexa watched helplessly as the station wagon rambled down the road, muddy from all the rain. She prayed until she could no longer see the car. Raising her face to the sky, she let the rain intermingle with her tears. "Lord, help them. Don't let the houses burn. Please, no." She slowly headed back in the direction of the dorm, her shoulders slumping, not caring that she was getting soaked all over again. It barely even registered.

"So, what happens now?" After drying off and changing into more dry clothes, Lexa dropped down onto Rebekah's bed beside her. Great sadness washed over her. It was similar to what she felt when she learned her mother had died. She hadn't been there, holding her hand when she left this world, and it still haunted her.

At this very moment, Sam and the other TeamWork men were at the worksite battling the forces of nature, trying to save the homes they'd labored over all summer. But houses could be rebuilt. That's why they were there in San Antonio, after all. Those houses were so important to Sam. As much as constructing homes, they were rebuilding lives. Lexa hurt for Sam, knowing how much he poured his heart into this mission.

"After we pray, we wait." Rebekah draped one arm around Lexa's shoulders. They looked at each other, wide-eyed, as they heard the distant sounds of emergency fire sirens.

"Where's a hammer?"

"What?" Rebekah's lips upturned. "Are you planning on doing some repairs, Miss Fix-It?"

"As soon as this rain lets up, I'm going over to Sam's office." Lexa walked over to the door. The rain was easing a bit. "It looks like there's a screen door calling my name." She felt proficient enough with a hammer and nails to do this. She had to try.

Walking across the room, Rebekah glanced over Lexa's shoulder. "Well, that's one way to do something to help. Sam's stronger than he realizes. That poor old door didn't stand much of a chance against the wrath of the mighty Sam."

When Lexa gave her a curious stare, Rebekah shrugged with a small, mysterious, smile.

Chapter 27

*S*AM FROWNED AND let out a loud grunt of frustration as he helped one of the men position the heavy hose. They aimed it in the direction of the flames licking at the walls of the first house they'd constructed. "Lord, don't let all our work here be in vain," he muttered under his breath. "It can't all have been for nothing." He shuddered, remembering the splintering sound he'd heard. It must have been lightning striking one of the houses, igniting the fire.

"Help us drag that line over to the next house," one of the firefighters yelled to Josh above the din all around them. Sam watched through narrowed eyes as Josh sprang into action on command, helping some of the other firefighters haul the heavy line a few hundred yards. Even though the rain was relentless as it pelted down on them, rivers of sweat coursed down Josh's face.

Sam swiped one arm across his brow as he released the hose. His eyes roamed across the worksite to where Kevin and some of the other TeamWork men worked alongside the firefighters as they hosed down another home. He was proud of his men. They were brave, every one of them, not afraid to jump in and help in any way they could.

He should have somehow prepared an emergency plan of action for something like this. Rampant wildfire was always a possibility in this region, especially because it had been so dry the last few weeks. This was the first rain since Lexa arrived at the camp. Funny how all his thoughts came back to the petite blonde.

"Pull it over a few more feet to the left!" the firefighter hollered to Sam. Following the man's lead, Sam did his best. Even though there were plenty of trained firefighters engaged in the battle, he couldn't stand idle while the fruits of their labor evaporated in a black cloud of smoke and flame. Even if it meant losing everything, he had to help, had to be a part of it. They needed to do whatever possible to try and save the houses.

At least one of the houses was already gone, seared down to the foundation, and another one was in serious danger, but it looked like the rest of the houses would survive relatively intact. It would take considerable manpower to start again on the burned houses and finish them before the end of the project in only a couple of weeks. Otherwise, he'd have to stay longer and do it himself. Which meant that he'd also need to take even more leave from his own work. Sam frowned at the thought although it was something he'd been considering.

An hour later, Josh and Sam stood shoulder-to-shoulder, surveying the damage. The rain subsided and only spit on them intermittently now. Lazy smoke curled in an upward trail from the smoldering remains of the two homes, an unwelcome reminder of their loss. But it wasn't as bad as it could have been, and for that, Sam was thankful. All the firefighters had departed, along with the rest of the TeamWork crew he'd sent back to the camp once they'd contained the fires.

Josh insisted on staying behind with Sam until the very end. Their clothes were drenched, and both of them were beaten down. Sam knew he must look as haggard as Josh after their efforts on the battleground front lines. He appreciated his help, but felt more disgruntled than ever. Working with Josh only seemed to exacerbate an already volatile situation.

"I'm sorry, Sam. Guess it's not as bad as it could have been, though. Only two are totally gone."

Sam didn't answer. He didn't trust himself. His feelings were too raw. He didn't like the attention Josh paid Lexa. He acted way too familiar with her, and Sam regretted not banishing him from the TeamWork camp three years ago. He started back in the direction of the station wagon with Josh close behind.

"Hey, wait up, Sam!"

The ride back to the camp was silent. After a few attempts, Josh finally gave up trying to engage him in conversation. Sam knew Josh wondered why he was so brooding and non-responsive, but other than saying a quick prayer under his breath, he couldn't muster anything more.

"Hey, man, it's not the end of the world." Josh slapped him on the shoulder as soon as Sam pulled the car into the makeshift parking space behind his office.

Looking down at Josh's hand on his shoulder, Sam fixed him with a cold, hard stare.

"Whaaaat?" Josh pulled back and lifted both hands in the air in mock surrender. "What's eating you, Sam? We'll rebuild those houses quickly."

"It's not the houses I'm worried about." Sam's voice was barely civil, his teeth clenched.

"Well, then, what's up?"

Getting out of the car and slamming the door hard, Sam paused. "Look, Josh, thanks for your help. I appreciate it." He inhaled a deep breath, forcing his voice to remain calm. "And yes, with God's help, we'll get the houses rebuilt in time."

"Sure, we will. Listen, there's something I've been meaning to talk with you about." Josh followed Sam as he headed toward the office.

"Shoot." Sam flung the screen door open, not bothering to wait.

"It's about Lexa."

At Josh's words, Sam whirled around and stepped back outside. He fixed the slightly shorter man with a hard, icy glare. "What about Lexa?" Sam's mouth formed a grim line, his curled fists moving down to his sides.

"Are you through with her? I mean, if you are, do you mind if I have a go at her?"

Sam's blood coursed through him. Lunging forward like a hungry lion, he tackled Josh. Pinning his torso between his knees, Sam pounded him with hard fists and grunted with each blow. A rage deep inside triggered, one never touched before that propelled him over the limit. Although he should stop, he couldn't. God help him, but Josh's reckless behavior had to be stopped. He needed to learn a lesson. Sam's relentless fist made solid contact with Josh's jaw.

"Get off me, Sam!" Josh growled as he tried to shove him away. "Stop it! Hey, man . . ." A thin line of blood trickled down the side of his mouth. Pushing against Sam with all his might, Josh rolled over on top of him and started to return the favor.

"Stop! Break it up, you two!" Kevin ran over to them, hauling Josh off him. Holding both men apart with considerable effort, he stared at Sam, wide-eyed. "What's going on here, guys?" The look Kevin directed his way conveyed his shock that he'd engaged in such a childish display of bad attitude and lost temper.

"You tell me and then we'll both know." Josh wiped one hand across his bleeding lip and glared at Sam. "Care to answer the man, Sam?"

He pointed a shaky finger at Josh. "You leave Lexa alone. I don't want to catch you near her again, Josh Grant." He tasted blood in the corner of his mouth.

"Oh yeah?" Josh fired back. "I'd like to see you make me do that. It's a free country, last time I checked. Why don't we let the lady make the decision?" he challenged, his voice full of contempt.

"Like you let Shelby make *her* decision?" Sam demanded.

Josh stared at him and then waved his hand at Kevin, dismissing him. "We'll take it from here, Kevin. Go. Sam and I need to talk privately."

Kevin had barely known Shelby, and had no idea what instigated their brawl. He looked over at Sam for his agreement. When he silently nodded, Kevin shook his head without another word and departed. He was such a quiet, peaceful man. He'd have to talk privately with Kevin later. Sam's heart sank even lower. How could he explain his actions without revealing more than he should?

He beckoned for Josh to follow him into the office. Even though they'd fought like wild dogs, he had to consider his position with TeamWork and deal with this situation like any other—in as calm, rational and objective a manner as possible.

"Sit down, Josh." It wasn't a request.

Dropping into a chair, Josh faced Sam across the wide expanse of the desk. Both were drenched through to the skin and caked in mud. They stared at one another, their breathing fast and labored.

"You weren't the only one who lost Shelby, Sam." Josh's voice sounded ragged, broken.

Sam's eyes narrowed and bore into Josh's. "I realize that. We all did. But how could you betray me, Josh? More importantly, how could you betray your own twin sister?"

"I didn't betray Beck. Shelby was going to come clean. We both were. We were going to confess our affair the next day. I swear it. You have to believe me. You . . ." he faltered. "You didn't know, did you?" Josh's green eyes widened.

"Know what?" His voice was a low growl, his jaws so tight he thought they'd snap.

"Shelby wasn't the sweet innocent you thought. She had lots of boyfriends before you." Josh fixed Sam with the intensity of his gaze. "I wasn't her first."

"I don't want to listen to this!" Sam brought his fist down hard on the desk. "Shelby's gone, so don't try to make yourself feel better by denigrating her memory. It's beneath you, and you don't know what you're talking about." He had to stop now or he'd erupt further. Closing his eyes tight, Sam prayed for the strength to deal with Josh. He clasped his hands together and tried to steady their shaking.

This situation was unlike anything he'd ever faced. This time it was too personal. He needed to apply biblical principles, now more than ever. That was also the hardest part. Sometimes all the prayer and Bible reading in the world couldn't stop his thoughts. He was human and failed so often. Sam lowered his head. *Lord, please help me find the right words.*

When he finally lifted his head again, Sam met the tears in Josh's eyes. Tears of an actor or tears of contrition, Sam couldn't be sure.

"I never meant to hurt anyone." Josh shrugged and shot Sam a helpless look. "Shelby was so beautiful. We were both consenting adults. It just happened."

The words were there, but Sam couldn't tell whether Josh felt true remorse. Had he confessed his sins to the Lord, asked forgiveness? That's what he needed more than anything else.

"I can't believe you just talked so callously about Shelby and Lexa. Women aren't playthings, to be bandied about and used, Josh. They're precious women God entrusted us to protect, honor and respect."

Josh shrugged again, but his green-eyed stare suddenly hardened. The look in his eyes was wild. "Man, has she ever got you twisted around her finger." His voice dripped sarcasm. "Lexa's just like Shelby," he taunted, "vulnerable and ready to be loved. What's wrong with showing them how gorgeous they are? Helping them see how womanly they can be?"

His grin was maddening, and it took everything within Sam not to strike the man down again. Finally, Josh's inner nature had emerged, and Sam glimpsed a different side of him he'd never seen before. A side that scared him, a facet of Josh's character that needed the kind of help Sam couldn't provide. Help from a trained professional, and more than a little from the good Lord Himself.

"Get out of my office, Josh. Leave my camp." It was hard to get out the words from between clenched jaws. "Don't bother reapplying for a TeamWork position unless you can prove you've repented and changed your ways. Go. Get the help you need." Shoving his chair back, scraping against the wooden floor, Sam rose to his feet. He stood his ground, facing him eye-to-eye.

"What are you talking about?" Josh demanded. "You can't throw me out of the camp!" He planted his hands on the desk. "Obviously, I gave Shelby something you couldn't, and I dare say Lexa . . ."

"Don't you dare say another word about Lexa!" Sam slammed his fist down hard again. "Enough! No more. As far as throwing you out of my camp, I can, and I am." Sam moved around the desk and hovered over the younger man, besting him by an inch. He fought to keep his hands at his sides. "It's something I should have done a long time ago. You don't deserve to be here. Now, get out before I have you thrown out!"

"I thought we were friends, Sam." Still no remorse.

"We are. I consider you my brother." His voice cracked. Sam stopped, swallowing hard. Josh had no idea how hard this was. It cut him like a knife that he didn't understand how much he'd hurt himself and others. Throwing him out of the camp was one of the hardest things he'd ever done. He cringed as he realized how much it would hurt Rebekah. "You have a deep problem, but you're too blind to see it. You need the kind of help I can't give you. Know I'll be praying for you, Josh. Always praying."

Josh refused his outstretched hand. That cut almost as deep as the betrayal. The Lord would have to deal with him now.

"I'll leave as soon as I get my things together." Yanking his TeamWork identification card out of his wallet, Josh shoved it under Sam's nose. "Looks like I won't be needing this anytime soon." When Sam didn't flinch and made no move to take the card, he slammed it down on the desk.

"One question." Josh hesitated at the door, his look hard and unyielding.

Sam's jaw tightened. "I'm listening." His eyes met those of his young friend one final time.

"Who's telling Rebekah?"

Chapter 28

_L_EXA WAS COMPLETELY dumbfounded. She had no idea what to make of the latest turn of events. Josh was gone, and according to the latest rumor, he'd been thrown out by a very angry Sam. Rebekah was sullen and weepy since her twin left, and the general mood of the camp was down. It was whispered that Kevin knew something about the quarrel between the two men that precipitated Josh's abrupt departure, but he was too discreet to say a word. Lexa hated the air of distrust and unspoken accusations so heavy in the air that affected everyone's mood.

If nothing else, the productivity of the TeamWork members increased. They'd already made good headway in rebuilding the two homes destroyed by the fire. From what Lexa heard, Sam hollered out orders and worked himself senseless, pounding away with a hammer and painting at all hours of the day and night. He barely ate, hardly slept. Sam must be trying to lose himself in his work. She wondered if Sam's insane work spurt might have something to do with their own tenuous relationship.

One afternoon, after dismissal of the classes at the makeshift schoolroom, Lexa walked over to the worksite with some of the other women. They wanted to help so they had a shot at finishing all the homes before the end of the mission. Rebekah opted to go back to the dorm. Lexa and Winnie tried to coax her into going with them, but she declined. Although Rebekah didn't say anything, Lexa suspected she wanted to stay as far away from the TeamWork director as possible.

One of the guys put them in charge of painting, and the girls set about their task as cheerfully as possible. Not wanting to appear obvious, Lexa looked around for Sam, but she overheard one of the men telling another that he'd gone into town.

It was much too quiet in the house. Dipping her paint roller into the pan, Lexa decided to get something started. "Anybody hear any good jokes lately?" She winked at Amy since she was the most outgoing. Being a journalist, she always seemed to have a good story or joke.

Taking the hint, Amy launched into an amusing story. Soon, the women and several of the men painting in an adjacent room shared a rousing exchange of everything from favorite old television stars and movie plots to the merits of televised football. They all laughed and joked as usual, the mood much more relaxed. It was a welcome change, and Lexa smiled with quiet satisfaction as she worked.

"Sam sure is a changed man," Natalie commented as they walked back to the campsite a couple of hours later. "Whatever happened between he and Josh must have been a real doozy." She shook her head. "Two Christian men should be able to work out their differences. I wouldn't have thought Sam had it in him to act so childish."

Lexa's spine stiffened at the comment, not wanting to pass judgment without knowing the facts. "I think Sam's eaten up about it. You've seen how despondent and withdrawn he is lately. It must have been something serious for him to force Josh to leave. Heaven knows, he needs all the workers he can get right now—especially good, faithful workers like Josh."

"What are you saying?" Winnie shot her a curious look.

Lexa shrugged. "I'm sure Sam had his reasons. If nothing else, I've learned he's a fair man. He may be a bit judgmental at times, certainly stubborn, perhaps impetuous . . . and grouchy," she murmured, shaking her head. "But overall, he's not a man to jump to conclusions and make rash decisions. That much I do know." Well, he *had* jumped to a conclusion about her, but that was an entirely different situation. How ironic

"I take it you and Sam aren't seeing each other anymore."

Lexa gaped at Winnie, not bothering to hide her surprise.

"What? Like you don't know you and Sam are the talk of the camp?"

"We are? I had no idea . . ." Lexa shook her head, dumbfounded. She shouldn't be surprised.

"Come on, Lexa," Winnie chided. "It was plain as day that you two were headed for the hot romance of the summer. For the record, I'm really sorry things didn't work out."

Lexa was silent, humiliated everyone in the camp knew her personal business. She imagined there'd also been speculation about why her relationship with Sam had soured. It was human nature to gossip, after all, even in the TeamWork camp.

Perhaps she should be grateful Josh's departure had taken precedence in the minds of the other volunteers in recent days and distracted their attention. She personally missed Josh's easygoing manner and his friendship. Her footsteps quickened, seized with the overwhelming urge to get as far away from the others as possible. She needed to distance herself so she could think and pray alone.

Lexa took off for the tree, bidding the others good-bye as they headed for the dorm. Sliding down to a sitting position, she crossed her arms on her knees.

"Oh Father, help Sam. I don't know what happened between him and Josh, but I know it must have been something very serious to have caused such a rift between them. Help them to look to you for guidance and wisdom in mending their fences and coming to a mutual understanding of how great you truly are. Help them know that you are the great healer of relationships. You can make things right again if they'd just get over their stubbornness long enough to see it."

A short while later, Lexa raised her head and started to stand. Stopping halfway up, she startled to see Sam sitting on the other side of the tree. She'd been so intent in her private time of prayer that she blocked out everything else around her. Sam's head was bowed, his eyes closed.

Lexa felt guilty, like an interloper invading Sam's private sanctuary. But the tree was their special meeting place, a place that held fond memories of shared closeness. All over again, her heart hurt. It would always ache whenever she thought of Sam and the TeamWork camp. Rising and quietly brushing the dust from her shorts, Lexa began to tiptoe away.

"Don't go."

Turning, Lexa looked down at Sam through veiled eyes.

"Please. I want to talk to you." Maybe it was his tone of voice, maybe it was the forlorn-looking expression, maybe it was those haunted blue eyes. She froze.

"Will you come sit down by me? It's kind of hard to talk to you when you're standing there glaring at me." The request was tinged with a hint of Sam's hidden humor. Lexa dropped down to sit beside him, her heart thundering.

"I suppose you're wondering what happened with Josh."

Lexa stared at the far distant horizon instead of looking into those incredible eyes. It was dangerous how she could so easily lose herself in them. She inhaled a quick breath. Her feelings for Sam were just the same as before. They hadn't changed at all. Even if he thought she was a wanton, loose woman, Lexa held special feelings for this man. In his heart, Sam couldn't believe she'd been having an affair with the same person as Shelby.

"I've heard rumors."

"I hope you don't believe them." He dislodged a dried clump of mud from the top of his boot and stretched out his long legs.

"I don't know what to believe, Sam. All I know is that I hate to see you, Rebekah and everyone else around here so down in the mouth. It's brought the whole spirit of the camp down. I'm sure that's not what you intended." Lexa drew a circle in the dirt by her feet. Both were doing a good job of avoiding eye contact.

"No, it's not."

When she dared look his way, Sam shook his head and ran a hand through his unruly hair before scratching his rough beard. He looked distracted, and she felt a tug on her heart. "Not to mention you're looking a bit shaggy there, Mr. Lewis," Lexa teased with a gentle smile. Sam chuckled. It wasn't full of the same humor as before, but it held promise and gave Lexa renewed hope.

"I was wondering if you'd go with me somewhere this Saturday. Just Saturday, and only for a few hours."

Lexa tilted her head, pretending to weigh the option. "I don't know. If I violate the terms of my probation, I could be in big trouble, mister. The director of this particular camp is pretty strict." When Sam cracked a small grin, her heart soared.

"Not a problem. The probation period is long gone. I know the director pretty well, and I know he'd give his stamp of approval. If it makes you feel any better, we'll throw in a little business on the side for good measure."

"I don't know . . ." Lexa repeated, looking up at him and meeting his gaze. Why did he want her to go with him? Did he want to rekindle their relationship? *Please, Lord, let it be so.*

"We don't have much longer at the camp, and I've made a decision."

"A decision?" Lexa blew out a sigh. Time for yet another surprise. Oh, joy. "You've got my attention now, so you might as well spill it." She had a feeling it was going to be another one of those surprises she'd rather not hear.

"I'm not going back to my financial planning business in Houston. I'm becoming a full-time director with TeamWork, supervising different projects around the world." Standing up and dusting off his hands, Sam started pacing beneath the tree. "Look, I didn't plan on just blurting it out like that, but I suppose there's no time like the present. This whole episode with Josh made me realize I need to be in a full-time, ministry-related position."

Sam gestured toward the campsite with one hand. "When I'm not busy being a jerk, I usually do a pretty decent job running these work camps. Don't judge me by this one. I've made some painfully obvious mistakes."

Lexa raised her head and rose to stand in front of him. Sam stopped pacing and they stood facing one another. Her heart was in her throat. She spoke quietly, forcing her voice to stay calm.

"Am I one of those mistakes, Sam?"

Sam stepped closer. At first, Lexa thought he would try and touch her, pulling her into the circle of his arms. But instead he stood about a foot away, his hands hanging at his sides. He watched her without speaking for what seemed like an eternity. He looked like he had so much to say, yet he said nothing for a long time.

"You might find this hard to believe, Lexa . . ." The lump in his throat was visible, the emotion evident in his eyes. "You're one of the best things to ever happen to me. But I blew it, big time. I'm so sorry I said those hateful, horrible things. So sorry I hurt you. You didn't do anything, and you didn't deserve my anger. You have to understand that I was overcome with a sudden, jealous anger. I didn't want to think lightning struck twice." Sam cleared his throat. "I pray in time you can forgive me."

"And why do you want me to come with you this weekend?"

The way he looked at her showed Lexa how much he cared. His eyes softened, and drew her in with their compassion. "I want to spend some time with you before you leave. I don't know when and if we'll see each other again. I know it's a lot to ask, but it's something I want. In here," he whispered, placing one hand over his heart. "Will you humor an old man, please?" His voice wasn't desperate, wasn't pleading, but it was deeply earnest.

Looking at him now, Lexa realized Sam really did want her company. To think she might not see him again after she left the worksite sent a spike into her heart. Lexa couldn't breathe. It was as strong—and painful—as a physical blow. She turned away from him and placed her arm across her abdomen.

"Lexa?" Sam was at her side in an instant, a light hand on her arm.

"I'm okay." Straightening up, she tried her best to recover her lost composure. Aware of Sam's concern, she couldn't reveal her true feelings. Lexa didn't want him to see how intensely she felt his words, how much she'd miss him when he wasn't in her life anymore. Not every day, not every week, month or possibly ever again. *Never.* Never seemed like such a crass, horrible word. It was so final, so abrupt.

She started to walk back toward the camp. As expected, he fell into step beside her. "I'll go with you this weekend, Sam."

"Good. And Lexa?"

"Yes?" She paused, looking up at him.

"Thanks for fixing my screen door. You did a great job."

"How did you know it was me?" She glimpsed those endearing smile lines.

A broad grin spread across his face, relaxing the worried lines etched on his forehead.

"Oh, I don't know. Maybe a little armadillo told me."

Chapter 29

$\mathcal{S}$AM PROVED A very knowledgeable, capable guide as he drove them into San Antonio late on Saturday morning. "San Antonio was founded in 1718 with the construction of the Spanish mission, the Villa de San Fernando, which was later called the Alamo." He turned left onto the main road that would take them into the city. "You might not know that San Antonio was also heavily influenced by a strong German immigration during the nineteenth century."

"Really?" Lexa's brows rose as she turned her head to gaze out the window. "That's surprising." She brushed a long strand of hair away from her face, and felt Sam's eyes on her. He'd been doing that a lot, but she didn't dare look at him. They might have an accident.

"You probably didn't make it to La Villita with the other ladies on your weekend off, did you?" When she shook her head, he continued. "La Villita is Spanish for little town, and it's the original settlement of Old San Antonio. It's on the east bank of the San Antonio River, developed in the mid-to-late 1800s, next to the Alamo. You'd really like it, and it's a shame I don't have time to show it to you. It's in the heart of the downtown district and has an active arts and crafts community."

He made another turn. "La Villita is similar to the Riverwalk with its restaurants and shops, but instead of a lot of hotels, there's this beautiful, dramatic backdrop of landscaped grounds and historical buildings that show the influence of the Spanish, Mexican, German, French, American and native Texan people who settled here. They have a big festival every year called The Fiesta to celebrate Texas's independence from Mexico."

"How do you know so much about San Antonio?" Lexa was impressed with his wealth of knowledge about most things in life, and it was clear he was a history enthusiast.

"My grandfather—my dad's father—lived here for years after my grandmother died." Sam's voice grew much softer at the mention of his grandparents.

"How long have they been gone?"

"My grandmother died about the time I started high school, and my grandfather died about seven years ago. They were both great people, full of life and active right up to the end. My grandfather used to rebuild the engines of old airplanes, and my grandmother made gorgeous quilts, and the best peach pie in the world."

"They sound wonderful. You must have loved them very much."

"I did. Grandpa Lewis used to love to come downtown with all us kids—all six of us, bless his heart, brave man—and he'd march us around for hours, showing us everything and pounding the history into our brains."

Lexa smiled. "Kind of a forced education?"

"I guess you could call it that," Sam agreed, laughing. "I'm the first to admit I never thought all that stuff would stay in my brain, but surprisingly, it has. Helps that I'm a history buff."

"Maybe it's also because you loved the teacher. It made the history lesson more personal. It helps you remember all those things."

Sam nodded, his appreciation for her comment reflected in his eyes.

"When did you decide to go to work full-time for TeamWork?" They sat in the car outside the lumber supply company after Sam picked up a few last building materials to complete the houses. After spending nearly an hour inside the store, the back of the station wagon was piled high with lumber, paint and other supplies.

"How much time do you have?" Sam pulled out of the parking lot. Although his tone was light, Lexa detected an underlying, serious undercurrent. "Want to have lunch before we head back to the campsite?"

It couldn't be a random suggestion. "I don't know. Our track record in public places isn't exactly the best."

His smile was infectious. "Well, then, we need to improve on it before you leave."

Sam kept bringing up the fact she was leaving soon. Did it really bother him that much? It was too late to do anything about it now. His decision had been made. Soon Sam would be traveling all over the world. Even if their romance had developed into something solid and strong, it would be nearly impossible to maintain a long-distance relationship under those less-than-desirable circumstances. Maybe it was better how things turned out, after all. But, the question remained—better for her, better for Sam, or better for both of them? It made her sad to think about it.

Looking down at his watch, Sam frowned, tapping the face a few times. "What time do you have?"

"Almost one o'clock. Why?"

He shook his head. "I think my watch has finally ticked its final minutes. I'll have to take the time," he said with a grin, "pun intended, to get a new one soon. But now, I don't want to be late for where I'm taking you." His sly grin said it all. "We're going somewhere special."

"So, you planned this all along."

"Would you expect anything else?"

"Not where you're concerned, Mr. Lewis." They shared a grin. "I certainly hope we're dressed appropriately." Lexa shot a disparaging glance at her shorts and casual top. Sam wore denim shorts, a black polo and his work boots. Although she tried to ignore them, it was hard to miss his well-toned, muscular legs. If only Sam wasn't so appealing in the physical sense, she wouldn't be so distracted. Not to mention his kisses sent her reeling at the mere thought of them. Which she often did. Which she tried to forget but never would.

Never—there was that awful word again. *I hate that word.*

"Are we going to McDonald's? Hey, you warned me you're frugal." Lexa loved teasing Sam, and adored the look on his face now. Kind of like a scrunched-up smirk. Totally irresistible.

He chose to ignore her barb. "I think we'll be all right. Besides, if they insist, they can give me a tie and jacket to throw on. I understand they always have a few hanging around on a coat rack somewhere."

"Oh, a fine dining establishment," Lexa cooed with a mock pout. "But what about me? Do they also keep skirts or dresses around?" A giggle escaped. Now she was getting silly.

"Well, they can just throw a jacket around your legs, although they'd be missing a spectacular view." Sam met her eyes for a second before returning his attention to the road.

Lexa's mouth flew open in surprise. It was the first flirtatious remark he'd made in weeks, and she was stunned. "Good to see you haven't lost your flirting instincts, Mr. Lewis." She slipped further down on the leather seat. Sam had thrown some old towels onto the seats to protect their skin from getting burned by the hot leather. Good thing.

"What about the supplies? I don't think you want the paint to explode." Lexa glanced over her shoulder at the various cans and boxes in the back of the car.

"I hadn't thought of that." Sam's brow furrowed as he chewed on his lip. "We actually only have a few items that might be in any real danger. Think they'll let me leave them in the coat check?"

"Maybe for an extra buck or two. If they even *have* a coat check at this time of the year. It's early August, you realize. I'm sure it's not in high demand."

"Then I'll just park them in a cool corner beneath a coat rack or under the table or something. But you're right. We don't want any paint explosions in the car." He looked over at her with a big grin.

"Oh, I don't know. It might actually liven up this old bomb."

Sam snorted. "Don't knock it, Miss Clarke. This old bomb, as you so fondly call it, has managed quite nicely, thank you." He reached out and patted the dashboard like he'd done when she first met him. Sam's car was like an old dog. Loyal and fairly reliable.

"It's gotten us where we needed to go during the last few weeks. I have some very fond memories of this car. Especially at *this* work camp." Sam's words dripped with meaning.

"Don't start getting all weird again about your precious old bomb." Lexa laughed. As much as she wanted to resist Sam, she was drawn to him more than ever. He was like a magnet. A big, strong magnet that attracted anything female within range. She scowled. This man would always continue to attract other women wherever he went. It was as inevitable as a bird finding its wings and learning to fly.

The saddest thing of all was that Lexa could have had Sam if she wanted him. And she did. But now it was too late.

Chapter 30

$\mathcal{A}$FTER DRIVING ALONG Scenic Loop Road for a short time, Sam exited onto a side road. "Close your eyes, please." He reached toward her with his right hand.

"I can do it myself," Lexa protested, covering both eyes. It brought back memories of playing hide-'n-seek with a playmate. *Catch me if you can*, she remembered taunting the other little girl. *Is that what I'm doing with Sam?*

She felt dizzy as the car turned a corner before Sam pulled to a smooth stop. "Okay. You can open your eyes now."

Lexa's eyes widened as she stared at the scene before her. She almost clapped in childlike delight, but clasped her hands together on her lap instead. "It's a castle!" She couldn't help it. She clapped anyway.

"It *is* something, isn't it?" Sam hopped out of the car and opened her door. As she put her hand in his, Lexa's hand trembled with the strong current of attraction as their fingers touched. She'd only read about such a thing happening in her romance novels. Until now. *Electrifying.*

Sam retrieved the cans of paint. "Don't want to forget these. And you're exactly right. This really is a castle." They approached the front entrance. "It's called The Green Manor Inn, and it was moved to Texas from England in the 1920s."

"Oh, Sam, now I really *do* feel underdressed." Lexa waited while he opened the heavy, wooden front door. "I should be Cinderella at the ball, but I'm dressed like a peasant woman."

"Ah, but that's the part about Cinderella I don't like." Coming through the door behind her, Sam's breath was warm on her neck. "You see, Cinderella didn't need the ball gown to make her the most beautiful woman at the ball."

Lexa rewarded his comment with a blinding smile. He deserved a kiss for that sentiment, but she wasn't sure how he'd react if she followed through on her impulse. Waiting as he took care of storing the paint in the coat check, she glanced about the charming restaurant, drinking in the ambiance. It was elegant and lovely. Her heart started its telltale thumping.

Lexa's fears of being underdressed were soon alleviated as they were ushered into the large, main dining area. Fresh flower arrangements adorned each pale pink, linen-covered table. Candles in the middle of the tables shimmered. Even with the light of day streaming in through the large vertical windows, it was still quite dim inside. Quite romantic, in fact. *Stop it, Lexa.*

"It's beautiful," she breathed. Sam walked beside her, one hand on her elbow. Following the hostess, Lexa smiled in appreciation as he pulled out her chair.

"Sure is," Sam said, taking his seat opposite her. He couldn't peel his eyes away from her. Lexa lowered her eyes first, fully aware Sam's comment did not refer to the restaurant.

"Don't, Sam," Lexa warned in a quiet voice. "Soon you'll be globetrotting the world for TeamWork. Besides, we're only here on business, remember?"

"Right." She heard the edge of agitation in that deep voice. "Thanks for reminding me." The waitress came to hand them menus and recite the specials of the day. Lexa couldn't remember any of them a minute later. As Sam thanked the pretty waitress, Lexa buried her face in her menu, her eyes blindly scanning it while her cheeks burned. The flirtatious glance the waitress gave Sam did not escape her notice. Bless his heart, he was either oblivious or preoccupied.

"You never answered my question." Lexa waited as a server delivered ice water to their table at Sam's request.

"Which question was that?" Sam's eyes sparkled.

"You know very well which question. When did you make this momentous decision to go to work for TeamWork full-time?"

He took a long, infuriatingly slow drink of his water before answering. "It's something I've been thinking of doing for a long time. I've just kept it on the back burner until now."

At least it wasn't a rash decision made in the heat of the moment. "It's quite a step of faith, Sam. I'm sure it will be tough, but I imagine it'll be a very gratifying decision in the long run."

He nodded. "I hope you're right. There's so much work to be done. There aren't enough men and women ready to give up their jobs to spearhead the projects." He shook his head and chuckled. "Not enough people *crazy* enough to do it is more like it."

"Not crazy. More like not enough people who are brave enough, smart enough and, more importantly—willing to trust God enough—to make it happen."

Sam smiled. "Thank you for saying that. Especially in the last few weeks, I've wondered if it's all a pipe dream." He leaned forward across the table. "Remember when I told you about my burden for the unsaved? That's what motivates me. I want projects that will put me in direct contact with the people. With this particular project, I've felt a little . . ."

"Stagnant?" Lexa remembered his use of the term soon after she arrived at the camp.

"Exactly. I want to be wherever God leads me, and where TeamWork sends me, of course. But my heart is in the projects where I'm working side-by-side with people who need to see the love of the Lord in action."

"You've done that to a certain extent here in San Antonio, Sam."

"I hope so." His eyes met hers. "The work projects are what energize me, keep me going, give me hope. Building churches in the Dominican Republic, starting schools in the jungles of deepest Africa, conducting open-air services in

South America, or staying right here in the United States providing flood relief." He shrugged. "Where He leads, I'll go. That's basically my philosophy."

Sam's eyes lit with enthusiasm as he talked. How great to feel so impassioned about following the Lord's will that he poured his energy, his very soul into it. "But . . ." Lexa began, hesitating.

"But what?" Sam took another drink of the ice water, watching her closely.

"What about a home?" She didn't want him to read too much into the question. She didn't want him to think she was asking for personal reasons. "I mean," she continued, clearing her throat, "what about having a place to call home? I mean your *own* home, not just the Lewis family homestead in Houston. Doesn't that mean anything to you?"

After a long moment, Sam nodded. "Yes, of course it means something to me. I want a home, and all that goes along with it . . . when the time is right."

"I see." Lexa sat back against the cushions of her seat and waited as the waitress placed her salad on the table. "But . . ." she started again. She avoided looking at him.

"Go on. Don't be afraid to ask." Sam tried to catch her eye again.

"I'm not afraid to ask." Raising her head and meeting his gaze once more, Lexa took a quick breath. "I'm just afraid of what you might read into the question." Might as well plunge right in. Sam was pretty good at reading her emotions.

"I guess what I'm trying to ask is how you ever hope to establish a permanent relationship, much less a home, if you're always somewhere out there," Lexa floundered, gesturing with one hand, "sleeping on rooftops and in makeshift buildings. It might be fine for a while, but don't you think you'd get tired of it at some point?"

"I'll have to answer that after I've done it for a period of time. For now, I'm only committing to a period of one year to see how it goes. No more, no less. When the year's up, I'll have the option of applying for more time as a TeamWork director. On the other hand, at the end of the year, I could also suspend or permanently terminate my working relationship with them."

"Oh." Even though she was relieved, Lexa wasn't sure she wanted him to see it.

"Sounds like you might have a personal interest at stake," Sam observed with a wry grin.

Snapping her head up to look at him, Lexa frowned. "Don't flatter yourself, Mr. Lewis. Why don't we pray for this food before it gets any colder?"

"Oh, I don't know. I think the conversation's starting to get pretty warm." Sam laughed at Lexa's frown, and bowed his head to ask the blessing.

She wished he'd grasp her hand for their prayer, but he didn't. But neither did she reach for his hand.

Their conversation flowed freely, without too much unease or awkwardness. He was almost the same old Sam, but without so much of the teasing. Today, he was a caring lunch companion. He asked polite questions, listened to her answers, and gave her his undivided attention. She liked this side of him, and appreciated his kind gesture in bringing her to this special place.

"How about you?" Sam stabbed another bite of his prime rib and plopped it into his mouth with a look of extreme satisfaction. It was gratifying to see his healthy appetite had finally returned. "What are your plans when you go back to Houston?"

"I haven't thought too much about it," Lexa admitted, wiping her mouth with the napkin. Should she tell him her job might not be waiting for her when she returned? "I suppose I'll go about my life as usual."

"You don't sound particularly enthusiastic about it."

"I suppose I'm not." She took another small bite of her chicken breast, chewing slowly. "It's not like I have many other options."

"My point exactly." Sam placed his knife across the edge of his plate, fixing Lexa with the intensity of his gaze. "Here's something for you to consider." He leaned closer across the table, covering her hand with his, lacing his fingers with hers.

"Come with me, Lexa."

Chapter 31

"I BEG YOUR pardon?" Lexa blurted out, shocked.

"You heard me. Come with me. Apply to be an assistant director of TeamWork. We can work together, and get to know one another better in the process."

"Are you . . ." Lexa started. Noticing the curious stares of other diners, she forced her voice lower. "Have you lost your mind, Sam? How on earth can I possibly do that? What makes you think I'd even *want* to do such a thing?"

She shook her head in disbelief. "The last time I checked, you spouted serious accusations that prove you don't trust me any further than you can see me. Has something happened to change your mind?"

Sam waved one hand in dismissal. "Have you already forgotten our conversation under the tree? I was wrong and knew it the minute those words came out of my mouth that awful night. You don't have a dishonest, cheating bone in your body. I know I have to prove to you that I trust you, but I *do* trust you, Lexa. Surely you must know that." He hesitated. "After what happened with Shelby, I've had a little trouble trusting people."

"You mean trusting *women*." Sam had been deeply crushed by Shelby's betrayal. It had been hard, if not impossible, for him to trust again.

"All right," he admitted. "You're right. Look, I hope you can forgive me, because I really care for you, Lexa. I'd love to have a relationship, a romance." Sam's expression was sheepish. "With *you*. But if all you're willing to give me is friendship, then fine. So be it. Above all else, I want to see you happy. It's more than obvious you're not particularly content with your life in Houston."

Sam leaned across the table again, his expression as earnest as she'd ever seen it. "You're also growing by leaps and bounds in the love of Christ. I'd love to see that continue. I'm afraid that if you go back to your old life in Houston, you're going to get stagnant, and what you've started here will wither and maybe die. I don't want to see that happen. I care too much about you."

His words were blunt and they stung, but what Sam said was true. "It'd be exciting and you know it. Think of all the fun we could have together." His brows rose in a provocative manner.

"You must have an awfully high opinion of yourself, or else a very low opinion of me." Lexa flung her napkin on the table, her appetite gone. "To think that I'd follow you . . ." Maybe her attitude was childish, but his words stirred her up inside, made her want to shout with anger. And jump for joy. All at the same time. Oh, it was maddening.

"I didn't say anything about following me. It's purely your decision. But we'd be working the mission together, side-by-side as much as possible. I can keep all the exotic animals away from you, and you can try to keep me in line." The smile lines surfaced, and the man had the audacity to wink.

Sam looked much too calm—and way too smug—for her liking. "You're incredibly infuriating!" Lexa started to rise from her chair. "I don't know why we can't sit and have one decent meal without me getting all steamed at you. You just . . ." she spouted, searching for the right words, "you just have this way of bringing out the worst in me sometimes!"

Sam surprised her by laughing. "Sit down, and let's talk about this rationally, like two adults. You can't keep flying off the handle and running away from confrontations, you know."

Lexa stared at him, open-mouthed. "How dare you talk to me like that?" Not wanting to cause another public scene, but not quite able to contain her extreme reactions to this man, Lexa slumped back down into her chair. "Contrary to what you may believe, you don't know everything about me. I'm beginning to realize you know very little, as a matter of fact." She crossed her arms.

"I know one thing. You're much more beautiful when you smile. That little frown thing you've got going on there doesn't do justice to your features." His words sounded as dispassionate as if he was repeating the weather forecast.

A nervous giggle slipped out. She simply didn't know how else to react. "Maybe I am acting childish. Point taken." The beginnings of a grin tugged at the corners of her mouth even as she tried to prevent it. "I'm not sure we'd make such a good team. Seems we're always pulling the wrong strings with each other."

"Well, for one thing, we could work on it," Sam offered, taking another long sip of his water. Lowering his glass to the table, he released a satisfied sigh. "I know I'm certainly willing to try, and I'd embrace the opportunity."

"You never stop, do you?" Lexa shook her head as she took another bite of her lukewarm chicken, not really tasting it.

"I try not to. After all, I have to keep you interested, don't I?"

"Flirt," Lexa accused, laughing again.

"Takes one to know one." The man didn't miss a beat.

"Just promise you'll think about it," Sam said a short time later as he drove them back into the camp. "Think about joining TeamWork with me."

"I don't know." Doubts clouded her mind, confusing her. "It's an awful lot to consider."

"Of course," he said, surprising Lexa by his ready agreement. Turning toward her in the car, Sam put his arm across the back of the seat. He was close enough to touch her arm and shoulder with his fingers if he wanted. Following her gaze, Sam moved his hand away, but not where Lexa hoped. She climbed out of the car and headed in the direction of the women's dorm with slow steps.

"Lexa?" She heard the hope, the optimism, in his deep voice.

Turning back around, she gave him a brilliant smile. "Okay, Sam. I promise."

A wide grin spread from ear-to-ear across Sam's handsome face. That incredible smile was getting way too addictive.

Chapter 32

*D*URING THE NEXT few days, all Lexa could think about was Sam's proposition about joining the TeamWork foreign mission. With him. It was only a week until she was scheduled to leave TeamWork and return to Houston. *Seven days.*

Sam talked more openly and freely with her again. Although they resumed much of their previous teasing relationship, he didn't make a move to reconnect with her on a more personal level. Lexa wasn't sure whether to be sad or worried. They both must have a problem trusting others.

Still, Sam wouldn't have asked her to join him on the TeamWork foreign mission if he didn't care about her. He'd suggested it as a way for them to spend more time together and get to know each other better. It was a big step of faith. *Am I ready to take such a big step?*

"How do you feel about it?" Winnie asked after Lexa confided in her. She wanted to talk about it with Rebekah since she was so close to Sam, but the younger girl had been quiet and withdrawn ever since Josh left the camp, and didn't talk much with anyone. Lexa wanted to help but didn't know how. She had the odd feeling the feud between Sam and Rebekah's twin had something to do with her, although she couldn't be sure and no one said anything. She'd been tempted a few times to ask Sam about it, but chickened out at the last minute. Especially if it had nothing to do with her, she'd feel foolish for asking.

"I'm not sure." Lexa slumped down onto her bed with a heavy sigh. "I'm tempted because, let's face it, my life's not exactly thrilling back in Houston. I love this work camp because I'm doing something to help someone besides myself. But, then again, I'm sure I could find a project back in Houston through one of the local churches." She waved her hand as though mentally dismissing the idea. "Besides, it's not like I need to go globetrotting halfway around the world to find a worthwhile project when there are so many at my own back door."

"Lexa, don't get mad, but I want to ask you something." Lexa looked over at Winnie in surprise, scooting over on the bed so she could sit beside her. Whenever anyone prefaced a remark with that particular phrase, she was always wary, knowing it usually meant a compliment was *not* forthcoming.

"Go ahead."

"You keep alluding to how dull your life is back in Houston. At the risk of sounding trite, life is what you make it." Winnie slid an arm around her shoulders. "Why have you settled for anything less than what you really want?"

Lexa frowned at the question, but she wasn't upset. "Maybe it's because I haven't known what it is that I want."

"And now you do?"

"No, but maybe working with TeamWork will help me figure it out."

"Sounds to me like it will help you decide if you and Sam belong together." Winnie squeezed her shoulder. "Are you afraid you'll lose Sam if you don't go with him?"

"I hadn't really thought of it in those terms, but maybe you're right." Lexa shrugged. "Between you and me, Sam's the most thrilling—not to mention the most infuriating—man I've ever met. He's got that charming smile, those witty comebacks, he's knowledgeable, he's strong in his relationship with the Lord, he's a great leader . . ."

Winnie giggled. "Yes, I know. Our Sam has many fine qualities. But, the main question here is, do you *love* him?"

Lexa's heart pounded at the question. She stared at Winnie for another long moment, not speaking, not daring to admit her feelings to someone else. She hadn't known Sam long, but she loved him with everything in her heart and soul. So much so it scared her witless.

Winnie smiled. "Sweetie, the look on your face tells me everything I need to know, not to mention the way your voice softens when you talk about him. Your eyes positively glow with happiness when you're around him. Don't even get me started on the way you and Sam look at each other. It's downright combustible between you two."

Lexa opened her mouth to say something, but nothing came out. Had she and Sam been that obvious to everyone in the camp?

"Maybe you should ask Sam why he kicked Josh out of the camp." The voice came from a dark corner of the room. Neither Winnie nor Lexa noticed Rebekah sitting quietly on her bed.

"What was that, Rebekah?" Winnie darted a quick glance at Lexa.

"I think Lexa should ask Sam why he kicked Josh out," Rebekah repeated, staring at the ground, shuffling her feet. Her hair was a bit disheveled, and dark circles rimmed her eyes.

"I think you should ask him that, Rebekah." Lexa tried to gain eye contact, but Rebekah avoided her probing stare. Pulling up her knees, she clasped her hands around them. She looked so forlorn and sad, as if she'd lost her best friend. Maybe she had.

"I don't know that it's any of my business. Since Josh is your brother, Sam might tell you, especially considering the fact that you're such close friends."

Rebekah snorted. "Right. Friends. I thought that's what we were, but then again, that's what Josh thought, too, until Sam ruthlessly stabbed him in the back." She shook her head. "No, thanks. Friends like that, I don't need."

Lexa bristled at Rebekah's harsh words, spoken out of hurt and anger. She took a deep, steadying breath. "I know I haven't known Sam as long as you, but he's a fair man. I know he must have had a valid reason for what he did. He takes his position as a TeamWork director very seriously."

"Yeah," Rebekah muttered. "Maybe too seriously. Maybe the power's gone to his head. He's got you and everyone else at this camp snowed under with his abundant charm and overwhelming personality." She rocked back and forth on the bed, staring at the floor.

"Have you tried asking your brother what happened?" Winnie's voice was gentle.

Rebekah shook her head. "No. I haven't talked with him since he left. I called Mom, but she said he hadn't come home and hadn't even told them what happened. We're all worried about him. Josh isn't a quitter and everything's always come easy for him, easier than for me." Rebekah's tone held not a trace of jealousy or envy. "He's not used to resentment and forcible ejection either. It must have been a crushing blow to his ego."

"All right then, come with me." Getting up from her bed, Lexa headed toward the screen door.

"What?" Rebekah stared at her, wide-eyed.

"You heard me. Let's go over to Sam's office right now. If he's there, you can ask him what happened with Josh. This situation is eating you up inside, and that's not good for anyone, especially you. It's time to clear this up so you can put it past you."

"I'm not sure," Rebekah protested.

"It's a great idea, Beck." Winnie jumped up and ran over to Rebekah and put a light hand on her arm. At least she didn't shrug her away. "Lexa's right, sweetie. Go straighten all this out with Sam. That way you'll finally know what happened. You know it's the only way to get past this anger and bitterness you're harboring." Pulling her off the bed, Winnie practically dragged her over to the door beside Lexa.

"How do you know I'm going to like Sam's answer?"

Rebekah's voice was so quiet, Lexa had to strain to hear the question. "Is that what you're afraid of? What Sam's going to say if you ask him?"

With a slow nod, Rebekah's eyes filled with tears as they met Lexa's. "Yes. You're right about Sam making careful decisions. I think there's a part of me that's scared of what Josh might have done to get himself kicked out."

"Well, instead of blaming Sam, let's ask him and get it over with. Then you can deal with it and hopefully work out this tension between you. Come on." Stepping outside and holding the door, Lexa paused long enough to make sure Rebekah followed.

The walk across the campsite to Sam's office was silent. Knocking on the door, Lexa's breathing grew shallow. If she was this nervous, she could just imagine how Rebekah felt.

Chapter 33

"COME IN." IT was dim inside the office, and Lexa hesitated, waiting for her eyes to adjust. Sam sat up straighter behind the desk and smiled. "Ah, two of my favorite workers. Come in, please. Have a seat." Removing his glasses, he motioned for them to take the chairs in front of his desk. "What's on your mind?"

When Rebekah remained silent, Lexa spoke up, getting right to the heart of the matter. "Rebekah wants to know why you ordered Josh to leave the camp."

"Is that right?" Sam looked from Lexa over to Rebekah. The latter nodded silently.

Sam put down the pen he'd been holding. "Lexa, would you mind leaving us so that Rebekah and I can talk privately, please?" He looked so earnest, and his eyes implored hers.

"Certainly," she mumbled, rising from her seat and heading to the door. This must be what it felt like to be dismissed from the principal's office. But she respected and understood Sam's need for privacy. He quickly walked across the room to pull open the door for her. With a lingering glance at Rebekah, nodding at her for reassurance, Lexa turned to leave.

"No, wait! I want her to stay. You can't say anything to me that Lexa can't hear." At Rebekah's words, Sam hung his head and muttered something unintelligible.

"Please, Sam," Rebekah reiterated.

"Are you sure that's what you want?" Sam shook his head. "You should talk to your brother. *He* should be the one to explain it to you."

Rebekah groaned and her eyes lit with anger. "No one knows where Josh is right now, so it's not like I can just call him up and talk to him. I'm sick and tired of everyone telling me to talk to Josh. I'm here to talk to *you*. I want some answers, and I'm not leaving your office until I get them." She crossed her arms and sat up straighter in the chair.

"I guess your mind's made up then." Sam's voice was resigned, and he eased himself back down into his chair. He nodded at Lexa to take her place again. "In a way, this actually concerns you, too, Lexa."

Her brows shot up in surprise as she once again sat next to Rebekah. Although she'd suspected as much, she couldn't be sure. A rising sense of dread stirred in the pit of her stomach. Sam appeared uneasy, chewing his lip, his brow furrowed.

"What do you want to know, exactly?" Sam watched Rebekah through veiled blue eyes. His mouth settled into a grim, straight line, but he held her gaze steady.

"Lexa just told you," Rebekah cried in exasperation, throwing her hands in the air. "I want to know what happened between you and Josh, and why you threw him out of the camp."

Sam sighed and raked his hand through his hair. "It has to do with Shelby."

"Shelby? What about Shelby?" Rebekah shook her head, surprise mingled with confusion etched in her expression.

"I wasn't the only one having a relationship with her."

Rebekah stared at Sam. "Josh?" She was incredulous. "You're trying to tell me that Josh and Shelby . . . ?" She hesitated to absorb this latest bit of information. "No way!" Bounding out of the chair, Rebekah stalked across the floor. Leaning back against a file cabinet, she shook her head slowly back and forth. "I can't believe it. I *won't* believe it."

"Not only did he have a relationship with her, but it was a physical one. Josh and Shelby were apparently deeply involved." The words were quiet but firm, leaving no room for doubt.

"You're crazy! I can't believe you've deluded yourself into believing these lies!" Tears streamed from her eyes and down her cheeks as Rebekah glared at him. "That can't possibly be true! You've made all this up to justify Shelby's death in some sick, twisted way."

"Beck, sit down and let's talk about this calmly." Sam's voice remained steady as he motioned for her to take her seat again.

"Don't you come near me, Sam Lewis!" Rebekah visibly withdrew and turned her head. Sam crossed the room and reached out in an attempt to draw Rebekah back over to the chair. He murmured quiet, soothing words, but Rebekah shook her head, putting her hands over her eyes.

Lexa didn't doubt the truth of any of it. Josh was the man with whom Shelby was involved. As horrible as it was, Sam spoke the truth. Her heart ached for them all.

"You were angry with Shelby that night. She told me all about it," Rebekah spouted, the words harsh and bitter, wounded. With the back of her hand, she sniffled and wiped the tears from her cheeks. Her eyes were full of hurt as she dared to look up at Sam. "You made her cry, and she ran off into the city with Jake because you pushed her away."

Sam hung his head and when he looked back up, Lexa saw his tears. "True, we quarreled the night she died. I gave Shelby an ultimatum. It was either Josh or me. I told her I was willing to forgive her relationship with him if she repented of her sin and asked forgiveness."

"Oh, you'd never forgive her and you know it! You wouldn't forgive a betrayal like that," Rebekah shot back. "You backed Shelby into a corner, and she felt like she had no way out. She was like this trapped, little scared animal at your will and mercy. You used her just like you use everyone else in your life!"

For a fleeting moment, Lexa glimpsed his deep hurt. Sam flinched, his jaw visibly tightened and his fists clenched at his sides. His voice was thick with emotion when he spoke. "It wasn't *my* forgiveness Shelby needed."

Sam's gaze moved over to Lexa. "She needed to repent and ask forgiveness from the Lord." He paced across the room, gathering his thoughts. Lexa knew he wanted to be as gentle as he could with Rebekah, softening the harsh truth to spare her feelings. "In my heart, I believe Shelby knew what she was doing was wrong. The problem is, Josh didn't think it was wrong then, and he apparently still doesn't."

Lexa fully expected Rebekah to erupt again, but she stood motionless, her eyes dull. When she spoke again, her voice was flat, eerily devoid of emotion. "How does Lexa fit into this picture?"

Lexa shrank back against the hard, wooden chair. This whole situation was unnerving. It should be a private exchange where she had no place. But Rebekah had asked the primary question lingering in her own mind, one she was afraid to voice.

Sam's eyes softened as they found hers again. "Quite frankly, Josh wanted to know if I was through with her, as he so crudely put it. Sorry, Lexa " Sam's focus darted back to Rebekah. "You know I never want to hurt you, Beck. I care deeply about both you and Josh, but your brother has some problems he needs to deal with, and I pray he gets the help he needs. He's a great guy—strong, intelligent and more than capable of doing anything he wants—but he definitely needs to put a leash on his behavior or he's going to get into even deeper trouble somewhere down the line."

"Why are you lying about this?" Rebekah accused, her anger overtaking her once more as she stalked toward the door. "Are you trying to protect your precious reputation? Trying to make it look good for Lexa?"

Sam made no move to stop her as she put one hand on the door. "I'm not trying to make it look good for anyone." He looked beaten down, desperate, his voice heavy with exhaustion. "I'm telling you the truth. I'm sorry. I never meant for you to find out this way. I think when you calm down and think about it, you'll realize in your heart that what I'm saying is true."

He blew out a long, ragged breath. "I have absolutely nothing to gain by lying. You and I have been through too much together, Beck, and you know it. Maybe you don't believe me now, but in time you will."

Without another word, Rebekah stormed out the door, and it slammed hard behind her. Sam was visibly shaken, his face pale, his eyes glazed as he slumped down into his chair. He hung his head, defeat in his sagging shoulders.

Lexa silently rose from her chair and moved behind the desk to stand beside him. When he looked up at her, his eyes shining, Lexa opened her arms. Reaching for her, Sam clung tight, his dark head resting against her stomach. His arms found their way around her. His hold tightened, and he closed his eyes. A tear escaped, followed by another.

"I'm so sorry, Sam." Lexa stroked gentle fingers through his thick, dark hair. She brushed a kiss over her the top of his head and leaned her head against his.

Finally surrendering to the overwhelming emotion, Sam wept. His shoulders shook, and he burrowed his head against her, muffling quiet sobs. She'd hold on as long as he needed her, thankful he wasn't embarrassed. Most men considered tears a sign of weakness, vulnerability and a concession to male pride. Sam Lewis was a giant among men in so many ways. But in that moment, he needed the comfort only a woman can give. A woman who truly loved him, heart and soul.

Chapter 34

THE NEXT EVENING, sharing leaning rights at the tree, Sam made yet another startling announcement. "I think you should know I never would have married Shelby."

Lexa couldn't hide her shock. "Why not?"

Taking a moment to compose his thoughts, Sam released a long sigh. "Shelby was all about trying to prove something to the world. But she was too young. It never would have worked out between us for the long haul."

"I don't know what to say." Lexa didn't bother reminding him that, being five years older than Rebekah, she was also Shelby's age. She also understood he meant something other than chronological age.

"I should think you'd be somewhat relieved." He chuckled and drew up his knees, his arms clasped around them. Leaning his chin on his arms, he looked over at Lexa with a thoughtful expression.

"Why?"

"I think you know why, Lexa. A lot of my friends were getting married at the time, so I figured it was also time for me to move on to that natural, expected phase of my life. Sad, I know, but true all the same. Shelby just happened to be there at the time, and she was certainly more than willing."

He shrugged and stared straight ahead. "She actually brought up the whole marriage thing. Out of convenience as much as anything else, I went along with it. We didn't date that long, if you can even call it that." He paused. "When we fought that last night, I think we both knew in our hearts that it was over. We were just kidding ourselves."

Lexa shifted. "Did you ever truly forgive Shelby for the affair with Josh?"

Sam's eyes never left her face. "I still struggle with that one. Put it this way—my head forgave her, but it's taken a lot longer for my heart."

"I'm sure it takes a lot of time to heal from something like that."

He nodded, and waited a long moment before speaking. "Before Shelby, I was too focused on my career and ministry with TeamWork to try and develop a lasting relationship with a woman. And after . . . well, after what happened with Shelby, I've poured myself back into the ministry so much that it's pretty much consumed me. Little by little, I'm learning to surrender my bitterness to the Lord. It's one of my biggest struggles." He rubbed his hand over his brow and leaned back against the tree, shaking his head.

Lexa settled beside him. "Thank you for sharing that with me. I'll pray that you can surrender those feelings to the Lord. I can't imagine what it's been like for you. To be betrayed by someone you love." She captured his hand in hers and ran a light finger over the callus on his palm. His hands were strong and yet so gentle. Kind of like the man himself—strong on the outside, but tender and soft on the inside.

"I think you know more about it than you realize." When she looked up at him, scooting closer, Sam leaned his forehead against hers. "Your dad, Lexa."

Lexa lowered her head to his broad shoulder. "I never thought about it like that. I'm sure he didn't mean to betray me. He just wasn't a sensitive man, and he didn't know how to show his love. But I know he did. Deep down, I know he cared more about me and my mom than he ever showed us. I hope he didn't feel betrayed because my mom died, leaving him alone with me." She shook her head, pushing wayward strands of hair away from her cheek. Raising her head, her eyes searched his. "I can't think that way. I know what my heart needs to know."

Sam kissed her then, stirring all of Lexa's senses. How long it went on, she couldn't know. It was more sweet than passionate, and as tender as she could ever imagine. Before he drew away, he sighed, and she felt his smile.

"I never felt about Shelby the way I feel about you, Lexa." Sam's lips traced a light path across her cheek. She gloried in his nearness, wondering if he'd take the leap of faith and tell her he loved her. If he did, how would she respond? They were quite the pair.

Closing her eyes, Lexa sighed in contentment. Tomorrow would take care of itself. She'd read a verse about that very thing in the Book of Matthew. It also talked about each day having enough trouble of its own. True enough. Better to enjoy this time of peace and quiet while it lasted.

They sat in companionable silence for a few minutes, hands clasped tightly together. Lexa snuggled against Sam, and he put his arm around her, nestling her even closer. At least it wasn't too humid, and a slight breeze ruffled through the tree overhead.

"What's your favorite movie?"

He chuckled. "What brought that on?"

"You can tell a lot about someone by the movies they like, you know. Kind of like learning about their fears."

"Is that so?"

"Answer the question, please."

"Okay. *The Ten Commandments*."

Lexa rolled her eyes. "Biblical epics don't count. They're a given."

He thought a moment. "Then, I'd have to say *Star Wars* is pretty cool. *Planet of the Apes* was fascinating." He snapped his fingers. "*Witness*! I loved that one." His lips spread in a wide grin. "Have at it."

"That's an easy one, cowboy." She stretched out her legs beside him and leaned back against the tree. "The whole fish out of water element appeals to you. Philly cop plopped down in the land of the Amish. It challenges you, gets your blood pumping through your veins. My Dad liked it, too."

"True. But the whole barn-raising thing is great since it's like our TeamWork project here in San Antonio. Neighbor helping neighbor." He smiled. "And your favorite movie is *The Sound of Music*."

"How did you . . . ?" She snapped her mouth closed.

"You mentioned it the first day we met. In the car. You brought up singing . . . and skipping. You like the idea of family, of belonging. Even though it's entirely unrealistic for people to burst into song at any given moment." He laughed.

It was Lexa's turn to laugh. "Right. And intergalactic wars and apes annihilating humans and taking over the world is realistic." She shook her head. "Do you remember everything?"

Leaning close, Sam whispered, "Everything, beautiful girl." The warmth of his lips sent shivers everywhere. It was amazing what a brush, a glance, a kiss from this man could do.

Lexa gave him a coy smile.

He laughed. "Oh, oh. I'm in for trouble now."

"I'm sure you left something out in the description of your dating history."

"Explain thyself, please." A smile tipped the corners of his mouth.

Lexa took a deep breath. "I'm sure you've dated your share of women. After all . . . well, take a good look at you." However lame it sounded, it was true. Although he looked surprised, she could tell he was pleased. "And you can't tell me the way you kiss is merely a God-given talent, Sam. It takes practice to be that good."

Sam looked at her with a look so loving it stole her breath. "No, Lexa."

"No . . . what, exactly?"

"It doesn't take practice. All it takes is finding the *right* woman."

Sam's statement would silence most women, but she couldn't let it go without comment. He shouldn't be surprised. "Are you actually telling me you haven't kissed many women?"

His jaw dropped. "Are you actually looking for a number?"

"Yes, I guess I am. If you can even count that high." Lexa didn't care if she sounded jealous. She loved teasing him as much as anything else.

He shook his head, as if disbelieving she'd even suggest such a thing. "Okay, Miss Clarke, you want a number?" When she nodded, Sam made sure he had her full attention. First, he looked upward as though taking a mental count. Looking back at her, he raised two fingers.

"You're giving me the peace sign?" Lexa laughed. "Oh, I get it. You're afraid to tell me how many. What is that, like a truce or something?"

"It's a number." Sam's voice was quiet, contemplative.

Lexa swallowed hard and stared at him sitting there—so handsome, strong, wonderful. "You've only kissed *two* other women in your life?" How was that even possible?

When Sam shook his head again, Lexa fully expected him to tell her he was teasing. She wouldn't be surprised. It certainly seemed more logical.

"No, not two other women. Two women total. And I'm sitting here tonight, against this tree, under the Texas sky, looking directly at one of them." The words were slow, full of purpose. "And with God's help, she'll also be the last one."

With those indelible words stamped on her heart, Lexa reached for him, pulling this precious man toward her. Cupping his face between her hands, she planted a long, very lingering kiss on the sweetest man she'd ever meet.

"Welcome home, Sam Lewis."

Chapter 35

"*I'M* SORRY I acted like such a jerk."

Again Lexa was surprised, but pleasantly so, by the turn of events.

Pulling Rebekah into a quick embrace, Lexa hugged her tight. "That's okay. I understand. You had quite a bitter pill to swallow." She released her. "I was afraid you might leave the camp after the meeting with Sam. I'm glad you stayed. I've . . . I've been praying for you." A couple of months ago, she'd never have said something like that. Now, the words practically rolled off her tongue, and it was natural to talk about such things.

"Call me Beck. My close friends do." She gave her a small smile.

"Thanks, Beck." Lexa returned the smile. "Have you heard from Josh yet?"

Rebekah nodded, a shadow crossing her face. "Yes, thank the Lord. He's finally back home. I asked him about Shelby, and he broke down and confessed everything. Our pastor back in Louisiana is going to counsel him about his, uh, problem. He's going to take some time off for a while, and get the help he needs, like Sam said. Law school will have to wait." She shrugged. "It'll be there when he's ready. I can't believe my own twin is a . . . a sex addict," she whispered, her cheeks coloring with embarrassment.

Lexa wasn't quite successful at hiding her shocked surprise. There had certainly been a lot of those lately. Enough for a good long while. "I don't know if I'd call him a sex addict because of one affair."

"There have been others. Lots, apparently." Rebekah's eyes traveled to the floor. "Shelby was only one in a long string of girls."

"Don't be embarrassed." Recovering her composure, Lexa draped an arm around the other girl's shoulder. "From what I understand, it's an addiction like anything else—drugs, alcohol, prescription drugs, and any number of things. Josh is a good man and . . ."

"But for a *Christian* man, it's especially embarrassing," Rebekah interrupted. "We have a responsibility to model Christ-like behavior. What use are we if we're known to be a Christian and then go around acting like some kind of wild, untamed beast?" Her words sounded bitter.

She glanced back up at Lexa. "I'm sorry. I'm taking out my frustrations with Josh on you. That's not fair. I still have a lot to resolve in my own mind, I guess. I'm mad as blazes at him right now, but I'll get over it. When I get home next week, I'm going to take the time to get reacquainted with my brother." She shook her head. "Apparently, there's a lot I don't know about him. And a lot I *should* know."

"I'm sure you want to do whatever's necessary to help Josh. Your encouragement will mean the world to him." Lexa squeezed her shoulder.

"Right." Rebekah sniffled and wiped away a few tears rolling down her cheeks. "I'm just thankful you weren't his next conquest. I knew the fight between Josh and Sam had something to do with you, but I couldn't be sure. At first, I thought Sam was upset when he lost his chance with you and was jealous because Josh was obviously interested. But now I know that Sam was protecting your honor, standing up for you." Rebekah stopped, making sure she had Lexa's eye contact. "I hope you know that man loves you."

Lexa's breath caught in her throat. "Did Sam tell you this?"

Rebekah squeezed her hand. "He didn't have to. Remember, I know the man pretty well."

"Are you going to talk with Sam? Set things right between you again?"

The beginnings of a smile curved Rebekah's lips. "I can't stay mad at Sam for long. I'm sure you know that's impossible. I've already apologized to him for saying those awful things." Her eyes glazed, and she shook her head. "I've never acted like that in my life, never said such horrible things. I love Sam, and I never meant to hurt him. That's the last thing in the world I wanted." Her eyes filled with quick tears. "But I couldn't believe that Josh had an affair with Shelby. I'm still having a hard time with it."

"Sam knows you were hurt. You were reacting to the shock of hearing about Josh, but you didn't mean to take it out on him."

Rebekah grabbed her hand, and Lexa held on tight. "Thanks for not being mad at me. You *do* love Sam, don't you?"

Lexa didn't answer, but her smile probably gave away any secrets she hoped to hide.

~

"Sam, I've made my decision." Although he'd been detained, Sam finally dropped down to sit beside her a short time later. He sounded tired but enthusiastic about the positive response he'd received to his message that night.

"What? No small talk first?" Sam stretched out and released a contented sigh. He patted the spot next to him and pulled her close.

"Please, Sam. I have to get it out now or I won't be able to do it at all." Lexa was afraid to look over at him, afraid of his reaction. She stared down at her hands twisting together in her lap. "This is hard enough." Unbidden tears suddenly blinded her, threatening to spill over.

"Well, that doesn't exactly sound like good news." He was quiet, but Lexa could see the tightness in his jaw when she dared to glance in his direction.

"You're not coming with me, are you?" He sounded disappointed, hurt.

She shook her head, her heart heavy. "I don't see how I can. Please know that it's not that I don't want to. You know what you want to do with your life. You seem so confident, so strong, so sure, and TeamWork suits your talents and interests. You've done it a lot longer than I have, and you're used to the lifestyle. To be honest, I'm not sure I could take it for an entire year, living out of a suitcase, not knowing if I'd be transferred to another project at a moment's notice."

"It's not exactly like that," Sam protested.

"You know what I mean." Lexa shifted her position. "I've been praying about it a lot. Maybe I need to grow more in my own spiritual walk." She hesitated, and lowered her voice. "Whatever it is, I know the time isn't right for me to go running around the world at this point in my life."

"Plus, you don't want to feel like you're following a man." When he looked over at her, Sam's expression was hard to read. "Admit it, Lexa. In case things don't work out between us, you don't want to feel . . . stuck." His eyes met hers. "Not that I think that's going to happen."

Lexa stiffened. "I guess that's part of it, but only a small part. Security's a big thing for me. I never told you, but I may not have a job at Alamo World Financial when I go back to Houston. When I left, they couldn't promise my position would still be there waiting for me."

"You gave up your job to come here?" Sam's voice was quiet, disbelieving. Reaching out with one hand, he anchored it under her chin, forcing her to look at him.

"Not exactly. But sort of," she stammered. "I didn't want you to think I was completely crazy," she admitted with a shrug.

He sighed. "That wasn't crazy. It was incredibly brave. I wish I'd known."

"Why? What difference would it have made?"

Sam looked at her a long time before slowly shaking his head. "Maybe you were following your dream like I'm trying to do by going on this overseas mission."

Lexa nodded. "I think the Lord is leading both of us. We have to be brave enough and smart enough to follow where He leads. You're obviously doing that, and I'm trying to do it, too." She shrugged. "Even though I might not have a job when I go back to Houston, I don't feel like going overseas with TeamWork is the right thing, either."

Even though it would be with you! She felt like screaming. Lexa's heart was heavy, and her eyes filled with tears. How could she agree to go when Sam couldn't find the words to tell her he loved her? Sadness threatened to carry her away in a sea of tears.

"I'll pray your job is still waiting for you in Houston."

"If it's not, I'll be okay." Lexa lifted her chin. "This TeamWork assignment has shown me that I'll be okay. No matter what happens. I trust the Lord to take care of me and my needs. I know I won't have a problem finding something else. It might not even be in financial planning."

"What then?" Curiosity lifted his brow.

"I have absolutely no idea. Maybe I'll become a pie maker and learn how to bake the best peach and apple pies in the world."

Leaning over, Sam pressed his lips to hers, allowing his lips to linger. "I think that sounds like a very delicious idea. I like a sweet girl, too, you know. To balance out the sassiness and the spice."

Lexa swallowed hard. She couldn't smile when her heart hurt so much. "Sam, you know how much I care for you, but I'm not sure how much of a future we can share with our differences in what we want from life, in our dreams and goals for the future." Her voice caught and she blinked hard to stem the flow of tears.

He didn't speak for a long moment. With his face bathed in the moonlight, he watched her with an expectant look. "Tell me about your dreams, your goals for the future. Tell me what it is that you *really* want, Lexa. You've avoided that question when I've asked before, you know. Time to tell me."

Lexa's eyes searched his before finally opening her mouth. Finding it suddenly dry, she swallowed hard and tried to find an explanation. "I suppose I want what everyone wants," she said slowly. "A home, family, love . . ." her voice trailed. "After being here with TeamWork the past few weeks, I know I want to grow in my knowledge and commitment of the Lord. There's an awful lot that I don't understand, but I *want* to understand. Does that make any sense to you?"

"Yes. It makes perfect sense. Do you know what I want?" He leaned his head back against the tree and closed his eyes.

"No," she said, shaking her head as though in a trance. "What do you want?"

He sighed and opened his eyes. "I want whatever makes *you* happy." All over again, he captured her heart. The man was uncommonly sensitive. Why couldn't he tell her he loved her? That might be a big step toward making her even happier. Surely he sensed that.

More than anything, Lexa wanted to reach out and take Sam's hand in her own. She wanted to pour out her heart to this man and tell him that she wanted him, that she loved him. But how could she do that? Something inside kept her from reaching out, just as it always had. It was like some self-protective mechanism that triggered within her every time someone started to get too close. Lexa didn't understand it, but it was undeniably a part of her. It only surfaced at the worst possible moments when she was just beginning to trust, snatching away hope and leaving her empty and lost instead of gloriously happy.

"Don't be afraid to reach out and grab what you want from life," Sam told her, rising. "Let me walk you back to the dorm. I can't walk away and leave you out here by yourself. There might be a wolf in sheep's clothing lurking about somewhere." He held out one hand and helped her to her feet.

"Josh is gone so you don't have to worry. I'm sorry," she said a moment later, shaking her head with regret. "That comment was mean-spirited. I shouldn't have said it."

"It's okay. You're right. I pray that Josh is getting the help he needs. He's a good guy, but he just has a problem. Don't we all?"

Lexa detected more than a touch of irony. "Surely you don't have problems, Mr. Lewis." She forced her tone to be light and teasing although her heart felt like deadweight all of a sudden.

Sam didn't answer, but walked along in the dark, kicking up dust with every slow step. He certainly wasn't in any hurry to leave her company, and in fact, seemed to dawdle purposely to keep it a little while longer. As they neared the dorm, Sam grabbed Lexa's hand, pulling her to the side of the building and into his arms. She could feel his heart beating, strong and sure, as he held her so close she thought he might topple them both.

"I don't want to lose you," Sam murmured, his lips on the top of her head. "I don't think our goals, our dreams, are all that different. Ultimately, I want those same things, too. I guess I just need to work some of this wanderlust out of my system first. If you don't want to go, I understand." Pulling back and looking down at her, he sighed. "All I ask is that you wait for me. Can you do that?"

"Oh, Sam," Lexa croaked, overcome with emotion. Raising her arms and then letting them fall awkwardly to her sides, she stared at him, her expression helpless. Her arms ached from wanting to hold and be held, but she couldn't.

"A year isn't the end of the world, you know," he continued in a quiet voice, filling the void caused by her hesitation. Taking her hands in his, Sam kissed her fingers like he'd done the day in his office when she'd told him about Sheila and Howard.

"I'll have a little time in Houston before I find out my assignment with TeamWork. We can spend some time together, get to know each other better. Then we'll take things a day at a time after that. I'll make it work between us." Stepping closer and reaching out to cup her face in one hand, Sam gazed at her with what Lexa could only call love in his shining eyes.

"Two hearts designed by God meant to find one another *will* find each other, Lexa, no matter what."

Overcome with emotion, Lexa nodded, swallowing her tears. "No matter what?" she repeated, looking back up at him.

Sam nodded. "No matter what," he whispered, leaning over to plant the softest kiss in the world on her forehead. His lips grazed her skin like a feathery brush, and Lexa leaned into the kiss. But as soon as he kissed her, it was over and he walked away, faster now.

Wrapping her arms about her, Lexa watched as he walked across the campsite to his own private quarters behind the office. It was almost as though Sam knew she was watching. When he reached the door, he turned and looked back at her. Reaching a hand up to his temple, he saluted. Lexa kissed her fingers and blew it in his direction. Although she couldn't be sure, Lexa thought she saw him smile.

Chapter 36

*P*LANS WERE UNDERWAY for a farewell party scheduled the night before most of the volunteers were due to depart. Somehow, Lexa was on the list of party organizers even though she didn't remember signing up. One of the other girls must have added her name to the list. Not that she minded.

Lexa glanced down at the list of needed supplies. "Looks like we'll need a lift into town later today." She caught Winnie's knowing grin. Finding reasons to visit Sam in his office had kept her preoccupied the last few days. Even if he sensed she was making up excuses to see him, she didn't care. Finding her time with TeamWork drawing to a close, she wanted every precious second with Sam to count. The thought of not being around him anymore made her extremely sad.

Sam's words about their being together if it was meant to be and designed by God reverberated in her mind. She loved Sam Lewis. She had no more doubts about that particular issue. And Sam must think he loved her since he'd asked her to join him with TeamWork, and then asked her to wait for him.

But, the fact remained that Sam had never spoken the words aloud, never told her he loved her. Lexa ached to hear the words. But even if he told her he loved her, she wasn't going to change her mind about going with him. Maybe he was the type of man who'd never be settled enough to marry, never be content to stay in one place for long. Somehow, though, Lexa's heart wouldn't allow her to believe it.

"Winnie, Natalie and I need to go into town sometime tonight, if possible, to get supplies for the farewell party," she announced after entering Sam's office late one afternoon.

Looking up from his paperwork, Sam shook his head. "Afraid I can't, Lexa." Shaking his head, he ran a hand through his hair. His voice was bothered, distracted. Removing his glasses, he rubbed his tired eyes.

"No, you can't or no you won't?" she teased.

"Very funny. I'm afraid I really can't, as tempting an offer as it is." Standing, Sam pushed aside the papers in the middle of his desk and faced her. His eyes were full of worry and his brow was furrowed.

"What's wrong?" Lexa hoped he'd share whatever made him so agitated.

"Something's wrong with the figures," he murmured, shaking his head again. "The numbers aren't adding up."

"What do you mean?"

"Someone's pilfering money from the safe."

"I can't believe that!" She didn't bother hiding her shock. There was a thief among them in the TeamWork camp? She moved closer. "I don't want to think anyone here at the camp would stoop to petty thievery. How much is missing?"

Sam retrieved his glasses and studied the ledger. "About five hundred dollars. At least I don't keep too much here in the safe on the premises. Most of it is in the temporary bank account I set up in the city."

Lexa shook her head. "How many people know about the safe, know the combination?"

"Just myself and a couple of the guys. Unfortunately, Josh was one of the guys."

"How long has the money been missing?"

Sam shrugged. "I'm not exactly sure. If you're wondering if Josh could have taken it, it's possible. But Josh isn't dishonest. And as far as I know, he doesn't need money. I'm the first to admit that I'm not the most meticulous person when it comes to checking and counting the money on a daily basis. At least in that area, I'm perhaps too trusting." He glanced up at her before returning his focus to the ledger.

"Oh, Lexa." Sam's shoulders slumped under the weight of his burden. "What am I going to do? If I call TeamWork and tell them I've lost the money, they probably won't reassign me anywhere else, at least as a director. This will only prove to them that I'm not responsible enough for a higher position."

"Excuse me for asking, but do you have to serve as a director?"

Sam frowned. "No," he said, drawing out his words, "I don't have to be a director, but it's a right I've earned and I enjoy it. But that's not the point." His voice was brusque. Lexa swallowed and lowered her gaze.

Strolling over to the tall filing cabinet, Sam stretched out his elbow and leaned back against it. "With only three days left in the camp, I'll have to work fast to solve this mystery. As if I even have time for something like this." Sitting behind the desk, he lowered his head onto his hands, but not before Lexa saw the bewilderment etched into his face. His shoulders sagged.

"Let me help you." Lexa walked over to his desk and planted her palms flat, leaning closer. "I want to help," she reiterated, willing him to look up at her. She waited until he raised his head.

"Thanks, but I don't want to involve you in something like this. It's my fault the money's gone, and now I have to be the one to straighten it out." The worry line surfaced between his brows.

"Fine," she snapped, heading for the door. "But I don't know why you think you can do everything yourself. It wouldn't hurt you to let somebody else help you every now and then, you know." She shoved open the screen door and heard something slam across Sam's desk as she departed.

"Here," he called when she was a few hundred yards away.

Turning back around, she managed to catch the keys Sam tossed into her hands.

"Take the car to get your supplies. Only problem is, I can't reimburse you right away. Keep your receipts, and give them to me when you get back."

"Aye, aye sir." Lexa gave him a mock salute.

"I'm sorry, Lexa." Standing just outside the office, hands in the pockets of his shorts, Sam gave her a helpless look. "I didn't mean to bark at you, but I've got to think this thing through. When you get back later, come see me. I'll try to think of some way you can help. We'll figure out a plan. Together." His words warmed her heart.

Lexa clasped the keys tighter in the palm of her hand and smiled. "Thanks."

Sam stood only a foot away, great tenderness in his eyes. "Don't tell anyone about this. It'll be our little secret. I don't want anyone else to know the money's missing. Maybe the person who took it is still in the camp and will try to make another move. Maybe I can toss out subtle clues there might be some extra money hidden in the safe in the next couple of days, and see if anyone makes a move."

"See," Lexa told him, pride in her voice, "that brilliant mind of yours is already formulating a master plan."

He grinned. "You ain't seen nothin' yet, sweetheart." The drawl was exaggerated.

"Sam?"

"Hmm?" he asked, turning back around, returning her grin.

"Your glasses make you look . . . very distinguished and scholarly. I really like them." And made him altogether appealing. Best not to tell him that little fact, though.

Sam laughed quietly. "Thanks. Guess I fooled you. I'll see you when you get back. Take care of the old bomb, though, will you please?"

Lexa laughed, turning to go. "Promise."

~

"I certainly hope one of us has a Triple A card. I don't know about you all, and no offense, Lexa, but I'd feel a lot better if Sam had driven us himself in this old bomb," Natalie grumbled, nonetheless climbing into the back seat of the station wagon a couple of hours later following dinner. "I'm surprised Sam even let you drive. He always insists on driving."

Natalie was right. Not since Shelby had he allowed anyone else to drive. "Relax. The old bomb will get us there and back." She grinned at Winnie as she slid into the passenger seat. For good measure, Lexa patted the dashboard as she'd seen Sam do.

"You sound awfully confident," Winnie commented.

"You have to be," Lexa muttered under her breath, inserting the key into the ignition with a silent prayer. The car's engine started with a roar. After a minimum of sputtering, it was ready to roll. The three girls chatted about the plans for the farewell party as Lexa drove them in the direction of a party store on the outskirts of the city.

"We need a gift for Sam," Natalie spoke up from the back a few miles down the road. "Any suggestions?"

"Hmm," Lexa mused. "Let me think about that one unless Winnie has any suggestions."

"Are we talking gag gift or serious?" Winnie twisted around in the passenger seat.

In the rearview mirror, Lexa saw Natalie shrug. "Whichever. I just need some ideas. We can get something tonight or else come back into town before the party."

"How about one of those Indiana Jones-type hats?" Lexa suggested after a few moments of silence passed. "Since he's going to work full-time for TeamWork." She was safe suggesting it since Sam announced his plans a few days ago to the group-at-large. "You know how he likes to wear his cowboy hat, so it's not like he hates hats or anything."

On her way out of the dorm, Lexa had tucked her credit card into her wallet. It might come in handy in case she happened to find just the right hat for Sam. Whether or not anyone else contributed to the cost, she'd just tell Sam the gift came from the entire crew.

"He'd look really good in one of those." Natalie sounded pleased with the suggestion.

"I think you're right. They can get rather expensive if we get the real thing, but if everyone pitches in, we should have more than enough for a really good one," Winnie agreed, nodding her head enthusiastically. "Sam certainly deserves something really terrific. Great idea, Lexa. Let's keep our eyes peeled. I know I've seen lots of hats in some of the area shops, so it shouldn't be too hard. The only challenge might be finding a store that's still open."

Winnie glanced down at her watch, triggering another idea in Lexa's mind. Sam needed a new watch. Maybe that was something she could get. Was it appropriate for her to give Sam such a personal gift? Considering the uncertain state of her relationship with Sam at the moment, she wasn't sure. Still, the man needed one for his overseas mission.

Two hours later, the three girls pulled back into the camp to find a flurry of excitement and activity. The bonfire devotions had just ended, and groups of young people stood clustered, animated, talking amongst themselves.

"What's going on?" Lexa asked the first group of volunteers she approached. She carried Sam's hat and new watch in a bag under her arm.

"Someone's missing. One of the volunteers," a girl standing on the edge of the circle told her.

"Really? Who is it?" Lexa shifted the bag and glanced over at Winnie to see if she'd also heard.

"Some girl. Sheila something."

Chapter 37

"OH, NO. WHERE'S Sam?" Lexa put a quick hand on the girl's arm to grab her attention.

"I'm not sure," came the vague reply.

Hurrying over to the dorm, Lexa stuffed the bag beneath her bed, shoving it way under. She prayed the same thief who'd taken the money from the safe in Sam's office wasn't watching her now. Darting a furtive glance around the dorm, Lexa wiped her dusty hands on a nearby towel.

Oh Sheila, where are you? Her bed was as neat as ever. Sheila was always so quiet and blended into the background. That's the way she liked things, not wanting to make waves or cause problems. Except the day Lexa walked in to find Sheila's husband fleeing the dorm. Howard had made her uneasy. If it was true that Sheila was missing, Lexa suspected the burly man no doubt had everything to do with her quiet roommate's disappearance.

Her heart pounding, Lexa walked outside, her eyes scanning the gathered crowd for any sign of Sam. In the background, she heard small group leaders making plans to break apart and canvas the area. *In Search of Sheila.* It sounded like the name of a book or a spy novel. Missing money and now a missing person . . . were they connected? If they were, it might eliminate Josh as a suspect regarding the missing money. That thought brought a small measure of relief. Lexa didn't want to think Josh was a thief, too. He had enough problems.

Spotting Rebekah, Lexa hurried over to the tall blonde. "Beck, what's going on?" She caught up and walked alongside her. "I hear Sheila's missing. Please tell me it's not true."

Turning to face her, Rebekah stopped, her expression grim. "Afraid so. One of the men saw her with some big guy a couple of hours ago. You and I both know it was Howard. He thinks Howard may have been forcibly making Sheila leave the campsite against her will. He feels horrible and wishes he'd done something more to help her." Her eyes traveled to Lexa. "But he didn't." She shook her head. "So much for our watch plan."

Lexa frowned. "Any idea where Sam is?" She hastened to keep up with Rebekah's much longer stride.

"I'm hoping he's in his office." A minute later, they stood outside the office. Knocking a few times with no response, Rebekah bit her lower lip and shrugged. "Seems he's missing, too, at least for the moment."

Lexa frowned. "You don't think Sam's gone to search for Sheila all by himself, do you?"

Rebekah shook her head. "I doubt it, but who knows? I suppose anything's possible at this point."

"Maybe he's gone to the police," Lexa suggested. "Although I don't know what good that would do. The police couldn't do anything, anyway, unless Sheila's been missing longer than twenty-four hours." The two stood talking in low tones outside of Sam's office.

As if on cue, Sam hurried around the corner of the office. His eyes lit when he spied them, and he nodded. "Evening." He unlocked the door and stood aside. "Come in and have a seat." He sat down behind his desk, linking his hands behind his head, leaning back.

"This is a familiar scene. I don't know about you, but I'm just about ready for this particular camp to be over." His voice dripped sarcasm, and he shook his head. "Since it's the two of you, I don't mind admitting I'm not sure how much more I can take."

Lexa's heart swelled, and she gave Sam a reassuring smile. "Can you tell us what's happening now?"

He blew out a breath and sat up straight, clasping his hands together on top of the desk. "As I'm sure you've heard, Sheila's missing. I'm convinced Howard Morris has taken her somewhere against her will. I seriously doubt she'd go anywhere willingly with him." His words were clipped and concise. "Howard's not after Sheila. He's after their daughter."

"So, it's a girl." Lexa hadn't realized she'd spoken aloud, and she glanced at Rebekah, noting her curious look. "I knew she had a child, but didn't know if it was a girl or a boy. Do you have any idea where they might be?"

Sam shook his head. "I wish I knew. I feel responsible for Sheila since she's part of my team. I'll tell you one thing. I'm not about to lose another TeamWork volunteer on my watch." He shot a meaningful look at Lexa and Rebekah as if to say, *This is all I need right now.*

"We'll find her, Sam." Lexa forced a confidence into her voice from somewhere deep inside. She had to be calm now, for Sheila, for Sam, for Rebekah, for all of them. Having seen the man, she was afraid of what he might do. If Sheila was Howard's way of finding his daughter, then he might very well have kidnapped her to lead him to their daughter. "How can we help?"

"Go back to the dorm. I give you permission to go through Sheila's things, anything you can find. See if she has a list of phone numbers, addresses, anything that might give us a clue who to call or where to start looking. I'll check her TeamWork paperwork, but I suspect she put down bogus information." He caught Lexa's look. "It was a self-protective measure as much as anything else."

The words were barely out of his mouth before both Rebekah and Lexa sprinted to their feet, headed out the door in only a few seconds. "Come to me first if you find anything!" he called to them. "I don't want anyone else to turn up missing."

"Right, Sam!" Rebekah called, throwing one arm in the air, signaling they'd heard. "Our fearless leader has spoken." She gave Lexa a half-grin as they hurried to Building Seven.

"I hope we can figure out where she is." Lexa pushed open the screen door of their dorm and hurried over to Sheila's bed. "You check the locker, and I'll check around her bed," she suggested, making quick work of stripping back the sheets. Rebekah opened the locker and started rifling through the bag inside. It was a good thing none of them used locks since they were among friends and saw no need.

"Looks to be just dirty clothes." Rebekah reached deep into the bottom of the canvas bag in her hands. "Find anything?" She glanced over at where Lexa sat reading. "Is that Sheila's diary?" Dropping down beside Lexa on Sheila's bed, she leaned over her shoulder.

"Yes. She's always got her head stuck either in here or her Bible, so I thought maybe it would give us a clue."

Rebekah nudged Lexa. "Don't you sort of feel like Nancy Drew right about now? I'll be George, and you're Nancy."

Lexa allowed herself to smile, lessening the tension. "Let's just pray we can solve this mystery in Nancy Drew fashion." Her expression dissolved into a frown. "Where did Winnie and Natalie go?" They'd disappeared after their return from the trip into town. "And Amy and the other girls?"

"I'm sure they're in the search parties." Rebekah walked over to the window. "I only see a few people milling around now, so I'm assuming most of them are out looking for Sheila. Not that there's really anywhere to go, and I'm sure Howard had a car." She ran a hand through her hair, mussing it. "It's so confusing." Her green eyes grew wide and she crossed the room, dropping to her knees. "Wait! Here's another case of some sort," she called, lying prone on the floor beside Sheila's bed.

Dragging a small black case across the cement floor, Rebekah glanced up at Lexa. Unzipping it, she withdrew a T-shirt and a pair of shorts, and then let her hand drop. "These seem awfully small," she mused, fingering the shirt. "Sheila's petite, but I seriously doubt she's *this* small." She looked up at Lexa. "Are you thinking the same thing I am?"

Lexa nodded, her heart pounding again. "Yes! These clothes belong to Sheila's daughter which means the girl must be somewhere nearby. Howard must know it, and that's why he's taken her. I'm going to read her diary some more. I feel guilty doing it, but what choice do we have if we want to help her?" Lexa shot a helpless look at Rebekah.

The other girl nodded, tossing her hair behind one shoulder as she sat down beside Lexa on Sheila's bed. "Go ahead. I think Sheila would understand since we're trying to find her. Read it out loud. Maybe together we can come up with something." Rebekah leaned one elbow on her knee and gnawed on a fingernail.

"It's worth a shot, anyway." Lexa flipped through the pages of the diary to find the last entries from the previous few days. It was perhaps the best place to start.

"This is Tuesday's entry. *Today was very unsettling. H. is here. I can feel his presence. It's like he's lurking on the outskirts of the camp, staring at me with those black eyes of his, seeing what I don't want him to see. I think he knows that A.'s here somewhere. I might have to leave before everyone else does. I have a feeling H. is going to make his move very soon. I'm scared. I pray every night that God will help me. I don't know how H. found me here. Still, I can't help thinking that if he could find me here, he can probably find me anywhere.*

"Wow." Rebekah stretched out on her back across the width of the bed, her long legs dangling over the edge. "Poor kid. Who's A., do you think?"

"Must be the first initial of her daughter's name." Lexa turned to the next page, eager to read another passage. "Let me skip to Wednesday. *I don't know what to do. I thought I saw H. standing behind the tree on the side of the camp watching me. I tried to blend in with a group of the women so that he couldn't catch me alone. I want to tell someone. Maybe Sam. I'm afraid. I don't want to drag anybody else into this nasty mess. I can't take that chance. If anyone's going to be hurt, it has to be me. I have to make sure that A.'s safe. I don't know how, but she's got to stay safe. Hopefully, God will watch over both of us now.*

"Oh," Rebekah said, rising to a sitting position again.

"What?" Lexa closed the small book with a frown.

"I have this awful feeling," Rebekah said, shaking her head. "If she saw him, then she's probably right. He must have made a move of some kind. I don't like this, Lexa. I don't like this at all."

"Neither do I, Beck," Lexa answered, her voice firm. "But we have to do something. We can't let Sheila suffer at the hands of this guy. We can't give up."

"Of course not. All I'm saying is, I'm more than a little petrified at the thought of coming face-to-face with Howard."

"Don't worry, Beck." She patted the younger girl's hand in a gesture reminiscent of Winnie. "Put your trust in the Lord. He'll take care of us." Again, Lexa was surprised at how easily the words came, and how comfortable she felt saying them.

Lexa glanced over at Rebekah and then back down at Sheila's diary. "Unfortunately, that was the last entry. Why don't we see if we can find the guy who saw Howard dragging Sheila away from the camp and see if we can get any more clues."

"Good idea, but first I've got to go make a quick stop in the other room," Rebekah told her with a sheepish look. "Be right back." A moment later, Rebekah burst back into the main room.

"That was quick," Lexa teased.

"Come in here a minute," Rebekah called, motioning with one hand. "There's something that doesn't make sense, and Sheila might have done it."

"Done it?" Lexa repeated, hurrying into the bathroom behind Rebekah. Staring in the direction where she pointed, Lexa spied a small pink heart in the lower right-hand corner of the mirror above the tiny sink.

"What in the world . . . ?" She walked closer to inspect it, touching the heart, smearing it on the mirror. Lexa rubbed her fingers together. "It's lipstick."

"Sheila doesn't wear lipstick." Rebekah shoved aside the plastic curtain in the shower stall and poked around the sides of the toilet.

"Maybe that's a clue in itself." Lexa rifled through the various cosmetics left in the bathroom by the other girls. "I'm sure none of the other girls made this heart. They'd have no reason. Let's think about it for a minute." She turned around, searching for any other possible clue, her mind working overtime.

"Suppose Howard surprised Sheila here in the dorm. She's usually here, anyway, unless it's time for work, dinner or the bonfire. She claims she has to go to the bathroom or else she runs away from him and shuts herself in here." Lexa's eyes focused on the pink heart. "Not knowing what else to do, Sheila makes this small drawing of a heart, hoping Howard won't notice it."

"But hoping we would," Rebekah chimed in, raising a brow.

Lexa frowned, silent for a long moment. "The only problem is, what in the world does it mean?"

Chapter 38

*T*HAT SMALL PINK heart was a clue, a sign, a plea for help from Sheila. It had to be. But Lexa felt helpless, not comprehending its meaning. "I don't know about you, but I find this all very maddening." Her hands rested on her hips. "It's the worst feeling in the world, not knowing what to do or how to help her. I hate to think about where that man's taken Sheila. She didn't do anything to deserve this kind of treatment. All she's trying to do is protect her daughter."

"Howard *is* her father." Rebekah shifted position, crossing her arms. "I hate to get in the middle of a nasty custody fight."

Lexa's glance was sharp and direct. "This is more than a mere custody fight." Her hands dropped to her sides and she released a long sigh. "Maybe I should tell you what happened to prompt the watch over Sheila in the first place. It was more than a mere threat. I happened to come into the dorm and surprise Howard once before. Sheila was scared to death. The fear in her eyes was almost palpable. I had to tell someone about it."

"Sam." Rebekah's eyes softened in understanding. "It makes sense since he's the TeamWork director. So, that's why you asked us to keep an eye on Sheila and to watch out for Howard. I wondered what that was all about since you didn't give us many details. We didn't question why. We knew you had Sheila's best interests at heart."

"Sam didn't feel comfortable telling everyone the circumstances," Lexa explained, "but we knew she might be in danger. Sam told me he'd discussed Sheila's situation with the board, and they made the joint decision to leave her here in the TeamWork camp." She frowned. "He might regret that decision now."

"So, she was hiding out."

"This guy has a record, and he's assaulted a woman before. It's more than a nasty custody fight. I don't think we should take Sheila's disappearance lightly. He could be planning something sinister, and we can't take any chances. We have to do what we can to find Sheila before . . ." Lexa's voice trailed.

Rebekah chewed her lip "Are you sure you're not just being melodramatic?"

Lexa stared back. "Do what you want, but I'm going to Sam and tell him what we've discovered. Maybe he can figure it out."

"Okay, okay," Rebekah grumbled, following behind Lexa and out the front door of the dorm. "I didn't say I wouldn't help. Sorry. You're right. Of course, we have to do what we can to help Sheila." She shook her head. "I suppose after what happened with Josh, I should believe anything can happen. This is all pretty surreal, though. This whole camp has been full of surprises."

Lexa couldn't agree more.

A few minutes later, after listening to what they'd found, Sam shook his head in exasperation. "A single heart drawn on a bathroom mirror with lipstick? That's our only clue? No names, phone numbers, addresses, anything? You couldn't find anything else?"

"No, and we looked over all her things," Lexa assured him, her defensiveness rising. "Do you have any idea what it means?"

"I haven't a clue." Sam threw down his pen in disgust and crossed his arms. "A heart can symbolize so many things, especially love. From all appearances, there's certainly very little love in Sheila's relationship with Howard, so that puzzles me greatly." He closed his eyes to concentrate, two fingers on his creased brow. "Let's try to think of every possible angle."

They all tossed out ideas until they looked at one another with helpless expressions. One by one, the leaders of the search parties came back to Sam's office to tell him they'd come up with nothing. No clues, no trace of Sheila. It was like she disappeared into thin air.

"Maybe we're all jumping to conclusions and imagining the worst?" Amy suggested as she, Winnie and Natalie joined them in the office a short time later. "It's not like Sheila really had any close friends here in the camp. Maybe she just decided to take off since it's almost the end of the project anyway."

"I don't think so," Sam answered. "She wouldn't have left her things, and I don't think she'd be the type to wander off by herself. Anyone who's seen Sheila knows the woman's practically afraid of her own shadow. I seriously doubt she'd make a phone call by herself, much less leave."

"I think Sheila's stronger than you give her credit for," Lexa interjected.

Sam looked up at her in surprise. "Go on."

"I've gotten to know her a little bit, perhaps better than anyone else here at the camp. She's got a firm inner resolve. Let's look at the facts. She ran away and hid herself in the TeamWork campsite, thinking she was safe from Howard. She managed to somehow successfully hide their daughter, at least until now. I don't know how, but he found her anyway. It took strength and determination to do what she did to protect her child. I think we need to give Sheila credit for more than simply being a quiet, timid doormat."

"I'm not saying that," Sam protested.

"Why don't we pray about it?" Lexa hated the feeling of helplessness. She couldn't sit still, knowing Sheila was out there somewhere, needing their help. It was enough to drive her crazy, but she felt powerless to do anything. "It's probably the best thing we can do for Sheila right now since we have no idea where she is. But the Lord knows, and I'd say an appeal to Him is in order."

Sam looked back up at Lexa with a gleam in his eye. "That's an excellent idea. Why don't we go round up the others and have a corporate time of prayer? In this case, I think there might be greater power in numbers." Lexa nodded and followed Sam outside as they made the rounds of the dorms to gather up all the volunteers.

Soon, they had a majority of the men and women gathered. They silently filed into the bonfire area where they sat together, their heads bowed. One by one, they lifted their petitions to the Lord, beseeching the Almighty for watchcare over one of their own.

"*Dear Father,*" Lexa prayed when it was her turn. Her voice was shaky with nerves. It was the first time she'd ever prayed out loud. "*Help Sheila find her way home. I don't just mean to us. I mean to find her way out of this situation. I don't know what the answer is, Father, but you do. You know what's going on in the hearts of both Howard and Sheila right now. You know where they are. Keep Sheila safe, Father, and help Howard see the error of his ways. And, if it's in your will, help us to somehow find them and bring them back safely so that this situation can be resolved peacefully.*"

After everyone else departed the circle to head toward the dorms for the night, Lexa and Sam sat huddled together. "Go get some sleep, Lexa. Maybe it'll all become clearer in the morning."

Lexa glanced over at Sam in exasperation. "How can I sleep? I can't possibly," she murmured, shaking her head. "I feel so useless. I want to help Sheila, but feel powerless. I want God to tell me what to do, where to go . . ." Eyes fiery, she looked back over at him. "I'm not mad at God, but I'm mad at this feeling I have. I hate it!"

Taking Lexa's hand in his own, Sam squeezed and held on tight. When she resisted, he increased the pressure of his fingers around hers.

"You're starting to hurt me," Lexa protested, trying to wriggle free from his grasp.

"That's how the heavenly Father holds you in the grip of His love." Sam relaxed his grip but still held her hand. "Sometimes He squeezes tight—so tight you feel like you're suffocating from the circumstances in your life crowding you in. But it's in times like that when we feel the power, the strength of His love, and know how very much He cares for us, how much He loves us. God loves Sheila and Howard, too. He won't allow anything to happen that He hasn't preordained or allowed to happen. Maybe that will give you some small comfort tonight as you try to sleep."

Lexa leaned her head on Sam's shoulder. "Maybe, but I doubt it," she told him, her eyes wide. "I appreciate your trying to comfort me. None of this makes any sense, does it?"

"No, it doesn't," Sam agreed, stroking her hair. "Unfortunately, there's a lot of things in our lives that don't make sense. Part of the mystery of life, I suppose," he murmured, planting a soft kiss on her forehead. It seemed like the most natural thing in the world.

"Any more ideas on the missing money?" Lexa asked as they walked away, hands clasped together, fingers intertwined.

Sam shook his head and released a heavy sigh. "No. With all the commotion surrounding Sheila's disappearance, I haven't had a spare minute to think about the money."

"Do you think it's all connected somehow? I mean, first the money's missing, and then Sheila."

Sam looked thoughtful. "It's possible, I suppose, but I don't really see how. Unless Sheila somehow convinced Kevin or Josh to give her the combination to the safe. And you and I both know Kevin Moore is as honest as the day is long. Like I said before, I know in my gut that Josh is honest."

"But unfortunately, Josh probably had his way of being persuaded," Lexa said, not daring to look over at Sam. "I hate thinking such a thing, but you and I both know it's true. The safe wasn't tampered with or broken into, was it?"

Sam shook his head. "No. That's one of the reasons I didn't know the money was missing for so long. Whoever took the money from the safe knew the combination."

"Do you have the combination written down somewhere? Could someone have gotten hold of it that way?"

"No. It's only written up here," Sam answered, pointing to his head. They looked at each other, knowing the other was thinking the same thing. Sheila might have taken the money, and used Josh to do it, knowing of his weakness with women.

"Oh, Sam," Lexa muttered, hanging her head, "I don't want to think such things about anyone."

"Sheila probably panicked and didn't know what else to do," Sam told her, opening his arms and drawing her to him. "A woman in desperate straits like Sheila might have slept with someone to get what she wanted. She probably didn't have anyone to turn to, and knew she could get her hands on some extra cash from the safe by cozying up to Josh."

"I don't think Sheila's a thief, but it makes no sense otherwise."

"I know, baby. I know," he told her, leaning his head against hers. "This is why I want you beside me."

Baby. Lexa always thought the term derogatory, used by a rough-cut kind of guy who clenched a cigarette between his lips, cursed frequently and sported a tattoo of a naked woman on his arm. But coming from Sam, she adored it.

Focus, Lexa. Raising her head, she met his eyes. "What do you mean?"

"I mean," Sam said, his voice quiet, cupping her face between his two strong hands, his thumbs making sensual circles on her cheeks. "I mean," he repeated softly, "I *love* you, Lexa Clarke. I want you beside me, talking things through, helping me make decisions and determining what course of action to take. There are so many times when I make the wrong choice about something because I'm quick-tempered and impulsive . . ."

What?" he asked, laughing as she looked at him as though he was crazy.

"Would you mind repeating what you just said?" Lexa nearly choked on the words. The words she'd been waiting to hear.

"You mean the part about being impulsive . . ." Sam stopped when she playfully swatted him. "I said I love you, Lexa. Madly. Completely. Forever." Drawing her closer into the welcoming circle of his arms, Sam's tender, inviting mouth claimed hers again and again as he deepened their kisses.

"What are we going to do?" In this man's arms was where she belonged. She never wanted to leave.

"I don't know." Still holding her, he graced her with a glance so loving it warmed her all over. "You could start by returning the favor."

She smiled. "I love you too, but I can't ask you to give up your dream." Lexa stood on tiptoe to kiss the place where those incredible smile lines deepened. She loved that spot, and gently traced it with a soft finger.

"And I can't ask you to give up your life in Houston." He looked lost and forlorn, like a little boy who'd lost his way home. "It'll work out, Lexa," he assured her. "I don't know all the details yet, but it will. Like I said, a year's not the end of the world and . . " his voice faded. They stood together in quiet silence for a long time, wrapped in one another's arms.

Oh, love does funny things to a person. Lexa couldn't help but wonder why, when she'd found the love of her life, he had to globetrot across the world. Sam had given his heart first to the Lord and then to her. It wasn't a competition, it wasn't a choice. It was a clear case of Sam Lewis following the Lord's leading in his life.

Lexa knew she had to let him go. What is it they say about the butterfly? Set it free, and if it comes back to you, it'll be yours forever. She'd hold Sam's heart forever, and he hers, but she had to let him follow his dream first. Then they'd have the rest of their lives together.

"Sam?"

"Hmm?" he asked absently, still holding her a short time later, the comfort of his arms warming her, making her heart sing.

"I'll wait, you know. I never had any doubt."

"I know, Miss Clarke." Lexa's heart swelled so fast she thought it might burst. "I never had any doubt, either."

Chapter 39

"I'VE GOT IT!" Lexa sat bolt upright in bed. Flinging aside the sheets, she wiggled out of her nightgown and tugged on her shorts before pulling on her bra and cotton top as fast as possible. Her hair was tousled from sleep, but she didn't have time for grooming.

Lexa shoved her feet into her tennis shoes and bolted out the door of the dorm, sprinting to Sam's quarters across the camp. Her fingers fumbled with the buttons on her shirt as she ran. She didn't know what time it was, but it must be sometime in the wee hours of the morning, judging by the position of the bright moon in the sky.

At first, Lexa knocked gently on Sam's bedroom door. "Come on," she mumbled, knocking louder with increasing urgency until she heard movement inside.

"Hold on a minute!"

She giggled as she heard him stumbling around inside, followed by a small crash. Leaning her ear closer to the screen door, she heard him mutter something unintelligible before he made it to the door. He flung open the inner door without looking. Turning away and running his hand over his face, Sam retrieved a light blue T-shirt draped over a nearby chair. His yawn was loud.

Lexa gulped, trying not to ogle this man's ripped, entirely masculine chest with unabashed fascination. It was obvious he expected one of the men to be standing on his doorstep at this unearthly hour of the morning. Closing her mouth with conscious effort as she opened the screen door and stepped inside, Lexa gave him a look that must defy description. That cover model on the romance novel could only hope to look as good as Sam did. She swallowed her grin.

Tugging the T-shirt down over his head, Sam's eyes widened in surprise when he realized it was Lexa standing on the doorstep. "Lexa! What brings you here at this hour?" His voice was groggy with sleep as he pulled the T-shirt down over his stomach with both hands. "This isn't exactly the proper time for a social call," he teased, stepping aside nonetheless. She noticed he left the door ajar in case anyone happened to be walking by. Sam needed to keep up appearances, after all.

"Nice digs," Lexa told him in appreciation, darting a quick glance at the room. *Not the time, Lexa. Get on with it.*

Sam snorted. "Did you just say nice legs?" He cocked a brow.

Lexa laughed. "No. Clean out your ears. But, now that you mention it," she said, eyeing him askance, "they're not half bad. I was complimenting your humble abode."

He shook his head, grinning. "Somehow, I don't think that's why you're here in my room in the middle of the night. You'd better state your business now, Miss Clarke, before others get entirely the wrong idea about us. This isn't the best move for your reputation, you know."

"I think I know where Sheila might be!" Lexa blurted out. She thought she'd keel over with anticipation.

"What? Really?" He tugged a pair of denim shorts over the shorts he'd been sleeping in. "I mean, where?" Sam had the grace to look embarrassed that she was standing in the middle of the room, watching him get dressed. "Do you, uh, mind?"

She obliged him by turning around as he zipped the shorts. It seemed a moot point after that glimpse of his incredible chest.

Lexa tried to keep her voice calm. "I don't know why I didn't think of it before. Can I please turn back around now?"

"Go ahead."

"I overheard Sheila singing in the shower a few times."

"Lots of people sing in the shower." Sam sat on his bed to pull on his socks. "I've even been accused of doing it myself from time to time. Not exactly the most pleasant of sounds," he told her with a wry grin. "And not exactly a unique character trait."

"Sam, please. Be serious," Lexa insisted. "And, for the record, I've heard you sing and you do it quite well. Like you do everything else . . . without much practice, apparently," she mumbled. "Anyway," she said, shaking her head to clear her thoughts, "just listen and try to stifle, okay?"

He mimicked zipping his lips, and she clamped a hand over her mouth when she realized her voice carried and was much too loud.

"Guess what Sheila was singing?" Sam shrugged, but remained silent.

"I Left My Heart In San Francisco!"

He shook his head as he tied the laces on his work boots. "Um, forgive me for being a bit foggy since it *is* the middle of the night, but I guess I'm not making the connection here. Are you saying you think Sheila's gone to California? San Francisco?"

"No, no." Lexa shook her head and pushed long hair out of her face. "You're not really going to wear those boots, are you?"

"Why not?" He stopped tying the second boot.

She frowned. "Don't you have a pair of tennis shoes or something? If we end up running around tonight, those boots are only going to weigh you down. Honestly, Sam, you couldn't keep pace with a turtle."

"All right. I suppose you're right although I'll have you know I was a pretty good track and field runner in college." He chuckled. "I can see how impressed you are by that tidbit. Hang on." Tugging the boots off his feet, he dropped them unceremoniously on the floor beside the bed. Going over to the closet, he grabbed a pair of tennis shoes and held them up. "I trust these suit you."

Lexa nodded. "Much better."

Sam eyed her as he tied the tennis shoes. "Nice hair, by the way."

"Not the time, Lewis." Lexa bit her lip not to laugh out loud.

"No, I mean it. It's all messy and . . . sexy. I definitely like it." Sam grinned. "And, I hesitate to mention this, but your shirt's a little cockeyed."

Lexa grunted. Picking up a pair of rolled socks from a nearby table, she tossed it at him.

"Good aim. Next mission, I'm signing you up for the TeamWork softball team."

"Come on. It's not the time to flirt. We have some rescuing to do! I've still got the keys for the station wagon. I'll tell you on the way to the car." She tossed him the keys as they headed out the door together. "I think Howard's taken her to one of the missions . . ."

"The Mission San Francisco de la Spade."

"Exactly!" Lexa beamed at him as they hopped in the car. She discreetly righted her blouse and buttoned it.

"Well, now that everyone in the camp is probably awake and alerted to our departure, shall we head for the mission?" Sam answered his own question by flooring the accelerator. "It's the southernmost mission of all the missions. I've only been there once. It's beautifully kept," Sam told her as they headed out of the campsite.

Lexa rolled her eyes. As if the mission's beautification efforts had anything whatsoever to do with the current situation-at-hand. "The main thing is, do you remember how to get there or do you have a map somewhere in the car?"

Sam nodded. "I think I can get us there easily enough. It's on Spade Road. But why would Howard keep Sheila at the mission? He could be long gone on the way to Mexico by now. What do you think his plan is?" He negotiated a turn onto the dirt road that would lead them back to the main road.

"I have no idea, but I know one thing. Like you said, Howard wants his daughter, not Sheila. He won't let Sheila go until he finds the child. Look, I realize I might be grasping at straws here, but I have this gut feeling they're at the mission. I need to find out if I'm right."

"You mean female intuition?" Sam chuckled at her grimace. "Hey, I've known it to work pretty well. You women are more in-tune with these kinds of things, I'll give you that much. Let's just pray we get there in time," he added, flooring the accelerator again. "And pray we don't run into any bored cops along the way. After all, I still have half a reputation as TeamWork director left to uphold."

Turning off the lights and coasting a short time later, Sam stopped the engine. The air was still around them, and Lexa shivered, bringing her arms across her body. "Here," Sam told her, reaching into the backseat and thrusting his jacket into her hands. "I keep it around for damsels chilled by the night air."

Lexa smiled her thanks. "You seem to have a bag of magic tricks in that backseat."

Sam grunted. "Yeah, well, come on," he said, stepping out of the car and looking around. "We'll have to walk from here. As it is, anyone in the immediate vicinity would have already heard this car announce our arrival. It's just too loud. The mission is about a quarter mile in this direction." He pointed ahead. "The Spade Aqueduct is right back there. It's part of the mission's original irrigation ditch system and dates from around 1740. It's one of the oldest Spanish aqueducts in the United States. What?" He stopped walking as he caught her incredulous look.

"I can't believe you're giving me a history lesson right now, Sam Lewis!" Lexa hissed. She wanted to laugh, but her nerves were taut. "What if Howard has a gun? What if he's done Sheila harm? What then? Are we nuts for coming out here in the middle of the night searching for them?"

"Hey, a good fact to know and tell never hurts," Sam protested in a low voice. "All right, if you'd rather not know your history . . ."

"Is this how you deal with stress? You start tossing out little history lessons?" Lexa demanded. "Well, then, I guess it's a good thing I'm finding out now." She shook her head in exasperation. "Unbelievable."

"You're the one who brought us out here on a hunch," Sam groused, picking up speed. "And now, apparently you're second-guessing yourself."

"Am not." Lexa quickened her pace to keep up with his ridiculously long strides. "How far are we from the mission now?" They'd half-walked, half-run a fair distance in silence.

"We're probably almost there," Sam whispered. "We'd better not talk anymore. Just stay by my side until we reach the mission." Lexa couldn't believe she'd dragged Sam off in the middle of the night for a probable goose chase. Still, as she'd told him earlier, she had to know if her hunch was right. After all, it's what Nancy Drew would do. Didn't the titian-haired sleuth solve a mystery near one of the missions?

"Sam!" The mission loomed in view ahead of them, majestic and dramatic against the backdrop of the moon.

"What?" he mouthed back, putting his finger over his lips.

He stooped down so that Lexa could whisper directly in his ear. "I saw something from the corner of my eye. Over there." She pointed in the direction of a far outer wall of the mission. Sam nodded and headed in that direction, pulling Lexa behind him. When she hesitated a moment, he looked back, squeezing her hand for comfort.

Lexa was glad Sam didn't want to split up as they continued their search of the area. His hold on her hand grew tighter as they neared the walls of the old mission. Lexa couldn't help but feel awed as she looked up at the imposing façade. Sam stopped, and bowed his head for a moment, closing his eyes. Lexa dared not allow her eyes to close, too, for fear they might be caught unaware. She lifted up her own silent prayer with eyes wide open.

I know you can hear this prayer, Father. Please watch over us and Sheila right now. Help us to find her and take her away from this place safely. Be with Howard. Give him a calmness so that he doesn't act rashly and do something foolish. You are a great God, and I know that you have everything in your control, gracious Father. Looking over at Sam, Lexa saw that he, too, had finished his prayer. Together they stealthily proceeded toward the outer wall of the old mission.

Slowly making their way around the façade, Sam kept his tight hold on Lexa's hand. She loved how holding hands was so natural for them now. At the moment, it comforted her. "Over there, Sam!" Lexa called to him a few minutes later as they rounded the side wall. "It's a man, and he's running!"

"Can you see if it's Howard?" Sam started running, tugging Lexa along behind him.

"No! But I don't think he's alone!" she called, no longer worried about being heard. The mere fact they were running was a pretty good indicator they knew they'd been spotted.

"Stop! All we want to do is talk to you!" They were gaining on the two, slowly but surely. Sam let go of her hand to move ahead with Lexa trailing slightly behind.

The man looked behind him to judge the distance between them and she saw something gleaming in the moonlight. "Sam! He's got a gun!" she hollered at the exact moment she heard a loud popping sound. In a sickening instant, Lexa knew it was the sound of the gun going off.

Chapter 40

*S*AM FELL TO the ground in one swift movement, yelling for Lexa to do the same. Daring to look up a moment later, she saw the man had taken off again. "Come on!" Sam muttered, sounding angry. Jumping back to his feet, he sprinted in the direction of the moving figures.

"Sam! Don't be crazy! He's obviously not afraid to use that gun!" She took off after him.

"Yeah, but he's a lousy shot," Sam called back over his shoulder, not slowing his pace.

"Is that supposed to be funny?" Lexa slowed her steps.

"I don't think he shot with intent to kill. He only wants to scare us. Just run, Lexa! Run!"

Run she did. Soon, they were gaining on the pair ahead of them. They ran in an open field with no protection should the man decide to use the gun again. Lexa's heart pounded in her chest but quickened even more when she realized that the second person running with the man was, in fact, Sheila.

"Sheila!" she called at the top of her lungs. It was an agonizing call of desperation. "Stop! We're here to help you!" They heard a muffled sound as the man clamped a large hand over Sheila's mouth. They were close enough now to see that it was Howard. Sheila's legs dragged the ground, and her husband had no choice but to drop her altogether or slow his pace. Sam reached them, and his hands raised in the air when Howard pulled the gun on him.

"I'm not afraid to use this, man," Howard warned in a surly, hoarse voice. "I ain't afraid to shoot Sheila either."

"Then why haven't you?" Sam sputtered, gasping for breath as he met the man's hard, cold gaze. Stopping behind him, Lexa leaned forward, hands on her knees, breathing hard. She couldn't catch her breath and breathed a silent prayer.

"You don't know nothin' about it," Howard spat, pulling Sheila up by her hair. When she cried out in pain, he laughed. "As soon as she tells me where Angelina is, I'll let her go. I don't really want her." He glanced down at Sheila with disdain. The dark-haired, petite woman shrank away from his touch and looked up at him with big, fearful eyes. "All I want is my girl."

"Let's talk about this like rational adults." Sam outstretched one hand to Howard. The big man laughed and spat again at him. "This doesn't have to be violent, Howard." Sam lowered his hand to his side.

"Hey! How'd you know my name?" Howard's voice was suspicious as he looked down at Sheila again. She hid her face in her hands. Lexa made a move to go to her, but Howard raised the gun again, his tone more menacing. "Stay away, girlie, unless you want an arm full of lead." His gaze traveled back over to Sam. "I don't think your boyfriend would want you then."

"Howard, I hope you know that God loves you," Sam began before being cut off.

"Don't even start in on me with that Jesus junk, man," he snarled, his voice fierce. "That's what got Sheila all messed up in the first place. She was fine until she got mixed up with those church people. Jesus ain't never done nothin' for me!"

"He *died* for you. Wasn't that enough?" At least it got Howard's attention for he turned his angry gaze away from Sheila and looked fully at Sam. Sheila lifted her head from her hands and looked up, still half-sitting on the ground in a stooped position.

"He ain't never died for me, man." Howard shook his head in disbelief. "You're as nuts as the rest of 'em. Now shut up and get away from me or I'll have to use this thing."

"You're not a violent man, and you know it," Sam began, taking a hesitant step toward him.

Lexa's heart was in her throat. *Lord, please help us!*

"Stay away!" Howard took a step back, yanking Sheila along with him, causing her to wince in pain. "I told you, I'm not afraid to use this gun!"

"All right. Take it easy." Sam held up his hands again and halted in his tracks. "Sheila, do you think you could arrange a court-supervised visit between Howard and your daughter? That way you'd know she'd be safe and protected."

Lexa stared at Sam, incredulous. Oh, that was rational. Howard didn't seem the type of man to sit and have a calm, quiet conversation in order to set up court-appointed visits with his daughter. No way.

Sheila looked up at Sam with the most fearful eyes Lexa had ever seen. "All he–he'd d–do is h–h–hit h–h–her li–li–like h–he b–b–beats m–m–me," she whimpered, cringing again.

"Sheila, I ain't never gonna hurt Angelina, and you know it," Howard protested, tightening his grip on her arm.

Sheila winced again and shifted her position.

"She's my little girl," he continued, his voice breaking.

Lexa knew in that moment Angelina was the key to this gruff man's heart. Everyone has a soft spot, and a little girl by the name of Angelina was his.

"Maybe Sheila and I can take you to Angelina," Lexa suggested, finding that inner strength again. It had to come from the newfound confidence derived from her faith. It was empowering.

Howard focused on her as if seeing Lexa for the first time. "You that broad in the building at the camp?"

"The same." Lexa tried to keep her voice as calm and unwavering as possible. Being called a broad was irritating, but she could live with it, considering the circumstances. "We have a car. We can take you to her, can't we, Sheila?" Lexa glanced over at her, and she nodded as Sheila turned large, frightened eyes in her direction.

"Sh–sh–she's ri–ri–right, How–Howard. We–we–we'll ta–ta–take . . . you t– t–to . . . An–Angel–Angelina."

"Now, that's more like it. I like her. But you watch your step," Howard warned Sam. He nodded at Lexa. "Tell you what, this little lady's going to take me to her." Lexa clenched her fists so tight at her sides she feared something might snap.

"You and Sheila are stayin' put," Howard growled. Lexa's heart lurched, and she looked over at Sam. Terror filled her heart like never before.

Sam nodded, but his eyes, too, were wide. "Take me," he offered, stepping toward Howard. "There's no need to involve her. She's only here because I dragged her here. I'll take you to Angelina."

Lexa tossed Sam a grateful glance but realized Howard wasn't buying it.

"Nah. It's gotta be one of the women. That way," he said with an evil-looking, leering grin at Lexa, "there's more at stake here. You'll make sure I get my girl, won't you?" He leaned close to Sam, almost nose-to-nose. "If you don't," he growled, "you can be sure you won't see *your* girl again."

"How–How-Howard, d–do–don't ma–ma–make th–th–threats." Sheila sounded more irritated now than scared. She cried out when Howard released her, and fell hard to the ground. Nausea rose within Lexa and she started toward Sheila, determined to help her. In a surprisingly fast move for such a large man, Howard grabbed Lexa by the arm and dragged her with him a few hundred yards. "Wait!" she called, trying to jerk her arm free. Lexa bit her lip not to cry out in pain as he wrenched her arm. Hard.

"Oh, for cryin' out loud," Howard shook his head in disgust. "Get a move on, woman! Don't make me lose patience with you." He shot her a look that told her he meant business.

"I need to talk with Sheila. Privately. For just a moment," Lexa stipulated, her voice sounding bolder than she felt. "I have to make sure I know exactly where Angelina is." She was trying to buy time, but considering the fact she really didn't know where Sheila had hidden their daughter, it was a valid excuse.

"Two minutes. I'll be standin' here with the gun on ya the whole time, so don't get any ideas, girlie."

In spite of her trepidation, Lexa stiffened at the term. It was almost worse than being called a broad. *Focus, Lexa.*

"You get over there with 'em so I can keep my eye on all of ya." Howard waved the gun around for emphasis.

Sam stepped toward the two women. "Lexa, don't do this," he hissed through clenched teeth. *"Please."*

"What choice do I have?" she shot back. "Sam, I promise you, I'll be fine. I'll be back." Shelby hadn't come back, but the circumstances were different this time. The Lord would keep her safe.

Sam's blue eyes pierced hers. "Wear your seat belt."

"No talking between you two!" Howard warned. "Just you and her." He nodded his head at Sheila. "Find out where my girl is, and then we're out of here."

Standing close to Sheila, Lexa turned and met the other woman's dark eyes. "Sheila, you've got to tell me where Angelina is. We don't have a choice if we're all going to make it through this. We can help, but we need your cooperation."

Sheila nodded and mumbled an address in a rundown section on the outskirts of the city. Lexa recognized the street name which was a miracle in itself. It wasn't far from where they turned off the dirt road onto the main highway when headed toward San Antonio.

"What happened to Howard's car?"

"Br–bro–broke d–down on th–th–the w–wa–way out he–here. H–he . . . a–aban–abandon–abandoned it, a–an–and . . . w–we wa–wa–walked . . . th–the re–rest of th–the . . . w–way."

Lexa frowned. They'd played right into Howard's hands by arriving at the mission when they did. But they had to help Sheila, so Lexa didn't regret any of it. Imprinting the address on her brain, she turned back around and swallowed her fear. "Okay. I know where she is."

Looking smug, Howard nodded in satisfaction. He kept the gun trained on them as he ordered them around the back wall of the mission. Telling them to kneel, Howard reached into a burlap bag he retrieved from the ground and pulled out a section of thick, white rope. He made quick work of tying their wrists and ankles, using a pocket knife to roughly sever the ends. Next he pulled out dirty cloths and forced them into their mouths but not before first reaching a hand down into Sam's pockets to make sure he, too, wasn't carrying a pocket knife. Finding one, Howard snarled and pocketed it.

Lexa's heart pounded with uncontrollable force as she watched Howard through terrified eyes. *Please, God. Help us. Don't let him do anything to Sam or Sheila. Not like this.* The scene was reminiscent of those movies where prisoners are blindfolded and shot while standing in front of a wall not unlike the mission behind them. Lexa shuddered.

"Come on! We've got some business to do." Howard threw a menacing look at Lexa.

With one last glance at Sam, who nodded and gave her a reassuring wink, Lexa allowed Howard to pull her along behind him.

Lord, please watch over us all tonight.

Chapter 41

"DON'T TRY ANYTHING funny," Howard warned, releasing his grip on her arm.

Lexa handed over the car keys on demand. "Don't worry. I won't." She climbed into the car beside him. He must not have bathed in a few days. Turning her head, Lexa exhaled slowly and tried not to breathe in. If only there was more of a breeze in the humid, still night air.

They rode in silence with Lexa speaking only when she needed to tell him when to turn the car. She prayed she'd remember the way. Howard wouldn't take kindly to being lost in the Texas countryside in the middle of the night.

"You one of those Jesus people, too?"

Lexa startled. She nodded but waited to see what he'd say next.

"Sometimes I'd listen to Sheila singing to Angelina at night." It sounded more like he was reminiscing out loud rather than consciously speaking to her. "She'd sing *Jesus Loves Me* and Angelina would start singin' in that sweet little voice of hers."

Lexa jumped as he slammed his big hand down hard on the steering wheel and muttered a stream of expletives. She slipped further down into the seat and leaned a bit closer to the door of the car. Her fingers gripped the door handle so tight they hurt.

"Get your hand off the door!" Howard roared, reaching over and shoving her arm. "Aren't you going to try and convert me?" he taunted, his voice full of contempt. "Try to tell me how Jesus loves me and wants me to be part of His kingdom or whatever that rot is you people are always talkin' about. Answer me, woman!" he bellowed when she didn't respond.

"Jesus *does* love you, Howard. Is that what you want to hear?" She shot a sidelong glance at him. "If I didn't know better, I'd say you're just dying to hear the truth about how He died for you and your sins. That's definitely something you should hear about," she muttered under her breath.

Watch it, Lexa. She needed to take it easy with this guy or he might lose his cool. She wanted to live past tonight if she had a prayer of a future with Sam. To Lexa's immense relief, Howard burst into booming laughter, amused by her wry sense of humor.

"Tell me why a guy like Jesus Christ should care about a guy like me." He made the Savior's name sound like a curse. But he'd asked the question.

Lexa sat up straighter in the car. Here she was being handed a golden opportunity to share the gospel, and she was about to let it pass her by. She shook her head at her own lack of perception and squared her shoulders, her mind searching for the right words. Sharing the gospel message was something

Sam and the other volunteers at the camp talked about a lot. But it was all new and foreign for her.

Even though she couldn't remember any complete scripture verses to save her life, she had to tell this man what she could. How ironic. It might be the only time Howard Morris ever heard the gospel message. The Lord had given her an awesome responsibility, and she couldn't let Him down. It wasn't the time to flee in the other direction. He had chosen *her* for the task.

You and me, Lord. Here goes.

"I'm a new believer myself." Lexa stole a glance. Howard appeared to listen. "It's all strange, but comforting in a weird way." Lexa couldn't believe she was engaged in conversation with a man who kidnapped his wife, then kidnapped her, and now intended to kidnap his daughter. "I've done a lot of bad things in my life that I'm sorry for, Howard." She hoped to reach him more on a more personal level by using his first name.

"Yeah, right," he muttered, turning onto a street where she directed. "Like you've done really bad things."

Now he was mocking her. She blew out a deep breath. "We've all done bad things. What you consider bad and what I consider bad—and what's considered bad in the eyes of the law—might all be different things. But you know what I mean."

She paused, and he nodded in agreement.

"You know, the things you do that you know in your heart are wrong." She hesitated a minute to let the effect of her words sink in. "I know you have a heart in there somewhere because it shows whenever you talk about Angelina."

"My little girl's the best thing that ever happened to me. I can't lose her." Howard slanted a glance her way. In that moment, he looked more curious than menacing. It went a long way toward soothing her trepidation. "What's your name?"

Lexa felt like lying but decided to give it to him anyway. "Alexis Clarke." She didn't bother telling him that most people called her Lexa. It was more a private name she didn't want Howard Morris to use. He grunted an unintelligible response, and she didn't ask him to repeat it.

"You're not a bad person, Howard. Why don't you stop all this hurting?" Her voice was quiet and calm. Maybe this is what it meant to have the Holy Spirit take over. He didn't answer, and she dared not look over at him. He slowed the car, but he kept going, much to Lexa's relief. She didn't know what she'd do if he stopped the car in the middle of nowhere. The insidious stirrings of fear began to rumble again in the pit of her stomach.

I will not be afraid. Lord be with me. I will not be afraid. She couldn't allow herself to give into paralyzing fear. It would serve no purpose other than perhaps getting herself killed. Deep down, Lexa didn't think Howard was capable of serious physical violence. She'd glimpsed the softness deep inside the man, but she didn't want to test his limits.

Talk about the Lord. Talk about something. Anything. Keep his mind occupied. You're almost there now.

"Jesus died for our sins, yours and mine." She forced a boldness into her voice so he'd hear over the noisy engine. It had started that annoying rumble. Lexa prayed the old Volvo would get them where they needed to go and then back to the mission. What in the world would they do if the bomb decided to give out when she was with Howard? She didn't even want to think about that one.

"Jesus was crucified and died a horrible death to take our place, Howard. He's our Savior because He died for the sins of man. All you have to do is confess your sins to Him and ask Him into your heart, and you'll have eternal life," she said, cramming it all in when it seemed he might try to stop her.

He started to interrupt her, but then stopped. Lexa could tell he was still listening.

"You'll live forever with Him . . ."

"I know what it means!" he shouted, slamming his big hand down on the steering wheel again. "You're crazy, lady. Just like Sheila, that boyfriend of yours, and all the rest of 'em," Howard muttered, shaking his head. "And I kinda had higher hopes for you."

"Maybe we're crazy," she rebutted in a firm voice, "but at least we know for sure we're going to heaven when we die. Can *you* say that much?"

"Shut up!" he demanded, turning to look at her with that menacing look in his dark eyes again. Lexa did as he commanded but turned her head, knowing she'd shared as much as she could with him and maybe given him something to think about and chew on.

Plant the seeds, Lexa. She couldn't expect to reap an immediate harvest with this man. But he'd heard what he needed to do to have eternal life. And he'd called her *lady* this time. The best thing was, it hadn't been hard at all to share about Jesus with this man.

"Turn here, and the house should be somewhere on this street" Lexa motioned with her arm, thankful they'd found it with no trouble. Howard turned off the noisy engine and they coasted down the narrow street. Steering over to the curb with concentrated effort, he ordered her to remain seated.

"What's the number of the house?" he barked in a gruff voice as he climbed out. He came around and yanked open her door, and motioned with his head for her to get out of the car.

"One-forty-two." Her eyes strained to see any house numbers in the darkness.

Pulling her along with a rough hand on her arm, Howard gestured to a house a few doors down. "Must be over here."

"I can walk by myself," Lexa protested. "I'm not going to run away. You can believe me." He looked at her long and hard before releasing her arm. She could still feel his rough fingers digging into her flesh.

"Make sure you don't." They made their way in silence toward the front door of the house, stopping on the front step. "What time is it?"

"I don't know." Lexa glanced up at the night sky. "Judging by the position of the moon, I'd say it's about four o'clock."

Howard snorted. "Ain't you the smart one? Well, then, it's time to wake some people up!" He rapped on the front door a few times, each knock louder and more insistent. A dog inside the house yapped, and soon they heard yelling and a door slammed.

From the back of the house, Lexa heard someone call out in Spanish. "Keep your pants on. I'm comin'," a disgruntled female voice called, this time in English. They heard the sound of a lock and then a deadbolt being unlatched before the door opened a crack.

"Yeah?"

Howard shoved Lexa in front of the door so the occupant of the house would only see her, not him.

"Yeah?" the woman repeated, staring at Lexa with wide eyes. "Hey, don't I know you?"

Lexa shook her head. "I'm sorry to disturb you at this hour, ma'am, but I'm in need of some assistance." She followed her gut instincts about what to say to this woman. "I need to use your phone if it's all right. Please."

The woman eyed Lexa, looking her up and down with one brow cocked. "Why? Some guy beat you up, sweetheart? You look okay to me." She started to close the door in her face until Lexa stuck her foot in the door, effectively blocking the woman from closing it entirely.

"You wanna keep the foot, you'd better move it."

"Look, I'm not a thief or a criminal, but I need a phone. Please," Lexa implored.

At least the woman didn't slam the door on her foot. Finally, she opened the door a crack and looked outside. In that moment, Howard seized his opportunity and burst past the woman into the house. Spouting a stream of loud profanity, the woman stared at Howard and then glared at Lexa with venomous eyes.

"I'm sorry." Lexa shifted to her other foot and captured the woman's eye contact. "I assure you, we don't mean you any harm." She kept her voice as calm as she could muster.

"Shut up! I don't wanna hear anything else outta the likes of you."

Lexa obeyed, knowing it was in her best interest. She stepped aside.

"What are you doin' here, Howard?" The tone was belligerent. She looked not in the least frightened or intimidated by this man. In fact, she looked meaner than he did, and downright menacing.

It was then that Lexa remembered where she'd seen this woman. "You're Margarita's mother, aren't you?" Lexa interrupted, stepping forward.

The woman laughed, but it lacked mirth. "Sweetheart, I ain't that girl's mother and I ain't never been. Only reason I'm keepin' that kid is 'cause she belongs to my sister. I'm doin' her a favor, keepin' that rug rat away from this good-for-nothin' lazy husband of hers. Howard," she said, returning her attention to him, "what do you think you're doin' burstin' in here at all hours of the night? You're a crazy idiot." Shaking her head, she plopped into a chair.

"Justina, go get Angelina now!" Howard yanked Lexa by the arm again and pulled the gun from the pocket of his pants.

The woman's eyes widened as she spied the gun, and she held up her hands. "Don't go and get all crazy on me. I'll get her for you. Hang on." She shrugged as she stood up again. "All she's been is a heap of trouble anyhow. I'm glad to get rid of her."

"Get her and shut up about it," Howard warned in a low, threatening tone. "If you don't, there's gonna be trouble. And, considering the amount of coke you've got stashed in your sofa cushions over there," he added, waving the gun, "I don't think you want the cops in here." At his words, Justina quickly departed the room without a word. In less than a minute, she was back in the living room with a small, sleepy girl in-tow.

Lexa cocked her head to one side, trying to get a better look at the child. Her hair was tousled and half in her face but there was no mistaking the haunted, dark eyes when they looked up at her.

Margarita.

Chapter 42

"MARGARITA?" LEXA HELD her breath as Margarita flew into her arms. Lexa held her tight. She stroked her hair and whispered that everything would be all right.

"Angelina, baby." Howard scowled in Lexa's direction. Stooping down, he opened his arms to his child. Angelina clung to Lexa, but stared with wide eyes at her father. "Come on. I won't hurt you, sweetie," he coaxed. At least he'd put away the gun. No need to scare the child with the weapon. Thank goodness he seemed like a halfway decent parent. That thought struck Lexa as highly ironic.

Angelina released her grip on Lexa and walked over to Howard. She laid her head on his shoulder. With gentle strokes, he ran his big hands over her hair, murmuring something into her ear. The child smiled her customary shy smile, and put a finger in her mouth, sucking on it in a familiar gesture. Watching Howard with his daughter, Lexa glimpsed a softer side of the gruff man. Yes, Angelina was his soft spot all right.

Margarita is Angelina. Sheila and Howard's daughter. Lexa didn't know why she hadn't put two and two together before. Same dark, silky hair, small hands and shy smile. But it was the big, sad eyes that were remarkable in their similarity. Sheila never worked with the children at the makeshift schoolhouse. She kept to herself, never talked about herself or revealed much about her life. This was all part of Sheila's plan to stay hidden and nondescript. Too bad it hadn't worked.

"Get a move on," Howard barked in Lexa's direction. She moved forward and grabbed the knob on the front door, aware that Justina's eyes bore into her back.

"Hurry it up," Howard repeated in a low voice. "We don't have all night." He followed behind Lexa, pulling Angelina along by the hand. "Come on, Angie. Your friend's comin', too." Lexa heard small whimpers and, as Howard passed her on the sidewalk, he picked up the child's slight form and threw her over one broad shoulder. Seemed men liked doing that.

Lexa grimaced as she started to climb into the back seat of the car beside Angelina. She was thankful he made sure his daughter was strapped in properly.

"Where do ya think you're goin'?" Howard kept his voice calm for Angelina's benefit. "Get up front, woman!" His small black eyes bore into hers.

Lowering her gaze, Lexa did as he ordered, giving Angelina a reassuring wink. She couldn't allow her to see any fear. She had to be strong enough for both of them. But all she wanted to do was hug the little girl close. But at least her mother would be able to do it soon enough if that was Howard's plan. Fear seized her again, squeezing tight.

"It's okay, Margar . . . Angelina." Lexa forced her voice to sound as soothing as possible considering the current circumstances. She was rewarded with a nod and a hint of a smile. Howard started the car again, and it sounded obnoxious in the quiet night. Cursing under his breath, he pulled the car around and headed in the opposite direction.

"You'd better tell me how to get back." This time, he made no attempts at conversation, and Lexa was grateful. Within fifteen minutes, they were back at the mission. Lexa felt like flinging open the car door and making a run, not to escape from Howard but to run toward the comfort of Sam.

If she wanted, she could have escaped on that quiet street. But Lexa couldn't leave Sam and Sheila at the mission, at the mercy of Howard. And she couldn't leave Angelina. She wanted to stay by Sam's side. The Lord put her in this situation for a reason, and she had to see it through. He'd protected her so far, and He'd continue to do so.

"Get out," Howard ordered said as soon as he turned off the engine.

Standing beside the car, Lexa held out one hand for Angelina. She crawled across the backseat and grasped Lexa's hand. Covering the small hand with hers, Lexa smiled. She loved when Sam held her hand, and she wanted to give the same measure of comfort and security to this frightened little girl.

Howard motioned for Lexa to move forward, following beside her as if to remind her not to try anything sneaky. Lexa moved in the direction of the back wall where he'd left his two hostages. Rounding the corner ahead of them, Howard motioned for Lexa to stop and keep Angelina with her. He disappeared. She guessed he was probably removing the gags and ropes from their mouths and hands. *He doesn't want Angelina to see her mother tied up.* The thought warmed her heart.

"Okay," he called to Lexa, gesturing with one hand for her to come closer and bring the girl. "Angie, baby, look who's here."

When they rounded the corner, Lexa saw Sheila stand up and wipe her hands on the sides of her shorts. She looked up with a trembling smile as Angelina went flying into her arms. "Mama!" the little girl cried, flinging her arms around Sheila's small form. They wept together, Sheila with her arms tight around Angelina.

Tears sprang into Lexa's eyes, and she turned away. It surprised her when Howard didn't interrupt their reunion. Maybe there was hope for this man yet. Looking over at Sam, she saw that he, too, was fighting strong emotions. Sensing Lexa's eyes on him, he moved his gaze over to her and smiled, nodding to let her know he was all right.

"Now, what am I goin' to do with you two?" Howard demanded with another one of his disgusting grins, his face twisted and evil with the moonlight streaming behind him. Frightened, Lexa instinctively reached for Sam's hand, moving closer to him as he captured her hand in his own firm grasp. When he squeezed it, Lexa felt small shivers running up and down her spine. Whether they were from fear or otherwise, she couldn't be sure.

"Let us go," Lexa pleaded. "Take the car." Ignoring Sam's elbow jabbing in her side and his grunt, she plundered on. "We're out here in the middle of nowhere, in the middle of the night. No one else is around, and it'll be a long time before we get to civilization. You could be halfway to Mexico . . . or wherever you're going by then."

"I'd keep her if I was you," Howard told Sam with another grin. "She makes a lot of sense. Seein' as how I really don't want to murder no one, maybe you're right. But, just to make sure," he added with a menacing leer, dangling the rope in front of him again.

"Sheila," he hollered over one shoulder, "take Angie and wait behind that wall over there. Go! Don't get any funny ideas because I'm right here, and I'm keepin' my eye on ya." Darting an anxious look in Lexa and Sam's direction and taking Angelina by the hand, Sheila started around the corner.

Howard made quick work of gagging Sam again and retying the ropes around his ankles and wrists. Then, with another one of his sickening grins, he turned to Lexa and did the same with her. In a flash, Howard was gone around the corner. Lexa scooted across the ground to lean against Sam. They both sat immobilized until they heard the distant rumbling of the Volvo's engine a few minutes later.

"Good job, Miss Clarke," Sam finally sputtered, spitting the gag out of his mouth. "You just gave away our only mode of transportation. Bomb or no bomb, it was *my* bomb." Leaning over close to her, Sam used his teeth to wrestle the gag free from Lexa's mouth. Winking, he shook his head and laughed.

"Well," Lexa huffed, staring at Sam in disbelief, "at least you still have your life, Mr. Lewis. Talk about gratitude," she grumbled, slumping back and frowning.

"You're right about one thing. Howard was no Boy Scout. He really doesn't know how to tie a decent knot. There," Sam added, breaking free of the ropes on both his wrists and feet and beginning to work on hers. "How's your thumb?"

"My thumb? Why?" Lexa pouted.

"Why, to hitchhike, of course."

"No, thanks," she protested, not bothering to thank him as he loosened the ropes binding her hands together. "I don't think I want to get into a moving vehicle with anyone who would be cruising around this area, especially, at this hour of the night." She untied the ropes around her feet.

"Suit yourself." Sam rose to his feet and started to walk away. When he realized Lexa wasn't right behind him, he walked back over to her. Reaching out with one hand, he helped her to a standing position. For a long moment, they stood and simply stared at one another. Without speaking, he moved closer. So did she.

"Look in the pocket of your jacket."

Sam looked at her with an odd expression. "My jacket? Why?"

Lexa's eyes never wavered from his, her voice steady. "Just look. In the right pocket."

"The jacket you're still wearing?"

"Yes. I promise it won't bite."

Sam stepped even closer and touched the bottom of the jacket. Feeling a heaviness in one pocket, he reached inside with tentative fingers, his eyes never leaving hers. His eyes grew large as he pulled out the gun. He held it as though afraid it might discharge.

"Don't worry. The bullets are gone." Lexa shrugged and grinned "What can I say? My dad was a cop."

Chapter 43

$\mathcal{H}$OW DID YOU get the gun away from Howard without him knowing it was gone?" Sam looked incredulous, but admiration for her shone in his eyes.

Lexa shrugged. "It fell out of his pocket on the drive back to the mission. He was saying something to Angelina and looking in the rearview mirror. I seized the moment, grabbed the gun and stuffed it inside the jacket." She laughed. "Good thing you're so tall and your jacket has such long pockets. As for why Howard didn't notice the gun was missing, I think we need to thank the Lord for that one."

"I feel a little better with Howard taking off with Sheila and Angelina knowing he doesn't have the gun," Sam admitted, raking a hand through his hair.

"Maybe we should find the nearest phone and call the police."

"Howard's still Sheila's husband, so I don't know that they'd do anything about it." Sam frowned.

"But he still kidnapped Sheila, and me . . . and Angelina," Lexa reminded him. This time, she didn't hesitate to smooth her fingers over the worry lines crossing his forehead.

"Sheila and I managed to talk, even though Howard gagged us—not very well, at that."

"Oh?" Lexa's hand moved to her hip. "Why do I have the feeling Sheila doesn't want us to report what Howard did? And you don't, either?"

"Put it this way. She's going to get away from Howard as soon as she can. As long as Angelina is with them, Howard won't hurt Sheila. And thankfully you have the gun." Sam shrugged. "I say we trust in the Lord to watch over them. Call it instinct, call it a gut feeling, but I think Howard will do something stupid and get himself caught tonight. Mark my words."

"And your precious bomb?"

"We'll see what happens. Something tells me that old bomb's not ready to die just yet. If it does decide to finally die, maybe this would be the right time." Sam took another step closer. He had that look in his eye she recognized and really liked. Full of meaning, and capable of making her giddy. "You are one amazing woman, Lexa Clarke. Come here. Please."

"I beg your pardon?" She giggled, feeling silly but heady with happiness. Maybe it was the emotion of the night. Maybe it was that the nightmare was over and they were safe. Maybe it was the man standing beside her and the overwhelming love she felt for him.

"You heard me." Sam's voice was low. Seductive. Inviting. Lexa took a step closer.

Sam smiled. "Come closer. *Much* closer." When she complied, he reached for her. Pulling Lexa to him, Sam held nothing back as he kissed her. One hand cupped her face, and his fingers ran through her long strands of hair. He whispered her name and caressed the back of her neck as he deepened their kisses.

"I was . . . so . . . scared tonight," Lexa managed to get out in-between kisses.

"Me, too," Sam murmured, covering her mouth with his own again, not able to get enough of her. He silenced her in the best possible way.

"You were so brave," she told him the next time she came up for air.

"Not as brave as you, my love. I do believe that after tonight, you're my hero." Sam's lips dropped down to gently nuzzle her neck with enticing kisses, causing quick shivers up and down her spine.

"Heroine," Lexa corrected, allowing him to help her shrug the jacket free from her shoulders as it slid to the ground in a soft heap at their feet.

"Right. Now, be quiet, my brave, beautiful heroine. Don't talk. Don't think. Just be quiet and kiss me back. Please," Sam pleaded with a soft laugh.

They collapsed to the ground together, their bodies intertwined. All the emotion, pent-up tension and longing of the past few weeks flooded out of Lexa as she clung to Sam, savoring the rawness of his mouth possessing hers, his strong body so close, wrapping her in the cocoon of warmth and love.

He moaned a little and kissed her with increasing passion. His hand traced its way in an achingly slow, gentle path along the curve of her face. His touch was feathery light as his fingers lingered on the small of her neck. His skin, his touch, warmed her everywhere. Hesitating a moment, Sam pulled back and gazed down at her with all the love he held for her.

"Should I stop? Tell me when to stop." His voice was huskier, deeper than ever.

Lexa answered Sam by pulling his head back down to her waiting lips, welcoming his own with everything within her.

He pulled her even closer to him. "I love you, Lexa," he whispered in her ear before reclaiming her mouth. There was no doubt in her mind this man was her destiny. She'd never been this close to a man, and she wanted to give herself totally to him—mind, soul and body. But as much as she loved Sam Lewis, Lexa couldn't cheapen what they had by making love with a man who wasn't her husband. Deep down, passion aside, that's what Sam wanted for them, too. It might be what they wanted in the heat of the moment, but it wasn't God's way.

Ignoring the warning bells in her head, Lexa lost herself in the moment. Sam's fingers flirted with the bottom edge of her thin cotton blouse. To his credit he was good, but if they kept this up, it was only a matter of time. The endearments he murmured under his breath were every bit as exciting. Heady. *Dangerous.*

It seemed like the most natural thing in the world, but when Lexa felt her body rising in anticipation, she knew they must stop. Especially when Sam shifted his position, Lexa thought she'd go mad. *This is dangerous, Lord, and we've got to stop.* She didn't want it to stop, but she shouldn't have let it go this far. She needed to be the stronger one. As strong as Sam Lewis was, he was still a man with passion and physical desires.

"Sam?" Summoning every last bit of courage, Lexa dragged her lips away from his long enough to gasp for air. "Sam . . ." Her fingers clasped over his, gently drawing his hand away.

"Hmm?" His voice was distracted as he found a delicious new place to nuzzle where the base of her neck met her shoulder. Lexa's eyes fluttered, and she inhaled a deep breath. When he started to withdraw his hand from hers, she held on tighter even though everything within her screamed to let his hand roam with abandon, wherever it desired. Sam wanted it, she wanted it.

Lord, give me strength, she pleaded under her breath. "Sam, we've got . . . to stop." She pushed against his chest with a gentle hand. "We've got to stop," she repeated. "I'm sorry. I shouldn't have let it go this far. What we're doing now is as dangerous as having that gun pointed at us tonight."

Sam stopped kissing the softest part of her neck and grazed her lips once more before releasing a low, guttural moan from somewhere deep in his throat. He collapsed on the ground beside her. Even though she'd never heard that particular sound before, Lexa knew without a doubt it was a groan of desire. Unfulfilled desire, but desire nonetheless. She wanted to groan, too. But they were right to stop.

"Lexa," Sam said, raising on one elbow as they lay side-by-side on the ground, "you are so beautiful in every way. And right now, every manly, earthly, lustful, sinful desire within me wants you more than I've ever wanted anything else in my entire life." He leaned in close for another deep kiss. Groaning again, he struggled to a sitting position. "It's also best if we stay upright. Safer that way. Rolling around in the dirt with you is fun, but it's way too tempting."

She felt dazed. It would take a moment to recover her senses and see straight. He helped her reach a sitting position beside him. Seeing that several buttons on her cotton blouse had come undone, Sam reached for her with trembling hands. His eyes caressed her, making her shudder. She'd never felt this intense a physical response before, and it both thrilled and scared her. Lexa watched him, her eyes wide and full of emotion.

"Are you buttoning . . . or unbuttoning them?" The night was so quiet and still. Surely he could hear how hard her heart pounded.

"Against my every instinct, my every desire, but abiding by my better judgment," Sam told her at length, closing his eyes as his fingers paused, "I am buttoning them for you. I love you too much to *not* button them."

Lexa watched in silence as this dear man opened his eyes and sat back to gaze upon her with a look all at once so loving and full of longing it made her heart stop. His adoration for her shone in every nuance of his face, his every movement, his every glance.

"There will be a time for us. When it happens, in God's timing, it will be spectacular, I have no doubt. But tonight," he said, a faraway glaze in his eyes, "and really for the first time ever in my life, I can understand why Josh and Shelby were so tempted. I'm very sorry I put you in that position. It wasn't fair to you."

She nodded. "Don't be. I wanted it as much as you, trust me. But I'm sorry if I did something wrong, tempted you in some way." She shot him a coy grin. "You were bound and determined to button my blouse tonight—one way or the other—weren't you?"

Sam laughed and pulled her close again. "You're always tempting, Lexa. You're like the peach pie cooling on the stove that can't be sampled until Thanksgiving dinner. The wrapped present under the tree that can't be opened until Christmas."

His sigh was deep and prolonged. "It was so tempting to throw caution to the wind, and make love to you tonight. Lord knows, that's what I wanted. You and I are both adults. Undeniably hot-blooded, passionate adults," he mumbled, shaking his head and running his fingers through his hair. Sam touched the side of her face in what was becoming a precious, sweet gesture. His fingers lingered as he held her gaze.

"Even though I know God is watching, I like to think He understands our struggles. Above all, I want to honor Him by respecting you enough to keep you pure. I've never been intimate with a woman, and it will be you, but in God's time. As hard as it is—and the Lord knows how difficult it is—I can wait." He winked. "Hope it's not too hard for you."

She smiled and laced her fingers through his. "Don't flatter yourself. But you're awfully hard to resist, Mr. Lewis. I appreciate your honesty."

Sam looked at her with a look of longing before shaking his head and letting his fingers drop back to his lap. "It's a beautiful thing how God knew that man needed woman, and then gave us the ability to love, emotionally and physically."

"All in good time, Sam. All in good time," Lexa promised with a soft smile, reaching with one finger to trace his lips.

"Trust me, beautiful girl," he told her, kissing her fingertips before leaning over to kiss her forehead, "it will definitely be well worth the wait, and God will honor our decision. Suddenly, though, this cowboy feels very old." His grin was wry, those smile lines never more endearing.

~

After leaving the mission and walking for the better part of an hour, they reached a convenience store where Sam called for a taxi. They rode in silence, and he dozed a little, leaning his head on her shoulder. She stroked his hair and closed her eyes, thanking the Lord for keeping them safe and praying for Sheila and Angelina.

Even though they'd been up all night, as the dawn started to emerge on the horizon, they sat together at the camp, leaning against their special tree. "I pray Sheila and Angelina are all right." Lexa rested her head against his strong shoulder. Her back was to him with his arms wrapped around her.

"I know, baby. I know." She closed her eyes as Sam prayed for safety for her roommate and her daughter, as well as for Howard. The night sky faded on the horizon as they enjoyed the quiet closeness without anyone else around.

As she turned to face him, Sam smoothed Lexa's hair away from her face and lightly kissed her cheek.

"I'm sorry I was so sarcastic. It's my instinctive reaction in times of stress, I suppose. Kind of a self-defense device. That and the history lessons." They laughed together. Sam's eyes searched hers for a long moment. "I'm so thankful you weren't hurt. In case I haven't told you lately, I love you, Lexa."

"I love you, too, Sam. More than you know."

He helped her reach a standing position, steadying her when she swayed a bit. Wrapping his hand around hers, they walked together toward the dorm and their uncertain future together, whatever it might bring.

God had a definite plan in bringing the two of them together. The relationship with Sam was right, and while it wasn't perfect, life didn't get much better. As they walked, she squeezed Sam's hand tight, releasing a long sigh of pure contentment.

Chapter 44

*T*HE NIGHT OF the farewell party was beautiful, warm but with enough of a breeze to make it more bearable than in recent days. Lexa sat on her bed with the wrapped gifts for Sam beside her. The brown suede Indiana Jones-style hat was in the bigger box to be presented to him in front of the entire crew. Picking up the smaller box containing the watch, Lexa tucked it beneath her pillow for a later time. It was something to give Sam in private.

"Ready?" Rebekah ran a quick brush through her long blonde tresses.

"As ready as I'll ever be, I suppose."

"You look really pretty, Lexa. But tonight is rather difficult for you, isn't it?" Rebekah was pretty perceptive about her relationship with Sam. "Have you two made any decisions about your future?" She shook her head. "I'm sorry for prying into your personal business. Just give me the Nibby Nose Award already."

They both laughed. "I wish I could tell you that Sam and I have worked everything out, Beck, but we haven't. It's true that only the Lord knows at this point."

They walked together in the direction of the dining tent where the party was starting and refreshments were being served. A portable CD player and speakers pumped out contemporary Christian music, providing a stereo effect throughout the entire area.

As they approached the tent, Lexa's eyes scanned the gathering crowd for Sam. While she didn't want to rush over to his side like a leech, she wanted to spend as much time as possible with him since their time together at the camp was dwindling. She comforted herself with the thought that he promised to call her when he was back in Houston a few days after the workers left the worksite.

"Lexa."

Turning, Lexa smiled into Sam's startling blue eyes. Tonight he wore a red, long-sleeved shirt, rolled at the cuffs and tucked into his jeans. He looked even more handsome in red. It intensified the gorgeous hue of those amazing eyes. The cowboy hat was conspicuous in its absence, his dark hair in need of a haircut after the summer spent at the camp. It covered his ears and fell in soft waves over his collar.

"You look lovely."

"Thanks. You don't look so bad yourself." Being dramatic, she sniffed. "Is that aftershave?" Lexa laughed as he gave her a shrug accompanied by a sheepish grin.

"Listen, I got some good news a few minutes ago." He took her hands and pulled her aside. "The state police called. It seems Howard stopped at a mini-mart outside the city last night, intent on relieving them of their cash. When he realized he didn't have the gun, the clerk pulled a gun on *him*." Sam grinned. "Long story short? Sheila and Angelina are safe and sound, and Howard will be in jail for a good long while."

"Sam! Thank the Lord you were right!" Lexa threw her arms around his neck in a big hug, not caring that other TeamWork volunteers watched. Sam embraced her, giving her a quick kiss. He obviously didn't care everyone knew they were an item, and it thrilled her. Who was she kidding? They all probably knew before she and Sam did, judging by the reaction of her roommates alone.

"There's more." Enthusiasm infused the deep timbre of his voice. "The police also picked up your favorite car. It's being delivered to me right here in the camp sometime late tomorrow morning. Which means I'll be able to drive you back to meet your bus after all—in style. In the bomb I know you love so very much."

Sam laughed again as he glimpsed Lexa's skeptical expression. "Love me, love my bomb. Seriously, Lexa, I love how you saw Sheila's underlying strength more so than any of the rest of us. Just another reason to love you." He dropped a quick kiss on her nose.

Lexa released a sigh. "I'll pray that Howard might see the light, so to speak, and realizes his need for Someone other than himself to help turn his life around. He loves Angelina without question. Hopefully, she can be the guiding light he needs." She shrugged. "Sounds like he'll have plenty of time for thinking now that he's behind bars."

Sam nodded. "Now, then, on to our party. Want some punch?"

"Why, I'd love some, Mr. Lewis." Taking his proffered arm, Lexa walked into the tent by his side. As she watched Sam, his eyes alive with excitement as he talked with his TeamWork volunteers, Lexa gloried in the fact this wonderful man loved her. He attended to her needs at the party—making sure her punch cup was full, including her in his conversations, listening with rapt attention whenever she had something to say. Hooking his arm through hers on several occasions, Sam made sure everyone knew how important she was to him. Lexa's head was spinning. The Lord had blessed her immeasurably.

The two of them talked and laughed with various members of the volunteer staff for over an hour until Winnie and Natalie sounded the dinner gong to get everyone's attention. Reaching beneath the podium, Winnie pulled out the wrapped package.

"We have a little presentation to make. Sam," Winnie called, looking around the crowd, "would you come up here, please?" It wasn't hard to find him since he was the tallest man in the group. He smiled as several of the men slapped him on the back and whooped, whistled and hollered as he headed toward the front.

Watching him, Lexa's eyes filled with tears. She turned away for a moment. Noticing her dilemma, another girl standing near Lexa handed her a tissue. Blowing her nose, Lexa smiled her thanks.

After the presentation was made, along with a few humorous awards, Sam strode back to Lexa's side with his new hat perched proudly on his head. "So, what do you think, Most Promising TeamWork Volunteer?" Acting silly, he postured in front of her with a big grin.

"I definitely like it," she told him with an admiring glance. "Just don't let it go to your head."

Sam laughed. "Beautiful *and* witty!" Grabbing her hand in his protective grasp, he leaned close, whispering in her ear. "What do you say we wrap this up and blow this popsicle stand?"

Lexa laughed and nodded her agreement.

A short time later, as most of the group started to disburse, Sam and Lexa walked together. "So, did you ever find out what happened with the money?"

"You know, it's a funny thing about that." He stopped walking and gave her an odd look. "I went into the office to write out my report and found an envelope on my chair. Containing exactly five hundred dollars." His eyes softened. "Seems there's no need to make a report. Know anything about that, Miss Clarke?"

Lexa hid her grin. "Not a thing except to say your volunteers love you, Sam. And no," she added, "no one else knows about the missing money. It's our secret."

"It's not *your* money, is it, Lexa?"

She shook her head. "The donations for your hat came in at exactly five hundred dollars more than we needed." She shrugged. "Call it a donation for TeamWork and enjoy the hat."

Sam smiled. "The Lord always has a way of working these things out, doesn't He?"

"In the most inventive and marvelous ways." Lexa beckoned him near. "Come closer, please. *Much* closer." She loved that he still wore his glasses from when he made his final remarks to the TeamWork crew at the party. All the more fun to remove those glasses.

The playful look she adored creased Sam's smile lines in a most charming manner, and it turned her inside out. In a very good way. "I really adore a man in glasses, but . . ."

He pulled back, teasing. "I hope you don't mean just *any* man?"

Lexa's heart swelled. "The man standing in front of me now. The man with the most beautiful *heart* I've ever known." With painstaking care, she inched the glasses down his nose.

"You're taking way too long." Sam yanked them off his face to spare her the trouble. "Save that for when we're old and gray." Taking her in his arms, he kissed her silly—so much so, Lexa needed his support. Or maybe she was holding him up. They definitely needed each other.

"Not to change the subject," Sam said a good while later, "but you don't really hate my bomb, do you?" He looked a little goofy with a hazy, besotted expression.

Lexa laughed. "You know, believe it or not, I've grown rather fond of that old station wagon. If your old bomb means that much to you, then I kind of love it, too." She leaned her head against Sam's chest, snuggling into him. His arms found their way around her, holding her close, secure and safe from everything in the world. Dwarfed by how tall he was, Lexa cherished how Sam made her feel statuesque.

"Glad to hear it." He sounded relieved. It was amazing how much that old station wagon meant to him.

"It's not the most romantic place, is it?" Lexa scanned the barren landscape around the worksite.

"On the contrary," Sam said, watching her. "To me, it's one of the loveliest places on earth."

Lexa stared at him, wide-eyed. "Oh? Had your eyes checked lately?" She grinned. "Maybe you should put your glasses back on."

Sam didn't laugh. "Considering it's the place where I fell in love with you, it seems full of its own unique charm."

Lexa sighed. "You're making this even more difficult when you say things like that."

Sam took her hands in his. "This is just the beginning, you know. It's not the end."

"I know." Lexa couldn't prevent the tears from forming and starting to slide down her cheeks. "I'm afraid," she admitted, looking up to meet his eyes.

Raising her chin with his hand, Sam smiled. "I'll never leave you, Lexa. There are two things you can always count on—the love of the Savior and *my* love for you."

As much as Lexa wanted to believe Sam's promise, it was difficult since her father had abandoned her when she was a child after her mother's death. Other than providing for her physical needs, he'd never been there for her in other ways, and she wondered if she could ever count on any man. But, if she could count on any man, it would be *this* man.

"I only have one regret," Lexa murmured, her cheek resting against the soft cotton of his shirt. She burrowed her head, taking a deep breath.

"Hmm?" Sam sounded far away. "What's that?"

"I never got to see the Alamo."

"You're right." He chuckled. "That *is* a crime. But," he said, "I'll make you another promise. One year from today, I will meet you at the Alamo. How's that?" He laughed at her incredulous stare. "I'm not kidding. No matter where TeamWork sends me in the next year, I'll meet you in front of the Alamo exactly one year from today. The TeamWork foreign mission will actually be a few days less than a full year. So, I'll be definitely be back in a year's time. To meet you here in San Antonio. At the Alamo."

"I don't know," Lexa answered, shaking her head with a slight grin as she looked back up at Sam again. "That sounds like a movie plot to me. You know, the one where the two star-crossed lovers agree to meet on the top of the Empire State Building a year later if they still have feelings for one another."

"I must have missed that one," Sam murmured, tenderly nuzzling her hair with his lips. "Do they meet up again?"

"Yes, but not without first going through tragedy and heartache."

Meeting her gaze once more, Sam placed tender hands on her cheeks. "I promise you I'll be there, Lexa—at six o'clock sharp," he added with a quick laugh. "The only reason we *won't* meet at the Alamo in one year's time is if you decide you don't want me."

"I'll always want you, Sam Lewis."

Lowering his lips to hers, Sam sealed his promise with another unforgettable kiss.

~

In the middle of the afternoon the following day, Sam pulled the station wagon up to the Greyhound terminal, twenty minutes before Lexa's bus was scheduled to leave for Houston. They were both silent during the drive from the camp, each lost in their own thoughts and dreading the actual moment of good-bye.

It had been hard enough to bid farewell to Winnie, Amy, Natalie, the other girls, and especially Rebekah, with promises to stay in touch. Since Amy lived in New York and Natalie in Boston, Lexa had no idea when she might see them again. She hoped it might be on a future TeamWork mission. With Winnie living just outside Houston and Rebekah in a small town near Baton Rouge, Louisiana, Lexa felt sure she'd reconnect with them. The group had formed close bonds during their eight weeks together, and she didn't want to let these wonderful people go forever

"Here, I forgot to give this to you last night." Lexa held out the small, slim box containing the watch as they stood facing one another outside the bus terminal.

Taking it from her with a curious look, Sam unwrapped it with quick fingers. Spying the watch nestled inside, his laugh was rich but subdued. "I love it." Removing it from the box, he fastened it on his bare wrist. "This is precisely what I need. Thank you, Lexa. It's very thoughtful. You always take care of my needs." When he looked up at her, those blue eyes mesmerized her all over again.

"You're welcome." She wanted to always take care of this man's needs. Smiling through tremulous lips, Lexa watched the bus pull up to the curb behind them. "That's my bus," she told him in a hushed voice. Sam nodded without speaking. Even though he made no move to touch her, his eyes spoke volumes.

A cough overwhelmed her, and Lexa succumbed. Putting one quick hand across her stomach and the other over her mouth, she coughed hard.

"Are you okay, sweetheart? Dust in your lungs?"

"No. *Love* in my lungs."

"Oh." He groaned a little, and they laughed together. Lexa was afraid she'd burst into tears and wanted to keep the mood light. When Sam bundled her close, she clung to him. Her hands gripped his shoulders, and she closed her eyes. She'd never thought of herself as a clingy female, but with Sam, she never wanted to leave the circle of those strong arms. A big part of the equation was that he'd soon be gone for the next year. It was her own bitter pill to swallow.

"I'm not going to say good-bye to you, Sam," Lexa whispered as he held her tight. She was becoming an emotional ninny around this man. But she didn't care.

"Then don't. I'll call you in a couple of days when I get to Houston." Sam tapped her chin with gentle fingers. "Remember, this is the easy part."

"Do you know where you're going or anything about your schedule for the next year?"

He picked up her suitcase to walk her over to the bus. The driver took the bag from Sam and told Lexa she needed to board as soon as possible. "No, but I should know more by the time I see you in Houston."

With a quick kiss and a murmured good-bye, Lexa hurried up the steps and onto the bus. Finding a window seat midway down the aisle, she dropped into the seat and waved out the window. A part of her wished Sam would simply climb in that old white station wagon and leave. It might make it easier for both of them. But another, deeper part of her, wanted him to stand there until the bus was out of view. He chose the latter route.

As the bus pulled away in a cloud of ever-present brown dust, Sam slowly raised his hand. As she settled back against her seat, wiping away a tear, Lexa knew it wasn't her imagination that a tear made its path down *his* cheek.

Chapter 45

$\mathscr{O}$PENING THE DOOR of her townhome, Lexa expected to see Sam standing on the doorstep. No Sam. Sticking her head outside, she looked one way and then the other. Hmm. She heard the distinct knock, and it was six-thirty on Friday night, the time he was expected to arrive. The man was always as punctual as clockwork. Then she saw it. On the ground, propped against the bushes to the right of her front door, was a long white box tied with a yellow satin ribbon.

Smiling, she crept closer and spied a small white envelope with *Lexa* written on the front. Scooping the box in her arms, she swept back inside her townhome and carried it over to the small kitchen. Untying the ribbon, she let the ends fall aside as she opened the top of the box. Parting the white tissue paper, she gasped in delight as she spied a dozen, long-stemmed yellow roses, along with baby's breath, nestled inside.

"They're gorgeous," she breathed, picking up one of the blooms and inhaling its scent. She'd never received flowers before in her life. Sam's loving sentiment was precious to her. Lexa felt like laughing with pure joy and bursting into tears all at the same time. The roses were the most beautiful shade of yellow she'd ever seen, symbolizing hope and sunshine, and a reflection of the way Sam made her feel inside.

How could he know they'd mean so much to her? Because he was such a caring, thoughtful man. Not to mention highly intuitive. Sam never asked about her past relationships, not that there was much to tell. Sam was so confident in his own skin. He trusted her to tell him if there was anything he should know.

Remembering she hadn't opened the card, she retrieved the small white envelope with shaky fingers and pulled out the card tucked inside. *My dearest Lexa, I might be in some far off land, but my heart will remain with you always. Trust in the Lord. He'll take care of you always and wrap His loving arms around you, holding you close when I can't. With great hope and expectation for our future together. Love, Sam. Ephesians 1:13-17.*

That did it. Oh, the cowboy could be so romantic. The tears started a steady stream down her cheeks. She'd even applied a little makeup, and now it was ruined. Never mind. Walking over to the mirror in the hallway, she wiped away a few last stray tears and tried her best to compose herself, forcing deep breaths.

It was great to wear something nice for Sam instead of the shorts and T-shirts she'd worn at the campsite. Not to mention they were both covered with a layer of dust or dirt at the work camp. Tonight she'd chosen a pretty, light pink cotton dress and high-heeled sandals. She'd never been one for frills and liked simple and elegant styles. She hoped Sam liked it. It was amazing how she suddenly wanted to dress to please a man, to please one particular man. Just eight short weeks ago, Lexa wouldn't have thought it possible. What a difference a TeamWork camp makes indeed.

This night promised the beginning of one of the most wonderful weeks of her life when they could explore their developing relationship apart from the demands and rigors of the work camp. The possibilities were endless. At the end of the week, she'd miss him something terrible. The thought that he'd be gone for an entire year almost broke her heart.

Lexa forced herself to concentrate on the here and now as she carried the gorgeous yellow roses into the kitchen and retrieved a vase under the sink. She handled it with care since it belonged to her mother. As unemotional and unromantic as her father had been, he'd given her mother flowers on the occasional birthday or Valentine's Day. Filling the vase with water, Lexa dumped in the contents of the preservative packet that had been tucked in the box along with the fresh blooms.

Another knock. Busy in the kitchen, Lexa knew this time it was Sam. Her heart pounded with anticipation although it had only been a few days since she left the TeamWork camp. She could only imagine what seeing Sam would be like again after an entire year had passed. She pushed that thought aside—again. Tonight, and the entire week ahead, was about enjoying being with the man she loved.

Smoothing her dress with a quick hand, Lexa fluffed her long hair and took another deep, steadying breath which proved futile once she saw Sam standing on her doorstep. He was making acquaintance with dear Clarice Swanson, her next door neighbor. Charming her from the looks of it. Goodness, the man could charm the shell off an armadillo.

"I was meeting your young man, Lexa." Clarice gave her a knowing wink. "Hang on to him, dear. He's a keeper."

"You think so?" Lexa practically hauled Sam over the threshold. With a wave as Clarice made her way down the front walkway, she closed the front door. Leaning back against the door, she was literally swept up in his arms as he pulled her to him and peppered her cheeks, her forehead and then her lips with light kisses.

"Is that the best you can do?" She pulled him toward her and planted one of the best kisses of her life on his expectant lips. At length, she eyed him with appreciation. He was dressed in khaki slacks and a gorgeous, medium blue, lightweight V-neck sweater. "I'd say you clean up pretty well, Mr. Lewis." Lexa always loved sweaters on men. Even though it was warm outside, the night air could sometimes get chilly.

"And you're incredibly beautiful, Miss Clarke."

Lexa sighed. "It's hard to know what to do with that, you know."

"Ah, but I thought you were getting much more adept at handling compliments."

"Speaking of beautiful, I was arranging a bouquet of absolutely gorgeous yellow roses delivered a few minutes ago. Have any idea where they might have come from?"

Sam chuckled. "Probably another one of your many admirers. I figured you might like yellow roses. After all, what woman in Texas doesn't?" Even as she acknowledged that sentiment, Lexa knew she'd love dandelions—weeds—from this man. She'd take anything he offered because it would come from the purest part of his heart.

"You're adorable when you giggle." Sam helped her put the last of the long-stemmed roses in the tall vase after first plucking away a few of the leaves and trimming the bottom. "Ouch. I knew that would happen," he complained after pricking his index finger on one of the thorns. He wrung his hand and raised his finger to his lips before smiling and holding it up. "Care to kiss it and make it all better?"

She laughed. "After you just had your germs all over it? Not on your life."

"The threat of germs didn't stop you from kissing me."

"Different and you know it." They laughed together and bantered back and forth as they prepared to go to dinner. Her momentary fear that they might not have anything to talk about at the end of the TeamWork camp was dispelled completely. Lexa remembered to grab her sweater as they headed outside, although she suspected keeping warm anytime in the week ahead wouldn't be a problem.

"So, do you still have your job at Alamo World Financial?" Sam wrapped his arm around her and pulled her close as they walked together toward the station wagon. Lexa appreciated how he kept his strides purposely short to keep pace beside her.

"Believe it or not, they hired someone else to take my place, but that person proved not quite competent enough to handle the workload."

"Are you going to bury yourself in work while I'm gone?"

"What do you expect me to do? Pine away for the man I love?" she teased, before turning more serious. "Yes, I'll probably pour myself into work. But don't remind me." Lexa buried her head against him, loving the feel, the smell, the everything of Sam. She wanted to savor every sense, every feeling, every emotion. "I don't want to spend this week talking about financial planning or anything close to it. But I know one thing I'll do while you're gone. I'm going to practice making peach pie."

He laughed, helping her into the car. "Let me take the most gorgeous woman in the world to dinner."

~

"So, did you pick out that blue sweater all on your own or did you have some help?" Lexa asked as they sat across from one another at dinner at The Grotto a short time later. It was romantic and elegant and featured a small, cascading waterfall in the middle of the dining room and a pianist played quiet ballads in a corner.

"My sister, Rachel, gave it to me for Christmas this past year. Said it would match my eyes." Although his smile was broad, Sam rolled his eyes.

"She's right. Tell me more about your family."

As they waited for their salads to be delivered, Sam reached for her hand. He squeezed, but did not relinquish it. "It's a big family with lots of stories." His eyes sparkled.

"Start by telling me about your mom and dad."

"This could take all night. I'm taking you to meet them later in the week, you know."

Lexa's heart beat faster. "Really?"

"They've been clamoring loudly for the honor of making your acquaintance. All right," he said, taking a deep breath, "I'm the oldest of six kids. I'm the namesake, which means my dad is obviously Sam, Sr. My mom is Sarah, and my siblings are—in order—identical twins Rachel and Emily, followed by Will, Caty and Carson. Rachel and Emily graduated from the University of Texas in Austin a few years ago and now live out on the west coast."

"Is that where you went to college?" Funny, they'd never even discussed their education. They'd talked about everything else under the sun.

"Yes. Degree in finance. You?"

"Same, but at Rice."

Sam nodded. "Will's a hotshot aeronautical engineer and Air Force pilot with grandiose dreams of working for NASA." Sam chuckled. "I think watching Grandpa Lewis tinker with all those old airplane engines started something with Will. He's a genius when it comes to scientific matters but lacks general common sense. My brother likes to tell God how things are going to be ordered in the universe. At least the universe according to Will. He also looks a lot like the person sitting across the table from you. Just a few inches shorter." He grinned.

"Catherine, or Caty, is my sweet Caty Bug, and I'm closer to her and Carson—the baby of all us kids—than the others. Those are the two you're most likely to meet, along with my parents, when I take you to meet them at the family homestead."

Lexa eyed him, curiosity written in her expression. "Why do you feel closer to Caty and Carson?" Since she never had any siblings, it was wonderful to think Sam had so many.

Sam shrugged. "Family dynamics, I suppose. They're all great, but Rachel and Emily always have this little twin thing going on between them. They've pretty much done everything together their whole lives—same schools, same schedules, even dated twin brothers for a while." He smiled. "Even though they have separate identities, I sometimes feel they're also too wrapped up in the other. It would probably do them a world of good to go off on their own and find out exactly who they are as separate individuals for a while. I hope that makes sense."

"It makes perfect sense."

"Caty will be a sophomore at Wheaton College in September. Of all my siblings, I'll miss her the most while I'm away on this TeamWork mission. She and I have always thought a lot alike and shared our thoughts with one another. I think she's always looked to me as her protector of sorts, although she's certainly very strong and independent in her own right." He chuckled, obviously remembering a fond memory.

"What are you thinking?" Lexa prompted.

"Caty called me one night during her junior year of high school and begged me to come to one of the downtown hotels and rescue her from an overly amorous prom date who . . . let's just say had big plans involving a hotel room. I picked her up, took her home and we spent an hour slow dancing together in our living room. She needed a prom date that night, not an overbearing big brother. Caty always asks me for advice and wants to know things like why guys grunt so much, slap each other on the back, smell their socks before putting them in the laundry hamper and wolf down their food so fast."

Lexa laughed. "And what about you, Sam?"

He lifted his brows. "Me?"

"Why will you miss Caty the most while you're gone?"

Sam sighed and repositioned his hand on the tabletop, intertwining her fingers with his. "Caty shares my passion for the Lord. She's a deep thinker. We can spend hours debating theological issues, and often do. We don't always agree, which challenges me all the more. I don't insist people agree with my opinion, but I like them to be able to adequately defend their position. Caty always holds up her end of the bargain in that respect."

"And Carson?"

Sam smiled. "Carson shares that fierce love of the Lord, too, but he's still very young. I believe he might pursue full-time ministry of some type in the future."

Lexa laughed. "Remind me never to get involved in a theological debate with you."

Sam gave her one of his irresistible, lazy grins. "I'd rather debate other things with you, Lexa."

"Such as?" She gave him a coy smile.

"Saved by the salads." Sam winked as their server placed them on the table.

"Why don't you pray that we can manage to get through this meal without causing a little scene," Lexa suggested. Sam laughed out loud, and they bowed their heads to pray. For the rest of the meal, they sampled each other's food, laughed, teased and enjoyed a wonderful evening. Every minute spent with Sam, Lexa learned something new or different about him. She'd always found it a ridiculous display when couples fed one another and stared like lovesick idiots across the table, but now she gladly joined their ranks.

"I feel like I should be leading bonfire devotionals or singing right about now." They sat facing one another a few hours later, her feet curled beneath her, his arm along the back of the sofa. The air between them was literally charged, and Lexa felt sensitized in every fiber of her being.

"You can give me a little Bible lesson if you want." Lexa kept her tone light, teasing. "I have an awful lot to learn. I don't expect to keep up with you, but I want to be able to hold my own in those theological debates." Maybe all the praying and studying she planned to do would also keep her thoughts a little more pure.

"I don't think I've seen anyone grow as much as you did at our TeamWork camp, Lexa." Sam's voice was quiet. His warm fingers inched a slow pathway to her shoulder, bringing a particular night under the tree to mind. The same night they'd shared such great conversation outside Maxie's.

"It's been such an eye-opening, wonderful experience for me as a director to see that personal challenge and growth. And, you," he added, shifting closer to her, quickening her heart the closer he came, "challenged me tremendously. I've learned more about myself because of your presence in the camp."

"Oh, I don't know about that."

"Oh, but I do," he murmured, pulling her chin toward him, "but I don't want to spend all night talking about it." Lowering his mouth to hers, Sam kissed her for all he was worth. He smelled so good, so masculine. It was different from his rugged, natural scent at the work camp, but every bit as appealing. The TeamWork Sam was the rugged, cowboy Sam. This man was the more professional, polished Sam, and it was good to see both sides of the man she'd come to love. Her hands moved to the back of his head, fingering the curls at the nape of his neck in the way he loved.

"What kinds of things did you learn about yourself, Mr. Lewis?" Her laugh escaped as Sam nuzzled her cheek.

"You're a very inquisitive woman, Miss Clarke. Enough talking. Why don't you be quiet and let me kiss you some more?" Sam's lids were heavy and she felt his staggered breath on her cheek. They had to be careful. His presence next to her on the sofa, and especially his kisses, did untold things inside her. The man was a potent drug, addictive and difficult to resist.

"In just a minute." Pushing him away with gentle hands, Lexa smiled but kept his hand anchored in hers. "I'd really like to know."

"Okay." Sam leaned back with reluctance, those full lips smiling in only the way he could. "First, I have no right to judge anyone. Only the Lord knows someone's heart and soul, and I need to leave it in His very capable hands."

When his smile faded, Lexa knew he was thinking about Josh. Sam leaned toward her again, his intent quite obvious.

"And second?" Lexa prompted, her own lids heavy. She blinked hard and tried to regain her faculties, but wasn't entirely successful. It was amazing what this man's kisses did to her. This night was so incredibly romantic. She never wanted it to end.

"Second, and as I know I mentioned before, a growing faith is better than a stagnant faith. What good is our faith if we allow it to sit idle? The way I look at it, our faith is like a garden. If it's not nurtured or tended to lovingly, it will wither and die. On the other hand, if that garden is cultivated and watched over carefully, it will thrive. But it needs water and sun and love in order to grow." He looked at her with a small smile. "Children are like that, too, you know."

"What? A garden?" She shook her head, confused.

He grinned. "Children have that completely honest approach to faith. It's fresh, and it needs to be nurtured, obviously. But look what happens when we feed them from God's word, when we share our love and model faith in action. I'll tell you something that gets me every single time is when the kids' choir sings at church. Those kids—with their shining faces, big eyes and willing spirits—open their hearts to what the Lord can do through them." Sam's eyes misted and he touched his chest. "It grabs this old heart every time. Just wraps itself around me and tugs away."

Lexa squeezed his hand. "*You* get my heart every time, Sam Lewis."

Sam looked at her for a long moment. "And you, Lexa Clarke, *are* my heart."

She grinned. "We're pretty sappy, you know, cowboy."

He winked. "Wouldn't have it any other way, beautiful girl."

"So, I take it you'd like to grow your own little garden of kids someday? So you can nurture them?" With a lot of men, a question like that would probably have them hopping away faster than a jackrabbit, but not Sam Lewis.

"Hmm," he murmured, pulling her to her feet to walk over to the front door together. Leaning against the doorframe, Sam studied her, not speaking for a long time.

On the opposite side of the door, Lexa tilted her head, trying to figure out what he might be thinking. It was a near impossible task. In a lot of ways, he was a complex and fascinating man.

"You didn't answer the question."

"Quite honestly, I can't wait to have children of my own. It'll be one of the greatest thrills of my life. I wholeheartedly welcome the challenge, but I also realize it's not the easiest responsibility." Sam pulled her to him, leaning his forehead against hers. "I want as many kids as the Lord wants to give me. But," he whispered, moving his lips down to brush a gentle kiss on her upturned cheek, "it takes two to create those children. And I look forward to that part," he said, moving his lips toward hers, "very, *very* much." His kiss stirred her all the way to her toes.

"Oh, Mr. Lewis, the things you say," Lexa teased, kissing him again before pushing him out the door with playful hands. She was tingling all over. It was going to be so hard to let this man go.

Chapter 46

$\mathcal{L}$EXA WENT THROUGH the motions of attempting to get some work done in her office every day while Sam attended to his TeamWork business. She ached to be together with him whenever possible. They had to squeeze in as much time—and make as many memories—as they could before he left Saturday on his flight overseas.

Sam met Lexa at her office, charming everyone in the process, and they shared lunches, picnics in the park, feeding the ducks at a pond near her townhome, and taking long walks. They sat together at the prayer meeting in his church where Sam proudly introduced her to everyone.

Sam showed her his small apartment not far from his family's home, but they didn't linger. It looked like a typical bachelor's home, used primarily for sleep. Sports equipment was stashed in every corner, and the man obviously loved books—they lined the shelves in the living room and were piled high on every available table.

They made a couple of dinners together in her townhome, sharing them by candlelight. Sam was surprisingly adept in the kitchen, preparing a delicious shrimp and pasta dish. Lexa watched, amazed, as he seasoned and sautéed like a pro. A man who looked as good as he did, and could cook, too? Not wanting to swell Sam's head, she hugged that thought to herself.

When he insisted on washing their dinner dishes, Lexa knew Clarice was right. She had a keeper. She also tried making a peach pie for the first time in her life. Sam claimed it was the best he'd ever had, which she rather doubted since he'd already told her that Grandma Lewis made the best in the world. Still, Lexa knew Sam appreciated her thoughtful efforts. When he came home in a year's time, she wanted to present him with the most mouth-watering peach pie he'd ever tasted.

Lexa told Sam more of her memories about her mother, and how she loved reading and writing stories when she was a teenager. They both shared as much as they could, packing in the memories and openly discussing their hopes and dreams. Sam included her in his hopes for the future, although nothing specific was said. It wasn't a matter of if, but a matter of timing.

Lexa met Sam's family on Thursday night. As he pulled the station wagon into the driveway of their sprawling suburban Houston home, Lexa felt intimidated when they all surrounded the car. But when they greeted her with open arms and the most welcome smiles in the world, she experienced an immediate sense of belonging.

"It's about time Sam brought you home to meet us!" Caty grinned at Sam as she hugged her close. Lexa warmed to her as she returned the hug. A lovely girl with long dark, wavy, hair, Caty's deep blue eyes were just a shade darker than Sam's. She was exuberant and charming, and Lexa could understand the closeness she shared with Sam. It wouldn't be a hard thing. Not at all.

And Carson. What a doll he was. He looked not a thing like Sam or Caty, and possessed innate charm in abundance. Blond with huge dimples in both cheeks and dark eyes, Carson was another Lewis man who could charm the hardest of hearts. Sam once more confided to Lexa his prediction that Carson might follow in his footsteps in some type of ministry one day, but he was much younger, and still a high school student. Being the youngest of six children, there was nearly a fifteen-year age difference between Sam and Carson.

"You're really pretty," Carson told her with unabashed admiration as he pumped Lexa's hand with enthusiasm.

"Carson!" Caty laughed, swatting him on the arm. "You're not supposed to say things like that, especially to Sam's girlfriend."

"It's okay," Lexa assured him. "A girl can never hear it enough." Carson's cheeks flushed beet red. Lexa adored being called Sam's girlfriend. All over again, she felt as giddy as a lovestruck teenager.

Taking her gently by the arm, Sam introduced her to his dad and mom. They were a lovely couple, and put her immediately at ease. Sam looked a lot like his dad, and the elder Samuel Lewis was only a half-inch shorter than his son. Caty told her Sam was the tallest in the family. Goodness, the entire Lewis family towered over her. Even the women were tall. If she married this man— and Lexa prayed in time she would—at least their children would have half a chance at not being height-challenged. The thought prompted a smile to her lips.

Sam, Sr. and Sarah ushered them into the living room after dinner for a time of private conversation. Of course, Sarah also baked a fresh peach pie using Grandma Lewis's special recipe. While he enjoyed his mother's pie, Sam took great pains to gush to his parents about Lexa's peach pie.

He showed Lexa some family photos and she marveled at how much his younger brother Will resembled Sam. "You could be twins!" She loved seeing photos of Sam in his highchair with cake smeared all over his face on his first birthday, in the backyard feeding a menagerie of animals, learning to ride his first bike, his school photos. In photos of his father, Lexa saw the son. It wasn't only the physical resemblance. The strength, goodness and deep faith of the Lewis men would be a family legacy to carry on through the generations.

～

Sam was proud of his parents. They asked Lexa polite, respectful questions and didn't express pity to hear she was an orphan. He'd told them about her background, and they were curious and open without prying. True to form, they showed Lexa the warmth and sensitivity he'd come to expect. The way they looked at her, by the respect they showed her that evening, they welcomed her into their lives. They understood she wasn't a temporary, passing fancy.

Caty told him she'd confided to Lexa that although he'd dated a lot in college, he'd never brought a woman home to meet them before. It was true. They'd never had the opportunity to meet Shelby. Lexa was the one they needed to get to know. His family would watch over her while he was gone. That eased the pain of leaving. Not that it was any easier, especially as the day drew nearer.

"She's a wonderful woman, Sam." Sarah hugged her eldest son before they departed at the end of the evening. "I can see how happy she makes you. Lexa's trusting the Lord to take you on this mission and bring you back safely. That's all your father and I need to know."

"She's charming, Sam. Witty, articulate. Pretty as can be." Sam's dad put his arm around his shoulders. "Lexa's a match for you in so many ways, son. Your mother and I are excited to see what the Lord's going to do in your life on this mission." The hand on his shoulder squeezed. "And after."

Sam walked alongside his dad while his mom lingered behind with Lexa. Probably telling her more about the secret peach pie recipe or some childhood scrape. Like the time he kidnapped the neighbor's dog and held her for ransom, thinking she was being overfed when all Pepper needed was a place to birth her puppies in peace. Or the time he brought home a companion for lonely Ears, and soon had lots of baby bunnies needing new homes. Maybe his fondness for helping animals—which Carson termed legendary—was another thing that endeared him to Lexa.

"I have no doubt the Lord holds many more adventures in store for you and Lexa in the future." Pulling back, his dad patted his shoulder. "It's going to be a long journey of love, laughter, and God willing, so much more. Enjoy the ride, son."

"I will, Dad. Thanks." Sam's eyes were moist as he thanked his parents. Lexa joined him, and he threaded his fingers through hers as they walked down the front walkway. The scent of his mother's rose bushes made him almost as heady as having Lexa beside him. Plucking a peach bloom, he stripped the thorns and bowed low, presenting it to her. When she reached for it, Sam grabbed her hand. Planting a gentle kiss on her open palm, he placed the gorgeous rose inside, wrapping her fingers around it. Her smile curled itself around his heart.

Oh, it was going to be torture to say good-bye to this woman for an entire year.

~

The moment they both dreaded arrived the next evening. Lexa's heart was so heavy she thought it might break. She tried her best to be brave, but succumbed to her tears as Sam held her in his arms. "I know you have to do this, but I hate it. I already miss you so much my heart hurts. It literally, physically aches."

Sam pulled her even closer, soothing her by stroking her hair and brushing feathery-soft kisses across her forehead. "Shh. I know, baby, I know. It's almost unbearable. But think how quickly the time went at the TeamWork camp. We'll both be busy, and it'll go by before we know it."

She pulled back. "You still haven't told me exactly where you'll be stationed."

He laughed. "It's not the Army, Lexa, although I know you like to think of the TeamWork camp as boot camp. All I know is I'm flying into Seoul and then moving on from there after about six weeks. They're not even telling me right now for whatever reason. I'll find out once I'm there. But no matter where they send me, I have the feeling I'm in for some real adventures."

She sniffed. "As long as those adventures don't involve exotic women." Although she acted the part of the sentimental fool, Lexa couldn't help it. Jealousy was a foreign concept to her. But, no matter how much she tried to prepare herself for this moment, she couldn't know how it would feel until faced head-on with the reality. And now, the truth staring Lexa hard in the face was that she wouldn't see this man, wouldn't talk with this man, wouldn't feel the arms of this man she loved, pulling her close and holding her tight, for a very long time.

"Lexa, look at me." Sam's voice was deadly serious and his eyes even more so as they sought hers. "I promise you," he told her, his voice even and steady, "the other most important lesson I learned in the San Antonio work camp is that you, my love, are the one the Lord intends me to spend the rest of my life with. No matter where He leads, no matter where I travel in the upcoming year with the TeamWork mission, I'll always be thinking of you and looking forward to our reunion."

"At the Alamo." Her smile trembled.

"At the Alamo. I hate to say it, but I must go." Rising to his feet, Sam pulled her up with him.

"I wish you didn't have to go," Lexa murmured, looking up at Sam with tentative eyes, her heart in her expression. They already agreed she wouldn't go to the airport. That would be too heart-wrenching for both of them. Not that it was any easier now.

"We've been through all this," Sam told her with a small smile.

"I meant tonight."

Sam's eyes softened. "You know there's nothing I'd love more, but I want to keep my promise to you and the Lord." He tipped her chin. "It'll happen, but in God's timing, not ours." He kissed her again. "If I stayed the night, it would make it that much more difficult for me to leave you again in the morning."

She sniffled. "I know. I'm sorry." It was a good thing Sam was being strong enough for both of them because tonight, she'd give him anything he asked. *Anything*. A sigh escaped. Obviously, she wasn't as strong in the faith as he was. She had a lot to learn in the coming year.

"Don't be. Hold that thought for a year, and we'll see what we can do about it."

Her gaze melted into those pools of blue. "I hope we don't have to start over again in a year's time."

"What do you mean?"

"Maybe this foreign mission will change you somehow. Maybe you'll decide . . ."

"Maybe I'll decide my favorite fruit isn't the peach after all."

"I don't think that's possible." She managed a small smile around the huge lump lodged in her throat.

"Always remember what I told you, Lexa."

"Which thing is that?"

"I love you. Tomorrow will take care of itself. I promise I'm coming home to you and will meet you at the Alamo. I've got the date and time imprinted on my brain, and it's what will keep me going for the next year. And I promise you something else," he whispered, drawing her to him for one last, deep, lingering kiss. He didn't hold anything back, and neither did she. He pressed her as close as possible, and probably more than was proper. Sam's fingertips lightly traced her face. His look was so loving, she thought she'd melt into a big old puddle of love.

"What's that?" Lexa barely restrained her tears. She bit her lower lip to stop its trembling.

"Once we're reunited, we won't wait long, my love."

Lexa memorized those incredible eyes and deep smile lines, imprinting them on her heart. "Please come back to me, Mr. Lewis."

Sam tweaked her chin with a wink. "See you at the Alamo, Miss Clarke."

He always knew what to say, but she heard the catch in his throat. If she didn't smile, she'd cry a river. His humor made it that much easier. Saying goodbye to Sam for a year was the hardest thing she'd ever done. But he managed to make her heart smile.

Climbing into bed after closing the door to that portion of her life, Lexa prayed the Lord would keep her love safe for the next year. Pulling out her Bible, she read verses of comfort and hope. The Lord craved her fellowship. It was an incredible discovery. The Lord accepted her just as she was, faults and all, sinful thoughts and all. He *loved* her. And she loved Him. She'd started a daily dialogue, telling Him the things most precious to her heart, the innermost longings of her soul. She'd started writing her thoughts and prayer requests in a prayer journal.

Sam gave her his own prayer journal he'd kept at the TeamWork camp. It was amazing to follow her own journey of faith written in Sam's words. He'd asked the Lord to draw her closer to Him. His journal was such a precious gift, and she'd treasure it always. He wrote of witnessing her growing faith in the questions she asked at the bonfires, in the way she interacted with Angelina and the women in the camp, and in the way she served others.

Lexa had already contacted the local TeamWork director about volunteering for some of their Houston-based weekend mission projects. That would be a good place to start, and it would also help her feel even more connected with Sam. Plus, it would help prepare her to be an even better partner for him when he returned home. It would be a year of learning about herself as much as growing in the love and knowledge of the One who'd brought them together.

No matter what else happened, the loving heavenly Father held them both in the palm of His hand. As Sam told her—and as she learned for herself at the TeamWork camp—they were such very capable hands.

Chapter 47

The Alamo - One Year Later

$\mathcal{L}$EXA LOOKED AT her watch for at least the fifth time in the last twenty minutes. At two o'clock, she was taking the quick flight to San Antonio and checking into her hotel on the Riverwalk. Hopefully, to start the next phase of her life. She couldn't even think of the alternative.

As she tidied her desk, her mind was a million miles away, as it had been nearly all day. Righting her calendar and stuffing her appointment book into her handbag, Lexa smiled at her secretary, her nerves ragged. She'd been on edge the entire last week and found it almost impossible to eat or sleep. Every time the phone rang, she jumped, wondering if it would be Sam. Lexa thought about calling his mom and dad, but decided against it. If he was back, why hadn't he called? She was nearly out of her mind with worry and anticipation.

"This is your big weekend, huh?" Jennifer flashed an understanding smile.

"I only pray that's true." Lexa turned off her computer and pulled her handbag over one shoulder.

Jennifer shook her head and sighed, holding a stack of file folders against her chest, a faraway look in her eye. "Well, if my opinion counts for anything, it's just about the most romantic story I've ever heard in my life. Straight out of Hollywood."

"Right." Lexa's smile was nervous. "Let's just hope it has a Hollywood-style happy ending."

"He'll be there, Lexa. If your Sam is anywhere near as wonderful as everyone says, he'll be there. I can't wait to meet him. He's practically a legend around here from what everyone says. So brave, so handsome . . ." She released a sigh. "You really haven't heard from him in six months, though?"

Lexa shook her head in regret. "Only one letter, and that's it." She treasured it and had memorized every precious word, carrying it with her and clinging to Sam's promises as well as the Lord's. "He's been out-of-touch, literally in the jungle somewhere in Africa. Most of his valuables were stolen or looted."

She blew out a sigh. "It was a mixed blessing hearing the news from the TeamWork office. But I suppose it was better than not knowing. That's the worst thing of all." At least Sam still had the watch she'd given him. He'd had that on his wrist and been away from the campsite when it was ransacked. Losing material possessions was hard, but the man she loved was safe. That's all that mattered.

"Wow. I can't begin to imagine what it's been like for him." Jennifer walked with her toward the door and held it open. "You sure he's back in the States now?"

Jennifer's question brought Lexa back to reality, and she shook her head. "No. All I know is that his mission should have ended sometime in the last week, and then he had a debriefing session for a few days, but not in Houston. I'll say one thing. Sam definitely has some very well-deserved R&R coming." Lexa managed a small smile and retrieved her suitcase parked behind the door.

"So, what are you doing standing here talking to me about it? You have a plane to catch!" Jennifer shooed Lexa from the office with a smile and good wishes.

As Lexa exited the elevator and walked outside the office building in downtown Houston, toting her suitcase behind her, her heart pounded. It brought to mind toting the same suitcase through the San Antonio bus station all those months ago. If she was going to make it to the Alamo without having a heart attack, she was going to have to get a serious grip on her emotions. Forcing herself to take several deep breaths, she headed toward the waiting taxi parked at the curb.

A few short hours later, she examined her reflection in the full-length mirror of her hotel room one last time. She felt satisfied she looked more than presentable. Running light fingers over her hair, Lexa fluffed her long curls before smoothing a wrinkle in the sleeveless, white cotton dress flirting around her knees. It was simple but elegant. Sam would like it.

Glancing down at her feet, she smiled as she eyed her new strappy, high-heeled sandals with her newly-pedicured pink nails peeking out. The pretty shoes highlighted her strong calves when she walked, not to mention giving her a little more advantage on her height. She wanted to look pretty in every way for Sam. If he was there.

"He'll be there," Lexa repeated aloud. Sam wouldn't forget his promise. Their time together in Houston before Sam left for the TeamWork mission had been altogether wonderful and special and served to solidify in their minds the Lord brought them together for a purpose. Still, there was that little nagging doubt clouding the back of her mind. It would be there until she saw Sam's face again, felt his arms encircle her once more.

With a deep sigh of longing, Lexa grabbed her purse and headed out the door. A year without seeing the man she loved, and the last six months with no contact whatsoever, was an interminable period of time. *Oh, he'd better be there, Lord.*

~

Biting her lower lip, standing in front of the historic Alamo, Lexa darted a glance at her watch one more time. Sam must be running a few minutes late, that's all. Ten minutes, to be exact. At the campsite and back in Houston, he'd always been punctual. Still, circumstances could have prevented him. Things like traffic, and . . .

Stop it! She almost said the words aloud. Glancing around, Lexa hoped no one was watching or they'd probably think she was a lunatic.

Feeling a soft tap on her back, Lexa jumped and whirled around with optimism tinged with cautious expectation. Surprise gave way to barely-disguised disappointment as her gaze traveled downward to focus on a small boy. He looked to be about eight years old, with dark hair and luminous brown eyes. Staring up at Lexa with a shy smile, he held a single, long-stemmed yellow rose in his chubby hands.

"For you." He extended the blooming rose closer to her hand.

Accepting the rose, Lexa smiled. "Thank you. Very much," she managed to mumble before turning back around so he wouldn't see the tears in her eyes. Lexa didn't want the sweet child to think he'd upset her in some way. To the contrary, it touched her that he wanted to give her the beautiful flower.

Putting her hand up to her face and composing her features, Lexa began to walk in the direction of the entrance to the Alamo, one slow step in front of the other. The last tours of the day would be starting soon. As long as she was there, and if the unthinkable happened and Sam didn't come, she figured she might as well fulfill her desire to see the Alamo. Even so, she wouldn't see anything. It would only be something to keep her busy, her mind occupied, so she wouldn't collapse from the unbearable sense of loss if he didn't meet her. Lexa's feet felt like dead weight. It reminded her of the heaviness of the work boots she'd worn at the camp.

Another tap on her shoulder. Pausing for a moment and taking a deep breath, Lexa turned around again. Another child. Another long-stemmed yellow rose. She wondered if these were local children trying to earn tips or make money from the flowers. Maybe they thought she'd give them something. Starting to reach into her purse, Lexa smiled. The small girl shook her head, pushed the flower further into Lexa's hand and took off running, giggling all the way.

Lexa spied a group of about twenty children eyeing her from about ten yards away, to the side of the front entrance. As she watched, they all started running toward her at the same time. Soon, the laughing children surrounded her, hemming her in the sweetest circle of beaming faces she could ever imagine.

One by one, they each presented her with the yellow rose they held in their small fingers. And, one by one, Lexa accepted the blooms they offered. She felt somewhat like a queen granting court to her subjects as they presented her with their very special offerings and gifts.

Soon, Lexa stood alone, clutching an overflowing bouquet of gorgeous, already-blooming yellow roses. Now what should she do? A sudden feeling of loss and abandonment surfaced. It seemed a bit suspicious that these children appeared as if from nowhere and presented her, of all people, with the flowers. Did she look so alone and desperate that they felt sorry for her and wanted to make her smile? Well, they'd accomplished that feat and more. But it wasn't as though she could exactly tour the Alamo with an armload of flowers. Should she return the favor, carry on the tradition, and start handing out the flowers to other tourists?

Then it hit her. Sam had given her yellow roses in Houston. Was this a sign? Was he telling her he was either here or on his way, prolonging the moment of reunion? The yellow rose was a familiar symbol of Texas, so anything was possible. By now, Lexa practically hopped up and down with anticipation. She couldn't wait much longer, and she'd never felt such urgency in her life. Not to mention how hard and fast her heart was thundering in her chest.

Approaching the entrance, Lexa stopped just outside the main gate. Glancing down at the ground, she spied yet another yellow rose lying at her feet. *What's really going on here?* She wasn't sure she could hold many more. Some of the other people were now stopping to stare at the woman with all the yellow roses. One young mother waved when her little girl pointed at Lexa and giggled.

Feeling another tap on her shoulder, Lexa tried to mask her growing confusion as she turned and looked down out of habit, expecting to see yet another small child offering up a flower. Seeing a pair of very shiny men's dress shoes, Lexa's eyes traveled an upward path, drinking in the gorgeous gray tailored suit, and white dress shirt with light blue silk, patterned tie. Finally, her gaze rested on the most intense, piercing, *welcome* pair of blue eyes she'd ever seen.

Chapter 48

The Reunion

$\mathcal{M}$OVING ONE HAND from behind his back, Sam held out another single yellow rose. His loving smile mirrored hers as Lexa stared in the face of her future. What a welcome face it was, with an incredible smile and perhaps a few more silver hairs at the temples. Her heart pounded.

"About time you got here. I need someone to carry all these roses for me." Lexa pivoted and headed in the other direction, with Sam close behind "Know anyone who might be interested in helping me out?"

Sam chuckled and reached for her. He pulled Lexa by the shoulders with his big, gentle hands, and turned her back around to face him. Sam lowered his head toward hers, hovering above her waiting lips. His eyes met hers and held them steady. This was becoming a very lovely habit with him. *Sam* was a lovely habit.

"Careful. I might drop all these gorgeous flowers."

"I'll pick them up in a minute," Sam murmured with a slow smile. "Right now, I need your complete and undivided attention. I'm going to kiss you now, Miss Clarke. Please be quiet and try to enjoy it."

Dropping the roses to the ground at her feet with lightning speed, Lexa's hands encircled Sam's neck as she pulled his head down. "Make me." The whispered words were silenced as his lips met hers for the achingly sweet, long-anticipated kiss.

Cupping her face between tender hands, Sam's tears of joy mingled with her own as he kissed her several more times, finding it hard to stop. They were drawing an audience now. In the vague recesses of her mind, Lexa heard romantic sighs and giggles all around, even a few claps. But she didn't care, and she could tell Sam didn't either It was as though the rest of the world ceased to exist, at least for that moment in time.

"You came back to me." Lexa buried her head against his chest, laughing and crying at the same time. His arms circled her as he held her close. She sighed. She was *home*.

Sam tilted her chin and brushed his thumbs with a featherlight touch beneath her eyes. "You did say please, after all."

"When did you get here?"

His hold on her tightened and he kissed her cheek. "Just now. I made a beeline for you. Missed me, did you?"

Lexa sighed. "Something fierce." She swallowed hard and looked up at him. He seemed even taller, and his skin was deeply tanned which only made those blue eyes more prominent. His dark waves looked freshly groomed. He looked incredible. Devastating. No doubt, he'd broken a lot of hearts between Africa and the United States. But he was *hers*.

"When did you get back to the States? To Texas?"

Sam chuckled. "Is there any *other* state? Just today, as a matter of fact. I was delayed a few days. Sorry I was a little late meeting you. I swore my family to secrecy, so please don't blame them. I'm just thankful I made it or you'd be standing here with Carson or my dad."

"I love them all, but I'm kind of partial to one Lewis man in particular." She ran her hands up to his broad shoulders, felt the powerful muscles beneath the suit jacket. The smile he gave her at that moment would warm her heart forever. It promised so much.

"Admit it, sweetheart. You were starting to panic."

Lexa stared at him, sniffling, one hand moving down to rest on her hip. "And how would you know that, Sam Lewis?"

"Because I know *you*. By the way, don't you think it's about time to merge our interests into a partnership of sorts?" He cocked his head to one side, his eyes twinkling. "I'm partial to Lewis and Clarke Expeditions. What do you think?"

"Hmm," Lexa mused, resting her chin on one hand as she pretended to ponder the option. "Not very original, but one I could learn to live with, I suppose. What do you have in mind?"

"I was thinking along the lines of a lifetime partnership, one full of adventure, fun, romance, and a ministry to others." He nuzzled her cheek. "And *lots* of exploration."

Lexa's cheeks flamed. Good heavens, did he just growl? "Mr. Lewis, the things you say!"

"Baby, you don't even know . . ."

She cleared her throat, interrupting him. "You've put a lot of thought into this, haven't you?"

"Indeed, I have. It's all that's been on my mind for the last six months, especially." Reaching into the inside pocket of his jacket, Sam pulled out a small, black velvet box. Taking her hand in his, he placed it in her open palm. When her hand trembled, he captured it and held it steady. Opening the box, he held it up for Lexa to see. A sparkling, emerald-cut diamond winked at her from its bed of black velvet.

Lexa's breath caught, and she moved one hand to her throat. "It's absolutely gorgeous, Sam." She stared at it in wonder, afraid to touch it. Could he be asking her to marry him? Right in front of the Alamo? Everything was happening at once. Her head was spinning with happiness.

"It belonged to my grandmother. But if you don't like it . . ."

She heard the earnestness in Sam's voice and hastened to reassure him. "It's perfect."

"It won't bite. Here. Let me do it for you." Sam pocketed the box after removing the ring. Taking her hand, he slid it quite easily onto her finger.

She wiggled her fingers to gain the full effect. "It's a perfect fit." Lexa loved his triumphant expression as she held up her hand for him to see.

"My sentiments exactly." His deep voice was husky. "Shall we depart to my makeshift office so that we can discuss this partnership in a little more detail?" Putting his hand on the small of her back, he guided her toward the street.

Lexa recognized—and loved—that telltale thickness in his voice. She held out her hand, staring at the ring as they walked. A moment later, she paused and looked up at him. "Just where is this makeshift office, anyway?"

Something long and white caught her eye. She turned toward the curb. "Oh, no." She broke into spontaneous laughter. "I should have known."

"Oh, yes, my love," Sam countered, taking her hand and leading her in the direction of the familiar white Volvo station wagon.

"The bomb. I'm surprised it started up again after a whole year."

Sam laughed. "I had Carson start it every now and again. Knowing my little brother, he tooled around town in it with his friends, too. Surely you must have seen it parked at the house. But, that's beside the point. This is *our* bomb now, Lexa. You know you've missed it. Remember, love me, love my bomb."

She just looked at him, shaking her head. But he was right, as usual. She had grown accustomed to it, and even missed it in a weird way.

Helping her into the car with the roses, Sam took her hand and drew him to her again for a longer, more impassioned kiss. "I've wanted to do that for so long." His fingers rested beneath her chin and, leaning forward again, he grazed her lips.

Lexa grabbed Sam's other hand and held on tight. She smiled against his lips, loving the fact that he didn't want to stop. When he pulled away and gazed at her through loving eyes, she loved the way he looked at her with equal parts love, desire, respect and admiration. He made up for lost time as his hungry eyes drank in the sight of her.

"How . . ." Lexa began before clearing her throat, "how did your trip go? I've missed you terribly, Mr. Lewis."

"It was . . . full. I'll explain more later. The main thing I want to tell you now is that I've made another important life decision."

She arched her brow and slanted a grin his way. "Do I really want to hear this?"

He smiled. "Oh, I think you do. I've decided that traveling around is great for a single guy, but not a married one."

"I see. Go on. Whatever will you do?" Lexa batted her eyelashes in dramatic fashion.

"Well, it just so happens that TeamWork's headquarters in Houston has an immediate opening for a full-time director. I'd be based there and only have to travel a few times a year to scout out locations for upcoming projects. Otherwise, I'll have an office and can coordinate things from there."

"Is that what you really want, or are you doing it because it's what you think I want?"

"I want *you*, Lexa, but you're right. Going all over the world is perfectly fine when a person's single and doesn't have any other ties to speak of. But when a man is thinking of settling down, finding a more permanent residence, starting a family, growing a garden . . ." He glanced over at her to gauge her reaction. "He has to start making plans."

"So, you think the wanderlust is out of your system, do you?" Lexa's heart was beating so fast, she thought it might burst.

"Well, if it isn't, then going on short scouting trips and working summer mission camps should take care of it. Besides, I might be able to talk the powers that be into taking my wife along. You know, to gain the woman's perspective and all that. My dad always told me that a woman's perspective is precious and invaluable. One woman's perspective, in particular."

Lexa leaned closer. "Your dad is a very wise man."

"In my mind, there's only one thing left to settle." Sam's voice was quiet, wistful.

"What's that?" His smile warmed Lexa down to her toes.

"I need your answer to my partnership idea."

"Oh? I don't remember hearing a specific question."

"Will you forgive me that I can't exactly bend down on one knee? Not to mention the fact that we've already given a lot of people plenty to watch today. Seems we've been the Alamo floor show tonight. After all, you're already wearing my ring."

Lexa smiled. "Nothing to forgive. Carry on, please."

Sam chuckled, then locked her gaze and her heart. "Alexis Clarke, will you please marry me, be my bride, and serve the Lord alongside me for as long as we both shall live?"

She didn't hesitate for even a second. "I will, Samuel Lewis. Especially since you said please. Oh, how I will," Lexa murmured, sealing her promise on his lips. "You know," she told him at length, "the first day we met, sitting in this very car, you asked me where my home was." She traced his lips with one finger, and he caught it with a quick kiss. "My home is wherever you are, Sam. *You* are my home. Wherever the Lord leads."

Sam smiled. "I think I knew the moment I met you that you were going to wreak havoc in my life. But in a very good way." He laughed as she swatted his arm. "I want to show you something."

Lexa watched as he pulled a creased, worn piece of paper from the inner pocket of his suit coat. Opening it out, he held it up. It was the photo of the two of them taken in his parents' home the night she met his family. "This photo kept me going for the past year, Lexa. I had you imprinted on my heart, but this photo has been incredibly precious to me."

When he looked back up at her after returning the photo to his pocket, Lexa glimpsed the tears shining in his eyes. She raised her hand to his face and traced the side of his strong, masculine jaw with gentle fingers. Sam leaned into her hand, kissing her palm. She loved how he possessed that rare inner strength of character and wasn't hesitant to share his true emotions with her.

"I want to show you something." Lexa reached in the skirt of her dress, finding the pocket. Sam's eyes widened as she pulled out the identical small photo. "Caty gave one to me. We've become very close friends. As a matter of fact, I've become a regular houseguest. Wait until you taste my peach pie now."

Sam laughed, holding her close. Lexa heard the joy in his voice, glimpsed the love in his eyes. He leaned his head against hers, and ran his fingers through her long hair. Sam whispered how beautiful she was, how soft her skin, how lovely her hair. Glorying in the warmth and pure joy of this man's love, Lexa felt like the most precious, treasured jewel. The Lord was so faithful. She belonged with this man.

Sam kissed the top of her head and pulled her even closer. She leaned her head against his chest, and smiled as his hold on her tightened. Loved hearing his strong, steady heartbeat. Loved *him*. "I've grown so much in the last year. Learned so much. Being away from you was incredibly hard, but I put the time to good use." Raising her head, she looked into his eyes. "The Lord's timing is so perfect, isn't it? I'm better prepared now, Sam. To be your wife."

At her words, Sam's brilliant smile reached his eyes. "For the record, what's your middle name, Lexa?"

"Mary." She didn't expect the hearty laughter prompted by her response. "Why? What's your middle name?"

Sam's eyes met hers in that direct way he had of looking straight into her heart, her very soul. "Joseph." He kissed her forehead again. "Just another sign from the Lord, I'd say, that we're meant to be together. I love you, Lexa. And," he murmured, his lips moving down to her cheek, "I think we should definitely make this partnership legal." The warmth of his lips seared through her as they moved to her mouth and then toward her neck.

Lexa broke out into a wide grin of pure joy. She'd never known such joy could be possible.

With a slight groan, Sam pulled away. "I want to start calling you Mrs. Lewis as soon as humanly possible. A year away from you was pure torture, and the last six months in the jungle made me positively certifiable, not being able to hold you . . . or even talk with you."

Settling back against the seat, he sighed. "The point being that we've waited long enough. I'm more than ready, and I believe you are, too. Besides, I don't think the Almighty wants us to wait much longer. It would be cruel and unusual punishment. However, if you need time to plan a big shindig..."

When Sam grinned, he captured her heart all over again. "Oh, admit it already, cowboy. You just want to enjoy the *benefits* of marriage as soon as humanly possible." Lexa could tell he was shocked by that statement, but in a very good way.

Sam erupted in uproarious laughter. "Well, don't *you*, beautiful girl?"

"Judging by the night at the mission, I'd say . . . yes. Definitely yes. What are we waiting for?" Lexa didn't even have to think any more about it. It made perfect sense. The Lord must be smiling at this little scene in the white Volvo station wagon. Parked in front of the world-renowned, historic Alamo, of all places.

Sam raised an eyebrow and grinned. "So, what do you say we go find ourselves a preacher and make this one of the shortest engagements in history? I have a friend who's ordained and licensed, and I've already called him. He can marry us tonight. We can always do a repeat in front of my family and our friends whenever you say. I've already told my mom and dad, and they're thrilled beyond reason that I'm finally taking a wife." Sam smiled, looking more than pleased with himself. "And Caty and Carson, of course. They've all fallen in love with you, too, you know."

She hadn't had a family to call her own in so long, and this day just kept getting better and more promising. "Here? In San Antonio? *Tonight?*"

Sam laughed and nibbled her lower lip. "Yes, my love. Right here in San Antonio. Tonight would be *spectacular.*"

His hold on her tightened and her heart thundered as she remembered the last time he'd used that word in terms of their relationship. She gulped and almost couldn't speak. "I hate to bring a hard dose of reality into this conversation, but from what I know, Texas has a three-day waiting period unless you're active military." Lexa could barely breathe. Sam wanted to get married *tonight?*

"Ah, but there's a little loophole, you see." Sam scooted even closer and took her hand in his. "Would you like to hear it?"

Lexa leaned her head back against the seat. "Of course, I do."

"A judge can sign a waiver foregoing the seventy-two hour waiting period, if you can show just cause."

"And I suppose you happen to know a judge?" She'd get to the other part of that statement in a moment.

"My grandfather was great friends with Judge Roy Branford, and I spent many hours in his company when I came to visit Grandpa Lewis here in San Antonio. I saw him late this afternoon, as a matter of fact. He gave us his blessing. Right after he signed the waiver. I have it in the glove compartment under lock and key. He also remembered my grandmother wearing the ring you're wearing now." He looked down a moment before meeting her eyes again. "He told me my grandfather would be very proud of me." Sam's voice caught. "And he said my grandmother would love knowing *my* bride would wear this ring."

She planted a gentle kiss on his waiting lips. "I'm honored to be your bride, Sam." She gave him a coy look. "Especially if that means I might inherit your grandmother's secret peach pie recipe." She laughed when he winked. "I'm not even going to ask what you said to persuade the kind judge to forego the waiting period. You're a very inventive and thorough man, Mr. Lewis. Those are very promising qualities."

He chuckled. "That's not all."

"I should think not."

"You see, I've also reserved a room on the Riverwalk the next three days. It's a honeymoon suite, and I'd really hate to stay there all by my lonesome. Remember when I left you in Houston, I told you I wouldn't make you wait long."

"You're also very confident, and a man of your word."

"It's a personal Lewis family creed."

"I'd say we're crazy," Lexa told Sam, "but I'd say it's about the best thing we can possibly do. After all, I already have the bouquet." She tossed a glance at the rose garden in the backseat. "The second thing we should do is go car shopping." Catching the look on Sam's face, she burst out laughing.

"What? You don't want to keep the bomb around . . . for old time's sake?" He leaned against the seat, shaking his head, feigning sadness. "I thought you'd grown quite fond of it. Or so you said."

"I suppose we can keep it around if you absolutely insist." Lexa wrapped her fingers in his, caressing the side of his hand with her thumb.

The lazy grin surfaced and those piercing eyes mesmerized hers. "I'm sure we can come up with a compromise. But, surely you jest. One thing I must insist on is that car shopping is not the second thing we do after saying our vows. I suggest we push it further down on the list of things to do. I definitely have more . . . intriguing things in mind."

Lexa felt the slow flush all the way from her scalp to her toes. It took a moment to regain her breath in order to speak a coherent word. Clearing her throat, she tugged on his tie and pulled him close. "By the way, that's a very nice suit you're wearing. I'd say it's a gorgeous suit in which to get hitched. You look incredibly handsome, cowboy."

"Glad you approve, beautiful girl." Raising her fingers to his lips again, Sam kissed them with a reverence that stole her breath. "And I can't help but notice you're wearing a lovely white dress. It's almost as though you knew." His brows rows before another grin surfaced.

Lexa smiled. "The Lord has blessed us so much, Sam. And I think He has a whole lot more in store, and TeamWork might have something to do with it. I can hardly wait." Catching the bemused expression on his face, she giggled. "What are you thinking? You're looking mighty devilish, I must say."

He laughed heartily. "I was just thinking, my love . . ."

"Yes?" Lexa smiled into his eyes. He hovered close in the way she'd adore the rest of her days. His eyes captured hers, drawing her in forever. This man promised her more than yellow roses on anniversaries and whispered sweet nothings in the secret places of her heart. Sam Lewis promised her children, love, and a family to call their very own.

It was beyond anything she ever hoped to dream. And to think it was all possible because she tried to help others rebuild their dreams. In the process, Lexa found her own. What a wonderful life it promised to be, with him by her side, holding her hand, protecting her, guiding her, *loving* her.

Sam planted a tantalizing, exquisite kiss on her lips, full of the promise of blissful things to come. He winked. "Stick around, Lexa. You ain't seen nothin' yet."

About the Author

Awakening is **JoAnn Durgin's** first published novel. A full-time paralegal, she lives with her husband and three children in southern Indiana. She is a member of the American Christian Fiction Writers, as well as its Indiana chapter, and was a finalist in the long contemporary romance category of the 2010 Romance Writers of America/Faith Hope & Love "Touched by Love" Contest. A winner and finalist in several flash fiction contests, JoAnn's passion for writing is fueled by her desire to touch hearts with the redeeming love of Jesus Christ.

Visit her at **www.joanndurgin.com**. She'd love to hear from you!

The *Lewis Legacy Series*

by JoAnn Durgin

A God-fearing man. A God-seeking woman. For Sam Lewis and Lexa Clarke, it proves a combustible combination. You'll keep turning the pages of this sweeping romantic adventure. With great characters, plenty of humor, enough emotion to make you shed a tear or two, and an ending that'll have you cheering, *Awakening* will leave you breathless. Hold on tight.

Paperback ISBN 978-0-9912252-0-0

Newlyweds Marc and Natalie Thompson have it all, but two months after the wedding, Natalie suffers a horrible fall. Not only does she not remember their life together, but now Marc has a personal timeline to reconnect with her—seven months. You'll root for them as they fight against the odds to find their way back to one another... the second time around.

Paperback ISBN 978-0-9912252-2-4

It's been more than four years since Josh was thrown out of the TeamWork missions camp, and he's still haunted by the bittersweet memory of his final meeting with another volunteer. When he also seeks her forgiveness, he gets the shock of his life. Could turning his deepest sin into his greatest blessing be God's answer for his hurting heart?

Paperback ISBN 978-0-9912252-4-8

The *Lewis Legacy Series* is available in paperback and eBook